PRAISE FOR THE FICTION
OF HEATHER JARMAN

"Heather Jarman's nar⋯ ⋯t it's
quite easy to become l⋯ ⋯folds
the tension builds con⋯ ⋯s of
satisfying release before ⋯ is like being on a
thrill ride that gives you moments to catch your breath before it races off again."

"Jarman illuminates important and poignant themes."

"World building is something Jarman excels at."
> —Jackie Bundy, TrekNation.com

"Besides writing well, Jarman knows how to keep the characters lively."
> —Kilian Melloy, wigglefish.com

STRING THEORY

EVOLUTION

Based upon STAR TREK®
created by Gene Roddenberry
and STAR TREK: VOYAGER
created by Rick Berman and Michael Piller and Jeri Taylor

POCKET BOOKS
New York   London   Toronto   Sydney   Exosia

An *Original* Publication of POCKET BOOKS

POCKET BOOKS, a division of Simon & Schuster, Inc.
1230 Avenue of the Americas, New York, NY 10020

ISBN-13: 978-1-4767-9122-7
ISBN-10:   1-4767-9122-8

This Pocket Books paperback edition March 2006

10 9 8 7 6 5 4 3 2 1

POCKET and colophon are registered trademarks of Simon & Schuster, Inc.

Cover design by John Vairo, Jr.

Manufactured in the United States of America

For information regarding special discounts for bulk purchases, please contact Simon & Schuster Special Sales at 1-800-456-6798 or business@simonandschuster.com.

To Sara, Allyson, Rachel, and Abigail, who kept saying,
"Mom, when are you going to write a book we can read?"

HISTORIAN'S NOTE

This story unfolds between the fourth and fifth seasons of *Star Trek: Voyager.*

"When I was a child, I spake as a child, I understood as a child, I thought as a child: but when I became a man, I put away childish things.

For now we see through a glass, darkly, but then face to face; now I know in part: but then shall I know even as I am known."

—The First Epistle of Paul the Apostle to the Corinthians, Chapter 13:11–14

STRING THEORY

EVOLUTION

Prologue

1365 A.D., Old Calendar: Delta Quadrant

"I won't allow you to go into the baron's fortress unprotected. You must conceal a weapon or allow me to carry one." Ced fastened the last clasp at the waist of Lia's heavy bronze breastplate, and then took a few steps back so he could look her in the eye. She wouldn't be able to deceive him face-to-face. When it came to the battlefield, Lia might be a cunning, unpredictable strategist, capable of wielding the elements like no seer in Ocampa's recorded history. Ced had discovered, however, after three rains serving her as her adjunct, that his liege was incapable of telling a convincing lie.

"We have nothing to fear, Ced. The baron is yet unallied. We have a chance to sway him to our side." For a split second, she held eye contact before turning away, shielding her thoughts from him.

I thought so, Ced thought, wondering what excuses or stories she would try to placate him with. She knew his doubts; her extraordinary telepathic abilities made it almost impossible to hide from her. But Ced wanted his liege to know his fears, hoping perhaps that they would dislodge her stubborn determination to go along with her foolish plan. *And I will stand by her, even to death.*

Kneeling down on the rug before her trunk, Lia searched among her weapons and armor for her rank insignia—a frontlet made of animal skin featuring a three-gem triad embedded in the center. She'd chosen to proclaim her status the ancient way, following the example of such notable warrior-seers as Sie, Mey, and the greatest of all, the female Ocampa Lav. Lav, too, had been born in a time of planetary tumult and had chosen to use her psionic abilities to wage battle against oppression, rallying her followers behind the standard of the three stars, represented by a triad of gems. Lia's deliberate invocation of Lav in the minds of both her followers and enemies inspired the proper amount of fear and trust. Ced had wondered, as did others, if Lia was Lav reborn, come to save Ocampa in what he believed would be their most desperate fight yet. At the very least, Ced believed that Lav must have been among Lia's knowledge-progenitors, with her lifetime of learning being among those engrams transferred to Lia during her first year.

Usually the sages kept careful records of who among them held the knowledge of illustrious forebears like General Lav or King Gran the Wise. The sages were supposed to be egalitarian and random about transferring such unique experience and knowledge to newborn Ocampa, giving all Ocampans equal access to their heritage. In practice, the sages hoarded their prestigious engrams, bestowing them far more selectively than they ought to. That someone of Lia's undistinguished parentage, who at the moment of her birth had been determined to have only the bare minimum psionic skills necessary to function in Ocampan society—a neutral—could emerge as the greatest warrior-seer of her age was proof to Ced that forces beyond understanding were at work in their lives. Ocampa certainly needed the help.

Already five moons had passed without any sign of the rains returning. Rumors had reached Lia and Ced that Mestof had warrior-seer advisors manipulating the planet's elements in such a way that the rains could be forcibly withheld. Lia and her followers saw the parched western continent as evidence of their power. Already, the moats and canals of their great cities had dropped to historically low levels. Aquaculture factories and processors shut down production as lakes and rivers became too shallow to cultivate. All feared shortages come harvest time. Rationing would address the worst of the problem; few would starve. The Ocampa were helpless, however, to prevent a more deadly phenomenon linked to the elimination of the rains: the ongoing erosion of the planet's protective cloud layer.

Ocampan evolution occurred in a nearly sunless environment, or so Ced had been taught. For the few rotations where the cloud layer thinned enough to allow more light and thus radiation in, the Ocampa typically lived indoors. Traditionally, the sunny seasons were known as the "hibernation times." While the low levels of light filtering through the cloud layer were critical to Ocampan growth and development, continuous, direct exposure to sunlight was deadly. Ocampans' physiology—from their lack of protective skin pigmentation to sense organs such as their radiation-sensitive retinas—wasn't equipped to handle heavy sunlight. Even neurological functioning seemed to be impaired when an Ocampa absorbed too much sun energy.

Whatever (or whoever, thought Ced) had stopped the rain had also begun dissolving the cloud layer. At first, preoccupation with planetside water shortages had prevented the researchers from focusing their attention elsewhere. All energies were devoted to solving the water crisis. Then the malignant skin lesions and miscarriages proliferated, and sunny days came with more frequency, forcing researchers to face the unthinkable: Ocampa was losing its water. It wasn't as simple as historical shifts in water distribution due to weather or other environmental factors. What researchers discovered was a steady downward trend in net planetary water resources: The water was slowly disappearing and wasn't reappearing in the form of water vapor, underground water table reserves, or ice pack.

Many refused to believe the evidence, attributing the changing climate to fluke circumstances that would ultimately reverse on their own. The spiritually minded believed that Ocampa was on the receiving end of supernatural punishment and that an apocalypse was upon them. Some in governing conclave councils believed that these "droughts" would pass. They wanted only to deal with the most immediate concerns: feeding their people and protecting them from the increasingly serious sunlight problem. Others, like those who followed Lia, believed that the planetary environment was being artificially manipulated by the power-mad Mestof and his followers. She vowed to do whatever was required to stop Mestof from systematically bringing all of Ocampa under his rule by this cruelest of blackmail. The most gifted seers dismissed Lia's allegations as being impossible; no one wielded the kind of power required to diminish Ocampa's water supply. They labeled General Lia crazy and dismissed her as a radical with political aspirations of her own. In some quarters, her military quests were seen as insane crusades against an imaginary enemy.

Ced, a retired soldier, had been a member of a conclave council that chose to avoid involvement in all conflicts.

He'd faithfully executed his council duties, believing he was in the right until a moon ago when he saw General Lia marshal her troops against Mestof's in an effort to prevent his conclave from being annexed to Mestof. He watched, horrified, as his fellow councillors made no effort to protect themselves or those who had elected them, so he had abandoned his post to fight beside Lia's troops. When the battle ended, he had pledged the service of his lance to Lia and had never looked back.

Now he functioned as her closest advisor; together they plotted stratagems that they hoped would lead to Mestof's demise. To this end, Lia would approach the last lineal baron of the western hemisphere to see if he would join forces with her against Mestof. Baron Var had land and resources that Lia would require should she attempt to mount a serious offensive attack on Mestof's forces.

At last Lia found the rank insignia, carefully wrapped and tied in a bundle of waterproof cloth. Ced watched as she reverently unwound the cloth and removed the insignia. It was no small feat for one of Lia's ilk to ascend to the command of an army at the young age of three. Centering the gem-encrusted piece in the middle of her forehead, she threaded it over her ears and tied the straps at the base of her skull, beneath the abundant blond plaits streaming down her back. "My gifts will protect us," she said confidently. "If they attempt to lay a hand on either of us, I'll invoke a shield around us."

And when you employ that tactic in battle, we have you surrounded with a squadron of warriors, protecting you from whatever mischief Mestof concocts, Ced thought. "But in the trance state, your self-defense options are limited—"

She placed a finger to his lips. "I trust you to help protect me." A slight smile softened her serious expression. "The baron will not grant an audience to one who shows up with a militia pounding on his door with fire lances. We go without the others." Taking a seat on a three-legged stool beside the trunk, she fished behind her mussed sleeping cot until she found her fire lance secured in its carrying case. She discarded the carrying case, slid open the lance's control panel, and began adjusting the weapon's circuitry, which she'd previously customized.

"How else can I help prepare for the journey, my liege," Ced said quietly.

Knowing you are beside me is enough, she spoke to his mind, and returned to her task.

Not for the first time, Ced studied his general's lovely, youthful face, wishing for all the rain of Ocampa that the sooths had found greater psionic abilities in him so he could be granted the right to offer suit to Lia. She hadn't yet taken a first, let alone the three or four mates that were the prerogative of one in her position. With her *elogium* soon at hand, Ced wondered at her continuing reluctance to choose a mate; he personally knew of several suitors with both the required mental gifts and the rank to court someone of Lia's stature. It had recently come to Ced's attention that suspicious conclave members, gossiping indiscreetly, had speculated that Lia was a fraud and would be unable to deceive a psionically gifted mate. *Perhaps she is simply waiting to see how events play out with the baron before she commits to anyone.* Even that didn't make sense to Ced. *Carrying a child should enhance her mental acumen in battle, so why delay? Could it be she hasn't found the right mate yet—that she might have formed attachments to someone not well suited to her?*

Like yourself, came the thought.

In your dreams, came the answer.

As was usually the case when these thoughts occurred, Ced quickly shuttled them aside. Why would a female of Lia's beauty and exceptional gifts desire a homely mate, one balding, advancing in age, and whose damaged body bore six years of battle scars and poorly healed wounds? He could hardly move without his hot, swollen joints shooting pain into his limbs. Serving Lia and her cause gave him the will to ignore his misery, to put aside his longing to transfer his meager engrams to a sage and embrace the Other Life. His reborn self might not return to location a time or place where he could be close to Lia as he was in this time so he would endure as long as he could.

Suddenly, the fabric door of the tent parted, admitting Lia's senior counselor, who was flushed and panting. He clutched at his abdomen in an effort to regulate his breath. *Not good news,* Ced thought grimly. He turned, met Tel's sober gaze. "Speak, Patriarch."

The counselor righted himself and inhaled sharply. "The messenger has returned from Palal," he said, his voice gravelly with fatigue. "The city fell to Mestof's forces less than a moon ago but our allies in the region have already been routed out and killed."

"Mestof must have sent in sooths to thought-probe the city's residents," Lia said. "That's the only way they could have so readily identified those who sympathize with us."

"Not possible," Ced said. "No sooth has the ability to ascertain such specific information." *If they can, our efforts to stop the war and fight the warning will amount to dust. There will be no place we can go where the enemy can't know our plans.* As Lia's adjunct, he had to always consider the worst possible potential outcomes, especially since Lia was such an idealist.

"And recall how I was designated a neutral when it came to the gifts. The sooths sent me to the factories, where I labored for several seasons before my gifts manifested themselves. These are strange days, Ced. Anything is possible."

"We can't risk going into the baron's fortress, General," Ced reiterated. "Should Mestof have spies in the court with the ability to thought-probe us, all our intentions will be known."

"There is something odd about how Mestof is proceeding. I believe if all his servants had the gifts displayed at Palal, he would have destroyed us already instead of engaging us in the occasional skirmish or minor battle. No, I believe that Mestof hasn't found a way to create an army of psionically gifted warriors, rather that someone in Mestof's ranks has abilities we've never seen before."

"There are stories, General," Tel said, "of two such warriors whom Mestof counts among his closest advisors. It is said that they can use their gifts to create hallucinations in the minds of many simultaneously. They can direct water from out of a streambed into the sky and call up fire from the ground."

"I've heard those rumors too, Tel," Lia said. "And while there are those that discount them, I'm inclined to believe there is truth in the stories somewhere. Just how much, I cannot say. We must persuade the baron to come over to the Alliance—that much is certain." *Are you ready?* she spoke to Ced.

For a brief moment, she unshielded her thoughts and Ced felt her anxiety.

I will defend you to my death, my liege, he said.

Should it come to that, Ced, we will die together.

As they traveled through the outlying villages and past the farms and factories on Baron Var's land, Lia felt reassured. Many Ocampans paused from their labors to wish them well. She could sense the stress the drought had brought to their lives and their desire for a quick resolution to the conflict they believed was the cause of the drought. They needed to look no further than to the eastern hemisphere to know what kind of autocrat Mestof was and how he threatened what limited freedoms these peasants had under Var's rule. Mestof took generous tribute for himself from every field tilled in his districts. Var wasn't nearly as greedy.

Though he was a generous and reasonable governor, Baron Var had granted little autonomy to those who worked his lands; they had a long struggle ahead to obtain the rights that those in Lia's district had obtained. Still, there was no question that all would suffer if Mestof won in the end. Lia counted on the baron having come to the same conclusion.

She and Ced were admitted almost immediately after they appeared at the gates. There was no question in her mind that they were expected, that the baron's spies had informed their liege of every move they'd made within his lands. He'd probably made up his mind whether he had any interest in their cause. Even utilizing her powers to their fullest, she'd yet to learn what the baron's intentions were. She'd have expected to overhear an indiscreet thought among those who lacked either the gifts or the mind discipline to protect their privacy. After a long winding trek through the grand and spacious palace, she entered the baron's inner chambers without any of the advantages that she usually had, a fact that she diligently hid from Ced. He worried enough without having to know how precarious their circumstances were. As was required, she surrendered her lance to the guards at the entrance. Then doors banged closed behind her, and she heard the security bars slide into their slots with a jarring clang and a click: there would be no easy escape from this place.

How she could move freely on a battlefield overrun

with spear-wielding warriors intent on slaughtering her and feel safer than she did now in this nearly silent place might be amusing were circumstances less dire. She looked around the circular perimeter and saw Var's advisors studying her intently, their beady dark eyes, buried in wrinkled pockets of pallid gray skin, intently following her every step from their perches on stiff, high-backed chairs. From above, a cold blue light pierced the translucent marble dome, shrouding the room in catacomb-like half-light. She walked slowly across the stone floor, her feet shuffling over the ornate inlaid patterns of green and gold and white. At the center of the room, at a point directly beneath the dome, she stopped.

Baron Var sat at the point opposite her on a dais, surrounded by his mates, his legates, and his household servants. She immediately felt his mind searching for hers so she shielded her thoughts.

"You want my forces to join your cause," he said finally. He leaned forward in his chair, resting his hands on his thighs and staring at her intently.

"If you want to protect your holdings from Mestof, yes," Lia said. "You will lose your sovereignty if you fail to act."

Var waved his hand. "Mestof has assured me that he has no interest in my holdings. I am in no danger from him."

"If you believe that, you are a gullible fool."

A gasp rose from the crowds. The advisors shifted in their chairs and a low murmur of chatter rose up from their ranks.

"You are the gullible fool if you believe you're among friends, General Lia." Var rose from his chair.

He had powers rivaling hers; she felt them pricking at the edges of her consciousness. Unveiling her mind, she fairly shouted: *Mestof makes fools of whomever he deals with. Ask King Tek—oh wait. You can't. Mestof beheaded him the day they were to sign their nonaggression treaty.*

Tek was a figurehead with no warrior-guard to speak of, never mind the man was a fool, Var argued back. *I will not form an alliance with one who cannot win.*

"Do not mistake me for one who cannot win, Baron," Lia said, walking forward until she stood near the base of the dais. "I am not here because I seek power." She fell to her knees. "Should you require it, I will swear an oath to give my allegiance to you when Mestof is defeated."

Var took a few steps down the dais stairs. "If I accept your allegiance, Mestof will surely make me a target for his next attack," he said gruffly. For a brief moment, he flooded her mind with his concerns for his people, his anxiety over the drought—his doubts about her personally—before abruptly shielding his mind again. He would not risk it. He would fight to the death to protect what he had, but he would not willingly taunt or engage Mestof in open war.

All that Lia had fought for came down to this moment. She could continue to pester Mestof and try to wear down his forces, but she knew that ultimately, she was merely a fingerfish to a leviathan. Unless Baron Var could be persuaded of the rightness of their cause. "Ocampa is dying," she said, imbuing her words with feeling but avoiding sentimentality. She would not win by emotion, but by reason. "I cannot claim to fully understand the mischief Mestof wields, but surely you cannot fail to understand what is happening on your own lands among those who call you liege. The rain is gone and with it, the crops. Within a season, your people will become weak from malnutrition. They will have to labor twice as hard for half the harvest, and in the end you will have nothing to offer the merchants who come in from the north. You will become vulnerable. How can you fail to see that this is exactly what Mestof wants?

"Unless the rains come, what's now verdant and arable will become inhospitable waste, and where once you were known as a strong but compassionate merchant prince you will find that you preside over a dying kingdom with no choice but to surrender all you have to Mestof." Lia raised her gaze to his face and wrestled his eyes until they locked with hers. "You will end your days in disgrace, leaving your heirs with nothing.

"Regardless of what you choose to do today, I will continue my fight. I will fight until Mestof's wizards destroy me with their evil sooth-doing and my blood drenches Ocampa's thirsty soil. I come to you seeking an alliance of like minds—those who refuse to accept the destiny Mestof is determined to foist upon us." Her head fell back and she raised her face to the light streaming through the domed roof of the hall. Opening her arms, she closed her eyes and invoked the trance, pushing away her surroundings. She heard protests—felt their animosity pushing against her, trying to disrupt her invocation. She received their angry energy, transformed it into fortification for her own thoughts, and then released.

A faint buzzing tickled her ears as she extended her awareness beyond her five senses and into the substance of the marble, ascertaining the character and cohesiveness of the bonds that gave it form until she knew each molecule and atom. Her thoughts sang to the smallest particles until they vibrated in harmony with her song. Slowly, the chorus swelled as each particle acknowledged and embraced the music she offered. She pushed through the stone and into the air flowing in and around the building, seeking to know each element individually; she acknowledged their uniqueness and bid the elements to seek for like elements. She called to the matter and gathered it together.

Beyond the edge of her consciousness, she heard an earsplitting crack, felt the air dislodging as large chunks of marble fell from the sky and crashed on the floor around her. There was a sting on her cheek as a stone pellet grazed her skin. Screams and shouts of protest made the air around her tremble. She maintained her focus, continuing her call to the elements, pushing her thoughts as far as she ever had. Slowly her strength was sapped from her limbs, but she refused to relent, focusing her will as far as her mind could reach—farther.

A breath of cool damp.

A faraway crack of thunder.

A gray shadow suddenly enveloped the sun; mist swallowed the room in a damp fog.

Droplets touched her parched lips.

The sky growled, convulsed.

The room trembled.

Rain poured through the shattered dome.

A weak smile touched Lia's lips; her awareness dilated, then contracted, diminishing into a pinprick of black.

Ced struggled in the grips of the guards who held him fast, preventing him from rushing to Lia's aid. "I want to help her!" He shouted to be heard over the rain rattling against the stone floors. His gaze never left the crumpled, unconscious form on the floor before him. He saw a rivulet of blood drizzling down her pale cheek and wondered what other injuries she might have sustained from falling debris. Around him, chaos reigned. Those racing to make a panicked escape from the chamber barely outnumbered those shocked by the miraculous appearance of rain within the baron's hall.

"What if an attack is next?" Ced heard one of his guards say to his compatriot.

Seconds later, the guard removed a knife from his belt with his free hand, briefly brandished it before Ced's face, and then pressed the flat side of the blade against the skin of Ced's throat. "We should kill him before he can help her—"

"If we anger her, she might kill us!"

"But we can't let him go—"

"Bind him!"

Without further discussion, the guards roughly threw Ced into a chair formerly occupied by one of the advisors and manacled his wrists to the armrest.

Ced threw all his weight forward, kicking at his captors' legs, trying to leverage himself off their torsos by pushing against them with his boots—anything to get the traction he needed to wrestle free. The knife-wielding guard turned angrily on Ced, throwing a hard punch against the side of his head—

Wait. Ced's body went slack, his eyes drawn toward a place over his guard's shoulder. He barely noticed that his guard's knife arm had dropped to his side and that his captor too had been distracted. Though Ced was a neutral, even he sensed the energy shift in the room, as if a pent-up sigh had been exhaled.

Something changed. . . . *No*, he mentally corrected, *someone has changed us.* A tall male Ocampa of unknown rank and position calmly parted the crowds huddled nervously around the baron; each serene step he took across the dais seemingly dissipated the crowd's turbulent mood. Ced had never seen anything like this ability to assuage a crowd—even during the meditations Lia led with the troops before battle. Anxious cries and talk diminished until only the rain, mingled with a small child's hiccoughing sobs, could be heard.

From the dais, the stranger walked down the stairs toward Lia's broken form, apparently unaffected by the rain and blustering winds. He paused where he stood. As his gaze swept the chamber, the rain slowed to a trickle—then stopped. Wispy, white vapor seeped through the stones, disturbed by the sporadic plinks of droplets.

Ced tensed, a surge of concern for his liege sending his pulse racing. And yet . . . Ced lacked the willpower to move—or even to cry out warning against those who would harm his liege. *Forgive me, Lia, for failing you,* he thought, wishing his liege could hear him. Panic gave way to a curious sense of trust: Ced knew, though he couldn't say how, that the stranger wouldn't hurt Lia.

Ced watched, mesmerized as the stranger bent down and scooped Lia up one-handed, cradling her as if she weighed nothing. He touched his free hand to the wound on her cheek: the blood disappeared and no trace of the wound was left behind. Ced blinked, certain that his eyes deceived him in the wan light, but no, a faint flush of color was returning to Lia's skin. The dark-haired stranger tenderly untangled the sodden mass of braids, and as he did so, Lia shuddered. To Ced's relief, her eyelids flickered, opened, and he heard her take in a ragged breath and cough. His heart sang out: *She is alive! Thank the maker!* A doting smile curled the stranger's lips as he cupped her face, gazing on Lia with what Ced could only call wonderment. The stranger began speaking but Ced heard nothing. The sibilant hiss of the stranger's unintelligible whispers became a counterpoint to the intermittent plip-plop of water dripping on the floor.

Even at this distance, Ced felt as if he were witnessing a private moment, though he lacked the strength or desire to avert his gaze. As he looked around him, it appeared the others in the room felt similarly. Those who just moments ago had been inclined to kill him stared dumbly at Lia and her rescuer.

Ced might have gawked along with the others had the buzzing, low-pitched thrum not distracted him. At first, he thought his hearing might have been affected by the guard's punch. He shook his head, hoping to disrupt whatever stimulus might be causing the noise. Instead, the thrumming became louder.

One possibility: Insects might have swarmed into the hall when Lia had broken the dome. Their troops had certainly encountered clouds of biting gnats and disease-carrying dust flies, now endemic to Ocampa since the rains had stopped. Because his hands were still bound, he rubbed his ear with his shoulder, hoping to discourage or brush off any flying pests that might be buzzing near his head. Around him, the air stirred as people on all sides shuffled and shifted. *The thrall of Lia's rescue must be wearing off.* He tensed, worried that the mob might reignite and the melee resume. Years of military service had finely honed his instincts, though, and he ascertained, without being able to fully survey his surroundings that the crowd's agitation wasn't antagonistic. Still, the rapidly shifting environment troubled him more than his own discomfort. A single command could rupture the peace, turning a complacent follower into a snarling attacker. He had to be watchful for the sake of his liege. Whoever this rescuer might be, it was Ced who had sworn an oath to protect the general and it was Ced who would give his life, if necessary, to that end. Deeply reluctant, he tore his eyes from Lia and looked around him. Misery appeared to afflict the entire room; the earlier calm had been completely banished. Some swatted their ears or shook their heads; others massaged their temples or pressed their hands against their faces. The baron shifted restlessly on his throne, pulling his cloak up over his head and burying himself beneath it. Ced, too, fought the impulse to shield himself from the sound. He longed to tuck his legs up against his body or huddle in a corner, though being shackled to the chair made such action impossible.

By now, the thrumming noise reverberated throughout the chamber, intensifying to a degree that he could feel the thrum in his bones until he ached. He groaned aloud. Constant vibrations sent twinges through his molars and jaw and sent pain radiating through his skull. He focused his will and pushed aside all distractions and for a brief moment directed all his thoughts, confused as they were, toward Lia. In spite of his limited capacity to initiate psionic communication with her, the combination of her gifts and her familiarity with him would make her especially susceptible to his thoughts. His fear, his concerns, his worries—his love—for her filed his mind; he willed her to receive his message and, in turn, send a message to his mind. *Answer me, my liege. Let me know all is not lost.*

Nothing.

And again, he extended his thoughts, directing them toward his liege. Instantaneously, the thrumming increased. First his hands shook, then his arms, until his body convulsed uncontrollably. *Where is this noise coming from?* His wrists jerked against the manacles, slicing his skin to ribbons. Blood drizzled onto his fingers. *Hear me, General!*

"Lia!" he cried out.

He remained alone in his thoughts.

A close-by child had doubled over, hands pressed over

her ears, shoulders hunched. The mother, face contorted with pain, muttered soothing comforts to her whimpering child even as involuntary tears streamed down her cheeks. He must spare his liege this pain. Throwing his legs forward, he scooted his chair a few centimeters. He repeated the action, and again, until he had nearly cleared the perimeter of the crowd. The pillars holding up the ceiling shook; the rock walls groaned and creaked. An earsplitting crack overhead warned of the building's probable collapse. A man off to Ced's side fainted. Fighting the effects of the thrumming drained Ced's strength; remaining alert and focused under these circumstances became more difficult with each passing moment. Only his pledge to Lia gave him the will to push deeper within himself to find the will to continue holding on. Pain eroded his grasp of reason. He despaired of his weakness, pleading for mercy on Lia's behalf.

An unfamiliar yet soothing voice whispered to his mind: *Take heart, good Ced. Whether you live or die, your liege will be well cared for. There is a greater plan . . .*

And just as abruptly as it had begun, the thrumming ceased and was replaced by a strange, golden-red glow from the center of the room. The stranger, still holding Lia, transformed before Ced's eyes. Though he still appeared to be as Ocampan as Ced, the stranger—and Lia— changed into varying monochromatic colors and seemed to flatten from three dimensions to two, as if they were shifting into another state. Their shadowy, ribbonlike forms undulated into slow, rippling waves, bending until their appearance was disproportionate and distorted, nearly beyond recognition. The outline of their bodies blurred, their edges began dissipating like mist rising off a lake. Beneath them, the stone softened into slate gray goo. The stranger's feet vanished, dissolving into the floor. For a brief second, Ced thought a hole had opened and would swallow the stranger and Lia. His heart skipped a panicked beat. He cursed his misfortune to be trapped in this chair. A bright, white light burst forth from the center of the room—as if a fountain of fire had erupted through the floor. He turned his eyes away from the blinding light; the thrumming resumed, quickly shifting into a high-pitched squeal. The vibrations cracked the surrounding walls. Deep in the earth, tremors boomed.

As abruptly as it started, the light was gone.

And Lia with it.

"I will find you!" Ced screamed, anguished. But the roar of collapsing stone drowned out his words. He felt the whoosh of stones and dust rumbling past, heard the terrified screams all around him. *I have to survive this. I have to survive this so I can save her!* he thought, throwing all his weight forward, hoping the chair would offer him a small measure of protection from the cave-in. He hit the floor face-first with such impact that he knew, from the instant he hit, that the blow would fell him. Warm blood gushing from his scalp coated his eyelids, poured down his cheeks. Tempestuous dizziness dislodged all his senses—he no longer knew which way was up or where he was; nausea twisted his insides. A single thought from an unfamiliar mind pierced the dark confusion swiftly overtaking him:

Your death will not be in vain, faithful servant.

Chapter 1

The Doctor floated in black so thick no sensation could penetrate. He tried moving his limbs, opening his eyes, seeking to touch, and failed to discern if his holographic body still existed. None of his programmed senses functioned as he was accustomed, and yet he knew he was *someplace* because *he* existed. When he was deactivated aboard *Voyager,* his sentience simply stopped—a suspended pause—until he was reactivated and his lifeline continued. Here and now, he knew only himself, as if the sum total of his existence had been reduced to self-awareness, nothing further. Not even his vast database could provide a reference point. Or had he even retained a connection to his database? He couldn't say for certain. So many of his thoughts were blurry and unfocused. He imagined his current state had much in common with what patients experienced post-anesthesia: aware, but not awake; cognizant of one's body, yet disconnected from it. Whatever force had ripped him from *Voyager* had sent his holomatrix into a state of shock, though the Doctor didn't know how that was possible.

Though he couldn't sense his limbs, he mentally directed his arms and legs to move, reaching into the darkness to find the parameters of his environment. The instant the thought left him, an impenetrable barrier, that he sensed but couldn't see, surrounded him. A force pressed right up against the parameters of his program. Drowsily he sought to lift his arm to touch his combadge. "Docplur . . . coo . . . sib . . . gib-blehb—" he muttered thickly, his tongue cleaving to the roof of his mouth. The incomprehensible garble emerging from his mouth was beneath one of his abilities. He tried again. When his third attempt proved futile, his determination awoke. The luxury of lolling about like some lazy lush on eternal shore leave wasn't granted to one of such vital importance as himself. He must return to his patients and a crew who desperately needed him. Exerting his will, he pushed against the unseen force that cocooned him in this blackness. The force pushed back, squeezing him into claustrophobic confinement. Dizziness assaulted the Doctor; he would not be deterred, though his body quaked from the effort. The slightest give in the resistant force imbued him with confidence. With persistence, he would free himself, of that he was certain. A nanosecond of warning alerted him to possible danger: a faint, warm sizzle brushed his back. Nothing specific about the sensation worried the Doctor, who routinely passed through forcefields that would cook the innards of a carbon-based life-form on contact. Believing the sizzling sensation to be evidence of progress, he increased his efforts. Clenching his teeth, he thought, *One last push. . . .*

Jagged energy threads sizzled and sparked, burrowing thorough his body at lightning speed. His matrix frazzled, splintering him into bits of matter; every particle in his being spun at reckless velocity, unleashing torrents of superheated, subatomic tornadoes, scorching through every millimeter of his form. Out of self-protection, his thoughts instantly retreated into a detached, drifting place. From a separate vantage he processed the searing torment coursing through every photon he was composed of. *It is odd,* he thought, *to have existed as long as I have and not understood pain before.* His matrix oscillated with such speed and force that he wondered if he would explode into billions of tiny bits. As reflex took the reins from conscious thought, he twitched uncontrollably, soon jerking with seizure force. A single thought lingered: *Save me.*

As instantly as the attack had begun, it ended. The forces coursing through him ceased; cohesion returned. The Doctor's consciousness lurched for a few moments longer until stumbling to a peaceful stop. He recovered quickly from his ordeal; his matrix hummed along as though it had never been disrupted. More importantly, he had been freed from whatever forces had bound him. Sensation returned to his body and he became keenly aware of being sprawled, flat on his back, his vertebrae pressing uncomfortably into a cold, hard surface. He blinked several times but the impenetrable, silent darkness still surrounded him. Clearing his throat, he touched his combadge. "Doctor to sickbay."

Silence.

He repeated the action, calling on the ship and half the members of the crew before he accepted, howbeit reluctantly, that he must be out of combadge range. A few of Lieutenant Torres's choicer curse words came to mind, but he believed he was above such impulses. As a thinking being, he would reason his way out. He eliminated being trapped in the Gremadian black hole (no out-of-the-ordinary gravitational pull) and being suspended in a space vacuum from the list of possibilities. He sensed neither motion nor mechanically generated noise, allowing him to rule out a presence on any starship or traveling craft.

Methodically, he contemplated every potentiality his mind could conjure until a strangely beautiful sight drew his attention from his ruminations.

Funnels of glowing specks swirled around him, casting shadows and illuminating, in flashes, rippling velvet black walls. He instinctively knew, as a distant relation, that the specks were individual photons. A steady stream of photons poured from an unseen place above him until a saturation point was reached, and the Doctor felt as though he was encircled by a glittery, golden tube. A transformation began. Sparkling white-yellow flecks danced, touched, and joined together in waves. In turn, waves braided with other waves, forming ribbons that became progressively brighter with each added strand until curtains of light revealed all. At last, the Doctor could see his surroundings.

The velvety black surface was not a wall, but hanging bloodred curtains; the hard surface beneath him was a floor of joined wooden slats painted matte black. High above, he saw row after row of red, blue, yellow, and white spotlights mounted on metal strips. A canvas backdrop painted with a typical pastoral setting—grass, trees, blue sky, and sun—stretched horizontally behind him and up past catwalks and hanging ropes. The ceiling was at least sixty meters away. *I'm on a stage,* he thought. The realization filled him with pleasure.

As he became more aware of his surroundings, he heard the faint strains of music playing somewhere beyond the curtains. He listened carefully. *String instruments. Repetitious, almost atonal melodies, though the key progressions in that last section are quite sophisticated.* Nothing in the style or sound of the piece recalled anything in his vast knowledge of music across the galaxy. He decided to investigate—in the interest, of course, of augmenting his database. Placing his palms against the floor, he pushed himself up to his knees, then onto his feet. He took a few careful, creaking steps toward the curtains, the music becoming louder by the meter. Recalling his recent encounter with near-dissolution, he surveyed his surroundings to assess the danger and found nothing more troubling than an abandoned backstage area furnished with light panels, props, and cast-off costumes thrown over chair backs and tables. He walked more quickly to the front of the stage, curled his fingers around the edge of the curtain, and pulled it back.

The magnificent trappings of an ornately decorated theater—perhaps nineteenth-century European—filled his view. Upward of two thousand people could sit in this auditorium, resplendent in its gold-leafed railings and red velvet seats. The Doctor's eyes glanced upward—and that chandelier! *Voyager*'s bridge could hardly contain it! Flickering candlelight glinted through the teardrop crystals, illuminating the ceiling painted in round-cheeked cherubs and gauzy angels floating among the clouds. He stepped through the curtains into the empty auditorium and for the first time saw the source of the music.

The orchestra pit was filled with a large string ensemble—as he had anticipated. What he hadn't anticipated was instruments playing themselves. He watched, fascinated by the bows seesawing over the taut strings, the plink-plink-plink of plucks by unseen hands. The Doctor, who didn't believe in ghosts, failed to understand why a creator with the brilliance to either perfectly automate an instrument or endow it with sentience would set his creations to playing rather obscure, purposeless music with no audience looking on. He was approaching the pit, hoping to study the curious technology, when the stage curtains parted abruptly and were pulled into the wings. The Doctor spun around and saw the pastoral backdrop, illuminated by spotlights calibrated to evoke the sense of dawn. Though the curtains had been drawn by an invisible hand, he was no longer alone onstage.

When the transformed Assylia emerged from the cocoon in sickbay, awe had filled him. Such beauty had been a flickering candle compared with the blazing sun that he witnessed descending from the stage's rafters. Creatures of light and wings illuminated the muddy gloom, radiating with serene majesty. One by one they emerged from a place beyond, until a dozen became a hundred, then thousands. In the lifetime he'd experienced since he'd been activated, he had come to know the fragility of life, both the steadily weakening flutters as a life was extinguished and the exuberant celebration of a life seized from death's grasp. Neither of those emotional extremes could compare to the rapturous wonderment he felt watching these astonishing creatures. Their wings beat rhythmically, up and down, with the strength of a massive sail catching the wind. The Doctor watched the creatures dashing around the vivid sky-canvas, feeling an unfamiliar longing to be freed from the restraints of his holographic existence, to live with utter abandon.

Tentative fingers of sunrise cleaved the blue. One by one, golden pink sunbeam spotlights heralded the day. Like angels, the creatures flew among tufts of clouds singing up the dawn. And the music! Had there ever been a more divine chorus? The Doctor, who prided himself on understanding the nuances and subtleties of the most complex music known to galaxies, satiated his senses on the glorious harmonies, soaking in each chord progression, each trilled treble note. With soul-starved intensity, he devoured the songs ringing through the sky, imprinting the memories into his holomatrix with the fervent hope that someday he might be able to join his voice with their song and, by so doing, reexperience the choruses he now heard.

A thought occurred. Tuvok's music, the music that drew him from *Voyager* and led him to Gremadia—this must be what he heard. Understanding—and empathy—overcame the Doctor as he comprehended what Tuvok had forfeited when he gave up his own transformation so that Assylia might join her people. Her people. . . . He mused on this for a long moment, and then realized, *These angelic beings are the Monorhan's Fourteenth Tribe!*

A shadow darkened the sky. The Doctor's holographic innards twisted.

A sextet of shiny black chitinous, segmented legs curled over the edge of a cloud. How such a thing could be conjured on stage astounded the Doctor. Attached to the legs was a globular abdomen, covered with coarse shaggy hair. Sharp pincers descended from the abdomen, flexing open and snapping closed. A pair of glowing eyes, the color of dried blood and mounted on slithery tubules, emerged from the abdomen and hovered, shifting from side to side, watching. Even from this distance, the Doctor could hear the insectoid creature chittering hungrily, tapping its legs together with a clicking crackle. Soon another insectoid followed, and then another, until they stained the dawn sky.

Ch-ch-ch-ch-ch-ch-ch. The chatter rained from the sky, pelting the stillness with angry hisses. Legs tapped together more rapidly and the hissing grew. The Doctor could sense the malevolent rage radiating from the insectoids directed toward . . . the angel creatures. The transformed Monorhans. But, why? Surely such lovely beings could hardly have malicious capacity—they would harm no one. From what the Doctor could see, the angel creatures sought only to play, to fly, to rejoice in their existence. To that end, the angel creatures continued their carefree play, seemingly oblivious to the storm gathering around them.

The attack came so swiftly the Doctor might have missed it if he looked away. The insectoids plunged over the cloud top toward the angel creatures. With their pincers, the insectoids ripped the wings from the angels' bodies, crushed them, and tossed them away with gleeful abandon, then grasped the wounded creatures between their three sets of legs before snapping the bodies into small pieces. Helpless, the Doctor watched as long as he could bear it before looking away, their pained cries tearing at him.

Just as their song had called the sun, their nightmare brought the storm. The sky darkened, rumbling with thunderous protest. The angel song became howling, mournful cries of suffering. From among the wails, the Doctor discerned that some of the angels fought back: he heard the shrill, insectoid squeals, the crunch of broken exoskeletons shattering to bits. He returned his gaze to the battle, hoping that the angels could defeat the insectoids swarming through the sky. Hope wasn't enough. He wanted to fight beside the transformed Monorhans. He opened his mouth to shout warning: what emerged was song.

The Doctor sang with all the conviction he could muster, pleading with the creatures to cease their fighting. Words he didn't know came to mind and he set them to music that came from a place deep inside. As he sang, the sparkling funnels of photons swirled around him, creating a spotlight. Their presence strengthened him. His musical commands slowly overtook the cacophony pouring from the painted sky. The demonstrable progress prompted him to sing as loudly and powerfully as he could. One by one, the combatants broke apart from their fighting until nearly half of the insectoids had retreated behind the clouds. *I've done it,* he thought, buoyed by confidence.

So filled with the power of his song was the Doctor that he almost didn't notice that the instrumental song from the orchestra pit had changed. With the decreased battle noise, he became keenly aware that the instrumental music behind him was playing counterpoint to his song instead of the odd music of before. As much as he felt compelled to continue forging peace, instinct told him he needed to see what was happening in the orchestra pit. He walked back to the edge of the stage, singing with each step.

His eyes went wide and his mouth dropped open. Each instrument in the orchestra had a player: him. There he was—many of him, in fact—attacking the violin with the expertise of a fifteen-fingered zessi, and again with the cello and bass. He had no idea where he'd learned to play the piano with such expressiveness, but there he was bent over the keyboard, making hand-over-hand runs with a finesse that even he didn't know he had. Curious as to the results, the Doctor continued his aria but transposed the notes into a different key. On cue, the instruments followed him, playing harmony. Satisfied, he smiled. He took a deep breath, prepared to embark on yet another measure of musical brilliance.

A female figure materialized beside him, her auburn hair flowing out behind her, like a figure out of a Raphael painting. The blue eyes, the high forehead, the full lips were familiar to him. . . . Then he remembered: the woman was a replica of one he'd met in sickbay. The captain had introduced her as Phoebe Janeway, but she was actually a Nacene taking on Phoebe's appearance. Could this be the same Nacene poseur? The version the Doctor knew from *Voyager* was off her rocker, to put in mildly. Presuming this redhead was Nacene might mean that he'd been transported to—*Exosia*. The thought of being in the realm of the Nacene chilled him, knowing that, thus far, he'd found the pandimensional species to be far from sympathetic creatures. Unbidden, the Doctor heard a refrain of the old air "When Irish Eyes Are Smiling" whistling in his mind.

Her eyes didn't smile; her eyes radiated cold rage.

"I want it transported to engineering." B'Elanna Torres studied the tricorder readout for perhaps the twelfth time in the last five minutes, enraged that the results, yet again, were useless. "I'll study it there."

"Lieutenant, I believe you have already obtained any diagnostic results that will be forthcoming from the remains of the tetryon transporters, " Ensign Vorik said, his voice an even monotone that made B'Elanna want to squeeze his throat until his vocal cords emitted a sound other than irrationally-calm-in-the-face-of-disaster. He studied the padd in his hand, which contained all the data they'd accumulated since Tom and Harry vanished nearly a day ago.

B'Elanna could quote every line on Vorik's padd chapter and verse. She knew the code and the frequency of every sensor and piece of communications equipment on the now-vanished shuttle. She also knew that Vorik was absolutely correct in his assessment of the situation: they already had whatever data they were going to get from the junk heap in the shuttlebay.

And she didn't care. There had to be something she'd missed even if she had to analyze that congealed glob of circuitry and metal one molecule at a time.

She touched her combadge. "Torres to Seven. Update me on the Blue Eye microsingularity."

"We have been able to conclude only that there may be a link between the growth of the microsingularity and the destruction of Gremadia and the subsequent disappearance of the Gremadian black hole. If our theories are correct about the artificial nature of this region, we may encounter more navigational or communication problems due to subspace destabilization, perhaps even deterioration."

"Subspace doesn't rot like a bad piece of fruit!"

"You are theoretically correct, Lieutenant. But the fact remains that if my current projections hold, subspace, as we understand it, will change—evolve—into something else, and no, I cannot explain it."

"Will *Voyager* clear this region before this evolution begins?"

"I cannot say."

B'Elanna balled her hands into fists and counted backward from ten, clinging to the knowledge that losing her temper now would get her nowhere. *If it's not one problem, it's fifty.* "Thank you, Seven. Let me know if you have any breakthroughs. Torres out." Turning, she noticed wide-eyed Ensign Matthews waiting nervously at her elbow, clutching a padd tight against her chest.

A sensor design specialist, *Voyager* had been Matthews's first posting on a nonscience vessel. She'd been used to quiet, respectful research laboratories. The constant chaos of *Voyager* had been an adjustment, to say the least, never mind the stress of working with a boss who lacked appreciation for the romance of pure science.

"Yes?" B'Elanna snapped, threading her arms across her chest, immediately castigating herself for her tone when Matthews flinched visibly. She took a deep breath and tried again, using a calmer voice. "You have the results of the latest sensor and communications sweeps searching for the *Homeward Bound*."

Wordlessly, Matthews passed the padd over to B'Elanna, who scanned them quickly, looking for a hopeful sign.

When she saw none, she cursed and kicked the remains of the transporter; the bones of her toes crunched like shells against rocks. An involuntary cry of pain escaped her before she clenched her jaw and forced any further traitorous noises back into her throat. A fiery pain surged through her tissues, shot through her leg muscles and into her torso before it diffused into throbbing stabs. *Breathe, B'Elanna,* she ordered her lungs. Through gritted teeth, she managed to dismiss Ensign Matthews before collapsing onto the deck.

"From the sound emitted when your foot came in contact with the transporter, I believe you may have broken the bones in your foot, Lieutenant," Vorik said. "Shall I initiate a site-to-site transport to sickbay?"

"No, transport these heaps of tetryon trash to the lab adjoining main engineering. I'll walk to sickbay."

"Is that wise?" Vorik asked.

"You don't get a vote in the matter." Squaring her shoulders, she started toward the turbolift, each excruciating step bringing tears to her eyes. A sudden, knifelike pain gave her pause; B'Elanna suspected it was a bone shard puncturing her skin. And yet, surprisingly, she felt liberated by the pain instead of crippled by it. It was as if the howling nerves in her feet sliced through her knotted-up insides, released all the pain she had carried since the shuttle disappeared, and allowed it to melt together into one big old seething mass. The emotional burden had been far more difficult for B'Elanna than her current physical predicament and now it was all indistinguishable. Pain was pain.

She entered the turbolift and after ordering the computer to take her to sickbay, she took advantage of the brief private moment. Her head dropped to her chest, she scrunched up her face and let loose a loud, visceral wail until her ears rang with the echo of her own voice. Exhaustion overtook her; she covered her face with her hands, slammed back against the wall, and slid to the floor.

She couldn't fathom her world without Tom. Whether she liked it or not, he'd become the emotional epicenter of her tempestuous existence. Slipping past her defenses using characteristically charismatic, clever ploys had been easy for a mercenary like Tom. Had it been the challenge of the impossible conquest that drew him to her? The place, the moment she knew he'd succeeded in making her love him—she couldn't name. She still hated herself for being stupid enough to fall for his gambit. And now she was stuck, sick with shock and nausea, wondering, worrying, waiting for answers that might never come. *Please let him be safe,* she thought. *Please let him come home.*

"Don't do it, Tom," Harry warned again, panic contorting his face.

Tom recognized the look. It was the same look Harry wore when Tom suggested that the captain really wouldn't care if he appropriated Chakotay's password to "borrow" from Tuvok's replicator rations to cover an unexpected gambling debt (unexpected because Ensign Tariq was obviously cheating: the way the chips landed on the wheel made a full-color quarto impossible!). Hypercautious Harry felt about risk the way Ferengi felt about loaning latinum. The irony of Harry's reluctance to wade into the unknown was that he, more than anyone in Tom's acquaintance, was most likely to be mutilated, squashed, or killed, regardless of how careful he was. So why be careful? In Tom's experience, most of the risky situations Harry studiously avoided had a component of fun.

Tom liked fun.

And he was hungry. If room service had food, he wanted some. He twisted the door handle and pulled the door back to admit the visitor. "Come on in!"

Harry cringed, scrunching up his eyes as if expecting a photon torpedo to detonate where he sat.

A uniformed server, a man wearing gold, purple, and black striped trousers with an antiquated military-style high-waisted solid purple jacket sporting rows of shiny brass buttons, wheeled his covered cart past Tom and stopped in front of Harry. His black pillbox hat with gold braid (being a holoprogrammer who specialized in "vintage" designs, Tom had an eye for such details) featured an ill-fitting chin strap. The syrupy light from the clown lamp failed to illuminate his face, which was bowed toward the cart.

Luscious smells wafted up from the cart. Tom's stomach growled impatiently. "I hope you've got pepperoni pizza in there—" Tom began.

The server yanked the burgundy drape off the cart, revealing a tray of hamburgers stacked with bacon, tomatoes, and lettuce; mounds of chili fries sprinkled with stringy, melted cheese; and two milkshakes as tall as Tom's forearm. "It's on the house, boys," the server said, meeting Tom's eyes and smiling predatorily.

"Q!" Tom's initial shock at Q's presence gave way to a backdoor sense of relief. The illogic and seeming randomness of their current predicament, with Q figured in, made more sense in kind of a Q-like way. How else could he and Harry have taken a test flight using the tetryon transporter and ended up in this stinky dive? He reached for a milkshake and took a long pull on a red-and-white-striped straw. *Mmmm . . . chocolate malt.*

"Don't eat that, Tom!" Harry said, his eyes wide. "It's probably—"

Tom paused in midsuck. Harry had a point. But he was hungry and this was the best malted milkshake he'd ever had; so what if it turned him into a tribble? He took another long pull, savoring the cold icy sweet streaming down his throat.

"Probably what?" Q leaned over, nearly touching his nose to Harry's. "What kind of Q do you take me for? I'm insulted, Mr. Kim." He held his hand—thumb touching his middle finger, poised to snap—next to Harry's ear.

Harry pulled back. "I didn't mean—I wasn't—I, um . . ." he stammered. Sweat beaded on his forehead and his face became a decidedly paler shade.

Q arched an eyebrow. "Gotcha." He glanced at Tom. "Is he always this easy?" he asked, jerking his thumb toward Harry.

Tom shrugged and reached for a chili fry. "Well yeah—" Tom said, hesitantly. "Pretty much."

"Have you missed me? I regret that I haven't stopped by since Q and I procreated, but the rigors of parenting and restoring order to the Continuum since the war have left me little time to socialize." Q took a seat on the edge of the bed beside Harry; Harry scooted over to put space between him and the entity. "What, pray tell is this? He lifted his arm, jammed his nose into the armpit, then inhaled extravagantly. Withdrawing, he wrinkled his upper lip and said, "Do I offend?" Shaking his head, he answered his own question. "No! Kathy's clearly failing to teach her kids how to demonstrate proper respect for their superiors. But more than that, we have history. I thought we'd be backslapping like old buddies!" He smacked Harry between the shoulder blades, who eked out a painful grunt in reply. Leaning over, Q peered up into Harry's hand-covered face. "Are you nervous, Mr. Kim?"

Harry shook his head. "This has to be a dream."

Q crossed his legs and looked over at Tom. "Regretfully not. Look, boys, I don't like having to involve myself in the troubles of lesser beings—"

Ply us with food, then start in on the insults. At least he's still the same old Q . . . Tom rolled his eyes and reached for a burger. He might as well be full before Q ruined his life.

"Oh don't start with me, Mr. Paris. There's nothing untoward about my intentions," he said snippily. "Fine. I confess: Toying with you lowly creatures can be amusing. But in this case I absolutely wish our rendezvous could come under more pleasurable circumstances. Inebriation, carousing, and other hedonistic pursuits might actually be fun with you two—" He glanced at Harry. "All right, maybe not him, but definitely you, Tommy. Let's wager half the galaxy and find ourselves some strippers from Plaranik V, shall we? I hear they're *very* flexible."

"What do you want, Q?" Tom asked. "Because, in spite of the food—"

"I knew *that* would win you over," Q said, obviously pleased. "You're a creature of very fundamental desires. Speaking of which, how's the little Klingon spitfire?"

"—it's been a long day and we're not in the mood," Tom concluded. "If there's no point to all this, send us home. *Now.*"

"Well, well! Your testy girlfriend's domesticated you, Tommy. Too bad. First Vash loses her sense of humor, now you're all work and no play. What's a Q to do?"

"Q," Harry said, raising his voice. "I'm with Tom. *Voyager*'s in trouble. We can't sit around here and make small talk."

Tom had to agree: Q's obvious enchantment with his own relentless prattling was testing his patience.

He cocked his head and offered Tom a put-out sigh. "Fine. I'll send you back after we take care of a few problems. Your esteemed captain really needs to curtail her humanitarian impulses and focus on the task at hand: namely, getting all you miscreants home. *Voyager*'s getting a reputation for not being able to work and play well with others. Kathy needs to learn to stay in her own sandbox or else there'll be a dustup." He paused. "Get it? Sandbox? Dustup? I keep throwing them, but you just stand there and watch the ball go by."

Tom suppressed a groan and struggled to stay on topic. "You're saying Captain Janeway caused a problem in the Monorhan sector?" he guessed.

Q smiled. "And it's a *doozy*. No half-measures for our Kathy! This time, she's managed to start the reversal of the Big Bang. Quite an accomplishment for such a primitive life-form, but nonetheless, ill advised in the grander scheme of things."

"Hold on there," Harry said suddenly alert, shaking his head with genuine incredulity. "That's quite a responsibility to heap on—what was it you usually call us, 'ugly bags of mostly water'?"

"That wasn't Q, that was—" Tom said.

"The *point* is," Q interrupted, rolling his eyes, "your species is mostly insignificant, but every once in a while you do something that makes your betters in the universal hierarchy take notice. Much the same way you might take note if a bunch of amoebas got together and built a tractor.

Something audacious and daring and, in this case—" He sneered at Harry. "—asinine."

Tom pulled a tipsy wood chair out from the desk where it was tucked and straddled it backward, facing Q. "Granted astrophysics wasn't my best subject at the Academy, but I'm failing to see how anything that *Voyager*'s done lately would have such catastrophic consequences."

A look of annoyance—or exasperation—flitted across Q's face. "It's always 'why this?' and 'why that?' with you corporeals. Patience, children. You'll have your answers soon enough. But we have to be on our way—"

Harry crossed his arms across his chest and exhaled loudly. "No. I'm not agreeing to go anywhere until you tell us where we are, what you want with us, and when we're going home."

Q sighed. "Think of this place as a suburb of the Q Continuum. There. Satisfied, Mr. Kim? The sooner we leave, the sooner we get back to that tin can you call a spaceship. Let's go." Q grabbed Harry's arm and tried—unsuccessfully—dragging him to his feet. "Be advised: You are moments away from becoming a newt."

"A suburb—not the Continuum proper?" Tom said. "Why? We've been in the Continuum before. Saved you from civil war last time we visited. Thought we'd be welcomed as heroes." Q's explanations weren't passing the "smell" test.

"The Continuum has a strict visitors policy these days. No riffraff." Q looked at them both disapprovingly. "Not to mention a dress code. Let's be on our way—"

A thought occurred. A wide, toothy grin split Tom's face. "You're in trouble."

"Am not!" Q said a little too quickly.

"You can't bring us into the Continuum because you don't want anyone to know. I'd say that puts us in a pretty good bargaining position. Say, we help you and you get *Voyager* back to the Alpha Quadrant." Tom removed the burger platter from the cart and passed it to Harry. "You really ought to try one. The sauce is outstanding."

"Don't mind if I do." Harry selected a double-decker cheeseburger with a large onion ring sandwiched between patties and bun.

Q threw his hands into the air. "All right! I admit that my reasons for bringing you here weren't entirely altruistic, but you have to believe me when I tell you that there wouldn't be a problem if it weren't for Kathy."

"Still falling back on that tired excuse, Q?" Harry said between bites. "If you've got that explanation, I'm all ears."

Q snapped his fingers. With a flash of white light, an enormous ear appeared in place of Harry's head.

"You really need to work on some new material, Q," Tom said.

Q frowned as he considered Harry. "Too predictable?"

Tom shrugged and nodded.

Q harrumphed and snapped his fingers.

Chakotay scrolled through the list of *Voyager*'s crew, studying their recent duty schedules, still amazed at the faithful service they continued to render, even under such strenuous circumstances. He didn't know how he could ask them to do more. There had to be another way he hadn't yet considered. He was just too damn tired to see it. Placing his hands over his face, he rubbed his eyes and rolled his neck around a few times to stretch out muscles cramped from sitting so long. Using a technique taught him by a shaman from his tribe, he cleared the clutter from his mind and revisited the task before him.

The list still looked the same as it had the last few times he'd studied it.

Slouching back in the Doctor's chair, he sighed aloud and looked over at Captain Janeway in her stasis chamber. Seven, after having done everything within her ability to help Janeway, had left a short time ago to continue her work in astrometrics. Not even the "miraculous" nano-probes would restore Kathryn to health.

"What would you do, Kathryn?" he said aloud. Being alone in sickbay meant he could indulge in a little crazy behavior—like talking to his nearly brain-dead command-ing officer. As acting ship's captain, he ought to be on the bridge, and he would be shortly. He just needed a little bit more time to think, without the eyes of every person on *Voyager* following his every move, worrying, seeking reas-surance that their deepest fears wouldn't be realized. Re-calling the worst of their recent near-catastrophes, from the war between the Borg and Species 8472 to the Hi-rogen takeover of their ship, Chakotay finally knew what it must have felt like to have the fates of these hundred and fifty people hinging on every decision you made. Janeway didn't have the luxury of being liked or being soft; she ex-pected the best from herself and would accept nothing less from her crew. He was trying to figure out if there was room for mercy in the equation too.

"I've examined every name on this list the same way I have since you gave me this job and for the first time in many years, I'm stuck," Chakotay said, glancing over at the stasis chamber. He wished for something, a miracle, perhaps. But he'd settle for an answer. He paused for a long moment, contemplating the silence, then said, "I guess I'll have to figure it out myself, which is probably what you would have told me if you could."

He asked the computer to change the sort parameters, providing him with each department's rosters organized by the most hours worked over the past week to the least. Within seconds, the reconfigured list appeared, and it was as useless as the previous one.

He recalled a time when each name on the list existed only as a rank and a department assignment. The names existed as pieces of this greater organism called *"Voyager"* and he would shuffle them around based on a host of easily quantified variables. Creating a duty roster was simple in those days, because the needs of the ship dictated his decision making. After four years of numberless hours living, working, and dying side by side with them, Chakotay couldn't look at these names without imagining the faces of the loved ones they left behind and the relationships they'd formed since arriving in the Delta Quadrant.

His eyes flickered over the engineering shifts and he discovered, not surprisingly, that B'Elanna hadn't slept in days. No wonder she was so ornery and short-tempered. The well-being of his chief engineer (or lack thereof) wasn't the only concerning factor in drafting the new duty roster. Years of scheduling Ensign Matthews taught him she was prone to anxiety attacks, especially when she worked more than two consecutive shifts. Sensors were vital to a successful exit from Monorhan space. Could he afford to let her take a break now? Take Crewman Crana, a technician. The Argelian had a tendency to become so absorbed in his work repairing gel-pack relays that he'd work three consecutive shifts before collapsing at his workstation. Crana's shifts had started after Sem had tampered with the gel packs. From what Chakotay could tell, he hadn't stopped working yet. Every individual on

B'Elanna's staff had a similar story. All of them needed a full two weeks of shore leave, not the extra duty shifts Chakotay was assigning them.

Scanning the list now in an attempt to organize the crew into a cohesive, functioning unit for the next several days was proving to be an exercise in futility. He knew, without asking, that virtually every person in every department had been working round the clock since they entered Monorhan space. In recent hours, he'd come across more than a few crew members curled up in the corners of their stations or slouched down on the floor, attempting to catch a little shut-eye between crises. Trying to organize a fair duty roster that took into account crew exhaustion when they lacked so many critical senior staff members was proving to be impossible.

"Computer, close file Duty Roster Charlie-Two-Six."

"File has not been updated. Do you still want to close?"

Before Chakotay could bark an affirmative answer, he heard footsteps behind him. He spun around to see who it might be.

"Why, hello, Commander," Neelix said. "Surprised to see you here. Figured you'd be on the bridge. Crewman Chell had an unfortunate mishap with a wok and a plesbrian sea urchin and I came by to get a dermal regenerator." The Talaxian craned his neck to look around to see behind Chakotay. "Looks like there's one over on the shelf. Do you mind—?"

Chakotay held out his hands as if to say "help yourself." "Crewman Chell's in the galley?"

"Helps him burn off some steam. Keeps his mind off things. Everyone's a bit on edge since—" Neelix nudged his head in the direction of what Chakotay was beginning to think of as a sarcophagus.

"Right." Chakotay understood the feeling. He'd rather

be anything but in charge at the moment. The screen filled with the unfinished duty roster nagged at him.

Neelix slipped the dermal regenerator into his pocket along with an analgesic hypospray. "Well, I'll be seeing you around, Commander," he said, and they exchanged waves before he started for the door.

Ambivalent, Chakotay watched him leave. Torn between the desire to get his job done and having an excuse to avoid dealing with his work, Chakotay wasn't sure how he felt about Neelix leaving.

Midstep, Neelix paused and spun about to face Chakotay. "So do you mind my asking?"

"What?"

"How the new assignments are going," Neelix said, resting an elbow on a console. "Everyone's talking about it."

"They are."

Neelix nodded. "With Tom, Harry, and the Doctor gone, everyone is curious who will replace them."

"You can let the gossip mill know, Neelix, that we're not replacing them," Chakotay said, wondering if his declaration sounded believable. Only the hope that he hadn't lost half of the senior staff was keeping him going. "We're just temporarily reassigning their duty shifts to junior officers."

"Of course they're irreplaceable! We know you haven't given up looking for them!" Neelix grabbed Chakotay by the uniform sleeves and squeezed his arms like a father offering reassurance to a child.

While he appreciated the Talaxian's enthusiasm, Chakotay needed to attempt to maintain the aura of command. "Thank you for your concern, Neelix," he said, calmly. "But let go."

"Just got carried away. My apologies." Embarrassed, he

stepped back, brushing away nonexistent creases in Chakotay's uniform.

"Not necessary, I assure you," Chakotay said. A long moment of uncomfortable silence elapsed. If he waited long enough, he knew Neelix's talkativeness would get the better of him and Chakotay would learn what he wanted to know about how the crew perceived their present circumstances.

Neelix rocked back and forth from his heels to the balls of his feet, then paused. "You know, Commander . . ."

"Yes?"

"As morale officer, I hear things—things that might be useful to you."

Chakotay smiled. "Such as?"

"The crew is in universal agreement that Clarice Knowles would be the best choice to take over for Tom. Unflappable, she is."

"Ensign Knowles is definitely that," Chakotay said. "And what about Harry?"

"Not quite a consensus yet, though the smart money is on Rollins. If Seven were Starfleet, she'd be the first choice."

Chakotay had actually been considering Ensign Vlar, but selecting Rollins definitely had its merits. He had the bridge experience Vlar lacked. "And the Doctor?"

"Lieutenant Nakano," Neelix said confidently. "Yuko might not have the Starfleet training, but who could doubt her after all that she went through during the guerrilla warfare in the Demilitarized Zone with the Maquis?" He waved aside what Chakotay presumed were any doubts that might be raised about Nakano's fitness for the position. "And of course, Commander Tuvok will be first officer—"

At the mention of Tuvok, the knot in Chakotay's stomach suddenly cinched tight, prompting a wince. He would have to deal with Tuvok; he hoped, however, to postpone the inevitable confrontation as long as possible. He had reviewed the Doctor's entries regarding Tuvok's medical condition as well as examined the brief log entry Janeway had made regarding Tuvok's reckless behavior. Intellectually, he understood that both the captain and the Doctor had concluded that Tuvok had been under the influence of forces beyond his control, literally "possessed" with some kind of alien transformative agent, and that there would be no disciplinary action imposed on him beyond a notation of the incident in his file. Telling his gut to accept Tuvok's exoneration was another matter. While he had too much trust in Kathryn's judgment to second-guess her decision regarding Tuvok, that didn't mean he had to agree with it.

Hindsight was always clearer than foresight, and one of the damnably annoying aspects of this space-time continuum was that you didn't have the luxury of going back and changing your mistakes. In this case, hindsight proved, without dispute, that Tuvok's choices (alien influence or not) had initiated a series of events that *Voyager* was not likely to recover from anytime soon. Chakotay's innate sense of fairness required that someone, namely Tuvok, should be held accountable. Noting that Neelix was waiting expectantly for him to speak, Chakotay said, "I find it interesting that the crew would assume that Tuvok would be my first officer. Do they trust him after his little field trip to Gremadia?"

Neelix scrutinized him, his forehead wrinkled. "No one else is as qualified. He's the senior officer behind you," he said matter-of-factly.

A sudden notion to play devil's advocate possessed him. "These are extraordinary circumstances, Neelix.

Perhaps I should choose someone more unconventional, say Lieutenant Torres—or Seven of Nine?" Chakotay shrugged.

"Pshaw," Neelix said, shaking his head and dismissing Chakotay's decision with a hand wave. "While I don't see the Maquis and Starfleet people sitting on opposite sides of the mess hall any longer, there might be some raised eyebrows if two Maquis commanded this ship. And Seven?" Neelix snorted. "She has a strong will to lead, but no clue how to get people to follow her."

Reluctantly, Chakotay had to admit Neelix was correct on all fronts, but he wasn't willing to let the issue go quite yet. "But what about his recent behavior? And by extension, what happened to the captain as a result."

Neelix threaded his fingers together, rested them on his chest, and pondered thoughtfully for a long moment. "You know, Commander," he said gently. "I don't think she'd hold it against Tuvok, so should you?"

Chakotay's gaze wandered over to the stasis chamber as he contemplated Neelix's words. Kathryn loved Tuvok, revered him and trusted him. She would always choose to see the best side of him, and in most cases she'd apply the same standard to anyone else under her command. He took a deep breath and exhaled the same, hoping to release some internal tension, but found his burden unchanged. Forgiveness would have come eventually. It was too soon for Chakotay to say when. Meanwhile, he would put *Voyager's* needs first.

Neelix followed Chakotay's glance across the room. "She looks so peaceful in there, doesn't she?" he said. "Like she's in a deep sleep, living in dreamland. I just wish she'd wake up."

Such a wish squeezed his chest so tightly that Chakotay lacked the voice to respond. He acknowledged

Neelix's words with a nod instead. The two of them stood together, side by side, looking at the captain. A nearly imperceptible touch on his sleeve interrupted his drifting thoughts. He heard the soft shuffle of Neelix padding across the floor; the door hissed open and closed.

Once again, Chakotay was alone with his thoughts.

The Nacene who once had taken the form of Phoebe Janeway settled on the second planet from the yellow star that still warmed Monorha. She, who was accustomed to manipulating every facet of her existence, quivered with outrage; she currently lacked the ability to fix her circumstances—or herself, for that matter. *Janeway* . . . White-hot energy rippled through her plasmatic tentacles. She . . . she . . . *hated* . . . no, *loathed* Janeway, and even that word failed to encompass the radiant heat surging through her.

Being forced to use humanoid words to explain what she was experiencing was yet another indignity to add to the humiliation she'd already endured. Lesser creatures had feelings. Biochemical responses and physiological inadequacies defined the lives of lower life-forms, not the Nacene. Janeway had reduced her to this pathetic state! And for what purpose? So that the abominations could traverse the gateway into Exosia?

Eighty thousand years confined in this space-time continuum, learning, growing, and absorbing knowledge had come to naught! Phoebe and her fellow outcasts had been denied their right to be reborn and return home. Her only consolation was that Vivia would now have to deal with the abominations.

Vivia would hate them. Even more than the exiled Nacene.

At least Phoebe wasn't alone in her suffering. The

human woman's body lived, but her life force had been drained from her. She would die. *Deservedly,* thought Phoebe, taking pleasure from the *feeling* of vindictiveness. But the momentary triumph would not compensate for the devastating consequences she and her fellow outcasts had suffered because of those pathetic, dull creatures from Monorha who had taken their spores. Aided and abetted by Janeway. She wanted them punished, demolished into their subatomic components. Revenge would have to wait, however, until she dealt with a more immediate situation. In their last encounter, Vivia had promised that her armies would come swarming out of Exosia if the gateway were broached.

Phoebe had no reason to doubt the veracity of Vivia's threat.

Thanks to Janeway, Phoebe was hardly in a state to survive such an attack. She recognized, from past experience, that her energy waves had taken on irregular, variable patterns. Consequently, she would have a difficult time sustaining any long-term transformation unless she wanted to risk taking on the transformation permanently. Aiding her fellow outcasts had depleted her far more than she had expected. Such a circumstance hadn't happened in a millennium, but now returning to Gremadia for renewal wasn't possible. Across thousands of lifetimes in more life-forms than those humans could fathom, she had always had the capacity to change herself or her surroundings to suit her. Her consciousness twisted restlessly, seeking a solution to her dilemma. Now, when she needed her abilities more than ever, she was denied.

She gathered her fragmented strength and focused on calling out to her fellow outcasts, bidding them to join her. One by one, they came from across the galaxy. She offered them comfort. They did not have Exosia, but they could find strength together.

We have been divided, she called out. *We can unite so that Vivia cannot stop us.*

One last time, they would join together and wage war. She would not easily accept defeat.

Chapter 2

Stop.

The voice in the Doctor's mind was as clear as if he were seated at his workstation in sickbay talking to a patient, and yet her mouth never moved.

She glared at him as if that should be all he needed to understand her, though what he could have done to cause such offense eluded him.

You have disrupted the strings. You must stop. Now.

There it was again: the voice in his head. It was disconcerting, to be certain—and somewhat rude—to talk to someone's mind without an invitation. The only sounds stimulating his auditory processors were the gradual winding down of the cloud battle behind him and the orchestral music. He was about to address the visitor when he was distracted by what was happening in the orchestra pit. *That's odd,* he thought. The disruption of his song seemed to have caused the disappearance of the musician "clones"; one by one, they evaporated into nothingness. When the last Doctor-musician vanished, the instruments resumed playing the number he'd heard when he first arrived. Or some version of it. The cello section sounded like their strings had gone a half-note flat.

She glided in front of the orchestra pit, her robes of continually shifting colors flowing out behind her like a living version of one of Michelangelo's frescoes. Her eyes blazed, her mouth set in a tight, pinched line. *You will die, insignificant creature.*

"Hold on there," the Doctor said, holding up a hand in protest. "That's no way to treat an old acquaintance. We've met before—back on *Voyager.* The captain introduced you as her sister Phoebe." The Doctor kept his tone light, confident that his joie de vivre could soften even the most cantankerous entity. It also might dispel any notion she might have of decompiling him on the spot. Upon meeting the "Phoebe" Nacene, he was nearly eliminated from *Voyager's* database to prevent him from exposing the Nacene's duplicity. "But we both know that you aren't the captain's sister. You're Nacene."

A scowl soured her face. *I am not this Phoebe. The one you know as Phoebe is Outside. This is the last form I took in your dimension. Your understanding of this place is formed by the lens of your experience, you see me as you need to see me to comprehend this place. The name I was given Outside will suffice. You may call me Vivia.*

"So Vivia, this place—" The Doctor indicated his surroundings. "—isn't Outside?"

Vivia frowned.

"I'll take that as a no," the Doctor muttered and sighed, now convinced that he was, indeed, in another dimension. "Since you don't seem too keen on my being here, perhaps you could show me the way out? Maybe, send me back to *Voyager?*" He offered her a hopeful smile.

You are an invader. You have contaminated Exosia. You escaped containment. Now you have tampered with the strings. You must be stopped. Vivia raised her arm above her head like a medieval sorceress conjuring the elements, hinting that she was prepared to strike him down.

The Doctor shielded his face with his arms and scrunched his head into his shoulders. Cognitively, he recognized that such a gesture was futile; he found, however, that his programmed instinct for self-protection was too compelling to ignore. A moment passed, then another.

Nothing happened.

Lowering his arms slowly, he peered over his forearm at the redheaded creature who appeared . . . flummoxed. *How odd. Unless . . .* The Doctor grinned. The creature wanted to hurt him, but apparently she couldn't. He may be a fly she wanted to swat but *he* had control of the situation. "It appears that you've reached an impasse. If you won't send me home, at least do me the courtesy of explaining why you're so keen on blowing my matrix into so many photonic bits. Though, at the moment, you seem unable to do that."

You are correct, she sneered, clearly peeved by his advantage.

"Then we will discuss our circumstances like civilized beings," the Doctor said. "These strings you speak of. I've done *nothing* here that . . ." His voice trailed off as he realized he *had* intervened in the battle. He'd stopped the insectoids from a attacking the Monorhan angels. Had he done something bad? "I didn't really mean to hurt anything. The angels . . ." He knit his brow and shook his head solemnly as he remembered what he had witnessed. "They were being *slaughtered.*" He opened his palms forward, pleadingly. "I was trying to make peace. Was that wrong?"

The abominations invaded as you did and polluted our realm. One from Outside opened the gateway between your dimen-

sion and our own. One who came from inside the container you live in.

Janeway! The Doctor thought. His last vision of the captain, as he was pulled off *Voyager,* made sense now. What had the captain done? Facilitating such a process as opening a gateway between dimensions must have required—his mind sorted through the possibilities—more than the physical capacity of simple carbon-based life-forms. A horrifying thought occurred. *Surely she hasn't sacrificed herself—what about the crew? Our journey home? I'm needed on* Voyager!

"I apologize for whatever disturbance I've caused, but I insist that by whatever means you have at your disposal, I must return to my ship. I assure you that my people will do whatever is required to fix whatever we've set amiss—"

At this, Vivia laughed. A laugh the Doctor could see not on her face but in his mind. And it was a mocking, brittle sound. *Your kind cannot fathom the damage you have done. Opening the gateway will only allow more photonic contamination. You disrupted our efforts to contain the abominations. Then you disturbed the strings! You must be stopped!*

"You keep referring to these strings." The Doctor threw up his hands in exasperation. "I'm sorry but I don't understand! How can I fix or stop doing something when I don't know what the problem is? As a fellow sentient, at least do me the courtesy of a civilized discussion." After an irritable exhalation, he assumed his best professional mien. "Let's start from the beginning. When did this problem start?"

Vivia gave him what could only be described as an amused look, one that said she'd tolerate him as long as he entertained her. Either that or she was determining how to rip his holographic arms out of his sockets.

You are a small being. You lack what is required to resolve a situation that has been evolving for—what unit of measurement is it that you creatures confined to three dimensions experience? Ah yes, time. You haven't existed long enough to solve this problem.

Frustration swamped all patience in his programming. He hadn't asked to be trapped in this place, to contaminate Exosia or to throw the strings—whatever they were—off balance. This Nacene Vivia clearly had no intention of being reasonable or civilized about this situation—and he was no longer in a patient mood. "Fine," he said calmly. "If you don't mind, I was in the middle of something before you so rudely interrupted me." With that pronouncement, the Doctor stepped away from Vivia, faced the orchestra pit, and launched into a rousing rendition of *"La donna é mobile."* The dozens of "Doctor" musicians in the pit reappeared and responded appropriately, accompanying his aria with aplomb. Immersing himself in the passion of the music, he closed his eyes, opening his arms as he reached his favorite measure—

STOP!

This time, her words shook the Doctor with the force of a photon torpedo. He dropped his arms to his sides and opened his eyes. The curtains flew closed, shuttering the angels' battle from view.

You allowed the abominations to escape! They invaded our realm and you allowed them to escape!

The Doctor wrinkled his forehead. *Abominations? Could it be—* "The insectoids?" he said aloud. "No, the Monorhan angels? No. It couldn't be."

You have tampered with what you don't understand!

"Then help me understand!" the Doctor shouted, his voice ringing through the cavernous theater. "Where I come from, we *talk* through problems and *solve* them together. As we've both seen, you can't compel me to comply with your demands and you certainly haven't made a case as to why I should listen to you."

We will negotiate. We will . . . talk, since your kind uses words. Vivia's lips twisted into a dour pucker and she dropped her arms to her sides. *You are not like the other photons. You have escaped containment; they cannot. This is why I cannot compel you to behave as I wish you to. They too are self-aware, but not like you. You are cohesive. You are . . . an individual.*

The Doctor swallowed hard, wondering if he had heard what he thought he heard. The stunning implications of the idea thrilled him. *Perhaps that explains me!* he thought. "Photons are self-aware in Exosia?"

This is why photons are dangerous to the strings. They have free will. They cannot be forced to comply, therefore they have to be stopped or the harmony of the strings is disturbed.

"The strings. You keep saying that word," the Doctor said, as if he were drawing out a history from a reluctant patient. "Could you be more specific?"

Strings are the underpinning of matter and force in your space-time. Their vibrations, their excitation modes, define the particles that allow you to exist and all the forces that define your dimension. Their music is your reality. We live among the strings in Exosia. We assure the strings have balance. Vivia's anger became earnestness, her words underlined with conviction. As her mood changed, so did the color of her robes, which were now a warm sapphire hue. *Look! See the strings!* She extended her arm out to the side and gestured toward the self-playing instruments in the orchestra pit.

Strings. Stringed instruments. I see the strings as musical instruments. When I sang, I influenced how the strings vibrated—I changed their music! A blush of embarrassment colored his cheeks as he realized the extent of his faux pas. *What subspace layers did I destroy by altering the string's song—or could it have been a newborn star? Did I alter the fates of worlds?* Remembering the quagmire *Voyager* encountered in

Monorhan space, the Doctor recognized that *he* might have created just such a mess elsewhere in the universe because of his carelessness. *No wonder Vivia wants to decompile me. The fact that I'm not reduced to photonic dust is astounding!* "I had no idea what how reckless my actions were," the Doctor said humbly. "From the bottom of my matrix, I apologize."

While his perceptions might be wishful imaginings, Vivia's countenance softened. She continued speaking to his mind. *Exosia is an in-between, linking place for many dimensions because of how the strings, entities that are expressed in many ways throughout many geometries, exist here. The strings create cohesion between dimensions. The Nacene exist to tend and care for the strings so that cohesion can be maintained.*

The Doctor realized Vivia had just explained the Nacene version of quantum reality. "The strings are a building block of matter and force in the universe, but they exist here in a form that can be seen and individuated."

A crude interpretation, but likely the best a finite nature such as your own can manage.

The Doctor continued: "And the photons. Photons don't naturally exist here?"

Photons first came into Exosia when some Nacene decided they were no longer content to care for the strings. They opened Exosia and entered your space-time as explorers.

This revelation tracked with what the Doctor recalled from their first encounter with the Caretaker.

At first there seemed to be no consequence to our having a gateway into your dimension. We came and went at our pleasure, playing with stars and planets. . . . Over time, however, photons seeped in among the strings. Photons are drawn to Exosia. She paused as if she were searching for the right term to describe the phenomenon. *It is like there is a magnetic pull between Exosia and the photons. Because photonic energy disrupts the harmony, the gateway needed to be closed. Difficult choices were required. Those like me chose duty to the strings above all else.*

As much as he loathed admitting it, the Doctor discovered that his complete and utter revulsion for Vivia, and those like her who had chosen duty over self-gratification, was softening as she told her story. "So what happened next?" he asked, though he suspected he knew part of it. Relatively recent encounters with the Caretaker, Suspiria, and "Phoebe" indicated that not all the Nacene had gone back into Exosia.

A war broke out between those who were willing to sacrifice all to serve the strings and those who cared only for their own pleasure. We, the caretakers of the strings, prevailed. The Exiles remained in your dimension.

"The Nacene called Phoebe was an Exile."

Vivia affirmed the Doctor's supposition, and then continued with her story. *A leader emerged among the Exiles. One among them called the Light, in honor of the power of photons, helped them devise a means by which they might return to Exosia.* Her lips twisted into an unattractive frown.

To the Doctor, it was obvious from the tone of Vivia's explanation of the Light that she considered that particular Exile to be distasteful at best, and heinous at worst.

The Light had built a place of rest where they would wait until the day when the gateway could be forced open using a key and a conduit should the Exiles weary of their choices.

The Doctor discovered, as he became more attuned to Vivia, that instead of words merely conveying her meaning, they had begun to form pictures in his mind. "Gremadia was part of the Light's plan, wasn't it?" The Doctor said, comprehension dawning. "The place of rest and waiting." A second, more horrifying realization occurred. "And my captain became the conduit."

That could be the only explanation for what he saw in his vision. He didn't know how or why, but the captain had forced open the gateway between Exosia and his own space-time, allowing the Monorhans—or the abominations, as Vivia called them—to enter in. She couldn't have known the damage she was causing, could she? His default position tended to be one that trusted the captain's judgment, but in this case, if what Vivia told him was true, Janeway's decision might have been misguided. This new understanding strengthened his resolve to fix what Janeway had inadvertently set awry. How many years, even millennia, of vigilance had been negated by *Voyager*'s actions? No wonder Vivia was angry; he could hardly blame her. "You have existed in Exosia since you cast out the Exiles. You tend the strings."

She nodded. *It was the correct choice for the Nacene. But exploration was a glorious life.*

Though he realized that what he saw was merely the Nacene world defined in terms he could comprehend, the Doctor believed he saw Vivia's form physically change as she communicated with him. It was more than her wistful sighs. Her vibrancy dimmed; to his eye, she became more human. Her sadness reminded him, initially, of a Lucia di Lammermoor. On further reflection, she became the tender Mimi of *La Bohème*. What a tragic life!

Lifting her sorrow-filed face, she offered him a pensive gaze for a long moment before drifting closer to him so they stood within touching distance. *A greater cause called us back to Exosia.* She drifted back and forth in front of the Doctor. *All we have done since the Exiles separated from us, all we will do, is in the service of the strings. To disrupt the strings is to destroy all.*

As one who was charged with the preservation and restoration of life, he had such empathy for the Exosia

Nacene and what a burden they shouldered. "Considering the vital importance of the strings, how could the Exiles be so cavalier about their duties here?"

Aren't there those Outside who, because of their newness, their youth—yes, youth is the proper word—rebel against their elders? Nacene kind are similar to Outsiders in this way.

His whole being filled with compassion, the Doctor began, "Let me help you, Vivia. Clearly *Voyager* blundered into something they didn't understand. I assure you that none of my people meant any harm to either the Nacene or the strings."

She arched a single eyebrow. *If the Exiles had never been able to open the gateway . . . no. That could not be undone by you.* Her skirts swished around her bare feet as she barely moved back and forth in the air. *If the source of the problem were eradicated before it became a problem . . . if the Light had been stopped . . .*

The Doctor saw his opportunity to negotiate and pounced. "Perhaps we can help each other."

Vivia cocked her head to one side and looked at him questioningly.

"You want to find this Light person and stop him"— the Doctor paused for dramatic effect—"and I want you to call off the attack on the Monorhans and ultimately go back to *Voyager*."

She responded instantaneously: *Not possible.*

"On the contrary. It *is* possible. You've already conceded that you can't stop me from—how did you phrase it?—*disturbing* the strings. Since you've made it clear returning home isn't an option, I'll focus on achieving my second objective: I *will* disturb the strings if it helps save the Monorhans."

Vivia narrowed her eyes. Scarlet stained her robes as she radiated progressively more intense waves of tension.

The Doctor shifted uncomfortably, refusing to be disturbed by her foul moods. She was quite like a blustering bully who couldn't make good on her threats but nonetheless was capable of making her victim miserable. Without having to be told, he knew that the Nacene wouldn't hesitate to fuse his photons together were she capable of doing so. Survival required that he parlay what little advantage he had into coaxing Vivia to act while avoiding enraging her. The universe might be combusting beyond Exosia—there was no question that his crew needed him. Standing around and chatting for eternity would get neither of them anywhere.

"You haven't demonstrated to me that they're a danger to Exosia. To destroy them just because you don't like them or don't understand them isn't right." He suspected from the contortions of her lips that his statements made her fume; he took her failure to respond as a concession that he'd made his point.

Gradually, Vivia's robes muted and the hostile energy she directed toward the Doctor diminished. *You would agree to help eradicate the Light at the source. You would prevent him from making the choices that created chaos.*

Now we're getting somewhere. The Doctor nodded encouragingly. A little voice he'd come to think of as his conscience (though Doctor Zimmerman hadn't included such a feature in his original programming) warned him about tampering in the time stream; the Doctor dismissed it. Nothing less than the stability of space-time was at stake here. Such a dire predicament warranted extreme measures, should they be called for. "I am a hologram of my word. Though I don't know how I can go back to the *source* of the problem. I may be a renaissance man, but time-traveling didn't come with the programming."

With a toss of the head, Vivia dismissed his concerns.

The rules that bind your space-time do not apply here. This barrier, you call it time, that confines you to a fixed spot in your three-dimensional world is irrelevant in Exosia. She paused, obviously searching for the right images to send to his mind.

Slowly, a conceptualization of the universe began unfolding in his thoughts that astonished him. Past and present existed simultaneously for Vivia. While she could sense the future, the currents of choice and consequence constantly shifted, making it more difficult to determine where all the disparate threads would lead. Still, she had the capacity to identify the nexus point of their current predicament and the subsequent consequences rippling to the present and forward to possible futures. Could she stop the problem from starting in the first place? Or maybe if the problem began on the Outside, *she* couldn't stop it (the Nacene weren't the Q, after all, and hadn't Vivia said that she would spend her existence in Exosia?) and that was part of her frustration.

But perhaps *he* could. "Tell me what I need to do to set this right," he said.

Stop the Light.

"Save the Monorhans."

Done. The curtains parted revealing the pastoral scene the Doctor had first encountered: the insectoids had disappeared.

He turned to Vivia. "Since the Light is Nacene, I'd appreciate having your insights into an appropriate strategy—" Cut off mid-thought, the Doctor once again felt the odd disconnected sensation he'd experienced when he arrived in Exosia overtake him. Before he could process his new environment, another transformation occurred, this one taking him deep within a cold and remote darkness. Prickles of fear needling his matrix allowed only a single coherent thought to form: *I am utterly lost.*

~

The sickbay doors hissed open and B'Elanna limped through. Upon viewing Janeway entombed in a stasis chamber, another wave of anxiety beset her, the latest in a succession of such waves that had plagued her nonstop since Tom and Harry had vanished. A brusque growl escaped through clenched teeth. Why couldn't there be somewhere she could go to escape this seemingly never-ending nightmare?! But no. That would be too much to ask. This whole damn ship was a reminder of what might go down as the longest bad day in her life.

She couldn't help but stare at the captain. From what she'd heard, Janeway was little more than a corpse with a pulse. Seven had done what she could to utilize the available medical technology and succeeded in stabilizing the captain, though little else. B'Elanna planned on reviewing sickbay's instruments to see if there were any tweaks or alternations she could make that would increase their functionality but she hadn't found the time. For now, healing Janeway's injuries was beyond the reach of anyone on *Voyager*.

Chakotay maintained vigil nearby at a workstation where the bridge had been sending him real-time updates as to their progress out of Monoharan space. She suspected that her friend needed privacy and quiet to sort through what his next action would be. Within less than a day, they would reach the boundaries of Monoharan space, and Chakotay would need to have determined a course of action by then. She didn't envy him the job. And perhaps he just wanted Captain Janeway to keep him company while he came to grips with all his responsibilities.

B'Elanna studied him for a long moment before alerting him to her presence. "Playing hooky from the bridge,

Commander?" she said, intending to invoke the teasing familiarity that had existed between them since their Maquis days. Instead, her words rang hollow to her ear, her voice thin and thready.

Startled, Chakotay turned away from his work to look at her, his eyes dull and lined with shadows, face gaunt from lack of sleep and from overwork. He looked more strained than she had ever seen him—even during the days of Seska's treachery.

She gasped involuntarily at his appearance, and then cursed her lack of tact. None of the crew was at their best, but there was no denying that Chakotay was in terrible shape. *Considering that he's taking the brunt of this mess, I'd say that's fair.*

"You don't look so hot yourself," Chakotay said, lacing his hands together on his lap.

"So we can exchange beauty tips," she lobbed back at him, "or you can tell me what's going on with my ship."

Composed into a portrait of Starfleet implacability, he said, "Talk to Neelix. These days he's the man in the know."

"I want to talk to my old friend." She hopped up onto the biobed closest to his workstation. "How bad is it, really—for all of us, for you?"

"My own well-being is irrelevant—"

"You sound like Tuvok. Or worse, Seven."

"I have to confess that today I especially envy their ability to disengage during a crisis," he said. "Personal concerns have to be irrelevant if we want to survive. For starters, critical personnel who serve at vital posts are either injured, like Captain Janeway, or missing, like the Doctor. Crew reassignments need to be made immediately, but everyone is overworked. There aren't any good choices."

She felt a flash of gratitude that Chakotay hadn't said

Tom's name aloud. She didn't know if she could hear it without flinching. *Focus on the tasks at hand,* she admonished herself. "You're working on the new duty roster?"

He nodded.

"You'll need to figure additional personnel for repairs. We still haven't entirely fixed what was damaged when *Voyager* was stuck in the subspace pocket." *A lifetime ago,* she amended.

"How long will those repairs take?"

B'Elanna paused, made a quick mental assessment. "If everyone who has an engineering certification one or greater worked in shifts around the clock, we might be done in three or four days minimum. Maybe longer."

"Identify the two or three most critical issues and what kind of crew support you'll need. All nonessential systems will need to wait until we've found a safe haven where we can work without having to take into consideration altered laws of physics."

B'Elanna nodded. She'd expected he'd say as much.

"As for command—I'll be frank. I don't have a lot of confidence in Tuvok's judgment right now. I know that if I follow the rulebook, he'll have to be second-in-command."

"That's right," B'Elanna said.

"This crisis has shown me that we have a serious shortage of command-ready personnel. We'll need to remedy that."

"As long as you aren't planning on changing my color to red, I think that's a fine idea." So far, she didn't understand what the big deal was. Chakotay wasn't saying anything that hadn't been raised in senior staff meetings from time to time. While they had plenty of crew members with Starfleet experience or education, very few of them had command-track training.

"So what do you think about me assigning Seven to shadow Tuvok for the purposes of bringing her leadership skills up to Starfleet standards?"

She hadn't expected *that*.

Her incredulous expression must have clued Chakotay in to how she felt about his suggestion, because he immediately continued. "I know and trust your judgment. After that episode on Monorha, you probably know Seven better than anyone on this ship. If you had a problem with that course of action, you'd tell me." He glanced away from B'Elanna.

She followed his eyes to the woman prostrate in the stasis chamber.

"You're a lot like Kathryn that way," he added softly.

"So's Seven, as much as I loathe admitting it," B'Elanna said. "I mean she's like the captain in her ability to grasp big-picture issues quickly and take action. She's not afraid to say what she thinks whether or not anyone will like what she has to say. She just lacks the polish and protocols that Starfleet officers are indoctrinated with. Tuvok would be the perfect teacher."

"I wish there were a way I could put you in the chair beside me. I know I could count on you in a crisis." Chakotay gritted his teeth.

B'Elanna hadn't seen Chakotay so bitter before. *He must be feeling incredible pain,* she thought. "Me in command?" she said, trying to keep her tone light. "That would last about an hour before I'd try to knock someone's block off. Probably Vorik's."

Chakotay's laugh dissolved the worry lining his face.

B'Elanna smiled reflexively. His momentary happiness was a small light on an otherwise dismal day. "I could join command just to shake things up."

He sighed deeply. "As much fun as the thought of you terrorizing the lower decks might be, I know better."

"The crew needs to know that things will continue to operate the way they've become accustomed—and that's by Starfleet rules—". B'Elanna paused in midthought, shocked by the realization that she actually believed what she said. "Wow. Professor Dunbar at the Academy would have lost at least one bet if he heard me say those words."

"Since when did two old Maquis become so stodgy?" Chakotay asked.

"Because of her." B'Elanna nodded toward Janeway.

Turning his attention back to his work, Chakotay said nothing.

Suddenly, she couldn't stand it any longer—pretending to be fine, trying to be positive for the sake of everyone around her when her own life was plunging into craziness. "I'm worried, Chakotay," she said, forcing open a discussion that neither one of them wanted to have. "The crew is demoralized—the ship is in terrible shape, we don't know whether the captain will live or die, we've lost—" She paused, feeling her voice catch. "—a lot of fine people in the last few days, and as a result, everyone is a little more anxious than normal. I don't know if I can keep doing it."

"Doing what?" he said gently.

"Being normal when nothing is normal."

"I'm more than a little anxious myself, knowing that my right-hand man is capable of vanishing without warning or thought to the damage he might do. I pray that we don't have any casualties on our way out of Monorhan space because I'm afraid we can't treat them. Never mind what losing Harry and Tom will do to my ability to run the bridge," Chakotay said. "Truth be told, I'm tempted to turn the ship over to Seven and take a very long nap."

Recalling the few rancorous days she spent sharing Seven's consciousness, B'Elanna couldn't help chuckling. "She'd love that for about half a shift and then she'd want to assimilate the whole crew out of frustration and in the name of increased efficiency. But if you assign Tuvok to advise her, he'll keep her in line." At the mention of Tuvok, B'Elanna thought she saw a shadow pass over Chakotay's face, so she quickly moved on. "If you quote me I'll deny it, but I trust her. Especially in a crisis. Don't be afraid to call on Seven to back you up."

"These are strange days," Chakotay said, "if you've come to believe we can trust Seven."

"No arguing with you there," she said grudgingly. Had B'Elanna been told several months ago that she would advocate for Seven, she would have pronounced such a statement ludicrous. Of course, she wouldn't have believed it possible that she'd lose Tom, either, in spite of the usual disasters that typically befell *Voyager*. A dull ache filled her at the thought of Tom. She hugged her arms close to her chest. Chakotay eyed her closely; not for the first time, B'Elanna had the strangest sense that she was transparent to him.

"All right, then," he said finally. "I'll call a meeting of senior staff in a half an hour if that gives you enough time to provide me with a complete engineering report."

"Yes, sir," B'Elanna said. She pushed off the biobed and dropped to the ground and was immediately assaulted by waves of pain. *Yeah. I kind of forgot about that little problem. . . .*

"What happened?" Chakotay asked, concerned.

"I kind of kicked the remains of the tetryon transporter. Broken toe. It's nothing."

Chakotay didn't appear convinced. "Can you set it without help?"

"I've got basic Starfleet paramedic training," B'Elanna

said, brushing aside his concerns. "I can manage an osteo-regenerator if you can find one for me—that and a hypo with an analgesic and anti-infective agent in it." She crawled back up onto the edge of a biobed. While Chakotay searched the Doctor's cabinets, she gingerly eased off the boot and peeled off her bloodied sock. As she suspected, a bone shard had punctured the skin of her big toe, but the blood flow had slowed to a mere seep, congealing around the wound.

When Chakotay turned back to hand her the tools, he physically recoiled, grimacing at the sight of the blackened hematoma spreading through her swollen tissues, her toes twisted and deformed from multiple breaks. "I suppose one of my first jobs will be to get someone down here to help out in sickbay until we figure out where the Doctor disappeared to."

"You mean you don't want me fixing everyone up?" B'Elanna asked. "But I have such a charming bedside manner." Bracing her injured foot against the base of the biobed, she bent over and held her ankle with one hand, then grasped the distended top of her mottled big toe between her thumb and index finger of her other hand. She gritted her teeth, then forced the broken bone segment back beneath the skin with her thumb, and jammed the broken segments back together, making a crunching, grinding sound. She smiled mischievously at her old friend, noting with dark amusement how he looked a little yellow around the edges.

"Pass," Chakotay said, and left B'Elanna to her work.

She activated the osteoregenerator and bent over to start mending her bone. She paused midway, resting her elbows on her thighs, her face rested on one hand so she could look at the medical instrument in the other. Her foot still throbbed from resetting the broken bone; pain pierced her calf and spread into her thigh. Chakotay had retrieved a hypospray containing a pain reliever. She could use it—*should* use it. The pain continued unabated—even intensifying as edema increased in her foot. Her skin stretched tautly over her bones and muscles as the tissues swelled with blood and water. Awareness of her injuries superceded thought. Her whole body hummed from the rhythmic firings of nerve endings.

B'Elanna liked how she felt. More specifically, liked the *pain*. The realization disturbed her, but she wasn't willing to make any moves to fix it.

Then she understood.

She *felt* the pain. Her body was alive. Pain broke through the numbness that had never fully gone away for what seemed like months . . . and it had been months, she realized. This dull flatness had shadowed her since the message from the Alpha Quadrant about the Maquis had arrived. The pain radiating from her broken bones had woken her up, even if it was temporarily. She savored *feeling* again, wishing she could prolong it.

She glanced at her chronometer. Unfortunately, duty called: senior staff in twenty minutes. Sitting around sickbay philosophizing about the sorry state of her life wouldn't get the engineering report done. Reaching over her leg, she waved the instrument over her foot, having mixed emotions as the warmth of the healing probe stimulated the mending of the damaged bone. *I actually feel pretty good, everything considered,* she told herself, hoping that a little more self-talk would be convincing.

Part of it, she realized, was that her injuries served as a distraction. As she put the tools back in the cabinets, a thought occurred: *Too bad I can't get injured more often. It would give me an excuse to see Tom during his sickbay shifts.* She laughed aloud at the ridiculousness of the idea. *Except Tom's not here.* Smiling sadly, she remembered him, regretting that the brief moment of self-deception had passed and wondering what she could do to escape from these interminable reminders. She didn't want to be one of those people who spent their time cooped up in a holodeck trying to escape their lives, but she certainly understood that way of thinking better than she did a week ago. *Are you out there, Tom?*

Tom blinked once. The world looked honey-tinted—like the centuries-old photos he often saw in museums. Apparently, this honey-colored world existed on a seafaring vessel—a massive cruising ship, from what he could see, looking down the polished wood decks spreading out on either side of him. Round portholes dotted the walls behind their deck chairs. A life preserver with the name Q E II painted on it in bold dark letters was mounted on the deck railing. All of it honey-colored. He blinked again and nothing changed. Still—

Harry, who was no longer an ear, yanked the tortoiseshell sunglasses from Tom's eyes and dropped them in his lap. "It helps if you take these off."

Tom's world immediately changed hues, though part of him wished he'd kept the sunglasses on. The pink and purple tropical flowers covering Harry's shirt reminded Tom of a hangover remedy his Academy roommate used to swear by. Dropping his eyes, he realized his attire wasn't much better unless you had a hankering for brown-and-yellow plaid Bermuda shorts with an orange T-shirt emblazoned with "Viva Las Vegas." At least the locale was pleasant. Too bad B'Elanna wasn't around to share it with him. She loved sunny climes. "I have to say," he turned to

Harry, "if you had to be thrown into the middle of nowhere by Q, this isn't a bad place to be thrown. Still, we need to find our way back to *Voyager*—fast."

"I hope you have better luck than I've had. Since we got here, I've tried to figure out where we are—even where Q is—and I've got nothing. I just end up wandering in circles."

"Maybe he's messing with your head."

"That's why I'm going to stay put until I'm summoned. Besides, all this dimension-traveling messes up my circadian rhythms. I'm going to take a nap, so stay out of trouble." He wriggled around in his rattan lounge chair until he found a comfortable position, and then closed his eyes.

"Right," Tom said. To his delight, a tall, bright green drink filling a carved-out pineapple appeared on the table beside him. The straw shaped like a hula dancer was the perfect touch. He'd have to remember to add it to the resort program the next time he began tinkering. Tom suspected that Q might be trying to get them intoxicated so they'd be more compliant with whatever schemes he was plotting. He took a long pull on the straw anyway.

Looking between his sandal-clad feet and through the white-painted railing, he saw an endless stretch of serene pink-gray nebula before him. Only swirls of particulate matter and the occasional spatial anomaly breaking the surface disturbed the perfection. *Wait. That can't be right.* Tom blinked. Rubbed his eyes. *Nope.* They were on a cruise ship churning through space. What did he expect, traveling with a Q?

Swinging his feet over the side of the lounge chair, Tom took in a deep breath, relishing the brisk, briny air filling his lungs. (The logical part of his brain wondered how briny air was possible in the vacuum of space, but who was he to care? The air, indeed, was briny.) A familiar, mocking laugh called to Tom like a beacon. He proceeded cautiously in the direction of the sound.

Down the deck from their chairs was a swimming pool surrounded by slot machines, roulette, *tongo*, dabo—every game of chance that Tom was familiar with and many games he wasn't. In the midst of the revelry stood Q, wearing a white captain's hat, a navy-blue-and-white-striped boat-neck shirt, and a jaunty striped cravat. He strolled among a crowd gathered at a craps table, shouting and clapping as a gambler shook and rolled the dice. A scantily clad Orion female was draped over his shoulders like an ill-fitting suit. Tom placed his tall, fruity drink with the hula dancer straw on the table between his and Harry's lounge chairs and started toward the gamblers. *Might as well go where the action is,* Tom thought, and moseyed over to where Q partied.

"I have to tell you, Q, this is quite a rig you've conjured up."

"It is lovely, isn't it? If we had more time, I'd sign you up for the Virgo Supercluster cruise. Unparalleled fun and frolicking. Alas, we have work to do." Q craned his head around Tom. "Where's Tweedle-dumb?"

Tom jerked his head in the direction of the snoring Harry.

"That won't do," Q said irritably, and snapped his fingers.

A splash from the swimming pool drew Tom's attention; Harry appeared, flailing madly, in the deep end. He eventually stroked to the swim ladder and sloshed up on deck, leaving puddles of water behind him.

"You can hardly take a nap when the fate of the universe is at stake. And you were the one so desperate for explanations," Q said, tsking. "Now, pay attention, Mr. Kim. There is no remedial version available."

Harry growled.

Q seemed not to notice. "You see, boys, there are two rules that determine the course of the universe: choice." He handed a cupful of dice to Tom and gestured for him to throw the dice on the green felt surface spread out before them on the table. "And chance."

Tom did as instructed and the dice came up snake eyes.

"You lose," Q said cheerfully. "Tom could choose whether to play and by playing he took a chance that he might lose. See how it works? A choice is made without knowing the outcome, because chance chooses the outcome. It's all so delightfully twisted, don't you think? And no matter who you are in the universe, whether you're a one-celled organism living in the primordial ooze or an omnipotent being like me, these two factors inevitably determine your existence. How choice and chance interplay is what determines destiny."

Wringing water out of his hair, Harry said, "Captain Janeway chose to explore the Monorhan system and the actions she took started a series of consequences."

"Very good, Mr. Kim. There might be hope for you yet," Q said, and snapped his fingers.

The scene abruptly changed again. Tom was starting to find Q's unorthodox style entertaining; he looked around to see what interesting location Q had brought them to this time and discovered he was on his back, looking up at four walls of white netting, too high for him to climb over. He smelled soap and talcum powder. Rolling over onto his stomach, Tom reached for a rattle shaped like a letter "Q," but it was snatched away by a chubby hand: Harry beat him to it. If that squatty, chipmunk-cheeked Asian baby with the pacifier jammed in his mouth was Harry.

Mortified, Tom squished his eyes closed, hoping to avoid seeing his own humiliating state. Woosh! A thick, hairy arm swooped in from the sky and scooped him and Harry up. Before Tom could start crying in protest, he looked up into the largest face he had ever seen.

"Daddy's going to tell you boys a bedtime story now," Q said, and placed Tom and Harry on the carpeted floor.

Seeing the sun glinting off a swing set outside, Tom immediately crawled across the floor, heading for the exit. "For most sentient species, the first choice is to explore the environment around them."

After butting his head against the slightly ajar door, Tom squeezed through the opening, crawled out onto the grass, and found he was face-to-face with a very wet, very smelly nose. He rolled back onto his haunches to stare at the puppy who was staring at him equally as intently.

"One choice leads to another and the world grows larger as a species seeks to push its boundaries and limitations," Q said, walking beside the crawling babies.

Tom couldn't believe how gigantic Q's shoes were. Terrified, he crawled quickly to keep ahead of the Very Large Feet.

Q lifted Tom and Harry off the lawn and placed them on the seats of two tricycles.

What kind of lunatic are we dealing with? Doesn't he know we're babies? Tom clung to the handlebars, assuming that he would fall off, but found to his surprise that his legs could reach the pedals. How was that possible? Checking out Harry, he determined that they must have aged at least two years in the last few moments. Apparently, Q was taking them through the early years of human development.

I need to stop being surprised, he thought. He pushed his sneaker-clad feet against the pedals and got the tricycle moving. Not quite as fun as a holocar, but what could he expect in a two-year-old body? Tom and Harry took off down the sidewalk, racing to see who would reach the end of the cement slab first.

Astride a pennyfarthing bicycle, Q peddled beside them at a leisurely pace, steering without gripping the handlebars. "Life is a series of increasingly more complex choices with increasingly more painful results . . ." At the end of the slab, Q stopped without warning.

Tom and Harry, who had been absorbed in their race, went careering toward Q. Tom frantically tried to stop, but the pedals spun faster than his feet could keep up with. The front wheel of his vehicle rammed into a lip of cement, sending Tom flying over the top of his handlebars. He winced, bracing himself for the crash—

And then they were on a lawn, wet with dew, again, lying side by side staring up a summer starscape. The sky rotated around them, constellations changing with a rapidity Tom could barely comprehend. Q was nowhere to be seen, but he heard his voice booming in his ear.

"Every once in a while, a sentient species comes along and really makes a mess of things. Their choices affect more than just their own limited sphere; they have a ripple effect on other species. For example, humanity's quest to understand its existence led you to the atom, which is all fine and well, but what you did with that atom almost destroyed you. Like humans, the Nacene went out and explored their dimension—they call it Exosia—and in the process they discovered a building block even smaller than the atom. You call them strings."

Harry sat up. "String theory. We've known about that for centuries."

"Have you?" Q's face replaced the wan, pale yellow moon.

"It's great to know we were right," Harry said hopefully, looking up at the sky.

"As if I'm going to fall for that old trick, trying to dupe me into answering a question you don't yet have a complete answer for." The Q moon heaved and shook with sneering laughter.

Harry folded his arms across his chest. "We do know string theory," he said petulantly.

Tom was thinking about how Harry needed to learn to keep his mouth shut instead of arguing with a Q.

"You may think you do, but as with everything else, what you think you know is dwarfed by all you *don't* know. You congratulate yourselves on your cleverness when you learn something new, arrogantly pressing on before you give yourselves time to fully process what you've discovered."

"Try me," Harry persisted.

"I don't think so. Don't worry, you'll get there—if you don't manage to annihilate yourself with the photonic core sequencing transformer—" Q suddenly put his fingers to his lips. "Oops. Was that out loud? Just forget I said that last part."

"I hate you," Harry said.

Snap.

Tom recognized the avocado-colored shag carpet he'd crawled on as a baby. This time, instead of being in a playpen, he was nose-to-nose with half of a cardboard box, its innards crudely painted with a facsimile of stars and planets. In his hand he held a white hard plastic spacecraft; at least, he guessed it was a spacecraft, since no planet-based aircraft looked anything like this saucer-shaped toy encircled with rows of lights, alternating blinking red and blue.

Tom discovered if he pressed a button on the bottom of the spacecraft, a muffled but high-pitched voice—a cross between Neelix and tribble—said, "Greetings, Earthling. We come in peace." *Cool,* he thought, and looked around to see if there were any other things to play with. He then realized that Harry was on the floor across from him. His friend wore a starched, short-sleeved orange-and-blue plaid shirt tucked into a pair of equally starched dark blue trousers. Blinding white socks, emerging from shiny brown loafer shoes, slouched around his ankles.

"Nice outfit, Harry," Tom said, smirking.

"I wouldn't point fingers if I were you," Harry said, putting his index finger and thumb together to flick smallish soldier figurines across the cardboard starscape.

Tom pulled on the braided red and white leather dangling beneath his chin and tipped his head forward. He discovered the straps were attached to a white straw cowboy hat with a thick red band. A shiny gold star imprinted with the word SHERIFF was fixed in the center of the hat. He looked down at his clothes: a red, black, and white kerchief tied around his throat, and a red-and-white checked shirt tucked into pants similar to Harry's.

"Quite the dandy," Harry said, teasing.

A figure seated in a yellow velour reclining chair dropped a newspaper to look down on them. Removing the tobacco pipe from between his teeth, he said, "Play nice, boys, or there'll be no dessert for either of you. Where was I? Oh yes. The Nacene. They began like every sentient species—wanting to explore, to understand their environment."

The plastic spacecraft in Tom's hand flew out of his grasp and into the cardboard space backdrop, where it hovered and blinked its colored lights.

"The Nacene discovered what you call 'strings' as part

of their natural exploration. All would have been fine if they'd left well enough alone. They didn't. The problem with their failure to keep their proverbial hands to themselves was that their happy-go-lucky carelessness with the strings affected more than just Exosia and your dimension, but every dimension that emerged from the Big Bang. You see, what you humans call 'strings' is a fundamental building block of the universe. All the dimensions are interconnected in a cosmic ecology that expands infinitely in all directions, and one of the key elements connecting all these pieces together are what you perceive to be 'strings.' The strings have different names, manifestations, and roles depending which dimension is being considered—"

"So the Nacene messed with the strings and everything got all knotted up," Tom said.

Q clamped his teeth around the pipestem and exhaled sharply, producing a small but perfectly shaped mushroom cloud from the bowl. "I'll handle the wordplay if you don't mind. But—to continue—yes, and not only in their dimension. They managed to manipulate the strings into altering the fabric of space-time of this dimension, allowing them to intrude into this existence. Initially, none of the damage they did was irreparable; the Q had a few nuisance clean-up issues to deal with, but nothing permanent.

"But like most sentient species that first discover they have power, they tended to abuse it."

Without warning, several light beams erupted from the bottom of the spacecraft, alighted on the plastic soldier in Harry's hand, and began incinerating the figurine. Harry looked on, forlornly, as the soldier melted into a khaki green lump in his palm, a curl of acrid smoke rising up from the remains.

"The Nacene possess abilities many species would envy and they developed even more—" Q snapped his fingers.

Still wearing the attire they had on in the living room, Harry and Tom stood before a series of mirrors, the plane of each mirror varying from the one beside it. The result was distorted reflections wherever Tom looked: Harry with a disproportionately large abdomen, Tom seeming as thin and tall as an evergreen. Each time he shifted his glance or walked in a different direction, he saw himself transformed into something he could only say was otherworldly.

Beyond the room where they were, slightly off-key calliope music played cheerfully; Tom swore he smelled salty buttered popcorn.

Q's voice reverberated through the chamber. "The Nacene developed a miraculous ability to manifest their energy as corporeal life-forms. Wherever they went, they adapted, explored, and manipulated their environment."

Tom's and Harry's bodies morphed before their eyes, stretching and contorting until they saw facsimiles of their faces mounted on alien bodies. Harry's skin had turned puce and he had four arms spouting out of a squatty, hair-covered torso; Tom had elongated into a knotty stick, with wiry limbs with eyes sitting one atop the other. Tom barely had time to assess his new body before he morphed into another, then another and another in increasingly rapid succession until . . .

He and Harry were back in the living room in their cowboy regalia, sitting cross-legged on the floor in front of Q, who held an open newspaper in front of his face.

"Because the Nacene could blend in wherever they traveled," Q continued, "they started interfering in the affairs of worlds, rarely seeking to better the circumstances of the aliens they visited." Q pointed to the headlines of his newspaper: LYRA GALAXY DEVOURED BY GREEDY SINGULARITY and, in smaller writing, NACENE BLAMED. Q tsked. "Not pleasant, is it? The plasma storms were particularly lovely in that system." He sighed. "Quite a loss."

Harry grimaced. "Why didn't someone stop them from doing so much damage?"

"Alas, there's that pesky fundamental principle called choice again. The Nacene had to be allowed to run amok for the same reason you're allowed to run amok."

A finger snap and . . .

Seven of Nine had information of vital importance. She felt it was imperative that she share her newly acquired knowledge as soon as possible. Commander Chakotay had agreed that Seven's discovery needed to be shared, but he also believed that Seven needed to wait until her turn came up on the agenda. "In this case, ten minutes won't change anything" had been his exact statement to her. Perhaps feeling the residual influences of B'Elanna Torres in her consciousness, Seven had wanted to throttle the commander. Agendas, Seven believed, could be partially to blame for the Federation failing to achieve total dominance in the galaxy. The Borg never used agendas. The Borg stated their intentions and executed the task without waiting for a vote. In this case, Seven had been reduced to taking her place at the table and keeping her mouth shut until the commander asked her to share her data. She glanced across the table at B'Elanna Torres, wondering if the engineer was equally as irked as she was. When Torres met Seven's gaze, she shrugged as if to say "Don't look at me," and dropped her eyes back to the padd sitting on the table before her. B'Elanna twirled her stylus absently between her fingers, staring off into space. Seven was disappointed that B'Elanna would not be her ally. She had come to count on her impatience to move meetings along.

Since being disconnected from the Borg, Seven had learned that successful interaction between species required the employment of specific behavioral niceties that she found inefficient. Small talk. White lies. Euphemisms. Success on Voyager required that she learn such unspoken social protocols. She hoped, however, that if she agreed, at least in theory, to adhere to such rules of etiquette, eventually she could persuade those in charge to see things her way. Given enough time and resources, she was certain she could prove to the ship's leaders that the Borg's stripped-down approach to assigning and completing tasks would improve all of their lives.

Regrettably, today would not be the day Seven would convert *Voyager*'s command staff to the virtues of Borg management. Unfortunate, considering that the crew didn't have a lot of time or resources to expend.

Commander Chakotay appeared to be determined to keep to the routine, carrying on with the meeting as if it were normal to lose half of the senior staff and trade them out with new personnel. Had Seven been in charge, she would have employed a more centralized, authoritarian leadership matrix until the crisis was over. No one asked her what she would do, however, so she was forced to sit here for as long as it took for Chakotay to go through the motions of reorganizing the staff.

Considering all that *Voyager*'s crew had been through in recent days, Seven believed the ad-hoc creation of a new senior staff was going as well as could be expected. Seven had learned that, as adaptable as most humanoids were, they tended to vary in their ability to adapt to change. Her consistency in this area due to her Borg nature was a distinct advantage she had over her compatriots.

Looking around the briefing room table, she saw that none of those seated around the perimeter had much of any reaction, including nervousness, to any of Chakotay's selections. *Perhaps so much has happened recently that they are desensitized to change.*

Lieutenant Ayala was an adequate replacement for Ensign Kim, though Seven believed she herself might have been a better choice for ops or sciences, in spite of her own "incomplete" credentials. She recognized, though, the merits of delegating responsibilities so that others could feel competent and needed. Her work in astrometrics would continue uninterrupted, however, and she would continue to report directly to Commander Chakotay or to Commander Tuvok. Lieutenant Rollins would be acting chief of security, though Chakotay hinted that he and Ayala might switch jobs as part of a cross-training initiative he would implement for the long term.

Seven was surprised but pleased with the choice of Lieutenant Yuko Nakano, who had field-medic experience with the Maquis, to supervise sickbay. She'd worked with Nakano on several away missions and was impressed with the woman's efficiency. Because of Seven's perfect recall and comprehensive knowledge of many species, Chakotay assigned her to supervise Nakano's certification in the basic Starfleet medical course from the computer's database. Seven understood that Nakano had a reputation for being rather chameleon-like among the crew, never building deep relationships or sticking with one group for too long. The adjective "Machiavellian" or "mercenary" had sometimes been used to describe her, though Seven had never found merit in that label. She appreciated Nakano's ability to do what difficult circumstances required rather than dithering on the way many crew members were prone to.

B'Elanna had a curiously indifferent reaction to Nakano's appointment, considering how little she cared for her former Maquis comrade. Noting the distracted look on the engineer's face, Seven concluded that B'Elanna must have known about the new assignments in advance. Or perhaps Chakotay's announcement that Ensign Clarice Knowles would be acting chief helmsman had been an unpleasant reminder that Tom Paris's whereabouts remained undetermined. Until the status of the missing personnel could be determined, all assignments were temporary, save one that remained unchanged.

As usual, Commander Tuvok was inscrutable when Chakotay made his appointment to the first-officer position official. The Vulcan acknowledged his new job with a perfunctory "Yes, sir." Furthermore, he gave no indication that anything was amiss when Commander Chakotay explained that Tuvok would be responsible for training Seven, ostensibly to increase the pool of personnel qualified for command track.

In the short term, Seven realized, assigning her to Tuvok allowed Chakotay to have a form of checks and balances. Should their present crisis be prolonged—should no solution to Captain Janeway's neurological deterioration be found—a confrontation between the commanders would be necessary and hard choices would have to be made. Her Borg perspective aside, sensible humanoids acknowledged that a command structure would be successful only if those in charge had a relationship underscored with trust. For the time being, though, Seven would have to ameliorate the situation.

Chakotay placed his hands on the table and said, "Seven of Nine has an issue that requires our immediate attention." He nodded to her, indicating she should begin speaking.

Seven rose from her chair and began circling the table. "As I've reported previously, the area we refer to as Monorhan space is evolving. The combination of the destruction of the Blue Eye, the explosion of Gremadia, and the disappearance of the black hole by Gremadia has destabilized the subspace fabric of the region."

"This isn't new information, Seven," B'Elanna said.

Inwardly, Seven smiled, glad that the predictably irritable and impatient engineer had remerged from her cocoon. "Correct. But the exact severity of the problem was unknown to me until just before this meeting. Within the next twelve hours, this region of space will become riddled with instabilities."

"Instabilities?" Rollins asked.

Seven searched for the correct words to explain her analysis. "Rips, pockets—"

"Holes?" finished B'Elanna.

"Exactly," Seven said. "This region will be virtually impossible to traverse."

"Are we talking phenomena similar to what we experienced when the displacement wave pushed us into the subspace pocket?" Tuvok asked.

"Perhaps some of the vulnerabilities will be similar, but I cannot say for certain. The clearest way I can explain what is happening is to state that space-time in this region is undergoing a transformation on the subatomic level." As soon as she concluded, she realized her explanation was overly simplistic. Seven paused, searching for the right words. Had a detailed mathematical analysis about particle spins and quantum reality been called for, she knew she could articulate the equations with breathtaking perfection. *How can I make them see?* she thought. She realized that she was the only one in the room with an in-depth background in theoretical scientific realms; this new awareness caused a sense of helplessness she was unaccustomed to.

"How does this subatomic transformation impact us?" Rollins asked. "Is it a situation where a quark is no longer going to be a quark, meaning that the personalities of protons and electrons will change?"

"And I second Lieutenant Torres in wondering how this is different from what we experienced when we first came into Monorhan space—we've known that subspace was different here since we arrived," Ayala said.

"No," Seven said adamantly. "This is not the same circumstance we faced a week ago. But I . . . am not sure the best way to explain what is happening." Kathryn Janeway would have known how to translate algorithms and formulas into word pictures that nonscientists could comprehend. This flustered feeling . . . this inadequacy . . . Seven found disquieting. In circumstances requiring expert social maneuvering, Seven had become accustomed to Janeway filling in where she lacked, whether it was softening Seven's customary bluntness or soothing the hurt feelings or egos of those peeved by her superior Borg knowledge. Simply put: Seven didn't know how to talk to people. Talking at them—ordering them—was far simpler, but ineffective. Though her communication skills had slowly improved, Seven would readily admit that she had a ways to go, but for now—

She missed the captain.

The revelation startled her. For the first time since placing Janeway in stasis, Seven felt a hollow ache in her abdomen that had no correlation to any physiological deficits nor could it be mended by nanoprobes. The routine loss of drones among the Borg was akin to the life cycle of cells in the body. As drones were eliminated, their functions were assumed by other drones. Termination wasn't . . . personal. She stood beside her chair, uncertain as to what she should say.

Her crewmates around the table looked expectantly at her. *Speak as the captain would,* she admonished herself. She reconfigured her thoughts, imagining talking through her discoveries with Janeway, and found that the words began flowing.

"Changes in the subquantum realm are, in turn, changing how particles express themselves. So yes, to answer Lieutenant Rollins's question, it is theoretically possible that a quark may become something other than a quark. I cannot provide specifics without further analysis, but my best guess is that an external event instigated a chain reaction that has stretched into subquantum reality."

"An external event like the destruction of the Blue Eye," Chakotay said.

"Precisely." A thought occurred to Seven. A metaphor Janeway had used in a discussion they'd had about why Seven couldn't continue carrying on doing whatever she pleased whenever she pleased because of how it affected the entire ship. "We have our own little social ecosystem on this ship, Seven," she'd said. "Your actions affect those of your crewmates. We have our own web of life on *Voyager . . .*"

"It is like . . . dominoes," Seven said, as she continued recalling Janeway's words. "When one is knocked over, it knocks over another, then another until there is a cascade effect. In this case, I theorize the destruction of the Blue Eye was the first domino that began destabilizing an already vulnerable subspace layer." Looking around the table, she saw, with satisfaction, the comprehension in their eyes. *Thank you, Captain.*

Seven continued. "The consequence of these changes is that our space-time boundary is becoming permeable.

How our dimension is expressed—how we experience it—is undergoing a metamorphosis."

"Could this transformation spread beyond Monorhan space?" B'Elanna asked, watching Seven intently.

Seven perceived that, not surprisingly, B'Elanna had started toward the same conclusions she had. "Yes, I believe so."

"Atoms, molecules," Rollins said. "Mesons, baryons, neutrinos—all of them would potentially change if there was a radical quantum-level reconfiguration."

"Gravity, electromagnetic force—how would they work?" B'Elanna asked.

"Reality as we currently know it could cease to be," Seven said.

Chakotay blinked, took a deep breath, and shook his head.

Seven knew she should have been first on the agenda.

Chapter 3

Tom and Harry, back in their normal forms, followed Q down a carpet-covered aisle, each side of the aisle lined with floor-to-ceiling glass cases. From what Tom could see, each case contained a rare or precious item with a flashing electronic price tag attached. He saw *wahahi* diamonds, figurines, works of art, photographs, icons, relics—he thought he saw a dodo from Earth in one case. They walked down several long rows before pausing in front of one of the cases where a sea of marbles was displayed on an artfully draped velvet cloth.

A cluster of marbles sparkled iridescently, hypnotically. Tom crouched down to study them more carefully. Within each of the miniature globes, Tom saw different celestial objects: swirling galaxies, wisps of nebulae, pulsars, quasars, and other phenomena that Tom had previous believed only to be theoretical. Amid the glistening orbs, Tom saw a familiar blue-white swirled marble that evoked a pang of homesickness. "Hey, Harry," he said softly, reaching across the shelf toward the "Earth" marble. "Come look at—" Unexpectedly, the shelf where the marbles rested tilted sharply, sending the marbles flying to the hard floor, where many shattered spectacularly. Rhythmic alarms blared. Tom jumped back, reflexively trying to gather up what few marbles survived. He grasped one—

"You break, you buy, Tommy," it said.

Tom held the marble up to his eyes and found Q's oversized eyeball staring back at him. "But I didn't do anything," he said to the eyeball, feeling for all the world like a little kid who had just been caught swiping a cookie from the cookie jar. "And I don't have anything to pay with."

"That's not the point. If something breaks, in this case a star system, a planet, or a nebula, someone has to buy. Ask any Ferengi if you doubt me. It's the direct corollary to the whole choice principle. You make a choice, there are consequences. Someone has to pay for it. Why else would I have brought you here to deal with Kathy's indiscretion?"

"Uh, what about *your* indiscretion," Harry said, smiling smugly. "We haven't gotten to that yet."

"You are an irritating toad, Mr. Kim," eyeball Q said, and promptly turned into a puff of smoke.

A prune-faced dwarf appeared at Tom's side with a square tablet in his wrinkled, liver-spot-covered hand. He took Tom's left hand and placed it on the tablet, which lit up in reply. "It's all yours, buddy," he croaked, and gave Tom a palm-sized box.

"How did I pay for this?" Tom said, dubiously studying his new possession.

"Loan. Guaranteed by Q. He's a vicious one to borrow from so I'd make sure my payments are on time."

Tom lifted the lid gingerly. Yep. The broken marble was inside. Engraved in small text on the lid was "Monorha" and a series of numbers that Tom believed must be its coordinates. "I own Monorha?"

Q materialized by Tom's side. "That is correct, Mr. Paris. Next time, perhaps, you should break something more interesting. I'd give you a chance, if we didn't need to press on." A finger snap and—

Tom, Harry, and Q stood on a plateau. Before them, a barren purple-brown field, blanketed in shadows and twilight, spread as far as they could see. To their backs, a slick obsidian wall curved over their heads like a sarcophagus lid, shielding them from bone-chilling wind whistling through rock teeth and down onto the open plain. Lightning cleaved the darkness; thunder answered in protest. The cacophonous sounds of war stormed in the distance.

Death lingered here; Tom felt it seeping through the ground, drifting on the dank air. He'd felt similarly back on Caldik Prime before his choices cost three Starfleet officers their lives.

"Before you ask, Mr. Kim," Q said, giving Harry a meaningful gaze, "this is the place where the Nacene finally settled their differences about whether they should continue to exist in two dimensions. One side favored locking themselves up in Exosia to 'fix' the unbalanced strings. The other side believed that exploration was their right and demanded to be allowed to come and go freely."

Vaporous outlines—ghostly armies—flowed over the hills and down into the plains. From the heights, the soaring, diving, floating phantasm looked like a tide pool of sea anemones with glowing tentacles waving with the tides. The Nacene did not wound, the Nacene annihilated. Tom found it impossible to look away from the horrible beauty of dancing colors and flashing lights.

"This place became Monorha, our own Mr. Paris being the latest in a long series of unfortunate owners," Q said. "All that Nacene destruction gave rise to life. An unforeseen *consequence* of the Nacene's *choices.*"

"I get it," Harry said dryly.

Directly opposite their position, a tall humanoid figure, more radiant than the Nacene below, appeared on a cliff, cloak flowing out behind him. He opened his arms to the starry sky above and cried out terrible invocations, calling on forces alien to Tom's understanding. Each spoken word caused Tom to tremble until his knees could barely support him. "Who is that?" he whispered.

Q studied Tom, with amusement or sympathy Tom couldn't tell, for a long moment before speaking. "The Exiles called their leader 'the Light,' and for a while it appeared the Light might be victorious. In the end, though, the Exosia Nacene won and the passageway was closed. You've met some of the Exiles—"

Without looking away from the Light, Harry said, "Suspiria and the Caretaker."

"Exactly. And lest you forget, the one who masqueraded as your captain's sister," Q said. "The wardens locked up Exosia by patching the gateway between the two dimensions, making it impossible for the exiled Nacene to reenter. The Exiles decided that they'd explore this universe until they found a way for them to exist safely in both places."

As the ramifications of Q's story sank in, Tom began making connections. "The Light and his followers built the black-hole array the Monorhans think of as Gremadia—as a place to refuel and renew their energy," Tom said.

Q raised his eyebrows, impressed. "Excellent, Mr. Paris. Perhaps Kathy is rubbing off on you after all."

"And the Monorhan system?" Harry said finally.

"It's not a system. At least, not a real one. Looks like space, feels like space. But it isn't. It's a construct that protects the gateway to Exosia. At least, that was its function up until recently, when the patch was dislodged and the boundary between Exosia and your continuum became porous again."

"The destruction of the Blue Eye—" Harry said, comprehension dawning. "That's what did it!"

"Give the boy a cookie," Q said. At which point a large chocolate chip cookie materialized in Harry's hand. Harry rolled his eyes and flung the cookie aside.

"This time, however," Q said, "the damage was so catastrophic that it disrupted some of the strings. Their vibrations shifted ever so slightly and as a consequence have started throwing all these interrelated systems out of balance. Soon, all the strings will shift vibrations and contraction will begin. All matter will come together, ending the universe prematurely."

"How soon is soon?" Tom said, worriedly.

"Twenty million years, give or take. I realize that's a future beyond any you can fathom, but that's practically a weekend vacation for a Q. Big enough problem for you boys?"

"But what happened to the Light?" Harry asked.

Q sighed and shook his head. "Studied with us for a while. Promising fellow. But he fell in love with a small-town girl—always had a weak spot for humanoids. Came up with the wacky idea that if they could mingle their matter together and create a child, their offspring might be able to undo all the damage the Nacene had done. Had to give up his life so that the little guy could be born, but born he was."

You have to admire a guy who gave it all up for love, Tom thought, though he had a hard time reconciling the frightening, powerful figure on the cliff with a vision of a lovesick Romeo. "Did his plan work?" Tom asked.

"Too soon to tell," Q said. "That's why you boys are here."

In the space of a heartbeat, the purple-brown field receded into the horizon until it dissolved into the haze.

Voyager's senior staff gathered around the conference room viewscreen where Seven had called up her research data. B'Elanna's eyes flickered over the equations and theoretical projections, and she felt the numbness seeping back into her body. Except as it related to engineering and navigation, astrophysics (especially the quantum side) had never been B'Elanna's expertise. Comprehending Seven's work, however, required only a rudimentary understanding of physics, so it was hard to discount her conclusions. Damn it all if Seven's data didn't appear solid!

The former Borg had extrapolated her theories based on sensor data collected over the past week. Under most circumstances—especially in physics, where time frames were measured in million-year blocks, not days—a week's worth of data would hardly be enough to base such a complex analysis on and produce credible results. It was like drawing conclusions about planetary geology based on a grain of sand! The rapid changes in Monorhan space seemed to negate any concerns over hasty conclusions, though. If anything, Seven's analysis was barely keeping abreast of the situation. B'Elanna's stomach crawled up her throat; she repressed the urge to throw up. Rollins and Ayala peppered Seven with questions. B'Elanna knew she should probably be paying attention to their discussion, but she found this whole situation so unsettling that she was having a difficult time convincing herself this wasn't a stress-induced nightmare.

Nakano, who was downloading the data into a padd for her personal use, asked B'Elanna if she'd like her to perform a similar download for engineering. B'Elanna declined. She'd come to the unarguable conclusion that regardless of what Seven's data said, they were inescapably screwed.

"So what do we do?" Chakotay said at last.

"I doubt that any of our efforts at reversing this quantum shift will be effective," Seven said. "My preliminary models indicated that beyond Monorhan space, the transformation would occur more slowly, taking perhaps tens of thousands of years."

"That's pretty quick when you figure a star's life cycle—" Ayala said.

"Or the orbital paths of some comets," Rollins said.

"How comforting—knowing we won't be around to witness the destruction of the universe as we know it. Especially since it looks like it's our fault," B'Elanna said cynically. "Nothing like having that responsibility laid at our feet." She walked away from the crowd gathered around the screen and dropped back into her chair. Slouching down, she buried her head in her hands, massaging her sinuses, where a headache had started gestating. Chakotay needed to end this meeting—soon. Her engines needed her.

The officers, one by one, returned to their chairs. Once everyone was seated around the table, the discussion resumed.

"It appears that our plan to evacuate the region immediately was the logical one," Tuvok said. "Perhaps we can devise a method to isolate or contain Monorhan space so that the destruction spreads no further."

Finally, a voice of reason, B'Elanna thought.

"Actually," Seven said, "we may not want to evacuate the region yet."

I didn't just hear what I heard. B'Elanna raised her head, mouth agape. The Borg had finally taken leave of her senses. Seven's obsession with the Omega molecule had been more than a bit crazy, but this was full-on delusional. Throwing her arms behind her head and smirking at Seven, B'Elanna said, "This I've got to hear."

Seven raised a single, perfectly arched eyebrow, sending what B'Elanna knew was wordless rebuke.

B'Elanna had been told that her system was nanoprobe-free, but moments like these made it hard to believe it: the odd connection between her and Seven remained. She frowned.

With a sniff, Seven turned back to the rest of the senior staff. "I have maintained surveillance of the microsingularity since it formed after the collapse of the white dwarf," Seven said. "While I've focused primarily our resources on the larger issues of the region, particularly as they relate to navigation, I have been able to delineate facts that may prove to be relevant to our current predicament. Computer, reduce lighting fifty percent." From where she sat, she activated a viewscreen at the front of the room.

With a yellow grid as a background, a rendering of Monorhan space appeared, indicating the positions of the planets, the stars, the microsingularity, the remains of the former location of Gremadia. *Voyager*'s current trajectory out of the system was indicated by a solid blue line swooping through the illustration. Also on the map was a blinking green dot indicating the most probable location of the missing shuttle. The green dot was six to seven hours away under present circumstances.

B'Elanna knew what she'd been told—that there wasn't any discernible sign of Tom within the region—but that didn't change her hope that he'd just show up at the rendezvous point with a wild and crazy story about where he'd been and why they hadn't been able to find him. She might have to kill him for his hijinks, but at least she'd know he wasn't squashed into billions of atoms some-where.

"Computer, add energy-distribution-analysis data to the Monorhan map," Seven commanded.

The computer chimed an acknowledgment, and a swirled red-and-white vortex appeared over the grid, the pinprick centered directly over the microsingularity. A key off to the side of the diagram indicated that the red color-ing mapped photonic energy; the white coloring indicated other energy. B'Elanna further examined the explanatory key and discovered that this was Seven's future projection for the distribution of light energy in this sector. In the near future, the Monorhan sun wasn't in danger of disap-pearing, nor was *Voyager* in danger of losing her own lights. But such an outcome was inevitable within months, maybe weeks if the subspace changes accelerated. This whole region of space would be snuffed out like a candle.

B'Elanna placed her elbows on the table, leaning for-ward to rest her head on the backs of her hands so she could get a better look. Narrowing her eyes, she studied the diagram intently, and then glanced up at Seven. The Borg looked far too smug. B'Elanna could practically hear Seven's words: *Good. I have your attention. You will come to the same conclusions I have and I will need you to support what I am about to propose.* To which B'Elanna anticipated responding, *Like hell I will.* The longer she looked, however, the more right Seven appeared to be. She muttered a Klingon invec-tive under her breath, ignoring Chakotay's withering glare. She took a deep breath. *Fine. I'll say it.*

"Over time, a disproportionate amount of photonic energy in the region will be swirling toward the microsin-gularity," B'Elanna said, looking away from the illustration and up at Seven. "I didn't believe the singularity had that kind of gravitational pull yet. It's still pretty small. To be drawing in photonic energy from all over the sector within several weeks—I thought only light that passed within the pull of the event horizon could be drawn in. This diagram seems to have a magnetic quality to it."

"It does," Seven agreed. "Something in the character of this specific object pulls photonic energy toward it. Take a look at another view, recorded by our sensors in the moments after Gremadia exploded." She ordered the computer to shift illustrations. Instead of a whirlwind of alternating colors trickling into the singularity, the display showed a solid red stream swamping the object like floodwaters over a levee.

"I don't understand it," Chakotay said. He glanced at B'Elanna, seeking her thoughts. "Why photonic energy?"

The engineer shrugged.

"A singularity with that strength should be pulling planets and all other cosmic detritus toward it," Ayala said. "But there's not even the subtlest of orbital shifts in any of the pathways of the planetary bodies or even the meteor belt when you compare the most recent data with the older data."

"Precisely," Seven said, obviously pleased.

Ayala might make a competent replacement for Harry after all, B'Elanna thought. *We're all replaceable, aren't we. . . .*

"I believe this isn't a singularity the way we understand singularities," Seven said. "To refer to it as such is a misnomer."

"That would certainly be consistent with everything else about this region—which is that nothing is consistent," B'Elanna muttered under her breath.

"Our hypothesis was correct," Chakotay said, methodically pacing the length of the room. "It isn't a singularity:

it is a destabilization of the boundary between this artificial system and whatever else it is connected to—"

"Exosia," B'Elanna said. "Home of the Nacene."

Silence smothered the room. The senior staff sat in contemplative quiet for a long moment. B'Elanna imagined that everyone was as sobered as she at the prospect of dealing with thousands, if not more, Nacene, should Exosia open to their space-time.

"Could we stabilize Monorhan space if we closed this boundary?" Ayala asked finally.

"Possibly," Seven said. "But more immediate to our concerns is my belief that the Doctor was pulled into Exosia as a consequence of the last major regional disruption—the destruction of Gremadia. If we want to find him, our best chance is to probe the rift to see if we can locate any traces of him."

The words had barely left Seven's lips before B'Elanna was out of her chair. She'd had enough of Borg madness to last her the rest of her life. Fists on hips, she stormed at Seven. "You're saying we need to reverse course and go back into the heart of Monorhan space."

"Yes I am." Seven's placid expression said that she'd anticipated this reaction, angering B'Elanna all the more.

B'Elanna opened her mouth, paused, blinked, and shook her head. "I'm speechless. After what you've just told us about this region turning into so much Swiss cheese, I don't know how in the hell you expect us to knowingly go back into the worst of it!" She gave in to the overwhelming need to escape her chair and stalked the length of the room several times, waiting for the other senior staffers to voice their objections.

"The Doctor's backup modules were irreparably damaged, Lieutenant," Seven said. "There's not a trace of his programming left aboard *Voyager*. We have to have a medical officer."

"What about Nakano?" B'Elanna argued.

"I'm not a doctor, B'Elanna," Nakano said softly. "I'm just a few steps beyond a nurse."

Realizing that no one else was going to speak up, B'Elanna stopped beside Chakotay, who leaned against the wall beside the computer. "Surely you can't be taking this seriously. The captain's last order was to exit Monorhan space!"

"At the time the captain gave that order, she had no idea that we lost the Doctor," Chakotay said. He turned to Seven. "How long can we safely remain within the boundaries of Monorhan space?"

"Less than a day," Seven said.

B'Elanna stepped back, leaned against the wall beside Chakotay, and watched the exchange. They'd all see reason once they started working through the practicalities of the situation. She knew they would. They had to.

Rollins asked, "Can we get to the rift and back in that time frame?"

"If we plan efficiently," Seven said.

"And the Nacene," Tuvok said. "We will need to have a defense plan in place should this rift indeed prove to be a gateway into Exosia."

"Good thinking, Commander," Chakotay said. "Make sure we have countermeasures ready to go if need be."

Nakano glanced up from a padd she held in her hand and over at Seven. "Any potential health side effects—lingering radiation from the Blue Eye or Gremadia's destruction, for example?"

"Nothing more than what we're currently dealing with," Seven said.

Chakotay inhaled sharply. "Are you confident we might actually find something?"

"No," Seven said. "But I am virtually certain that if we don't go back to the rift we may never locate the Doctor."

"If we can trace the Doctor, how will we extract him from wherever he is?" Ayala said.

"*Thank* you!" B'Elanna muttered.

"Watch your tone, Lieutenant," Chakotay said, then turned to Knowles.

"Presuming that subspace's deterioration is ongoing, can we even navigate away from the rift once we get there?"

"I'd need to study the astrometrics data in order to plot a course," Knowles said, scooting her chair away from where B'Elanna hovered. "But I suppose anything is possible. We might nee—"

B'Elanna's patience ran out. "Is *anyone* here the least bit concerned about my engines? Anyone?" Visions of her breaching warp core exploded before her eyes. Fast, shallow breaths made her light-headed. Seven had no right to send *Voyager* into harm's way in pursuit of her crackpot theories. Dangling the possibility of Janeway's recovery before them was no different from a Cardassian archon offering empty promises of clemency to a condemned criminal facing a death sentence. "You tend to be insensitive, Seven, but giving false hope falls into the realm of cruelty. The Doctor is likely obliterated into zillions of photonic pieces and the captain is little more than a breathing corpse!"

"*Lieutenant,*" Chakotay said, the sharp disapproval in his voice making her flinch.

Accepting that she'd lost this round, she looked away. "Yes, *sir.*" She crossed her arms over her heaving chest.

The throbbing tempo of her pulse in her ears. Her limbs trembled. She squeezed her arms to still them. Steady, focused breathing did nothing to quell her anger.

Out of the corner of her eye, she watched Chakotay look slowly around the table, meeting each member of the staff in the eyes before ending with B'Elanna. She knew what he was doing. His motives were transparent to her: he wanted to know who was with him as he made a difficult decision. She kept her face forward, refusing to look at him.

"Fine then," Chakotay said. "When we're done here, I'll issue the order to head for the rift to look for the Doctor."

If B'Elanna's heart had been pounding before, it abruptly stopped now. Her hands went cold and any hope she had of ever breathing again ended. She thought of the green dot on the map. The hopeful green dot where Tom might be waiting for her. She wanted to scream but couldn't find her voice. She closed her eyes, swallowed hard, and found the strength to speak.

"What about the *Homeward Bound?* At this point, the only chance we have of finding Tom or Harry is to get out of this hellhole," she said, her voice husky. B'Elanna fixed her gaze on Chakotay. He had to know that their friendship hung on this moment.

In his face, she found sympathy, but also resolve: Chakotay would not budge.

"You've got to be kidding me." Her mind blanked from shock. They were abandoning Tom. Thoughts tumbled out, each with increasing vehemence as her frustration gained momentum. "You think finding the Doctor is more important than finding Tom and Harry. The Doctor is software. We can rebuild him. We can't replace Tom and Harry. There's not a holobuffer we can pull them out of."

Chakotay said nothing.

"Lieutenant Torres, the best chance we have at finding a cure for the captain is if we locate the Doctor," Tuvok said. "Otherwise, her death will be assured. And you, more than anyone, are aware that any remaining data relating to the Doctor's program has been corrupted beyond recall."

"What about the rest of us? Do we sacrifice all of our lives for the chance of saving her?" B'Elanna loved the captain as much as the rest of them did, but she couldn't believe that Janeway would endorse such an all-or-nothing strategy. *Or maybe she would,* B'Elanna thought. *She wouldn't give up on any of us.*

"Overall, the crew as a whole stands to benefit from a skilled medical practitioner in their midst," Tuvok said. "No doubt everyone in this room has had an experience where only the Doctor's extraordinary capacities saved their lives or the lives of another crew member. Lieutenant Nakano, while adequate, lacks the abilites of an EMH."

"This fool's errand could get us all killed," B'Elanna said. "And then what good will the Doctor be?" In desperation, B'Elanna turned to Clarice Knowles. Clarice and Tom were friends. It couldn't just be her, Tom's lover, fighting for his return. Someone else had to fight for him. Clarice averted her eyes from B'Elanna. In profile, B'Elanna could see the pilot's eyes glistening brightly.

No, she was alone in her battle. The sorry truth was that for anyone but Tom, she probably would have sided with Chakotay and the rest of the senior staff.

But this *was* Tom.

She inhaled a deep, ragged breath and rose from her chair. Quietly, she said, "Maybe today is a good day to die. I'll be trying to keep my engines from blowing up before we meet our deaths in glorious battle." B'Elanna then crossed the room and was out the door. Let Chakotay send Rollins after her. Confine her to quarters. Throw her in the brig. To B'Elanna, it didn't matter anymore. Nothing did.

In the space of a thought, the Doctor's mind reconnected with his holographic form—wait. No. This didn't feel like a holographic body. Whatever the case, the data stimulating his sensory receptacles felt glorious! Ah, to be alive and—uncomfortable. He was definitely uncomfortable. Cramped shoulder muscles, hard sharp points embedded into his forearms. Cold, damp, and hard. He smelled fermenting plants, no, rotting flesh. His eyes flickered open and he discovered that he was definitely on the ground, facedown on a stone floor, surrounded by dust and unidentifiable debris. Turning his head, even slightly, proved challenging: he was trapped beneath something solid—might it be wood?—that curved over his head and touched the ground in front of him, essentially creating a barrier between him and whatever was above him. Moving his limbs proved equally difficult. Weight on the backs of his legs, especially the calves, pressed them into the floor. Gingerly, he shifted his legs, jostling his knees back and forth to test the boundaries of their confinement. He succeeded in dislodging objects of various sizes and weights; from the sound made when they moved and what little texture he ascertained through his clothing, he guessed he was partially buried by rock or some other building material. He did find it odd, however, that he felt such pressure on his limbs. Not that he was one to show off superior physical skills, but he knew from a few discreet practice sessions on the holodecks that he could bench-press at least ten times what a typical humanoid could lift without any adjustments to his program. Unless a starship had landed on him, nothing he currently faced should pose much of an obstacle to him.

He could definitely tell he was in a small air pocket of some kind, because his upper body wasn't confined by the same weight his legs were. The hollow space above his back and head, probably created by the same object that shielded his head, provided him with enough room to push back his shoulder blades and fan out his elbows. He met immediate, painful resistance when he tried moving his wrists. (He made a mental note when he returned to *Voyager* to adjust the parameters of his matrix so that his "skin" sensors were not quite as acutely tuned to reproduce every human nervous-system response.) Unlike his legs, his hands had been purposefully restrained, most likely by manacles. Manacles had to be attached to something to be effective. He analyzed the angle of his arms, the position of his body, and concluded that most likely his wrists were manacled to armrests. Armrests were generally part of furniture, ergo the object on top of him must be a chair. The quantity of fine particulate matter in the air as well as the detritus on his person—specifically his legs—led him to believe that the chair had likely prevented his torso from being buried after . . . what? An explosion? A cave-in? An earthquake?

Annoyed, he sighed. He was no closer to knowing where he was or what relation this place had to his quest to escape Exosia. Vivia had indicated that she would send him to the problem's point of origin. Perhaps he wasn't as advanced as a Vivia (his thoughts tinged with cynicism) but he failed to see what his present circumstances had to do with the Nacene, never mind the imbalance in Exosia. He considered the possibility that Vivia had tricked him into believing they had a deal when in reality she had merely engineered another means to *contain*. That *would* be a clever tactic. Given the chance and the means, he certainly would have tried it.

Weak gray light seemed to be creeping in off to his right; his eyes followed the light's trajectory until he noticed a gap between the floor and the chair that trapped him. Focusing beyond his immediate area, his eyes gradually acclimated to the dim lighting until he could accurately discern more about the pie slice of the room he could see. Wherever Vivia had sent him, he was currently in the interior of a circular chamber, and a fancy one at that.

Exhibiting a sophisticated level of craftsmanship, the paved floor appeared to be composed of tightly interlocked pieces of polished granite. Rubble, primarily broken pieces of pale-colored stone; the Doctor guessed it might be similar to alabaster, as it reminded him very much of the luminous rock hewn from the Tuscan hills. Dark puddles stained the floor like carelessly spilled ink; he heard irregular drips plopping hollowly onto the ground. Inhaling deeply, he drew in a large breath of musty air. Dust trapped in his nose incited a loud, body-shaking, openmouthed sneeze; the sneeze's momentum caused his face to slam into the floor, his lips and tongue becoming coated with gritty dirt. An unexpected shivery, ticklish sensation shuddered through his body as soon as the air burst through his mouth. He spit and licked his lips, trying to remove the distasteful metallic taste from his mouth and teeth, but didn't succeed. Immobilized by the chair, he couldn't reach his tongue to his shirt sleeve or his shoulder. Before he could formulate another strategy to rid himself of the unpleasant sensation, his nose scrunched up and another sneeze blew threw.

His thoughts stopped. He blinked. A sneeze.

A sneeze by itself was not an unusual phenomenon.

The Doctor regularly treated patients for such physiological symptoms, which were typically prompted by allergic reactions. Such a reaction was not programmed into his holomatrix, however. Holograms didn't have allergies, nor did programming them to mimic symptoms of humanoid ailments serve any purpose, as he had discovered when he had given his matrix a "cold." Mucus-filled noses, rashes, warts, bunions, acne, headaches, backaches, and other such minor annoyances hadn't been part of Dr. Zimmerman's design. The sneeze confused the Doctor—greatly. He had little time to ponder what might have prompted such a malfunction when the sneeze repeated itself, this time generously laden with spittle.

Holograms definitely didn't have saliva. Secretions weren't part of the programming. The Doctor lingered on his disgust for only a brief moment (thoughts of the mad hologram Dejeran flitted through his mind) before he initiated proper empirical procedures to try to figure out what had prompted such a *physical* response.

The Doctor was forced to consider the possibility, one that he wasn't sure terrified him or intrigued him, that he might have been given an actual flesh-and-bone body.

Such a transformation would explain why he couldn't dislodge the debris on his legs. Without the almost limitless possibilities of his holomatrix, he would be confined to the same limits his humanoid compatriots had. Utilizing all the intellectual capacity he could muster—that certainly hadn't been attenuated by whatever had happened—he catalogued and analyzed every sensation he could define and some he could truthfully say he had never experienced before. The steady glub-dub of circulation. Heat radiating off his skin. Lubrication in his eyes. And an itch! He felt an itch, though he couldn't reach it, damnable annoyance that it was. A blunted, gnawing sensation in his innards insisted on being addressed; at best he could define it as achy. At first he thought he might have sustained internal injuries, but upon further evaluation he determined that the underlying sensation of lethargy that plagued him might be due to reduced cellular energy output. Put simply, this body suffered from low blood sugar, an uncomfortable but hardly life-threatening condition that could be addressed by ingesting food.

He felt hungry.

The alternating burbling and tightness in his belly made him think that this body had recently missed many meals. He could imagine how gratifying it would be to assuage this uncomfortable feeling. Ah, to eat! He paused, smiled, and thought, *No, the real prize is to* taste.

As intriguing as the possibility of becoming the equivalent of a holographic Pinocchio was, he knew, without being told or having proof, that he wasn't entirely transformed. Though he certainly had physical limitations that hadn't encumbered him previously, he still had access to his memories, his medical knowledge, and facts and skills relating to the various hobbies he had cultivated over the past few years. The essential elements that defined his identity appeared to have survived his removal from *Voyager*. He, the individual known to the crew as the Doctor, had exceeded the parameters of his programming to the degree that he could exist outside the holobuffers or his mobile emitter. *I think, therefore I am.* The realization struck him profoundly; he savored the thought: *I am. I am more than a matrix and programming. I have evolved.*

And yet he retained parts of his original nature. Weakened versions of his holographic capabilities lingered with him in this form. With concentrated effort, he could stretch the limits of this body's senses and have enhanced visual, auditory, and olfactory capabilities. But what he could muster couldn't compare to what he was accustomed to. He lacked the ability to effortlessly shift his vision between ultraviolet and infrared light spectrums or analyze the chemical compounds of whatever came in contact with his skin. The organic material that housed him placed limits on his ability to express his holographic nature. He concluded that he wasn't entirely humanoid nor was he entirely holographic. Rather he'd become a hybrid, a synthesis of two, seemingly incompatible matters, photons and flesh.

While he wasn't entirely certain what rules governed this new state of being, he knew that changing his current circumstances should be his chief priority. Slight decreases in the temperature and an increasingly fresh smell in the air indicated to the Doctor that the chamber opened to the outside. Probably not purposefully, he guessed, betting that walls had crumbled or a roof had caved in. Unexpected circumstances had to have wrought the destruction he could see, but whether it was an act of war or nature he couldn't tell. He knew from the smell that many dead bodies lay buried beneath the debris; all too soon the stench would be stultifying.

Shadows moved in the room outside; the Doctor saw the shifting shades across the floor and knew he wasn't alone. He was unable to discern words in the unintelligible, sibilant whispers he heard echoing outside. A glimpse of a sleeve, the glint of steel—a weapon or tool, he couldn't be sure—and the footsteps, alternately sounding a ringing clackety-clack or a muted shuffle against the stone, gave no definitive clue as to who or what was outside. He recalled from his brief time with Vivia that a grating whirring field exuded from her—like a discordant energy aura. While her energy didn't prompt any discomfort in the Doctor, it was distinctive and he knew he'd recognize it if he encountered it again, even with his new physiological makeup. Thankfully, he didn't sense it here. He heard multiple sets of footsteps, different vocal intonations; he guessed there were two or three individuals in the room. He almost called out to them to ask for help.

Almost.

In this moment, the Doctor realized he had a decision to make. A Starfleet hologram came programmed with an encyclopedic knowledge of rules and regulations coupled with a strict dictum to adhere to those regulations. Practical experience had taught the Doctor that sometimes rules needed to be fudged; Janeway had taught him that when circumstances called for it, rules needed to be tossed. While the Doctor hadn't known what to expect when he accepted Vivia's challenge to find the Light and stop him, he now knew that most likely, he had been sent to a pre-warp civilization. Whether he lived in the past or present he couldn't say; he supposed it was somewhere in the past. Not only were there Prime Directive issues to consider, there was the conventional thinking about contaminating the timeline to consider as well. The Doctor prided himself on being a model officer, one who upheld the procedures that made Starfleet the outstanding organization it was. Yet . . . here he was. With a decision to make: to break the rules, or not. Theoretically, he could find a way to extricate himself from the wreckage and then stealthily search this world for evidence of the Light. He might be able to perform his mission with a minimum of interaction.

Or he might not.

He had a new appreciation for Janeway, who navigated this ethical gray area with far more confidence than he felt at present. So he decided to follow Janeway in making his choice. In the years he had known her, she had first erred on the side of assuring her crew's survival; second, she examined the humanitarian or moral issues of a situation; and finally, she considered how the consequences of breaking the rules would impact her first and second priorities. If what Vivia told him was accurate, not only was *Voyager* in danger, the stability of the fabric of space-time across the universe was threatened.

If that wasn't a justification for fudging the rules, he didn't know what was.

When one set of footprints came close enough for him to believe that the individual might be in earshot, the Doctor took a calculated risk and exposed his presence.

"Ho, there!" he called out as loudly as he could. "I need help!"

The footsteps halted and turned back toward him. A pair of stained animal-skin boots, peeling apart around the seams, blocked out what little light he had.

"Hello," the Doctor said, trying to sound friendly. "You think you might be able to help get me out from under all this rock?"

The boots walked closer to him until the muddy toes nearly touched the Doctor's face. "Over here, Nual!" a decidedly male voice said. "Someone managed to stay alive when the ceiling collapsed!"

"Can you tell what side he's on?" the one called Nual, the owner of a gruff, older voice, said. The Doctor heard him shuffling over in his direction.

The owner of the boots paused, clearly seeing something the Doctor couldn't. "From the crest on his fire lance, he looks like he owes allegiance to the witch. He's probably one of her Shadows."

The Doctor didn't like the way the owner of the boots spat out the word "witch." He was a doctor, a man of science, not a superstitious simpleton.

Nual snorted. "I'd hardly call the general a witch. A mighty powerful warrior-seer, but there's nothing dark about her successes. She might reward us if we help her man."

"I assure you there's nothing magical about me," the Doctor said cheerily. "I'm harmless. Especially since I appear to be manacled to this chair."

The steps shuffled closer to him. "Get him out, Din."

Piece by piece, the Doctor felt the weight on his lower back and legs decrease until he could shift his legs around and dislodge what little remained. One of the men who was unburying him applied gentle pressure to his chair, indicating that he was preparing to right it. The Doctor situated his body so that moving the chair wouldn't rip the skin from his arms. As the chair tipped back, he scrambled to his knees, then scooted backward until he sat flush against the chair back.

The taller of the two men removed a vicious-looking hunting knife from the leather belt slung over his hips. "Make your hands into fists," he said.

The Doctor's heart thudded a bit faster: the man had a very large knife. He swallowed hard, considered his options, and realized he had none. But the Doctor sensed no malice in his voice, so he complied, fingers crossed that he wasn't about to be gutted like a trout.

Stepping behind the chair, the tall man slipped the blade between the Doctor's wrist and the manacle, sawing back and forth with a high-pitched *zzZZ-zzZZ* until the metal band had been weakened enough to snap in half. He repeated the same action on the Doctor's other manacle.

The Doctor, once again, breathed freely. Grateful to be unencumbered, he stretched out his arms, linking his fingers together in front of him, and pushed his hands out, stretching cramped muscles. He'd never before known that such a simple behavior could have such pleasurable results; he flexed again. Cocking his head, he looked up at his rescuers. "I can't thank you enough," he said, really seeing the pair for the first time.

While Nual and Din had been removing debris, the Doctor had formed a picture of them in his mind—soldiers of some sort, clearly on the opposite side from him judging from their comments when they found him. His conclusions had been wrong. The two individuals standing before him obviously weren't soldiers, or if they were, they had to be the rattiest, dirtiest recruits he'd ever seen.

Coarse, rough-hewn, long-sleeved tunics, soiled with dirt and sweat, hung off their shoulders like carelessly cut bed sheets. Breeches, sewn from animal skin, still reeked of tanning oil and rotted carcass. The Doctor shuddered to see the dark brownish splotches at the seams, imagining that it was likely caked-on blood that he hoped came from last night's dinner and not a murder. Gauzy lengths of black fabric, similar to long scarves, covered their heads, wrapping across their foreheads, around their cheeks, and over their mouths before the ends vanished into their tunics. The Doctor found their clothing so distasteful that he initially missed what should have been their most distinguishing feature, especially to a trained medical professional.

Around their wrists and on whatever exposed skin the Doctor saw were red-brown warty lesions, some as large as his hand; they appeared to be a hybrid of psoriasis and a mole. Viscous fluid—perhaps pus or discharge from a fungus growing on the skin—formed a scabrous crust over the wounds' most raw areas. The borders of the lesions were red and enflamed. Dried epidermal patches scaled off like flecks of mica off a rock. He knew without any diagnosis or further triage that the lesions were malignant—likely related to radiation poisoning—and this pair had only a short time to live. Compassion for his rescuers was tempered only by the realization that he, too, had flesh that could be exposed to whatever contaminant had caused their cancers. Gone were the days when he could stroll in and out of any environment he chose. He quickly looked at his hands—discovered them gloved—felt his head and realized that he, too, wore some kind of head scarf, as well as a cloak. Relief filled him as he didn't see any visible evidence of the same ailments that plagued his rescuers. As soon as he could, he would need to give himself a thorough examination.

The taller of the two, whose face was barely distinguishable under a grimy layer of soot and grease, touched his palm to his chest and said, "Hail, adjunct, I am called Nual." He swung his elbow out to the side, indicating the shorter, and obviously younger, man. "And this is Din, my son."

The Doctor, having no idea how to introduce himself, fell back on the first logical excuse he could think of. "When the ceiling collapsed, I hit my head. I believe I've lost my memory. I don't know who I am, save that I serve the general." *Whoever the general is,* the Doctor thought, wondering exactly how steep his growth curve would need to be if he had any prayer of surviving. He hoped that their concerns about the general being a "witch" weren't enough to warrant killing him on the spot.

Nual and Din exchanged knowing glances, apparently satisfied with his answer.

"I see you have been wounded. Do you need aid or may we finish our work here?" Nual said, gesturing to the wreckage. "We may be able to help you rejoin your regiment when we're done." The unspoken caveat being *we'll help you rejoin your regiment*—for a price.

Though he had no idea what he could offer these men, the Doctor assured them he was fine, expressed appreciation for their help and told them he would do whatever he could for them. He also felt relief that attention would be turned away from him. Before too much more time passed, he needed to come up with a plausible backstory or he doubted that either Nual or Din would help him find his way out. The true story—that he was a holographic sentient, kidnapped from a starship—strained credulity, even to the Doctor's way of thinking. His plan would have to be well formulated, though, and he wasn't terribly confident that it would be.

One of the annoying aspects of his new hybrid self was that he simply didn't process information as quickly as he was accustomed to. Neurons lacked the instantaneous processing his holomatrix did, because so many of their resources were dedicated to dealing with other stimuli. *Like being tired,* he thought, *as well as being hungry, injured, and aching all over after a building fell on me.* He discovered a newfound respect for humanoids, who accomplished a great deal considering how much they had to cope with, moment to moment. What he really needed was to sit down and think. He discovered a stone block, smooth side up, that appeared to be stable enough to sit on, a few steps away from where he'd been found.

As he walked, he happened to notice his reflection in water pooled on the floor and was taken aback by his appearance. *No wonder he asked about my wounds,* the Doctor thought, seeing for the first time his bloodstained sleeves and head scarf. *I must have taken quite a blow*—he noted the bruises mottling his face and touched them tentatively—*or series of blows.* Peeling away his scarf, he squatted down beside the water to get a closer look at his new form. The Doctor didn't care for the barrel-chested body or the balding head, fringed with a ruffle of thinning gray-brown hair. The curved beak nose wasn't too attractive either, especially with pocked jowls and nonexistent cheekbones. He turned his head to get a better look at his profile—

He blinked, swallowed hard, blinked again. His hands went to his ears; he ran his fingers over the contours and knew instantly that the reflection didn't lie. *How is this possible?* It was all too fantastic to be believed. He searched for more evidence in the rubble surrounding him, glanced over mud-soaked tapestries and collapsed columns.

He studied his own clothing: a bronze breastplate embossed with the crest of a lilylike flower over a suede black jerkin stitched with a fine needle. The insignia Din referred to were a series of gold bars pinned on the jerkin's upper arm. Not far from him, he saw a corpse whose tunic sleeve bore the crest of a cluster of wheat shafts bound together by an openmouthed creature, fangs exposed, that looked like a cross between a snake and a centipede. He'd seen these images before, but where?

And then he knew. The insignia confirmed it.

The Doctor blamed the fusion of his holographic and physical natures for slowing his cognitive abilities. Otherwise, he might have quickly identified his current circumstances. Armed with his new understanding, he studied the room, examining architecture and artwork; he analyzed what climatological data he could discern from inside a building. As he organized and catalogued facts, they complied perfectly with the knowledge Kes had shared with him during her years on *Voyager*.

Vivia had sent him to Ocampa.

One by one, the outcasts answered her call to come together one last time for the final battle. Some of them were in worse condition than she was, but none were stronger. All of them looked to her for guidance. Perhaps lingering too long in a human form had tainted her perspective, but she perceived them as being *tired*. How long they had labored, seeking the solutions that would liberate the captives that dwelt in Exosia? The conviction that they would return triumphantly, that even detractors like Vivia would accept them as saviors, had sustained her since the Great Battle. Now the best they could hope for was to survive Vivia's wrath. How odd that she hadn't yet made an appearance. What could possibly be preventing her from launching her promised attack? Phoebe could not devote too much of her precious energy to attempting to predict Vivia's behavior. No, her fellow Exiles needed her— pleaded with her for wisdom.

In choruses, they communicated with her. "What now?" "The Key is lost. Gremadia is gone. How can we be renewed? Will our lives drain away?" Their desperation filled her. Janeway had forced this destiny upon them. She had robbed them of what was rightfully theirs! Without a key, they could never return to Exosia. If only that primitive simpleton of a Monorhan Kaytok had a concept of what havoc he had wrought. If only they had a key . . . if only . . .

A key.

Surrounded by her fellow exiles, Phoebe felt buoyed by their strength. Her ability to make connections and assess her environment steadily improved. Perhaps circumstances weren't as dire as she'd believed. Vivia's failure to act immediately had provided them with an opportunity that they hadn't believed possible—the chance to seize the momentum, to choose the time and place of their war. She saw the options afforded her here in this place where they had once fought against those in Exosia. Long ago, the Light had used what resources he had available to him to create the Key; she would have to do the same.

A key. . . . If we join together . . . yes, it is possible. Revenge is also possible and I can fuse my purposes into one. . . . We may yet return to release those enslaved to the strings.

The realization thrilled her. She told them all: *Yes, we can create a key.* Her fellow Exiles shared their satisfaction with her plan. Yes, sacrifices would be required. But only small lives, and she would not allow small lives to hinder her destiny any longer.

Chapter 4

Seven watched B'Elanna leave, along with the rest of the senior staff. After issuing padds with the duty rosters to the department heads, Chakotay dismissed them without comment. The customary chatter that typically accompanied the end of meetings was nonexistent. None of the officers even looked at each other as they left for their respective departments until only Chakotay and Tuvok remained behind with Seven. She studied Chakotay, anticipating that the tension between him and Tuvok would return now that the staff had departed. Interpersonal relationships were too complex for Seven's liking. She eagerly anticipated her return to the astrometrics lab, where her colleagues, the computers, neither threatened to punch her nor seethed beneath the weight of unexpressed feelings.

"Commander Tuvok, you will accompany Seven of Nine to astrometrics for the time being," Chakotay said. "Assist her in prioritizing analyses and distributing the data to the proper parties. You will also be in charge of any weapons reconfiguration that needs to be done to protect *Voyager* against possible Nacene attack."

"Ensign Knowles will need a real-time datalink between helm control and astrometrics," Tuvok said.

"Seven will work with Lieutenant Rollins to facilitate such a link."

Seven nodded, acknowledging the assignment. "I will go to work on it immediately." Linking her hands behind her back, she turned toward the door and took two steps before Tuvok asked her to wait.

"If we reach the rift without a plan as to how we will search for and retrieve the Doctor, our efforts will be futile," Tuvok said.

"I recommend that we move ahead on testing the multispatial-probe design," Seven said. "I believe it is our best hope for finding the Doctor."

"Once you have a strategy, I'll notify engineering," Chakotay said.

Imagining B'Elanna's reaction, Seven said, "Lieutenant Torres may not be a cooperative contributor toward such an assignment."

"Lieutenant Torres will work through her emotional turmoil in her own way," Tuvok said. "I believe her desire to see this task done quickly and correctly will outweigh any reticence she may have."

A thought occurred to Seven, a way she might be able to rid herself of the disquieting feeling she'd had since B'Elanna departed. "Let me discuss the matter with Lieutenant Torres."

For the first time since convening senior staff, a hint of a smile curled Chakotay's lips. "As you wish. I'll be on the bridge if you need me."

"Thank you, sir," Seven said, then turned to Tuvok. "It appears we will be working together."

"Indeed," Tuvok said.

They exited the room behind Chakotay, walking to the

turbolift with a bare minimum of transactional communication passing between them. Once a plan had been settled on, neither of them spoke. Seven welcomed the quiet after the emotional upheaval of the staff meeting. The silence continued until their arrival at astrometrics. Tuvok stood by while Seven received Ensign Brooks's report and dismissed him. Tuvok maintained an unobtrusive position off her elbow while she resumed her customary position at the control panel, studying the datastream pouring into the computer for analysis. The subspace shifts had become more pronounced in the short time she'd been away from astrometrics. In the millions of lifetimes of knowledge she'd acquired during her Borg existence, Seven had no recollection of a phenomenon such as the one she observed in this sector occurring. *Engineering should see if these quantum variables will impact the engines.* She dismissed her first impulse: *No, helm control first. But do the changes have more than statistical significance?* Her fingers flew over the panel, inputting a new algorithm. The computer spewed more data, but none that illuminated her thinking. Her body vibrating with tension, she shifted her weight back and forth between her feet several times trying to alleviate her discomfort.

"One of your first lessons in command," Tuvok said, "when facing a plethora of variables, is identifying what items are most critical to the functionality of your crew and ship."

Seven cocked her head and examined Tuvok, impressed that he discerned her state of mind without her expressing it. They stood side by side as Tuvok talked her through the best way to prioritize the data and distribute it accordingly. His voice rarely deviated beyond a careful three-or-four-note range that Seven found curiously reassuring. The tension wiring her shoulders released and her thoughts flowed freely once again. By the time they were finished updating, Ensign Knowles had her datalink and Seven could start formulating ideas on how they might find the Doctor as well as the missing shuttle.

"I will begin the weapons modifications," Tuvok said, and took a seat at a vacant workstation behind her.

"Of course." Seven quickly became immersed in her work. Devising a means to recognize specific photonic signatures wasn't difficult. She first located traces of the Doctor's organizational patterns in the ship's computers, and then filled in the patterns with the most rudimentary elements that composed his identity. For example, the visual parameters of his holomatrix—his appearance—was an easy place to start. Anything that remotely complied with those definitions could be detected by properly calibrated sensors. Identifying the Doctor was simple by comparison with what would be required to extract him from the rift. Seven perceived removing the Doctor as a problem that required a technical solution—an engineering solution. But before she approached B'Elanna, she wanted to make one last attempt to find Tom and Harry. Seven knew that B'Elanna believed that by returning to the rift Chakotay had given up on Tom and Harry. Seven wanted to show B'Elanna that this belief was in fact not true.

In the day since Tom and Harry disappeared, she had focused her efforts on calibrating the sensors and devising new data-collection methods that would allow them to find the missing shuttle out in regular space. Seven had finally developed the necessary calculations to help the sensors compensate for the irregularities and interference of Monorhan space. She was confident that the readings they'd recently taken would be more accurate than any they'd had so far. Thus far, it had been easy to blame their inability to contact/find Tom and Harry on the regional oddities that seemed to thwart them at every turn. There were no such excuses any longer. Seven studied the latest readings hoping that she'd have good news for B'Elanna.

From her experiences sharing B'Elanna's consciousness, she did know that the complex and often illogical relationship B'Elanna had with Tom Paris was one of the stabilizing forces in B'Elanna's life. Losing him permanently could have a seriously detrimental impact on one of *Voyager*'s most vital crew members. *On one of my . . . friends,* Seven thought, still not entirely comfortable with the term. Unfortunately, the longer she worked, the more she believed that a positive outcome for Tom and Harry was impossible. She decided to persist a little while longer in the hopes that she might find a piece of data she'd overlooked. She input another long series of formulas, then stood back to wait for the operation to run its course.

Tuvok had remained silent for such a long moment that Seven had forgotten he was with her until he asked if he might speak with her about a situation unrelated to their current assignment.

His request surprised her: of all the members of *Voyager*'s crew, Tuvok was the least likely to socialize on duty. Recalling Captain Janeway's behavior at moments such as these, she encouraged him to speak freely. "I am presently waiting for the computer to finish its calculations," she added, lest he feel she was too busy to listen.

"In the immediate future, there will not be time to have such a discussion, nor will it be appropriate," Tuvok said, employing the same steady voice he'd used before. "I apologize in advance for taking time away from the matter at hand, but I believe your insight into my personal situation may be valuable."

"I doubt that my limited experience as an individual

can provide you with understanding you have not gained in more than a hundred years of living," Seven said, continuing to study the sensor datastream. She wondered if she should ask him to join her in consuming a beverage or to stand beside her while she spoke. Such behavior seemed to be customary among crew members when they wanted to "talk." Except Tuvok. She didn't know what he found customary.

"I believe I have recently acquired knowledge that has facilitated a greater understanding of your life with the Borg."

Curious, Seven turned to look at him. His face, as usual, revealed nothing. "Proceed," she said.

"During my experiences on Gremadia I discovered what it is like to live in the presence of many. To know and be known by many minds and to freely exchange understanding and knowledge," Tuvok said. "Before this experience, I knew only the linking of several minds, and in that process, I never surrendered my individuality."

"And on Gremadia?" Seven said softly, suspecting that she knew what he would say next.

"My individuality was augmented. I believe I glimpsed the Vulcan ideal, *Kol-ut-Shan*—" The carefully modulated tone diverged by a note. He paused, his entire body still save for the rise and fall of his chest taking a sequence of identical, deep inhalations.

Seven identified the deliberate rhythm as a meditation. Whatever he was attempting to express had affected him deeply.

The calm veneer renewed, he continued: "I became more and I expanded. A solo flute expanded beyond its singular capacity that became part of a symphony creating music that I didn't know was possible."

His words evoked memories. Seven did indeed understand what he spoke of. For once, she was not on the outside of a conversation; she allowed herself the tiniest of triumphant smiles over this small, social victory. "Based on your metaphor, I believe what you experienced was more beneficent than the Borg collective. There was nothing in the collective that I would describe as 'music,' as it is more of a hive-mind state. However, it is difficult to explain the merits of such a unified state of mind to those who haven't had such an experience," Seven said.

"Until I lived with all those minds being part of my own, I admit that I failed to recognize what an isolated and contained existence individuals have." He met her gaze directly.

"That is true," she said, and added mentally, *You may not say it, but I will: It is a lonely existence.* In the long moment she held his gaze, Tuvok's Vulcan self-control never wavered. She perceived, however, that beneath the calm surface he projected, he had experienced a loss. She acknowledged to herself that she might be projecting on Tuvok her own sense of alienation after being severed from the Borg. Even so, Seven felt oddly comforted to know that at least one person on *Voyager* could relate to her past life.

"The adjustment—after you were severed from the Borg—did it take a long time before you felt whole as an individual?" Tuvok said.

"Truthfully, I cannot say that I've ever felt whole as I did when part of the collective. But I have come to think of my life in different terms."

"Such as?"

"Instead of considering what I lack, I have made peace with my separateness. I have come to appreciate the merits of free will."

"Indeed. Having control of one's mind and body can

be satisfying and provide a tremendous sense of accomplishment."

"My independence meant more to me after I had the contrast of being an individual for a time, then sharing my consciousness with—"

B'Elanna. Remembering what she had been doing before Tuvok had begun speaking to her, Seven returned her attention to the console. Moments later, the computer chirped that Seven's equations were complete. She became engrossed in what she read, uncertain of its meaning.

"New information," Tuvok said.

Seven nodded. "Concerning the missing shuttle."

"My first recommendation in your command training is to deliver this news, good or bad, in person. It is the most considerate choice given how important it is to Lieutenant Torres."

It was Seven's turn to take several deep steadying breaths. She touched her combadge. "Seven to Torres."

"What do you want, Seven?" She sounded exhausted.

"I request a meeting with you about several items, including using the multispatial probe for the Doctor's recovery."

"I have the specs here. Send your modifications over and I'll have Joe pass it to me as soon as it comes online."

"I believe we should discuss this in person." Seven glanced over at Tuvok. He nodded his approval.

Another long pause, then, *"Fine. Main engineering in five minutes."*

A longing to remain entombed in astrometrics filled Seven. She hated dealing with people.

"While you are gone, I will continue my work on the weapons systems," Tuvok said, nudging her along.

"Should there be any developments—"

"I will contact you." Tuvok stood looking at her, making no indication that he would return to his work until she departed.

Seven took the hint. She downloaded the probe data onto a padd and departed. Taking the longest route to main engineering would give her time to consider how she should approach B'Elanna.

Just as Tuvok understood her as he never had before, Seven had recently come to understand B'Elanna. This news would not be received well by the engineer. Unfortunately, she had the data to support her assertions; no ambiguity remained. Indeed, what she learned was a setback to all of *Voyager:* Tom and Harry were nowhere within light-years. They, and the shuttle, appeared to have vanished without leaving a single clue as to where they might be. The most obvious conclusion was that the shuttle had been destroyed. What gnawed at Seven, however, was the utter lack of any evidence of the shuttle's destruction.

Most likely, the shuttle would have been destroyed as it launched off *Voyager.* Neither she nor B'Elanna had found the slightest physical trace of the shuttle's remains—not so much as a random neutrino from the warp core blowing up. Her ongoing surveillance of the designated transport location showed the same result. Even in this sector of space, where the rules had been rewritten, Seven had seen no proof that a fundamental, Newtonian principle didn't apply: even in Monorhan space, matter was neither created nor destroyed. Mass could change form, but it still existed. It was as if the shuttle had been scooped out of their shuttlebay and taken someplace beyond *Voyager*'s ability to find it. But where?

Tom blinked and discovered he once again stood on the *Q.E. II.* His gaudy tourist attire had been replaced with a navy blue jacket over a stiff white button-up shirt. A length of red-and-blue-striped fabric was cinched tightly beneath the collar and tied with a choke knot at the throat. The khaki trousers scared him. The fly fastened with some horrific device with nubs of metal teeth that looked like it shred any skin unfortunate enough to get caught in its jaws. He had some vague recollection of clothing like this in the World War II holoprogram the Hirogen had had so much fun exploiting. Over his shoulder, he caught a glimpse of Harry, also dressed in a jacket and trousers, standing with Q at the top of a gangplank, waiting to disembark at an unknown destination in space somewhere. As far as he could see, the *Q.E. II* was still sailing around stars and nebulae. The gangplank terminated near a particularly grim-looking moon that, from the observable atmosphere, bubbled over with highly acidic gases. *That Q—always up for a good time,* Tom thought as he jogged over to join Harry.

"You look smart, Mr. Paris," Q said.

Realizing that Q was similarly attired, Tom wondered if this was a time-travel trip and if the *Q.E. II* was dropping them off at an interstellar space-time juncture. "Are we somewhere on twentieth-century Earth?"

Q snorted. "Hardly. We haven't left the Continuum. No, we're paying a visit to Q U—my alma mater, located just outside the Continuum boundaries. Finest facility of higher education in the universe and definitely not a place to go slumming in artificial fibers." He flicked Tom's lapels with his finger.

"This is how they dress at Q U?" Tom asked.

"To you it is." Q started down the gangplank with Tom and Harry following close behind. "Like most things in this universe, reality is relative to how you perceive it. You perceive the Continuum in terms your little brains can wrap their neurons around. The truth is, you aren't really wearing what you think you're wearing but your brain is limited in its capacity to translate Q reality into human reality."

As they approached the end of the gangplank, Tom looked over the sides cautiously. A meteor drifted by lazily. Otherwise, he saw a whole lot of nothing.

"Back to this whole Nacene guy called the Light," Harry said with an undertone of impatience.

Q spun on his heel and glared down at Harry. "Are you really so eager to begin your life as a cold-blooded invertebrate, Mr. Kim?"

"I get how *Voyager's* choices brought consequences to the universe. What I don't get is why you need us to solve the problem. Why we just can't go home." Harry stared calmly up into Q's eyes. All signs of "crawl-under-the-bed" Harry had vanished.

Tom was impressed. After the ear gag, he wasn't sure if he would tempt Q into making good on his promise to turn Harry into a newt.

Q seemed to agree with Tom. He said, "Much better, Mr. Kim. You've grown a pair. And you've proved that you deserve to exist in the vertebrate taxonomy." Q glanced nervously (to Tom's eye) around the crowd streaming down the gangplank, then exhaled vociferously, muttering, "You might as well know. I misplaced something and I need you two to help me find it."

Harry snorted. "You think two humans can do better than the Continuum?"

Placing an arm around Tom's shoulders, then Harry's, Q pulled them aside, then drew them close in so they could both hear him whisper. "The Continuum doesn't know there's a problem and none of us will tell them, is that understood? Trust me, Mr. Kim, the recent appearance of your backbone will not stop me from turning you into a plate of escargot—with butter sauce—if necessary."

"I thought the Q knew all," Tom said.

"Compared to you, we do. But that doesn't mean that a certain measure of choice and chance doesn't apply in our realm too."

"Can't you just do some of that finger snapping hocus-pocus and conjure whatever it is?" Harry said.

"It isn't an 'it.' It's a 'who.' And since the 'who' has the ability to choose for himself, the little bugger's gone missing just as the whole universe is looking to him to fulfill the mission he was born for." Shaking his head, Q sighed.

"The little what?" Harry said.

"The Keeper of the Light, Mr. Kim," Q said. "Offspring of the Light, conceived to save the universe from destruction. The kid took off from school last week and I need to find him before the Nacene do."

At first, her fellow Exiles resisted Phoebe's suggestions. Time in this dimension had made them weak and confused—so many had lost the vision of their purpose. She made them see that her way was correct, in part by reminding a Nacene who lacked the energy to change out of his Hirogen form how much pain she was capable of inflicting.

You have forgotten your purpose, she told him as he twisted and convulsed in the midst of them. *You have forgotten your promise to liberate the captives of Exosia!*

His attempts at resisting her attack (instead of accepting it, stupid creature) had sent his Hirogen form into even worse paroxysms. Even in his miserable state, he refused to relent.

Too long a separation from Exosia had made him stupid, Phoebe concluded. *Stubborn creature!* She accelerated the vibrations of his subatomic structure until his sporocystian structure began liquefying.

The others had watched his convulsions impassively, but she knew they realized they would be next should they fail to embrace her vision. When she sensed that they had accepted the inevitability of her dominion, she released the Hirogen from her attack. After all, draining his energy reserves wouldn't help their cause much: she acknowledged this. It would take all of their power fused together to accomplish the task before them. Her authority, however, was demonstrated by making an example of him. Otherwise, she would have faced endless questions and input from the rest of them. Nearly a hundred thousand years in this space-time hadn't necessarily changed their Nacene tendency to be caught up in minutiae. She wouldn't tolerate such time wasting. The longer they delayed, the more likely they would lose their opportunity to return to Exosia with answers that would save their people.

One by one, they gathered around Phoebe until they formed a circle larger than she had the ability to see with her limited senses. Their circle spanned from the refuse belt created by Gremadia's explosion and around the system's star. Many Exiles she recognized; many she didn't. Those that retained the capacity to revert to the Nacene's natural state in this continuum did so. The weaker, more vulnerable Exiles retained their less-evolved guises. Gazing around their circle, Phoebe saw many primitive species whose forms and life cycles she too had assumed. She found it ironic that after all the time that had passed and the exploration she had undertaken she was compelled to return to Exosia as a refugee.

When the Exiles had all joined the Light at the great

decisive battle and fought the Exosia Nacene for the right
to be explorers, she had imagined she would one day return in triumph. She had envisioned showing Vivia and all
those like her who were slavishly devoted to caring for the
strings what the Nacene were truly capable of. Now . . .
Now, she thought, *I am forcing my way to the gateway out of
desperation.*

Mingle essences, she ordered the thousand gathered
around her and immediately, she felt their confusion.

Where to begin? they asked her. For too long they had
been Exiles, communicating as individuals.

Let go, she urged them, *of what you know. It is only what
you are that matters now.*

As her fellow Nacene complied, at first clumsily, their
energies gradually found one another. Steadily increasing
power radiated from their bond. She felt their strength
pouring into her; her strength poured into them. Understanding flowed in unimpeded streams. She had forgotten
this glorious sensation of oneness, of being whole. Her
appetite whetted, the desire to once again partake of
Exosia's glory overwhelmed her. Lost friends became
known to her as the knowledge gained over thousands of
centuries illuminated her. The conviction that she had
made the right choice for them gave her the strength to
issue the command: *Go to the refuse world, Monorha.*

The war had begun.

In her mind's eye, Vivia observed the Exiles joining their
essences in what would be a futile attempt to storm the
gateway. There was no question in her mind that Phoebe
would fail.

Granted, she had yet to dispatch her armies. She had
yet to decide if such a tactic was necessary, especially if

Phoebe insisted on bringing the fight to them. The future was still forming, so much was in motion. All the choices had yet to be made. As soon as the probabilities became clearer, Vivia would be ready to fight if necessary.

In the meantime, all the Nacene that could be spared from the strings had another issue to deal with. The regional destabilization caused when the Light's pretentious contraption exploded had forced her to deploy her resources to pull the black hole singularity through the subspace layers and into Exosia, where it could be safely controlled. Had she left it Outside, the strings would have been thrown out of kilter so quickly that what was left of the membrane protecting Exosia from the Outside would have dissolved. Any chance the Nacene had of protecting the strings would be gone. Such a risk could not be tolerated.

And then there was that photonic creature. The one from the container on the Outside. He had been a nuisance to deal with but at least she had found a use for him. Vivia had many extraordinary powers but placing herself into a primitive, carbon-based body in the time stream Outside was not one of them. She could, however, manipulate circumstances so that someone else could perform this errand for her. In this way, the photonic creature had come in handy. She would risk it muddying up the time stream if it meant ridding the universe of the Light in the process.

Should the photonic creature fail, Vivia had a contingency plan playing out in the present as well. She had carefully chosen emissaries who had fanned out through the galaxy and into other dimensions searching for the Light's offspring. Thus far, the child's whereabouts had eluded her, but she would not be discouraged. She would not fail.

Either the photonic being would take care of the Light or she would destroy his offspring. Her victory could be assured without ever having to begin the fight with Phoebe.

But Phoebe did not know this. She believed that Vivia was marshaling for war, and this incorrect assumption had allowed Vivia to put off making her choice. She would wait to see what Phoebe would do next. Vivia resented having to base her decision on that inconvenient dimension: time. The Exiles' existence in a dimension bound by time required that she figure in such limitations. At least it would be over soon, the gateway sealed and Monorhan space dealt with once and for all.

Yet she had yet to understand why she felt so restless when all of the momentum appeared to be flowing in her favor. Phoebe would sow the seeds of her own destruction—Vivia was certain of it. Something she observed nagged at her. She would be bothered until she rid herself of it. So she conjured up the vision of the Exiles before her, replaying the events the way they had transpired. How typical of Phoebe to be so cruel, especially to prove that she deserved to lead them. Phoebe would be dealt with. The Exiles would know what suffering meant before her existence was complete. The universe had a way of enforcing consequences; Vivia knew this to be part of the balance.

A presence beside her disturbed her focus. She turned to see who or what would dare approach her in this moment. No Nacene would be such a fool. A lustrous, flowing being floated beside her. One of the abominations, naturally. The photonic one had found them . . . beautiful. To Vivia, beauty was harmony and this creature embodied chaos.

You are fortunate to still be living.

The abomination fluttered its wings with what Vivia

could only perceive to be pleasure. *I am. And it is a joyful existence. If only I knew that my* rih *had passed over with me. Until the end, she thought only of her tribe.* The abomination curled its wings thoughtfully. *The one you watch. She thinks only of herself. As, I suppose, is the Nacene way.*

What do you know of the Nacene way? Vivia increased the height of her form until she towered over the fluttering abomination.

Only that you tried to destroy us the moment we passed through the conduit. The abomination flew up to where it could look Vivia in the face.

The balance—the harmony—the strings!

The ugly-faced abomination swooped and dove, beating its wings with a rhythm that found sympathy deep in Vivia's sporocystian core. *We have no interest in the strings,* it thought, *save to listen to their song. We came from you, so we share your purpose. Why do you want to destroy us? Why do you want to destroy all you touch?* The abomination extended its wing, indicating the tableau playing out before Vivia. This time, the vision of Phoebe attacking her kindred Exiles seemed different to Vivia, though she could not say why. She considered her own choices, her own behavior in light of Phoebe's. Vivia had always been so different from the selfish, vindictive creatures who had remained Outside. Or so she believed.

After the abomination flew off to explore the glorious energy and thought that was Exosia, Vivia pondered and watched the flow of future streams shift and change as the future became the present, then the past. Soon she would choose and her choice would enter the stream, thus shaping the future. Either the photonic creature would stop the Light or the fabric of space-time that protected the gateway would be destroyed, by her and those who kept the strings, as a way of preserving balance.

Vivia split her focus between the preparations of the Exiles and the photonic creature. She held out hope that the course of its mission might make her choice for her. *Such an outcome would be fortunate,* she thought, though her sudden willingness to surrender her choice to another troubled her.

Ocampa. Of all the places in the universe, this was where the past needed to be fixed. The Doctor couldn't be absolutely certain of his exact geographical location or historical era, though he surmised Vivia had sent him back at least a millennium, to when the Ocampans still lived on the planet's surface. The presence of water affirmed that the Nacene hadn't annihilated all nucleogenic particles from the atmosphere, though he suspected that time was close at hand. Either the Nacene were already here working their mischief or they would arrive shortly, of that he was certain. Finding the Nacene should be as simple as looking for evidence of their presence by the damage they caused. The knowledge he'd gained from Kes would provide him with enough of a map that he should be able to navigate this time without being hopelessly lost.

Strange . . . he hadn't revisited his memories of Kes for a long time. He never thought the information would matter beyond his sentimental attachment to Kes and pure academic interest in Delta Quadrant species among scientists at that time when *Voyager* would eventually return home. Now, however, he would have to devote a good part of his time to scouring his recollections, searching for clues as to how he should proceed on this mission for Vivia.

After Kes's encounter with Suspiria's Ocampa, her latent psionic abilities began manifesting themselves with a degree of strength she hadn't experienced up to that point in her life. A side effect of stirring these latent abilities had been her ability to access memory engrams that didn't belong to her and had been dormant since her infancy.

One of the fascinating aspects of the Ocampa life cycle was how they learned. A shortened life span necessitated that knowledge be transferred efficiently; the luxury of spending years in the classroom studying and analyzing simply wasn't afforded them. The Ocampa who demonstrated an increased psionic strength by comparison with their peers, as well as the superior cerebral capacity, were designated by Ocampan leaders as sages, whose primary role was the mind-to-mind transfer of knowledge engrams.

Along with knowledge of history, mathematics, language, and culture, some memory transfer occurred, most accidentally. Rarely did memories received as part of the transfer process impact Ocampan life in a meaningful way, save the occasional flash or dream. A few Ocampans, usually those who had undergone psychological trauma or who had been subjected to extreme duress, would experience more complete manifestations of memories not belonging to them. These Ocampans were said to have experienced the "second life," because they had the perspective of living not only their own lives but also the lives of those who had gone before. Rebirth or reincarnation wasn't a part of their belief system, though those who did have the second life were revered and honored.

From the Doctor's analysis and studies, he determined that the Ocampans had little in common with the Trill except the ability to build on the knowledge acquired by previous generations in an organic, physiological fashion as opposed to the experiential methodologies employed by most humanoid species. The Ocampans, from a purely scientific standpoint, were a relatively ordinary species who displayed psionic abilities similar to those exhibited by Vulcans or Betazoids.

Not surprisingly, Kes was exceptional. Little about her complied with the "generally accepted" beliefs about her species.

As her abilities grew, so did her capacity to fully access residual memory engrams. She had flashes of experiences she'd never had—saw vistas she'd never visited. At first, the memories had frightened her, confusing her sense of what was real and what was imagined. Time and careful tutoring helped her refine her powers of discernment. She developed the capacity to not only separate inherited engrams from her own memories but to study and learn from them.

Now, sitting here amid all this destruction, the Doctor recalled the day when Kes asked if she might begin sharing her memories with him, as a way of preserving her heritage. Her relationship with Neelix had long since ended and she'd just survived a dramatic journey from her future to her past. Hoping to spare *Voyager* from future catastrophe, Kes had discussed the future she'd experienced with Janeway. She knew, as a consequence of her "spoiling" the future, that she had cast her own destiny in doubt. Having a new awareness of the totality of her life had caused her to question her assumptions, one of those assumptions being that she would someday have a child.

"All of my life, all the experiences I've had and those of my predecessors will be lost if I can't pass these engrams on to someone," she'd said. "There are no other Ocampa I can give them to and I don't want them to be lost entirely."

"Someone" turned out to be the Doctor.

And so began their long discussions in sickbay, shift after shift passing all too quickly as the Doctor listened, entranced by her recollections. Being a hologram gave him the capacity to record her every word in his database. In the months since she'd left, he'd indulged in replaying some of those conversations, as he found himself longing for more refined company than Mr. Paris. Her stories had kept him company, assuaged his loneliness, and now Kes's stories would be critical not only to his survival but to *Voyager*'s as well.

The Doctor surveyed the chamber one more time, determining that he'd learned all he could from his current surroundings. He would be able to pinpoint his identity and location and time with more specificity once they departed. The sooner he could catch up with the general, the sooner his questions would be answered. Impatience seized him. He hopped off the block where he'd been sitting, brushed off his clothes. "How soon can you help me find the general?"

Din looked up from his scavenging. "The troops are in the mountains. More than a day's travel from here. The journey is not easy."

"I will compensate you in whatever way I can, I promise. There will be a greater reward if we leave immediately." The Doctor had no idea how he would make good on his promise. He would use his genius to figure out something.

Nual stood staring at the Doctor, his face thoughtful.

"Is there something wrong?" the Doctor said.

"Most of those in my community have radiation sickness—too many sunny days spent in the fields," Nual said. "I'd forgotten what health looks like."

The Doctor felt chastised by Nual's words, and his posture softened. "I know something of various treatments for the poisoning you describe. Perhaps as payment for rescuing me I can look over your injuries and see if I can—" He paused, searching for a word other than "cure." "—help you be more comfortable."

Din's eyes widened. "Are you a healer?"

"One learns things when one is in the service," the Doctor said.

"As soon as we're done here," Nual began, "we'll place you on the road to Silver River. Once the baron's people come back and discover him dead, I suspect they're going to blame your general—"

"And they'll take their frustrations out on me," the Doctor said, not liking this conclusion.

"I'm finished here, Father," Din called out from the far side of the room.

An idea occurred to the Doctor. "I'll formulate a treatment plan for your illness as we travel so you can get started when you arrive back to your community."

Nual paused, and then said to his son, "Do you believe we can trust him?"

"We can't know," Din said. "But the general has power. If we return her man, she might help us."

At last, Nual nodded his assent.

It was the middle of the night when the Doctor left the chamber in Nual and Din's company. The baron's forces hadn't yet returned to the fortress, so they moved uninhibited, though stealthily, through the various levels of the eerily quiet structure. Only the wind whispering in the draperies and the hollow shuffle of their footsteps against the stone could be heard. With no lighting, artificial or natural, to speak of, the Doctor could discern little of the baron's home, save its opulence and ancientness, in the bruise-colored duskiness. He longed to study and absorb the details of this clearly advanced society, but he knew such wishes were folly at this critical time. Thanks to Kes's detailed recollections, he could content himself with being able to identify various artifacts, architectural styles, and cultural details.

They passed through a drooping curtain of desiccated vines into a large, circular courtyard paved in geometric patterns of light and dark stone. The Doctor noted the empty fountains, the sculptures stained with mineral residue and dried moss. Shriveled plants in crumbling soil dangled limply out of hanging pots. Further examination revealed that barren basins and gutters lined the perimeter of the courtyards and terraces. The bottoms of the gutters were marred by the occasional flea-covered skeleton—presumably some water-based creature. Once, this place must have overflowed with aquatic life. Nual walked from water outlet to water outlet until he found a weak burble in the shade of a shriveled tree. He removed an animal-skin bottle from his utility belt and fitted the mouth of the bottle over the water source and waited for it to slowly fill.

Night breezes stirred the dirt film coating every surface into a low-lying dust fog. Din wheezed asthmatically; the Doctor raised the scarf draped around his head so that it covered his nose, though it failed to filter out all the particles. Each inhalation drew in a layer of dirt into his nostrils that caked uncomfortably around the rims of his nose. *We must be close to the end of times for Old Ocampa,* the Doctor thought. *The drought is already far-reaching for dust storms to be a problem.* He guessed that along with their observable medical problems, Din, Nual, and millions of others had also developed respiratory problems ranging from simple asthma to emphysema and pneumonias.

As with most species, Ocampan physiology was ill-equipped to deal with such sudden, drastic climate changes. Less catastrophic events had forced the extinction of species across the galaxy. The Doctor suspected that if the Caretaker hadn't built the Ocampans an underground world, life on the surface would have ceased to exist, even without the decimation of nucleogenic particles. The Ocampans of this age had been born on a verdant planet, lush with diverse plant life.

Din touched his sleeve: time to leave.

After traversing several similarly situated terraces, the threesome exited the compound through unguarded gates, past vacant sentinel posts and into the yard outside. Low-lying buildings formed the yard's boundary; the grunts and growls of animals could be heard through open doors, the sour, acidy aroma of waste wafting on the wind. The realities of Ocampan life in this age held little promise for the Doctor. A twinge of longing for his twenty-fourth-century life squeezed his chest.

He followed Nual and Din to where they had left their traveling animal, a *lumwa,* in a stable. Much to his relief, several mechanized vehicles, reminiscent of Federation hovercars, were parked outside the stable. The Doctor had enough general technological knowledge to believe he could both activate and pilot the crafts. At least this place wasn't entirely barbaric.

"We'll move faster if we take one of those," the Doctor said hopefully, pointing at a vehicle that didn't have tangles of wires hanging out of the hood and bent fins scraping the ground.

Nual refused to consider the idea. "What gives us ease now will cause suffering later. The baron's men will hunt this vehicle down and extract payment for it from what little profit we make from our failing crops. Combined with the seasonal tribute we owe the baron, we will be in debt till we die."

As was usually the case, the Doctor had considered his own comfort before the possibility of retribution against Nual and his people. His own selfishness nauseated him. He had much to learn before this journey ended! The hardship endured by these people touched the Doctor. He could tell from watching Din that he was a young man accustomed to manual labor, his body hard and wiry from continual exertion. Walking beside a *lumwa* for the ten kilometers back to their community would be nothing compared to day after day working in fields that, owing to the drought, were no longer arable. The Doctor simply couldn't understand how the baron could justify living as he did when those who made it possible for him to retain his standard of living suffered. Without further complaint, he asked what he could do to help them get on the road.

He helped Nual and Din pack their scavenged treasures into several saddle packs on the weak-looking four-legged animal they informed him was named Mur. The *lumwa* had smooth, mottled brown skin, in texture more like the skin of an amphibian than like the skin of mammals humans had used in their past. His four stumpy legs featured heavily muscled thighs, tapering down to webbed feet that would be useful on boggy land—possibly even equipping the creature to swim. Having heard a bit of Ocampa's evolutionary history from Kes, the Doctor was aware that the planet had a water-based ecosystem with much of the landmass being heavily waterlogged. Bog and swamp-based crops had been their primary sustenance.

Glancing up at the clear star-flecked sky, he was reminded that part of the planet's water cycle had been the nearly continuous presence of a thick, protective cloud layer that functioned very similarly to Earth's ozone layer. The brief "light" seasons had been the Ocampan's indoor time as they avoided prolonged exposure to the sun's radiation. Now the occasional wisp veiled the stars, but nothing more substantial.

He gritted his teeth angrily, cursing the careless, irresponsible Exiles who had wrought this mess. The Nacene might be inadvertently responsible for his existence; after all, had *Voyager* not been taken from the Badlands he never would have been activated to replace the deceased medical officer. Gratitude, however, wasn't among the emotions he felt when he thought about the Nacene. He'd had enough dealings with them to find them a reckless, selfish species who failed to see beyond their own needs and desires. The Doctor glanced at the *lumwa*'s hide, discovering, unsurprisingly, that the animal too had sores indicative of radiation poisoning. It wasn't enough for the Nacene to wreak havoc on a planet; they had to make life miserable for every living thing within their touch. He patted the *lumwa*'s back comfortingly.

Mur had a long curved neck with highly flexible cervical vertebrae that allowed him to twist around so his smaller cone-shaped head could face nearly backward. The animal did just this when the Doctor touched him. Mur's deep-set eyes stared out at the Doctor from where they were mounted at the top of his skull in a position very similar to the position of a horse's eyes. The *lumwa* studied the Doctor, his head angled to one side, for a long moment. Abruptly, a forked tongue snaked out of his wide mouth and flicked rapidly beside the Doctor's ear, his breath smelling of rotting swamp reeds. The Doctor wrinkled his nose.

Noticing the Doctor's discomfort, Nual said, "He's trying to get to know you."

The Doctor accepted this, but still didn't enjoy being tongue-flicked by an overgrown lizard.

Once Mur seemed to have adjusted to the Doctor, the three men shored up their packs by tightening the girth around Mur's abdomen.

"We will go now. Follow me," Nual said, taking Mur by the reins and leading him down a cobbled road leading away from the baron's fortress.

The sooner the better, the Doctor thought, looking forward to what might happen during his inevitable confrontation with the Nacene. *They can't be allowed to get away with this,* he vowed. *I will find the Light for Vivia and she will destroy him.*

The two-day journey to Silver River was, thankfully, uneventful. Compared with some of the Doctor's sickbay shifts, it was positively boring. Kilometer after kilometer, they walked or took turns riding, following dusty trails through scabby clumps of brush and anemic trees bending over meandering, dried-out riverbeds with hardened mud crusts cracked like shattered glass. Climbing steadily upward, the trail took them through terraced foothills, toward a toothy gray rock mountain range. Granted, Nual told him they were taking an indirect route to the general's camp to avoid any confrontations.

The Doctor believed it likely wasn't the favored route for good reason. Beyond the lackluster scenery, the monotony of trail life was magnified by the swarms of newly hatched sand flies nesting in splintering reed husks. Itchy, oozy red pimple-bites blossomed on all exposed epidermal surfaces. He resisted the impulse to complain; Din and Nual were hardly more comfortable than he was. His longing for his replicator, with its extensive list of anti-itch creams and insect repellents, grew daily.

They lived off the land, scavenging berries and edible plants. Din proved to be an adept hunter who was limited only by the scarcity of game. Traveling the majority of the distance in the early-morning and twilight hours, while attempting to move swiftly and far in long stretches, proved challenging. Once the sun reached its peak at midday, they retreated into the shade until the highest radiation levels passed. Closer to the mountains, old-growth forests with their towering timbers facilitated longer travel times, but traversing around fallen branches and logs and through dense undergrowth slowed them down considerably. The Doctor took advantage of these breaks to treat the Ocampans' ailments. Working in sickbay with Kes for three years had given them plenty of time to compare notes on how medical problems were dealt with on Ocampa. Kes's detailed stories had proved valuable in helping the Doctor identify herbs, minerals, and other substances that would have therapeutic value. He'd never imagined preparing salves over an open fire, using fireweed oil and soot as binding agents. Based on how gratefully Din and Nual received his therapies, he believed his efforts weren't entirely fruitless. The Doctor knew that even minimal relief was better than none; neither did he discount the possibility of a placebo effect with these ill patients.

During their midday rest on the second day, the three of them talked at length. The Doctor used these discussions as a means to gather current information about Ocampa. He discovered Vivia had sent him to the decade before the planet's atmosphere and ecology collapsed irreparably. The Ocampans lived under three governments: the figurehead monarchy of the Prince of Runland that was actually controlled by Lord-Prefect Mestof; a republic of free states that coalesced under a parliamentary government a century previous; and the last of the feudal-style baronies, governed by Baron Var.

Several seasons ago, before the warming had started,

Mestof had begun annexing free territories that adjoined Runland, asserting that they posed a threat to Runland's stability. Treaties were negotiated but Mestof's aggression continued unchecked until those living in the Freeland formed militias and began pushing back. Quarrels in parliament prevented the formation of an official military force as well as a declaration of war. The people fought on their own without government support. Mestof made few inroads during this time until the appearance of the wizards. The mention of these supernatural entities piqued the Doctor's interest. He believed he'd finally found the Light's hiding place.

Neither Nual nor Din seemed to be particularly superstitious, but the stories they told of Mestof's "wizards" had a strange, surreal quality that had more in common with fairy legends than factual accounts. If they were to be believed, Mestof's wizards had the ability to conjure swarms of biting gnats to feed on their enemies, to call water out of a streambed to create mists to camouflage his troops, and to strike down combatants with what Din called the "waking death," a condition that sounded suspiciously like a comatose state to the Doctor.

The Doctor carefully probed his companions' recollections, seeking to align what he knew about history and the Nacene with their stories. The longer they spoke, the more convinced the Doctor became that Mestof had Nacene in his ranks. No other explanation made sense when considering the dramatic spectacle created when Mestof's troops went to battle. Based on *Voyager*'s experience with the Caretaker alone, the Doctor knew the Nacene possessed not only transformational abilities but sophisticated technology that would seem magical to a species at the Ocampa's level of development. He found nothing questionable in the stories related to him by his traveling companions. Their conversation wound down as the sun began falling toward the horizon. Nual smothered the fire and the *lumwa* was brought back from grazing. Time to depart.

A rougher climb awaited them as the elevation increased. Amid the scrawny evergreens jutting out from shallow soil, they jumped from rock to rock. Finding secure footing was tricky, and the Doctor nearly twisted his ankle on three separate occasions. The thinning atmosphere combined with his exertion caused the Doctor's breathing to become labored. Moments like these made him long for the relative ease of a holographic life. Nual indicated that once they cleared this slope, they would be on flat terrain within a kilometer of the reservoir's southern boundary. Wiping the sweat beading on his forehead, the Doctor had a hard time believing some of *Voyager's* crew would consider this kind of hike recreational. As they cleared the summit of the hill, he heard the half-awake murmuring of water burbling through the woods for the first time since the Doctor left Baron Var's land. Din led the *lumwa* to drink. Nual refilled the water skins. Cupping his hands, the Doctor dipped into the stream, splashed water on his face, and drank until he felt swollen. He hadn't realized how parched he was until his thirst was satiated.

Shadows lengthened on the forest floor as the curtain of twilight began to fall. Because the stream originated from the reservoir, they followed along the meandering bank to find their way through the forest. The Doctor was surprised that they had yet to see any sign of the army. He had just begun to wonder if perhaps the general and her troops had already left when he felt faint rumbles in the ground beneath his feet. A whiff of weapons' smoky discharge on the north wind confirmed that, indeed, military

forces occupied the region. In the distance, a rapid-fire
crack reverberated, disturbing the forest calm. He quickly
calculated an approximate distance, based on the echoes,
between them and the armies: not fifteen kilometers away.
The sober expressions on Nual and Din's faces confirmed
the Doctor's guess that a battle lay before them. Silent,
they moved through the tree groves, the Doctor following
Nual's deft footing as he picked through the brush. The
closer they came to the reservoir, the clearer the sounds
of weapons fire became. The muffled pop-pop-pop of
the artillery followed by a faint boom continued even as
the sun dropped below the rugged, sawlike silhouette
of the silver peaks and the wan crescent of the new moon
rose drowsily, casting only a sliver of light.

Nual reached into one of the saddlebags and tossed a
long-sleeved, lace-up tunic to the Doctor. "Put it on over
your armor," he said. He then ordered Din to tie up the
lumwa and remain hidden in the trees while he and the
Doctor scouted out their surroundings.

Din protested, pointing out that his mother needed a
stable provider and he, the younger one, had greater
strength than his father. Nual would have none of Din's
rationale and presented just as many reasons why it was
better to risk his own life.

As the argument continued, the Doctor slipped the
garment over his head, his nose wrinkling at the musky
tang that saturated the fabric; he didn't complain. They
had no idea, unfortunately, which side controlled the region they hiked through. Should Mestof's followers
stumble upon anyone wearing the general's crest, they
would attack first and ask questions later. As much as the
Doctor longed to stay far behind the lines with Din, he
knew the answers would be found ahead of him. He laced
up the tunic and then checked his person to make sure

that all other evidence connecting him to the general had been disguised. Satisfied with his appearance, he glanced over at the father and son to see when they'd be on their way.

Throwing up his hands, Nual started up the bank, muttering unintelligibly as he walked, seemingly unconcerned that the Doctor wasn't behind him.

Apparently the discussion had ended. The Doctor sent a small hand wave in Din's direction and hurriedly followed after Nual, wondering if he would ever see the younger Ocampan again.

The thrilling fusion of fear and anticipation quickened his pulse; he was barely able to maintain smooth, deliberate movements; his limbs quivered from the adrenaline surge stirring his veins. Stealthily, they crept through the brush. A misstep onto a branch and the resulting snap sent a rush of birds flying from their nests. Scrunching up his shoulders and closing his eyes, the Doctor stood stock-still, his heart hammering, waiting for a legion of Mestof's goons to come rushing through the woods like the Gauls on the Romans. Save a glare from Nual, it appeared that they remained undetected.

When Din was about fifty meters behind them, the Doctor and Nual emerged at the boundary of the forest onto a scrub-covered bluff overlooking the reservoir. In the gathering darkness, the smoke rising across the way formed a gauzy, cobweblike curtain that ascended from the land to the sky. Nual dropped onto his belly and crawled close to the bluff's edge. He removed a distance lens from his utility belt and held it up to his eyes, thoroughly scanning the opposite shoreline.

"There," he said finally, pointing to the northwest corner of the reservoir where sandy beaches yielded to a relatively flat, tree-covered plain at the feet of the mountains.

"I see movement in the trees." He handed the lenses to the Doctor.

The Doctor squinted through the device. At first, he saw only dense evergreen brush interspersed with the occasional spindly birch poking through the crowded canopy. His eyes adjusted and he studied the shoreline. Neat rows of canvas tents, doors and walls flapping with the winds blowing off the water, lined up against the tree trunks. Solid patches of dark shifted at irregular intervals. The longer the Doctor studied the shadows, the more readily he was able to distinguish individual silhouettes. Soldiers! "I see them," he exclaimed excitedly. "Can you tell what side they're on?" He passed the lenses back, indicating that Nual should look though them again.

Taking the lenses, Nual studied him, his eyebrows knit with puzzlement. The Doctor remembered that *he* was supposed to be—*was*—one of the general's fighters. If anyone could distinguish one side from the other, it ought to be him. He shrugged, embarrassed, trying to cover. "Head injury, remember?"

"Can't be sure 'cause of the poor lighting, but I believe it's the general's encampment."

"How will we get over there?"

"*We?*" Nual said, questioning. "There's a battle going on over there. Seems I kept my promise and brought you up here. You should be able to follow the shoreline and link up with them." He continued to scan the surroundings with the distance lenses. "Besides, there doesn't appear to be any fighting between here and there. You should be able to travel with little problem."

The Doctor's innards twisted nervously. He was a doctor, not a mountain man. "There'll be extra in it for you if you'll take me to the camp."

"I don't know . . . your treatments are all I require in

payment," Nual said, his voice trailing off. "Wait. Down there. By those rocks—"

The Doctor followed where he pointed toward a finger of smooth metamorphic stones—perhaps granite—jutting out from the land into the water. The outcropping, obviously built by the Ocampa, turned a natural cove into a small marina and simultaneously served as a dock. What had caught Nual's attention was a two- or three-person watercraft moored near a log jutting out of the water.

"If you took that across the water, you'd save time," Nual said. "Follow the shoreline where the shadows can hide you and you could make the northeast side of the reservoir within a few hours."

The Doctor took a deep breath. Of all the options available to him, this one took the right balance between risk and playing it safe. After all, he didn't have the luxury of an impervious holographic body to protect his programming. He assumed that he could actually *die* in this body. Theoretically, Vivia could rescue him—if she wanted to. The Doctor wasn't interested in taking the particular risk. What use would he be to *Voyager*—or the Nacene, for that matter—if he managed to get himself killed before the mission was done. "Tell you what. If you'll guide me down to where the boat is, I'll be fine."

"Fair enough," Nual said, obviously pleased. "But we should first scout out the adjacent areas to make sure that whoever left that boat isn't around any longer. I'd hate to be surprised down where we wouldn't have any escape."

"Agreed. I doubt any surprises awaiting us would be pleasant ones." Artillery rounds whistled through the air at various shrill pitches until they detonated with syncopated crackles. Seconds later, the kettledrum-like BOOM-BOOM-BOOM shook the sky. *And I'm willingly heading in that direction,* the Doctor thought, the now famil-

iar tension of fear settling on him. He waited impatiently
for Nual to complete his reconnaissance, feeling far too
exposed up on the ridge.

Once Nual was satisfied that they wouldn't encounter
any foot patrols on their trek down, they walked along the
bluff until the terrain began a gradual descent back into
the forest. No words passed between them; the only
sound the Doctor could hear besides the steady, nearly
soundless padding of their soft-soled boots on the soil was
the thudding of his heart, a wholly disquieting sensation
that only served to remind him of his own nervousness.
The Doctor followed behind Nual, his ears pricked, his
eyes flickering over his surroundings. It would be nearly
impossible to see anyone lurking in these deep shadows
until an assailant was upon him. That he too could hide in
the shadows cast by densely foliated overhanging limbs
should have offered him reassurance, but instead the fore-
boding sense of the unknown haunted him; if his enemy
was out there, would that they would reveal themselves
and be done with it. The waiting made him crazy! *Being in
a flesh-and-bone body has caused me to take leave of my senses.*
Understanding—and empathy—for his patients' irra-
tionality filled him.

For the entire length of the bluff and passing about
twenty meters into the forest, neither of them saw any
sign of any living creature, animal or Ocampan. Not even
a skittering rodent or nocturnal avian. *Too still,* suspected
the Doctor, but he was the amateur on this journey and
wouldn't think of second-guessing Nual. His hair prickled on his neck when he felt someone watching him.
Turning about quickly, he saw a pair of glow-in-the dark
yellow eyes the size of sunny-side-up eggs peering
serenely at him out of an oval face, at the base of an im-
pressive rack of antlers. The Doctor and the animal had a

brief staring contest, the Doctor swallowing hard, wondering what the thing might be and whether it was carnivorous. The creature yowled—sounding bored, of all things—-and moseyed off, fallen leaves rattling with each leisurely step of its eight large, hairy legs. *At least it wasn't hungry,* thought the Doctor. The duration of the hike passed without any further encounters.

When they reached the rock outcropping, Nual told the Doctor to remain hidden in the woods until he checked out the boat and gave the all-clear signal. The Doctor watched, agog, as Nual stripped off his tools and gear pack, then dove silently into the water. No sign of him appeared until the Doctor saw his head bob to the surface beside the small rowboat. Nual rocked the craft back and forth and slapped the planks. Apparently satisfied, he pulled himself up on the side so he could examine the boat's interior. In an instant, he vanished again.

Nual broke the water's surface, startling the Doctor. "She's seaworthy. Can't tell if the engine's been used recently, but I wouldn't turn it on anyway—don't want to draw needless attention to yourself." Pressing his palms onto the ground, he locked elbows, shifted his weight onto his arms, and swung himself up onto the beach.

While Nual wrung the water from his clothing, the Doctor glanced across the water, determining that any journey would take him several hours. As much as he loathed the idea of traveling alone, he rejected any notion that Nual would place his life in danger any longer. "I'll start off immediately—"

A high-pitched zing startled him; Nual tipped over sideways, blood pouring out of his mouth, and toppled into the muddy shore.

Reflexively, the Doctor grabbed Nual by the arms and dragged him into the forest. He conducted a cursory triage—pulse, respirations, bleeding—ducking and shifting as a shower of zings shrieked past his ears. Little sparks scattered whenever the projectiles hit. Whoever had targeted them had far too good an aim for the Doctor to feel safe. He pulled Nual farther into the woods, careful to avoid further damage to his neck and spine.

The best he could tell, a projectile had entered the back of Nual's head, passed through his brain and a primary circulatory junction located between the throat and brain and lodged there, thus the hemorrhaging from the mouth. Without any medical accoutrements, the Doctor had no chance of saving him. There was a slim possibility that he might be able to tamp off the bleeding long enough to let Din see his father before his death. The Doctor had that hope in mind when he squeezed backside first into a rotted-out hollow in the trunk of a gargantuan pine, clutching Nual in front of him like a shield. He shoved his fingers into Nual's mouth, feeling his way past the man's teeth back into his throat, where he found the spurting vessels. He pressed hard against the wound and the bleeding momentarily stopped. Waiting for the attack to subside would be torturous—he didn't know how he could do it, sitting there, helplessly anticipating his own death as well as that of his patient. Several breaths later, the assault ceased.

The Doctor paused, listening for any sign of his attacker; initially, he heard nothing save gurgling in Nual's throat. The death rattle, as it was commonly known. The wounded man's respirations became more shallow and irregular—then a gasp. The Doctor remained still, feeling Nual's life drain away within the circle of his arms; he focused on controlling the anxiety surging through him but found it increasingly difficult to think clearly. To even consider the possibility appalled him, but if Nual couldn't die more quietly, he might have to hasten the process. He cursed his circumstances. Unshed tears pooled in his eyes—from anger, from fear, from the crippling helplessness that kept him from treating Nual.

A single crackle in the underbrush caused him to sit up sharply, all his senses on alert.

Whether Din approached or his assailant, he couldn't guess. The Doctor would be killed if he was caught here. If he perished, many more—including *Voyager*—would follow. He made the painful choice, removing his thumb from the back of Nual's throat. The geyser of blood resumed. Gingerly, he resituated himself so that Nual was hidden inside the trunk. He made a quick check to see if Nual carried any weapons he wasn't aware of: the Ocampan had been unarmed, so he would be unarmed.

The Doctor moved quickly from shadow to shadow, looking for places to hide. He almost tripped over a fallen branch that, if wielded with force, might be an effective weapon. Yanking it out of his way, he tucked it up beneath his arm and continued his escape. Behind him, the whoosh-whoosh of shaking brush picked up tempo. No sign of civilization or assistance caught the Doctor's attention. Theoretically, he could run along the reservoir's eastern boundary for several kilometers before he'd connect with the general's troops, assuming that he survived the journey without being shot or his legs giving out beneath him. He didn't believe he had a choice—

His foot came down with a splash, his boot sinking up to his ankle in slimy murk before he had the sense to take two large steps backward into the forest. A deep whiff of brackish air and he knew he'd reached a swampy area. Reeds and clumps of grass extended as far as he could see. He headed away from the shoreline, but discovered the ground to be increasingly boggy with each subsequent step. The only thing he had in his favor was the inability of his assailant to track him in the dark: it wasn't like his footsteps were visible. With neither the time nor the familiarity with the landscape to traverse the area with any speed, his assailant had run him into a dead end.

Unless . . .

The Doctor turned abruptly toward the reservoir, taking large steps until he reached the water. He inhaled deeply, sat down, and pushed himself into the water as soundlessly as he could. Repressing the urge to stop moving as the cold water soaked his clothing, he persisted until he was in the reservoir up to his neck. The deep water made it easy to move about without splashing. Meter by meter, he stroked over toward the reeds. The crashing from the forest continued unabated. Any minute now, his pursuer would be upon him. He gently parted the reeds and swam, ever so carefully, until he was surrounded on all sides. Lowering his foot, he felt around the bottom until he found a rock to shift his weight onto. He then lowered the other foot so he could stand and watch without having to tread water.

While he was certain that he'd temporarily eluded certain death, he wasn't sure how long he would remain undetected. He doubted he had the capacity to remain in the chilly water indefinitely—he had maybe six hours, seven at the longest—before hypothermia set in. Making his captor give up searching for him was the challenge. The Doctor had limited resources to create a diversion or to hide himself. A thought occurred. He saw a reed that had recently become uprooted floating in the water nearby. Under the water, he broke off the bottom and the top. A quick glance revealed that, as he hoped, it was hollow. Crouching down so he was submerged under the water, save his chin and above, he placed the base of the reed to his lips and tilted his head backward. The reed stood erect above the water while his head remained under the water. He sucked in deep breaths through the reed stem, in and out, in and out, trying to ignore the mud and other detritus coming into his mouth. *Perhaps he's given up,* the Doctor thought hopefully.

The loud splash from several meters away told him differently. A silhouette darkened the water as a few sloshing steps came closer.

The Doctor stood still as stone. He allowed his rib cage to expand mere centimeters with each inhalation for fear of disturbing the water. *One and two and three air in; one, two three, air out . . .* he counted. Aching fingers clutched the reed, the cold water stiffening the muscles; his splinter-filled lip swelled. Each breath dried inside of his mouth. Salivary glands squirted into his throat but he couldn't swish the liquid around for fear of disturbing the reed. A current change in the water nearby alerted him. Only his desperation to remain alive gave him the strength to endure.

The slenderest beams of moonlight illuminated the masculine features of the person stalking him. The Doctor saw the outline of the four-quadrant crest on the shield: a notched sword, a bleeding sun, an openmouthed feline with vicious canine teeth, and a soldier figure, one foot placed on the back of a victim. The pursuer could only be one of Mestof's men—it was the only conclusion that made sense. He twisted to the side, the relief of his face etched against the paler black-blue of the sky above the water. With a swish, he turned away and vanished from view.

The splashing sounds became fainter as the assailant went away from his location. *He must have decided to give up.* The Doctor permitted himself a luxurious swallow before resuming his disciplined routine. He counted, allowing several minutes to elapse before determining that he was in the clear. Exercising the same caution he had thus far, he swam out into open water and then to the shore. Scooting backward, he leaned against a tree trunk, coughing until the dirt cleared out of his throat. He bent over to remove his boots, intent on emptying the water out of them.

Mestof's assassin had a knife blade at his throat. "Tell me where the rest of the witch's troops are and I'll allow you a few more minutes of life."

Chapter 5

Q had explained that Q University wasn't so much a university in the way that Harry understood the term (after all, the Q were omnipotent). Rather, it was an organization that provided opportunities for the Q to exercise and refine their "Q-ness" under the auspices of the most esteemed Q in the Continuum, "including myself," he'd added. The Q who matriculated at Q U acquired enhanced status within the Continuum. Q had informed Tom and Harry that anyone who had any desire for power and glory with the Continuum had to endure examination at Q U, even though it meant surviving their studies with curtailed Q powers. "Part of the challenge," Q had explained. After such a description, Harry hadn't been sure what to expect from an institution of higher learning geared toward all-powerful beings. His imagination ran wild with the possibilities.

The reality was, well, pedestrian.

But it was, right up to the flying buttresses on the library, exactly what Harry would want in a university.

Q University reminded Harry Kim a good deal of the crumbling, ivy-covered institutions he'd grown up dreaming of attending. Oxford. Princeton. Deneva. The

Institute at Ursa Prime. Cleveland University. Students of all heights, widths, skin tones (and a few without skin), dressed in their black robes, flooded the walkways, eagerly engaged in deep philosophical conversations as they moved across the quad between classes. The clock-tower bell tolled sonorously, marking the hour's arrival. The three of them passed by oaks with trunks the size of *Voyager's* nacelles, beneath graceful leafy branches curving over the cobblestone paths and through archways. Even the ugly gargoyles—staring down from their perches atop detached Ionic columns—made Harry smile.

Then he reminded himself what Q had said about reality being relative to personal perception, and he decided that his brain was translating Q University into his academic dream world. If he started looking in the professors' directory, he guessed he'd probably find Aristotle, Euclid, Michelangelo, da Vinci, Newton, Mozart, and Cochrane too—all teachers he'd jump at the chance to study with. Too bad it wasn't real. At least, not real the way Harry wanted real. It was like finding out that the dessert you'd been craving for days was, in actuality, a ration bar dressed up to look like dessert. He sighed and continued trudging dutifully after Tom and Q.

All three of them had slipped black student robes over their blazers and khakis, so no one gave them a second look as they raced past clusters of students arguing, eating, and discussing. *What* does *a pandimensional student body look like,* he thought, trying not to be too obvious about his curiosity. His eyes widened as he thought he saw . . . *Whoa. Is that anatomically possible?* Finding it difficult not to stare, his steps stuttered to a halt.

Q hooked an arm around Harry's neck and dragged him, stumbling, forward. "Eyes on the prize, my boy, eyes on the prize."

Gagging, Harry extracted his throat from the crook of Q's elbow and took a place walking on Q's left. Tom was on the right.

"We'll start in his suite. The Keeper of the Light might have left behind some indication of where he's gone to," Q said, making an abrupt turn down a pathway that veered out of the main areas and branched off in the direction of several shabby two-story buildings constructed of decomposing rust-colored brick. As they approached the central building, Harry noticed a couch with stained flowered upholstery sitting on the lawn, springs and stuffing popping out of a cushion. An upward glance revealed red lace lingerie hanging from a tree branch. Harry sniffed: a distinct fermented aroma drifted from an open second-floor window. He exchanged puzzled looks with Tom, who shrugged. Harry was trying to decide whether it was related to booze or bodily eliminations when an explosive POP rattled the glass, followed by a shower of shards and drifting smoke. Arms over his head protectively, Harry glanced up from his crouch at Tom, who appeared to have a disturbing degree of ease amid the refuse of debauchery.

A frieze embossed with Q HALL was mounted above the porch. Harry kicked aside several empty bottles and wrappers as he climbed up the stairs. On the porch swing, a figure buried beneath a moth-eaten blanket stirred, then resumed snoring.

Q guided them through a nondescript lobby, up a flight of rickety stairs, and down a hallway past several doors, one of which was barely hanging on to its hinges. When they reached the door at the end of the hallway, Q didn't bother to knock. He threw open the door and stormed into the suite, his robes fluttering out behind him. "Where is he?" he shouted.

Harry's first thought upon entering the Keeper of the

Light's suite was that he wished he were eligible to attend a pan-dimensional university, because these quarters made his Academy dorm look like the backwaters of Farius Prime. Fur-covered chaises sat atop aquarium foundations. Music floated in via unseen speakers, and the sound quality made his audiophile's heart weep for joy. Sculptures carved from iridescent stone—might it be extinct pink marble from Teanak III?—were set amid striped lilies, and orchids cascaded out of floor-to-ceiling cylindrical planters. To Harry, whose soul was drawn to all things beautiful and artful, this place had been decorated with an eye to quality, not opulence; with a sense of carefully composed line and color as opposed to finery for the sake of showing off.

Tom appeared to be absorbed in examining a floor-to-ceiling viewscreen displaying a menu of entertainment choices ranging from a roleplay channel to an intergalactic gaming net. With a room like this, why bother going to class?

After a moment, Harry realized that a slight figure clad in black student's robes stood beside a desk, bent over a computer station, fingers tapping furiously. Apparent anachronisms in worlds as complex as the Continuum barely registered now, but Harry was wondering what a computer could possibly offer a Q.

Q bellowed a second time, prompting the student to turn a placid gaze on the trio. "Do you ever knock, Q?" Her hood fell away, revealing a pair of wide violet eyes framed by short straw-colored hair, punctuated by a lock of bright blue that draped down the middle of her nose. Full, rose-colored lips turned up in what could only be described as a *sarcastic* half-smile.

Involuntarily, Harry grinned. Like an idiot, he recognized, but a grin nonetheless. Okay, she probably wasn't real the way he wanted to experience real, but this was an illusion he could adjust to.

Noting Harry's appreciation, the blonde sent him a sideways glance and then surveyed him from head to toe with a frank gaze that made Harry wonder if she could see through him.

He smiled winningly, further inviting her attentions.

She dismissed him with a sniff.

Shaking his head in an I-told-you-so way, Tom winced.

The blonde placed her fist on a cocked hip. "The Keeper's not here. I informed you of that fact when you contacted me yesterday."

"It wouldn't be the first time you've hidden him from the Continuum," Q said, systematically lifting the chaise's fur-covered cushions and checking beneath.

"Like he'd hide in there after you found him last time," she said derisively. "He's too clever to repeat himself."

Harry moved past wondering how the Keeper of the Light would hide himself in a couch cushion and returned to appreciating to the petite blonde. Once you got past the don't-touch-me vibe, she had a wide-eyed wholesome look to her that reminded Harry of spring-break trips to the Mars caverns with his parrises squares team and barbecues on his parents' backyard deck with the neighbors' children. "You're Q too?" Harry asked the female Q, making sure that he closed his mouth after he spoke. Gaping—and subsequently drooling—would be a turnoff.

"No. I'm q," she said, emitting a burdened sigh. "Can't you hear the lowercase?" She shrugged her robe off her shoulders, tossed it on the chaise, and then smoothed and straightened her bright pink tank top.

Harry wasn't close enough to discern the tattooed pattern that covered most of her left shoulder and upper arm, but it had a decidedly geometric flavor. He could picture himself lounging beside her, tracing those lines as far as they might go, over her shoulder, down her back . . .

Tom cleared his throat.

Harry chose to ignore him. Tom wasn't going to ruin his daydream. He knew how to look and not touch.

"Look wherever you want, Q. You aren't going to find him here. I haven't seen him for a few days now." When q flopped stomach-first onto the couch, her black skirt rode up around her thighs, revealing a pair of shapely, tanned legs. Manicured fingernails, painted chartreuse, combed through her hair, ruffling the short locks on the back of her neck.

The blood rushed from Harry's head. He placed a hand on an end table to stop him from toppling over.

Cupping a hand over his mouth, Tom leaned down and whispered, sotto voce, "Don't do it, Harry."

"What?" Harry said, eyes never leaving q. *She really is something.* Had that perky cute beach-girl exterior with a definite undercurrent of devil-may-care Q-ness that intrigued the hell out of him.

"Fall for a Q. Your track record with alien women isn't the greatest."

"I hardly think that's fair," Harry said. "Besides, who says I'm falling for her?" He resented Tom's assumption that he was a naïve schoolboy who needed protection.

"The giddy expression on your face." Tom chuckled softly. "Never gamble, Harry, unless you're prepared to lose."

As Q continued poking about, generally wreaking havoc, q watched, her face etched with annoyance. "He's not stupid. The Nacene sent their representatives poking around the Continuum boundaries a week ago and he wasn't about to risk letting his blobby half-relatives sniff him out."

"Which blobs were they? Do you recall?" Q asked.

"One of them took a form like *them*—humanoid," she said, nodding in Harry's general direction. q rolled onto her back with a sigh, reaching her arms above her head in a decidedly feline stretch. "Why do you keep bringing these carbon-based bipedals around, Q? I mean, aren't their kind supposed to stay in the suburbs? They can't have had their shots."

"Living dangerously can be exhilarating, my dear," Q said. "Haven't you learned yet what a fun college town the Milky Way can be? You need to get out more often." He threw open a closet, revealing stacks of magazines, sports accountrements, assorted gadgets and gizmos that Harry could tell must be light-years ahead of Federation technology but of course he wouldn't have the opportunity to examine. Q spun around and stood behind the chaise. "All right. He's not here."

Tilting her head, she glanced up at Q. "What gave it away?"

"Where is he?"

q hesitated.

"Tell me or I'll report your extracurricular neuro-chemistry projects to the Student Oversight Board."

She glowered at Q. "Talk to the Oversight Board and I'll tell the Continuum you lost the Keeper of the Light!"

"Where is he?" Q shouted

As the contentious seesaw of rhetoric continued, Harry decided to wander around. He wouldn't touch anything that appeared to be beyond him; Q's newt threat still rang in his ears. If q wouldn't have anything to do with him, it couldn't hurt to see what kind of delights existed in the pandimensional world. Besides, Tom always told him that the best way to ingratiate himself with a woman was to show an interest in her life. Having no frame of reference for what a female Q's life consisted of, Harry thought it best to nose around to see what kind of conversational topics he could dig up. He half paid attention to the ongoing discussion between Q and q.

Still sprawled out on the chaise, q shifted so she lay on her side, her elbow bent, head resting on the palm of her hand. "He accumulated some fines he couldn't pay. So he took off."

Harry found this latest position to be very alluring.

"Fines?" Q raised an eyebrow.

She shrugged. "One too many thermonuclear whoopee cushions in the professors' lounge . . ."

"An oldie but a goodie," Q said.

"He didn't have the credits to bribe the Oversight Board. A few games of Trinity gone bad . . ."

"Wait a second," Tom said. "The Q use credits? What for?"

"This isn't the time for a lesson in Continuum economics, Mr. Paris," Q said in exasperation. "Just remember what I said about processing what you see and hear in ways your limited brain can handle, and you'll find the need to ask fewer questions."

Harry paused his prowling in front of the desk that held the computer station q had been working on when they first arrived in the suite. A mangy, one-eyed tabby cat perched atop the terminal, the name FELIX engraved on his collar. Harry extended a hand to pet the cat between his ears. Hissing and spitting, Felix batted at Harry's hand with his paw, his sharp claw drawing blood, and then jumped off the terminal, vanishing beneath the couch.

"Good riddance," Harry muttered.

Beside the computer, a clear cube held a 3-D image of q standing arm-in-arm with several aliens, only one of whom Harry could properly identify as humanoid. The presence of Felix on the humanoid's shoulder, the cat's tail coiled around his neck, was a pretty good indicator of the humanoid's identity. Hadn't Q said that the Light had created a child with a Milky Way humanoid? The humanoid must be the Keeper of the Light. He certainly was a handsome fellow by human standards, bald, with a brown goatee. Upon closer scrutiny, Harry discovered that the Keeper had a hint of Nacene about him—like the glowing tentacles emerging from his back. He watched fascinated as the image shifted from moment to moment. Sometimes the tentacles appeared behind the Keeper, sometimes they didn't; sometimes q laughed, other times she inflicted a good-natured punch on her suite-mate. Apparently, an entire moment in time had been captured and stored in the cube.

The Q University logo rotating on the viewscreen's background drew his attention away. A series of stacked bars with various labels ranging from METADIMENSIONAL COMMUNICATIONS SYSTEM to PERSONAL covered the left-hand side of the screen. He had questions about q; the computer offered answers. Harry contemplated his options and then decided, *What could it hurt?* Not daring to use voice commands, he touched the bar that said PERSONAL. The logo dissolved and was replaced by two tiles, one said Q the other said KOL (Harry assumed that Kol was the acronym for Keeper of the Light). He glanced away from the viewscreen at the pair of Qs whose heated arguments over Kol's whereabouts continued unabated. A thought occurred. While he would have a hard time explaining why he felt it was acceptable to invade q's privacy, he knew he could rationalize invading Kol's. He might score points with Q *and* impress q. He touched the screen to bring up Kol's personal account.

Admittedly, most of the content scrolling past appeared to be in a mathematical language that, given a lifetime, Harry probably couldn't crack, but he noticed a few icons that might be useful, including "accounts" and "correspondence." He touched the latter. For a long moment, he perused the contents, noting the thumbnail-sized pictures of who had recently contacted Kol. One guy—Fest—had sent the last message Kol had watched.

"Who's Fest?" Harry looked up from the viewscreen at Q, who was pacing the length of the room while arguing with q.

Q paused, his eyes narrowed. "What are you doing, Mr. Kim?"

"Searching for Kol," Harry said. "Fest was the last person who contacted Kol before he disappeared."

"Weren't you paying attention during the whole 'you break, you buy' demonstration? I told you: Do. Not. Touch. Anything." Q strode over to the viewscreen and smacked Harry's hand before shoving him aside and examining Kol's correspondence file. He ordered the computer to replay the last message Kol had viewed. A holographic projection of a creature with an eel head and a weasel-like body appeared and began describing, in physiologically explicit terms, what Kol's fate would be if a certain debt wasn't repaid.

Imagining a fate similar to the one promised Kol by the eel, Harry linked his hands protectively over his midsection. Yikes.

"Explain, q," Q said.

The contents of her empty lap suddenly became fascinating; q dropped her eyes, fiddling with her beaded bracelet with her hand from the opposite arm. "Fest is a kind of account specialist. Deals in credits, transactions of goods and services."

"He's a two-bit hood," Q said, hands on hips. "That stupid boy has a loan shark after him."

Tom and Harry exchanged looks. Harry, for one, couldn't imagine what kind of horrors a Q-level loan shark might inflict.

"I told you he didn't have the credits to bribe the Oversight Board, I just didn't tell you why," q said.

"So what's his poison?" Q asked.

"Kol has a fondness for games of chance."

Q shook his head. "If he needed credits, why didn't he come to me? Uncle Q is nothing if not generous."

"Oh please, Q, your interest rate is worst than Fest's."

Harry raised a hand, trying to get Q's attention. "Pardon my interruption, but could we safely assume that if Kol needs to pay a debt, he's probably somewhere trying to get what he needs to repay Fest?"

"Or," Tom said, "at the very least hiding from Fest."

Q beamed at them. "I told you humans could be useful," he said to q.

Standing up straighter, Harry grinned and squared his shoulders. "Anything else I can help with?" he asked, giving q a meaningful look. *She had to be impressed.*

She returned Harry's eager overture with a withering gaze before yawning indifferently. "Is he housebroken?" she asked Q.

"Mostly harmless. You can keep him for a pet when this is over, if you'd like," Q said.

Rising from the chaise, she strolled over to where Harry stood and, crossing her arms, gave Harry a thorough once-over. She smoothed his hair, traced the outline of his cheek until her finger landed on his lips, then sent Q a look that indicated she'd consider his offer.

Harry wasn't sure how he felt about the possibility of being kept by a q. On one hand, she was hot. On the other hand . . . Harry decided there wasn't another hand: q was hot. She sent his blood rushing to all the right extremities.

"Where would Kol go to make some fast credits?" Tom said.

q paused for a long moment, her forehead wrinkled in concentration. "I'd heard he was playing particle tag in the wormholes. Someone in my matter-creation lab hangs out there on the weekends. Said he was node racing on the side. A good racer can pick up two or three thousand credits a night if the action is good."

At the mention of racing, a decidedly intrigued expression appeared on Tom Paris's face. It was Harry's turn to frown and shake his head. "Don't even think it, Tom."

Tom scowled. "Come on, Harry. I don't even know what 'node racing' is. Don't begrudge me a moment of professional curiosity."

"Kol was always a thrill junkie. Do you still have your racing gear or do you need me to procure some?" Q said, throwing open the closet doors. He began rummaging through the shelves, tossing aside gadgets he didn't find useful.

"No way. I'm not going with you," q protested. "I'm not. I have exams. That whole magnetic core stabilization exercise is a bastard."

"Then the boys can go," Q said, smiling far too warmly for Tom's comfort. *"Won't* you, boys?"

"But we want to go back to *Voy*—!" Tom began.

"After you find the Keeper," Q said. And before either Harry or Tom could protest further, he'd snapped his fingers.

~

Chakotay sat in the captain's chair on the bridge, watching the alpha shift bridge crew efficiently performing their jobs. *Voyager* had about another three hours, by Ayala's estimation, until they reached the point where they'd launch the probe into the rift. Thus far, their passage had been uneventful. All that they had learned about navigating this strange region had been utilized.

From what Chakotay could observe, everyone across the ship, by unspoken agreement, kept their heads down and focused on doing what was necessary to facilitate finding the Doctor, thus hastening their ability to hightail it out of this "hellhole," as B'Elanna had described it. Chakotay wasn't one to believe in jinxes or curses, but he wouldn't believe this waking nightmare was over until *Voyager* was humming along at warp five at least a parsec away with Tom at the helm and Harry absorbed in, but thrilled beyond reason by, an utterly boring, predictable interstellar phenomenon. The Doctor would be back in sickbay working on restoring Kathryn to health. The crew could go back to complaining about Neelix's food and trading replicator rations for holodeck time.

He knew the odds of finding the Doctor were slim to none. But he also knew that he would never have a sound night's sleep if he didn't at least attempt to find the one entity he knew that might have the capacity to save the captain. The captain aside, he owed it to the crew. Imagining the aftermath of their first firefight without the Doctor in sickbay was sobering. He was prepared to take risks now if it meant he could move forward with no regrets.

What happened after they searched for the Doctor seemed straightforward enough: Kathryn's last order to him was to get out of Monorhan space, resume their journey to the Alpha Quadrant and not look back. Following that order meant they would accept Seven's findings that

Tom and Harry's shuttle was nowhere to be found. Though he had continuously kept abreast of Seven and B'Elanna's data analysis for the last day, Chakotay wasn't comfortable with accepting their bleak conclusions yet. Facts were facts, though. He wouldn't have a lot of maneuvering room when he gave the crew their orders several hours from now. Thankfully, he didn't have to make any immediate decisions. *Voyager* could continue swimming upstream through Monorhan space, and her crew could continue pretending that everything would be fine on the other side of this day. A little self-deception could go a long way in helping them remain sane in the short term.

Their situation reminded him of a story from his childhood about a clever fox who played dead so that a warrior would place him inside a bag full of fish he had caught to impress a prospective bride. The warrior believed that bringing a fox to his bride-to-be would prove his great hunting skills and impress her into marrying him. While the warrior was busy congratulating himself on his successes, the fox gnawed a hole in the sack, pushed out the fish and escaped after them. The fox had dinner; the warrior was let with an empty sack, humiliated in front of his bride. Chakotay wanted to believe he was the fox, but he couldn't help but think he'd soon discover he was the warrior.

A shrill beeping noise from Ayala's companel disrupted his thoughts. He spun to the side. "Report," he said.

"Sensors have picked up three vessels off to the starboard side. All Monorhan."

Chakotay's stomach convulsed. *We didn't need this.* "Life signs?"

"Five thousand, sir. But no indication that any technology beyond the barest life-support is functioning," he said. "They appear to be stranded."

A simple beeping indicator had thrown them back seven days to the moment when Harry's innocent observation of an anomalous star system had started a cascade of events none of them could have foreseen. Chakotay keenly felt the expectations of the bridge crew weighing on him. *Five thousand Monorhans. Nothing but life-support. They're waiting out here until they die.* He couldn't imagine a more horrible fate.

"Set a course for the Monorhan ships," he said, rising from the chair and heading for the turbolift. "I'll be in main engineering organizing an away team." He didn't allow himself time to determine whether or not the bridge officers agreed with his decision. As long as Kathryn Janeway drew breath, he believed he had an obligation to follow the standard she had set. More importantly, he would not dishonor the trust she had placed in him by ignoring the needs of five thousand innocent people simply because *Voyager* was too tired or too hassled to care.

B'Elanna hunched over the workbench, examining the prototype multispatial probe's rewired circuitry with satisfaction. *You still have the magic touch, Torres,* she thought. When Seven had first approached her with the project, B'Elanna had thought searching for the Doctor had more in common with trying to capture a specific *gl'ebagh* worm in an entire mountain forest full of nests than with a rescue mission. Seven's theories were solid, though, so B'Elanna was quickly able to adapt their technology to the necessary specifications. Next up she was going to try an experiment with a wide-spectrum light, a character from a holodeck program, and the Doctor's mobile emitter. If the probe could definitively identify a specific photonic signature amid a flood of photons, *Voyager* might be able to determine if the Doctor was somewhere inside the rift. She'd retrofitted the probe to carry a smaller, self-powered module containing the equivalent of sickbay's holobuffers. *If* they could find the Doctor and *if* they could transfer him to the probe, the smaller secondary device could be launched out of the rift should the primary device be damaged or rendered otherwise unable to exit the rift.

All of B'Elanna's plans assumed that the Doctor's consciousness was active and that his program was still intact. If he was trapped—or, heaven forbid, decompiled—she didn't know how they would extract him.

From B'Elanna's perspective, *Voyager*'s crew was working as hard as they ever had to achieve objectives that they had little chance of accomplishing. They were basing their hopes on a lot of unknowns and "what if" scenarios that B'Elanna wasn't thrilled with. Then again, she had seen enough go wrong in her lifetime that her expectations tended to default to the worst-case outcome; she was pleasantly surprised if the results were more positive. Tom was the gambler in their relationship; he'd take any odds if the potential payoff was worth the risk. Part of her wished she had Tom's optimism about now.

Seven had tried her best to show B'Elanna the reasons why no news was good news in the case of Tom and Harry. No evidence of their destruction, ergo, maybe they aren't dead. B'Elanna's immediate response to Seven's postulates was to dismiss them as a means of self-preservation. After all, even a Borg equipped with nifty nanoprobes would prefer to keep her ocular implant and other limbs attached to her body: Angry B'Elanna equals Broken Borg. Further thought, though, convinced B'Elanna that Seven was attempting to offer reassurance, however meager. B'Elanna appreciated Seven's efforts.

Suddenly, the thrum of the conduits stopped. The engines halted. *What the*—She stopped. No alarms that accompanied systems failure sounded. Panic, for the moment, had been averted. Whatever had stopped the engines could wait. She reached for a vial of coolant and injected it into the coils surrounding the probe's processors. Backflow spilled onto her palms and drizzled onto her uniform. *Lovely. But at least it's nearly ready to be transported to the launch tube.*

She glanced up from her workbench to reach for a rag to wipe off her coolant-smudged hands when she saw the doors of main engineering open. Chakotay stepped through and scanned the perimeter of the room, presumably looking for her. Apprehension for the well-being of her engines filled her. B'Elanna slid out of her chair, onto her knees, so she could observe unobtrusively without *being* observed. He better not ask her to subject them to any more abuse than he already had. She was almost out of mechanical miracles.

Chakotay turned to Vorik, who subsequently pointed to the "corner" where B'Elanna was sequestered. *Traitor,* she thought, vowing to put Vorik on conduit-scrubbing duty as soon as possible. Chakotay immediately started walking in her direction.

B'Elanna quickly dropped her eyes and focused on making her final adjustments to the probe. *Not good,* she thought, *when the boss decides to deliver bad news in person.* For an instant, she considered whether she should save time and hurl the hypospanner at Chakotay now. Locked up in the brig, she might get the time off she deserved.

She noted, with dark humor, that the engineering staff had collectively put a few more meters between themselves and her location. Ensign Titus looked like he wanted to burrow through the deck plating with his bare hands. She almost laughed aloud: her close friends understood that stories of B'Elanna's angry outbursts were exaggerated. She didn't dispel the rumors because a certain amount of fear was an effective way of keeping her team in line. Still, it was tempting, this one time, to give her staff what they expected. . . .

And then, without warning, any will she had to fight back dissipated. She released an audible exhalation; her shoulders slumped and the need to curl up with a soft pillow and take a nap overwhelmed her. Detachment replaced the cynicism. She drifted far, far away from her body. Working by rote, her fingers found the last empty connector and slid the chip into place. She slid the faceplate onto the probe until it clicked.

By the time Chakotay reached her, she'd become indifferent to the drama. What did her objections matter? What did her purported anger matter? Chakotay would do whatever Chakotay wanted to do—or needed to do.

When he was several steps away, she said, "Just get it over with. Crisis of the hour. Unreasonable request. Bad news. Take your pick."

Chakotay's eyebrows shot up.

"If you were expecting a repeat of senior staff, I hate to disappoint you but I'm fresh out of theatrics," she said, and tossed her soiled rag in the general direction of the recycler.

"We need to mount a rescue mission," Chakotay said.

"I'm not lucky enough that it's for the *Homeward Bound?*"

"Sorry. We've encountered three stranded Monorhan ships. Five thousand refugees. No engines, just life-support. We're going to lend them a hand."

It took her a minute to wrap her brain around what Chakotay had said. When his words did sink in, she discovered her resolve to passively agree to whatever he requested had altered somewhat. Instead of rage, however, she felt overwhelmed by the futility of her life. "Haven't we reached the point where we've given enough yet?" B'Elanna sat back on her heels. "At what point do we say to the universe, 'We accept that we are your slaves and will be fated to this *Gre'thor*-like existence if we ever attempt to look out for our own interests'?" She blew a mouthful of air and shook her head.

"Pretty fatalistic approach, even for a half-Klingon."

"From where I sit, we'll bleed ourselves dry before this is over and for what, a species that may not have the capacity to heal its lingering radiation sicknesses before it becomes extinct?"

"Should we be less compassionate?"

B'Elanna snorted. "Now, that's Kathryn Janeway talking."

"That's a compassionate, caring individual speaking."

"Am I dealing with Commander Chakotay speaking on behalf of Captain Janeway or am I dealing with *Captain* Chakotay?"

"Are you questioning my authority?" Chakotay said, visibly bristling.

Struck a nerve, did I? B'Elanna slowly climbed to her feet, crossed her arms across her chest, and calmly said, "No. I need to know who's asking me to put my staff's lives on the line."

"An order from a superior officer is an order, Lieutenant," Chakotay said.

She shrugged. "Fine. What do you need: supplies or personnel?"

"I need an engineer to go on the away mission to the stranded Monorhan space vessels. Tuvok will be in command. Nakano's picking out a medic."

Her decision took only a second. "I'll go," B'Elanna said softly.

"I'm not certain that's wise under the circumstances," Chakotay said, narrowing his eyes to study her. His doubts about B'Elanna's state of mind were clear from the hardened expression on his face.

"Under the circumstances, I'm the best person for the mission." B'Elanna unbuckled the tool belt strapped around her waist and tossed it casually into a storage bin beneath a workstation. "If we're going to get out of this mess once and for all, our best chance is to get the job done right the first time." She shouted a series of orders to Joe Carey, who poked his head out from behind the warp core long enough to nod in acknowledgment before she returned her attention to Chakotay. "Besides, if someone is going to die in this round, I'd rather have it be me than someone who actually has something left to lose."

"I travel alone," the Doctor calmly said to Mestof's assassin. "I was separated from the general at Baron Var's estate. I've traveled two days to rejoin her."

An angry hiss sounded through his teeth. The knife sliced a stinging line across his flesh. "I don't believe you."

I may actually die here. "You killed the peasant who guided me here." The Doctor's mind raced. He had to disarm his attacker. Tension poured off the soldier; the Doctor sensed his fear. "Tie me up, take me back to your camp as your prisoner, interrogate me."

The soldier hesitated.

"Check the insignia on my sleeve," the Doctor said, praying that Nual knew what he was talking about when he identified him as a high-ranking official.

The knife bobbled only a little as the soldier pulled up the tunic sleeve. He gasped. "The adjunct to the general!"

The Doctor felt a shift in the air behind him as the soldier toppled backward, surprised. *Now!*

With lightning reflexes, the Doctor spun around and pinned the soldier's arms to the ground, squeezing his wrist and forcing him to drop the knife. He kicked the weapon into the water with his shoe. The soldier kicked one of the Doctor's legs out from beneath him, throwing him off balance, but the Doctor grabbed on to the soldier with both hands and pulled him down at the same time. They rolled around on the shore, dangerously near the dropoff to the water. A blow to the Doctor's mouth, to his eye.

Don't make me kill you! The Doctor gouged at the soldier's face, then ground his teeth into the hand that smashed into his nose. The soldier squealed, his grip slackened. Survival instinct drove him but it warred with his Hippocratic oath. The Doctor pushed the soldier down onto the ground, sitting on the man's waist, and wrapped both of his hands around the soldier's neck and compressed his trachea just enough to deny him air and make him disoriented. Somewhere near the base of the ears, there were nerve bundles that would collapse the man if they were compressed hard enough. Taking a risk, the Doctor released his grip on the soldier's throat.

The Doctor pressed his thumbs against pressure points beneath the man's ears, instinctually knowing that doing so would cause pain—violent waves of it. The man's eyes bulged; a burst blood vessel stained his iris. Unwavering, the Doctor continued compressing the points—even when the hoarse screams began—until the soldier blacked out. The Doctor paused, becalmed himself, closed his eyes and tried to wipe the memories from his mind. He opened his eyes and stared at the soldier for a long moment, wondering who he was and why he had attacked with such viciousness.

He wanted you dead, came the reoccurring thought as the Doctor counted the assassin's shallow breaths. *He will kill you if he has the chance.*

The Doctor dropped his branch, stumbled to the nearest tree and braced against it for support, his insides convulsing. Bent from the waist, he retched up his stomach contents until he dry-heaved bile. He wiped the vomit from his mouth with the back of his hand, then turned back to the unconscious soldier. Rifling through his pockets, the Doctor removed any item that could possibly be used as a weapon or might be as of use to him. He found, in the soldier's rucksack, a coil of rope that would be useful in binding the would-be killer's feet and hands. Once that task was accomplished, the Doctor started back through the forest toward Nual's corpse. He would drag his friend as far as the outcropping, strip him of his valuables and personal goods, and leave them at the base of the bluff, in case Din should come looking for his father come morning. Knowing Din's passion and youthful impulsiveness, the Doctor wouldn't give him a choice whether to follow him to the general's camp. He would disappear across the water and not look back.

The slow, methodical trek across the reservoir's eastern edge took him well past the hour when the moon had begun its nightly descent. Rumbling artillery and explosions continued as he rowed. The Doctor found the regular, rhythmic beat of the oars in the water soothing. Focusing on the physicality of the task allowed him to avoid mulling over the pointlessness of Nual's death. Guilt for robbing Din of a father would come later. For now, he would row. He reached the opposite shore in the hours before dawn. He walked, following the sounds of battle, as long as he had strength before he stumbled, his legs giving way beneath him. He picked himself up and continued walking a bit farther. At the base of a slope, he crawled under a hollow created by a berm and fell into a dreamless sleep.

The Doctor pulled his cloak tighter around him, ignoring the persistent tapping on his shoulder. He rolled away, turning his back on whatever was pestering him, and faced toward the matted grass, now warmed by his body.

The tapping became shaking and continued unabated. A loud whisper joined the assault on his rest. "Adjunct Ced! Wake up! Wake up! The lines are shifting. You're going to be cut off if we don't leave soon."

Wait. Through the befuddlement of sleep, the Doctor heard a name. A name that had the vague ring of familiarity to it. He mumbled something incoherent, requesting that he be left alone. The speaker kept repeating the name, his tone tinged with urgency. And then the name connected with knowledge, a puzzle piece connecting with its mate. Kes had told him the story of the great female general and her most loyal adjunct, an aging Ocampa named Ced. The Doctor's eyes flickered open.

Crouched down beside him was an Ocampa wearing a lily crest that matched the one on his own armor. She ceased shaking him as soon as the Doctor's eyes opened. A dark shape, silhouetted against the daylight sky, filled his view. Mist crawled over the grasses, coiling into sleepy curlicues and clouds.

"Beg your pardon. Mestof's troops will be here soon, Adjunct. We need to be on the move," she said, lips quivering. "The general thought you were dead."

The Doctor nodded. "So did I." He rolled over onto

his belly, pushed himself up on all fours, and arched his back in a feral stretch. "I don't—I can't recall your name."

"Iga. My name is Iga, sir," she said. "Beyond this rise, we can walk upright. We should stay down until we reach the forest edge. Mestof has spies everywhere. They say even the avians and animals will share their secrets with him."

"Lead the way, then."

Mimicking the zigzagging, back-and-forth gait of a water bug, Iga darted all along the length of the hillside, using the knee-high, thick-bladed grass for cover. The Doctor followed close behind her, trying to avoid half-buried rocks and insects swarming into their nests.

The Doctor contemplated whether he should start thinking about defining himself in Ocampan terms. After all, he now had an identity, at least who he was on Ocampa in this era. Ced, son of Pran, adjunct to General Lia, leader of the unified forces of the free republics. He knew Ced was at least eight years old at a time when the Ocampa typically lived into their teens. The Doctor also knew why he'd been in the baron's fortress. Kes had told him the legendary tale of Lia's and Ced's visit to Baron Var to ask him to join the alliance against Mestof.

What a strange state to be in, to live in a body not one's own. The Doctor, as he followed Iga, analyzed his memories and responses; he failed to find evidence of Ced's life force lingering in this body. The life that was Ced must have ended when the fortress collapsed. Vivia had sent the Doctor into Ced's body and the Doctor's sentience reanimated the Ocampan.

When they reached tree cover, they began walking. The Doctor followed Iga, who moved swiftly but soundlessly through the woods, reminding him very much of Nual. Observing the Ocampa's natural, instinctual interaction with their environment added to the Doctor's growing conviction that the destruction of the planet's surface had stunted Ocampan evolution. He could only imagine what traits and abilities might have emerged had they not been forced underground.

Periodically, Iga looked back to see if he kept up. The Doctor's sleep had been restful, however, so he discovered renewed vigor as he tramped through the brush. Glancing above him he discovered that the previous night's transparency had been blanketed in gray-black. A momentary thrill brought by the hope that a storm might be coming gave way to the realization that weapons smoke coated the sky. He'd become oblivious of the incessant detonations, rattles, booms, and tat-tat-tats disturbing the morning calm. Or was it noon? He couldn't tell. Iga guided him about a half a kilometer farther, crisscrossing to avoid briars and the prickly shrubs in the undergrowth. The battlefield sounds magnified with each meter covered. A brief bout of panic seized him: What would he do when he reached the fighting? He was a doctor, not a soldier. He had neither the skill nor the stomach to be a killer.

And then, without warning, he realized they had arrived. A thick curtain of smoke rising from below them dramatically decreased their visual range. Iga slowed her steps. Her alert, intelligent eyes rapidly shifted back and forth as she scouted out the ghostly terrain. The tree line came to an abrupt end a short distance ahead, giving way to a clearing of unknowable size. Beyond that, the Doctor discerned what appeared to be a sheer dropoff.

"The smoke has assured that we cannot be certain who controls the field," Iga whispered. "If we approach through that copse of brush over there, we might be able to observe the fighting from the overlook." They moved deliberately, realizing that an enemy could emerge without warning. They dropped down onto their bellies. The Doctor peered through the haze and discovered that they overlooked a natural basin—perhaps a dried-up lakebed. Soldiers swarmed over the terrain like Denebian dung flies. He couldn't tell which side held the advantage; the glowing barrels of the fire lances flashed through the smoke but none could be linked to a specific army. Sky bombers, soldiers who wore mechanized wings and carried acid grenades, swooped off the rims of the basin. The wing markings were unmistakable—each was adorned by the four quartered crest of Mestof. The Doctor had to concede that Mestof's side had an advantage if they controlled the air.

Iga handed the Doctor a pair of distance lenses she'd been using. "Can you see her? I've tried, but I can't locate her in all the confusion down there."

By "her," the Doctor assumed Iga meant General Lia. He surveyed the field, adjusting the lenses to give him a panoramic view.

Suddenly, a jolt, all too similar to an electric shock, ripped through the Doctor's body. He grunted, clutched the lenses to his chest, and rolled over on his back. His mind blanked and he knew only pain. Once the effect subsided, he realized: Nacene were nearby. Suspiria had used a technique similar to the one he'd just experienced when she came aboard *Voyager*. The Doctor had treated those who had tangled with her, so he knew, firsthand, the effectiveness of Nacene warfare.

The pain gradually faded, replaced by an uncomfortable tingling sensation that he intuitively understood indicated Nacene presence. He'd felt similarly around Vivia but he'd been a mere hologram then, not a flesh-and-bone individual. He would find the Light here—he knew he would. Eagerly, he searched the battlefield.

The Nacene gift for transformation made it nearly impossible for him to determine which of the dark figures swarming in the smoke might be an extradimensional alien. But he believed that he'd be able to identify the *signs* of their involvement if he saw them. So far, nothing struck him as out of the ordinary as he watched the Ocampan version of war play out below. He'd experienced war games with Mr. Kim and Mr. Paris on the holodecks, not to mention during the Hirogen takeover. Save different weaponry and attire, the fundamental goals of this real-life scenario varied little from what he'd role-played.

Rolling back onto his stomach, he focused every molecule of his matrix on the battlefield. Oh, how useful his holographic gifts would be at a time like this! He could drop from the heights and walk the field, impervious to threat. Being organic was horribly inefficient. Mentally, he sectioned up the battlefield using a grid. He moved the lenses from sector to sector, evaluating every soldier— every weapon—he could see; nothing out of the ordinary struck him. A commotion drew his attention back to an area he'd just examined. Soldiers under the banners of both sides scattered, running as if their lives depended on it. Not that the Doctor blamed them once he saw glowing orange magma oozing out of a rift.

Molten fingers crept over the ground, ensnaring all those who failed to outrun it. Burbling out of the earth caldron, the ribbons of fiery rock fanned out, nipping the heels of a platoon of Lia's soldiers whose terrified shrieks rose above the mechanized noise. A web of radiant filaments fanned over the ground, veins carrying fire and destruction. *Odd,* the Doctor thought. The longer he watched, the less arbitrary the flow appeared to be. Some under the four-quarter banner had fallen, but comparatively few when examining the whole. The elements had been called up to fight on Mestof's behalf.

Another, slighter electrical shock bored through him. He winced, fused his lips together, refusing to allow a sound to escape his lips. He would not expose their hiding place and thereby be the cause of yet another senseless death. The pain passed. He resumed his search. Scanning the immediate vicinity and the battlefield, he discovered nothing that hinted of a hidden alien presence. *Damn!*

Then the light came.

At first, the Doctor thought the sun had finally broken through the veiling smoke. When he saw the beams radiating from out of the murk below him, he knew he was witnessing something extraordinary. The hair on his neck prickled: whether he felt fear or amazement was unclear. Awestruck, he trembled. Iga, beside him, cried out, repeatedly jabbing her finger at the air, "Look!"

An orb, like a small moon, rose above the soldiers' heads and suspended in midair. Brighter than midday, the white light shining from the orb overcame the gloom and illuminated everything it touched. Tree canopies glowed as if they were aflame. Mestof's soldiers dropped to their knees, burying their faces in their hands.

The Doctor could neither look away nor bear to look on the light; its searing purity pierced him to the core. The light knew him, he felt certain, and could expose his innermost secrets. Whether he should stand and flay himself before the light or whether he should hurl himself off the precipice in despair, he didn't know. He knew pain, though. The flashes of pain he'd had before had nothing on the agony he felt now. It was as if the light was a laser carving away his flesh layer by layer, leaving him decimated. No doubt about it, the Nacene were here—perhaps many of them—and they were angry about the wielder of the orb.

"Make them stop!" he shouted, rolling back and forth along the ridge, begging for relief.

If Iga had thought his behavior strange, the Doctor couldn't know. She had curled into a fetal position and had covered her ears with her hands.

In the midst of the pain, the Doctor looked down on the field and saw, at the epicenter of the light, an Ocampan woman, red-blond hair flowing out behind her. Her eyes closed, arms outstretched as if in a trance, the Doctor believed he could see her mouth moving. He knew she spoke an incantation that guided the orb. He stared at her, and for a horrified moment, wondered if General Lia was Nacene.

On every side, the soldiers shrank, cowering from the all-present, all-knowing light. Mestof's men ran screaming from the battlefield as if their lives depended on their escape. Casting aside their weapons, they scattered into the forest. In the distance, the Doctor could see them hurrying away like agitated insects fleeing a disturbed hive. A few of Mestof's soldiers stood on the field defiantly, arms raised in a mirror image to the general's. The Doctor's view of those soldiers shimmered and rippled like a mirage conjured by a great desert heat. *They must be the Nacene,* he thought. *They seem to be fighting back against the orb. . . .* Thought faded.

The pain became so great that the Doctor lost his ability to withstand it. Beside him, Iga seized, her eyes rolled back into her head; the Doctor was helpless to assist her. It took all his self-control to keep the pain from driving him mad. Hurting in his bones and ligaments, the Doctor crawled to the very edge of the embankment. Death would be kinder. Voyager . . . Voyager . . . *I have to hold on for* Voyager. *Must find the Light* . . . His eyes drooped closed, he teetered—

The light vanished, snuffed out.

The Doctor fell backward onto the ground. His energy sapped away, and the Doctor wondered if his flaccid muscles would ever contract again. He felt like a marionette whose strings had been cut. *Iga had a seizure.* Turning his head to the side, he searched wearily, finding her a few paces away.

Iga's body slackened; her rapid, but shallow, breathing indicated shock. A dull sheen of clammy perspiration glossed her pale face.

Undeterred by weakness, the Doctor dragged himself over to Iga's side, assessed her airway and circulation. "Slow down. You'll hyperventilate." He placed a hand on her shoulder to calm the woman. "In and out, in and out." Soon, her breaths followed the cadence of his words. He unfastened his cloak and covered her with it.

The worst appeared to be over. Even the battle—that only moments before had seethed with heated fury—seemed to have dissipated into nothingness. Soldiers staggered around the basin, weapons cast aside, field positions abandoned. Mestof's forces, save the corpses, had vanished.

For whatever reason, the orb appeared to have had less impact on those wearing the white-lily crest than Mestof's army, a corollary to the magma that had a preference for Lia's troops. He could only guess that Lia had extraordinary psionic gifts that allowed her to wield the orb. Given time, the Doctor assumed, cynically, that he'd find scientific basis for the phenomenon. Hah. Science Nacene style. For now, he felt grateful to have escaped with his life and mental faculties operating reasonably well. He had a new appreciation for the day-to-day struggles of organic life-forms.

Fastening his cloak around Iga's shoulders, he wrapped his arm around her waist and hefted her to her feet, resting her head on his shoulder. The Doctor discovered a deeply grooved switchback trail that led from the ridge down to the basin. He lost track of the minutes, then number of steps he had to take. Stumbling, he made his way down until he reached the flats. He stepped over bodies, careered back and forth with the coordination of a drunkard, but moved forward, imagining in his mind's eye where the general stood commanding the orb. A sharp tingling—like blood returning to a numb limb—alerted him to Nacene presence, but he lacked the wherewithal to search out the source. His mission to heal took precedence, though he craned his neck about as he walked, searching for any clue that might lead him to find the Nacene meddlers.

A murmuring rose around him as he passed through the crowds. He heard his name being whispered. "Ced has returned from death," they said.

And then he saw them. There were two of them. A woman and a male. They looked like Ocampa but the Doctor knew better. The sharp tingling coursed through his limbs to the point of discomfort. "Who are they," he asked a page who pushed a cart beside him.

"Mestof's wizards, Adjunct," came the boy's answer. "The general and her lieutenant captured them using their magic orb."

He smiled. All the Doctor's pain and misery—and that suffered by Nual and Din—to this point had been worth it. The Light had to be among those prisoners. He had to be. What was it Mr. Paris was fond of saying? Pop-pop-pop: fish in a barrel.

Several soldiers bearing a stretcher wove around smoking piles of battle refuse. Believing that they were running a patient to a field hospital, he tried to follow them, hoping they would lead him to help for Iga. The young woman needed medical attention; he would move on and accomplish his mission for Vivia once she was taken care of. Realizing that the stretcher bearing soldiers approached him, he stopped.

The Doctor began. "Iga here needs—"

"Sir, the general," a soldier in blood-spattered clothing said.

A small, crumpled body buried beneath blankets stirred. One of the soldiers running beside the stretcher pushed away the dusty covering to reveal the profile of ashen-faced General Lia, her face partially covered by red-gold hair matted with filth. "Ced, you've come back to me."

"I'm here, General, to serve you." The Doctor attempted to maneuver so he could approach Lia without dropping Iga, but found it difficult.

"May I, sir?" The soldier who had announced the general stood beside Iga, offering to care for her so the Doctor could talk with Lia. The young Ocampan male slid his arm around Iga's waist and began walking her toward a tent in the trees that, from the activity surrounding it, the Doctor surmised was the medical area. He observed the pair until he felt comfortable that Iga was being handled appropriately.

Lia grasped Ced's arm with her quivering hand. "I've missed you, friend." In spite of her weakened state, her grip was firm.

A tall, broad-shouldered, helmeted soldier standing beside her gently pushed her hand back down to her side. "Easy, *meshanna*. You must save your energy to recover." He turned to the Doctor, his soot-covered features indiscernible in the helmet's shadows. "She will not relent until she has seen you, but she needs to have treatment."

The sharp tingling had magnified. *The prisoners must be moving,* he thought. *I need to find the Light before he is removed from his place.*

"Ced?" The soldier spoke again.

Startled, the Doctor said, "Of course, I will speak with her." He crouched down beside his liege, though he reluctantly turned away from the helmeted solider. Something in his voice, the melodious timbre, sounded so familiar. He stole an upward glance.

The soldier's hazel eyes flashed. Though the helmet covered most of his face, the Doctor could see from the line of his cheekbones, the fullness of his lips, that this was a handsome individual.

"Did we capture Mestof's wizards?" Lia asked, reaching for the hazel-eyed soldier.

He entangled his fingers with Lia's. "For the moment, they are contained. I will deal with them when I know you are safe."

Contained. Something about how the soldier said that word . . . Shivering involuntarily, the Doctor looked away from the soldier and focused on the general. *Odd,* he thought. *I don't believe I've experienced such a sensation before.* Though déjà vu wasn't part of his matrix, the Doctor felt a disquieting familiarity with his circumstances. How could he know a place he had never been, feel a connection to a person who he'd never met?

As unusual as his experience had been so far, the Doctor was ill prepared for his first, close-up view of the woman bundled on the stretcher. Momentarily struck, he must have hesitated—not out of alarm, but from surprise. The Doctor smiled, struck by her elfin features, smudged with weapons grease and dirt. Hardly the warrior striking terror into the hearts of her enemies that he'd watched from afar. The Doctor permitted her to touch his face.

Her cool, fragile fingers fluttered over his face and lips. So taken by her resemblance to Kes was he that he couldn't stop staring at her. The longer he studied her, though, the more he noticed the differences: Lia's sinewy arms and chiseled bone structure, her crooked lower teeth and a small hook-shaped scar beside her nose.

"We will fight another day, Ced," Lia said softly, and with a shuddering breath, drifted back into semiconsciousness.

The hazel-eyed soldier, the one who had used the endearment, reached for the Doctor, touched his sleeve. "You have returned. All is as it should be."

For a brief flash, the Doctor felt as if he had returned to Vivia's imprisonment; every cell in his body oscillated with violence that forced him to his knees.

"The adjunct! Help him!" an unfamiliar voice cried out.

The Doctor wanted to answer, say he was fine—but he wasn't. The sharp tingling reached a pitch in his shaking hands. White light filled his vision. Just as he believed he could endure no more, the pain receded. Exhausted, the Doctor collapsed face-first onto the ground. He clung to the one truth his misery had revealed to him.

The hazel-eyed soldier was Nacene.

The Monorhans never saw the Nacene coming. Phoebe made certain of that. She used every technique she'd learned over thousands of years to mask their presence. Even in their weakened state, the Exiles—especially when their wills joined together—had tremendous power. Phoebe wanted to avoid exposure lest their purpose be compromised. She would not tolerate such a development. Already, too much had been lost for the barely sentient creatures that populated this planet to thwart what was the Exiles' right.

Granted, by cosmic standards the Monorhans were crude, poorly evolved creatures, but that didn't make them stupid. After all, it was Nacene essence, left behind after the Last Battle that had allowed the miserable planet to give rise to life. Nacene influence, however minuscule, on Monorhan DNA had endowed them with unusual capacities—such as their psionic abilities—that made them sensitive to their sires' presence. Practically speaking, could the Monorhans do anything to stop the Exiles from accomplishing their stated purpose? Probably not. Dealing with them might, however, require the Exiles to deplete their energy reserves. Phoebe would not arrive at this critical apex and risk being unprepared.

Small group by small group, Phoebe's ragtag collection of Nacene outcasts assembled on the northernmost section of an uninhabitable continent just as the remains of tepid daylight were overpowered by gray gloom. The slimy, brackish marsh waters could sustain only algae and single-celled animal life: they would be undisturbed here. Shallow waters polluted with rotting biomatter emitted offensive hydrogen sulfide gas that Phoebe found distasteful. With so many lovely places to visit in the galaxy, it seemed a shame that they had to end their travels in such a nasty place.

Phoebe flitted about, watching and studying the behavior of each Exile as they alit on the stagnant marshlands. She would need to choose soon. By her calculations, only a hundred or so remained in transit. They would expect to begin as soon as they arrived, unaware that there was one outstanding issue that needed to be resolved before they created the Key. She'd hidden the complete truth from them, knowing that their apprehension—their fear—would cripple their will to follow through on the plan. Because she had superior strength and control, she had successfully withheld one critical piece of information from the others: the Key would be useless without spores to enable their transformation back into pure Nacene energy. Phoebe knew how to create the spores; that wasn't the issue. Compelling the others to go along with the creation was the issue.

At last, the final cluster of her fellow Exiles arrived. They looked at her expectantly. Phoebe closed her eyes, basking in the abundance of strength that was hers for the taking. She savored the power, knowing that the Exiles' dependence on her to show them the way back to Exosia would allow her to challenge Vivia and those like her. Upon her triumphant return, she would offer hope to those who had lost lifetimes to serving the strings. She would be celebrated as a liberator and Exosia would be her domain. More than any experience she'd had since leaving so long ago, the possibilities open to her thrilled her. And it was so close, so tantalizingly close that she could barely restrain her eagerness.

She surveyed their faces, searching for the one. *The time has come. Our return has been foretold and now we will seize our destiny.* Floating above the ground, she drew upon her still-formidable transformative powers to increase her size, to imbue herself with a terrible beauty that she knew would instill fear and awe within them. At last, her eyes alighted on the most vulnerable among them: a diminutive Enaran female whom Phoebe recognized as a former companion she believed lost in the destruction of Gremadia. Together, they had traveled galaxies from one end of the universe to the other. Sad that she must be sacrificed. *Knowing her as I do will be to my advantage, for I can exploit that if necessary, if she needs persuading,* Phoebe thought.

Come forward, in front of all of us, Phoebe ordered her oldest friend.

Sadness softened the Enaran's face, but she complied with Phoebe's request.

For the good of all, you must offer yourself.

The Enaran lifted her chin, staring at Phoebe defiantly. *No.*

Effortlessly, Phoebe hurtled an energy wave at her oldest friend, watching with satisfaction as the creature recoiled from the blow, then collapsed onto the ground, writhing with pain.

The circle of Exiles hummed nervously.

Within moments, the Enaran had righted herself and stepped out of the circle to stand before Phoebe. *You will have to do better than that.*

Phoebe smiled. Her friend wasn't easily cowed. She had counted on this. *I won't*—she opened up her arms, indicating the thousand Exiles standing in a circle—*because they will. They know what is required to return to Exosia. They will not allow you to deny them what is their due.* Phoebe called out to those in the circle, showing them her vision of what the future she had planned for them, allowing them to see what was possible *if* they could open the gateway. Phoebe lulled the Exiles away from their confusion, seduced them with promises, and she found their weak wills bending beneath her vision. *She must be sacrificed to complete the transformation.*

The circle around Phoebe tightened as the Exiles closed ranks. She saw in their expression the conviction required to do this horrible deed. The Enaran, too, must have sensed the inevitable, because she expended (regretfully) all her remaining energy with urgent, though futile, pleas.

You will not fully be lost. You will live on forever as part of each of us—in Exosia. Phoebe smiled. When the first attack on the Enaran began, she left the circle to float in midair, watching the sickly Monorha sun set behind the horizon. Alas, her last experience in this dimension would be unpleasant—a dismal location with such nasty business required for their departure. She heard the garbled screams beneath her, followed by the sizzle and pop of the Enaran's matter being compressed. The combined will of a thousand Nacene would not be denied.

From the elements of the air, Phoebe wove a sac to hold the spores. The delicate filaments caught the light. The screams faded. In a moment the task would be complete. *It would have been so much easier if she'd been able to retain her Nacene form,* Phoebe realized. She sighed. *Too bad. More work for the rest of us.*

An unexpected jolt startled her: an unwanted presence stirred not far from here. She had been so consumed with creating the spores that she'd almost forgotten about the nosy creatures who had forced this fate upon them. *Your turn will come,* Voyager. She had taken no pleasure in having to destroy her friend to form the spores. Difficult times called for sacrifice, however painful.

Dealing with Janeway's crew, however—she would have no regrets there.

The gnashing beneath her had ceased. Phoebe swooped down into the circle and began gathering the spores.

Chapter 6

Seven waited outside main engineering for Chakotay to emerge. At the commander's request, she had prepared a perfunctory briefing for the away team destined for the Monorhan ship: an engineer yet to be selected; Tuvok; Crewman Estella Luiz, a medic; and Neelix. The selection of the last individual had puzzled Seven; after all, beyond preparing nutritive supplements for the crew, she wasn't entirely sure what function Neelix performed. He assisted Samantha Wildman in caring for her child, Naomi Wildman. And he talked a great deal.

Seven suspected that the Monorhans wouldn't be in much of a talking mood.

When Seven had expressed her reservations, Chakotay had informed her that her concerns were noted but that the assignment stood and dismissed her. The commander would have liked to believe that he had hidden from her what might best be referred to as a bemused smirk when their discussion terminated. Seven, however, had noticed the smirk and had felt irritation. She noticed most things. She chose not to comment on them because her fellow crew members behaved more naturally when they believed her to be oblivious of their whispers, their pointing, and, in this case, their amusement at her expense.

Seven did not believe her role was to inject humor into social situations. That was Lieutenant Paris's job. She sighed. Whatever was taking Chakotay so long in engineering was keeping her away from her own work. And for what—a relatively useless report.

She had tried to establish communication with the vessel, but had received only a recorded message. What she knew about the ship's problems came only from sensor readings; on-site inspection would be required. Her briefing, in summary, said, "The ship is broken and Monorhans will die if we don't fix it."

The engineering doors opened. Chakotay, in deep conversation with B'Elanna, emerged.

Seven blinked her surprise. Commander Chakotay had apparently selected B'Elanna to go on the away mission. "Commander, Lieutenant—would you like me to discuss my report on the way to the shuttlebay?"

Chakotay nodded. "The other team members will meet us there. B'Elanna can fill them in in-flight."

"From what we can tell, their propulsion system is nonfunctional," Seven began as they started walking toward the turbolift. "If possible, Lieutenant Torres should undertake repairs that will allow them to start back to Monorha."

"And if the system is beyond repair?" B'Elanna asked.

"Your job will be to help them attain momentum that will put them on a trajectory close enough to Monorha that a rescue is feasible," Seven said.

B'Elanna nodded her head approvingly.

Seven could guess what she was thinking: *As long as we're not repatriating them on Monorha and getting bogged down in regional politics again.*

"You'll need to wear environmental suits," Chakotay said. "The ships are flooded with radiation. I've allotted you three to four hours to assess the damage and make the repairs. Beyond that, we'll give them a little push and be on our way. Fair?"

"Will *Voyager* continue traveling toward the rift?" B'Elanna asked.

Chakotay nodded. "But we've determined we don't need to go much further for the probe to be successful. We'll only be a few thousand kilometers ahead of you."

"So we can return to *Voyager* to resupply or treat wounded . . ." B'Elanna said.

"If that's what Tuvok orders, yes. Satisfied, Lieutenant?"

When B'Elanna didn't object, Chakotay wished them well and started back toward the bridge.

As they stepped into the turbolift, B'Elanna asked Seven, "Who else is coming with us?"

"Crewman Luiz will be your medic and Ensign Tariq will pilot the shuttle. Neelix will be coming along—" Seven paused, searching for the words.

"To make everyone feel better," B'Elanna said, as if it were obvious why this was important.

"As you say," Seven replied. Under the current circumstances, Seven questioned the necessity of squandering resources on emotional needs when providing medical care, breathable air, and a functioning ship were vital. But what did she, who had been rescued from a collective with the capacity for total galactic domination, know? Perhaps if the Queen had consulted with her unimatrices before she launched assimilation efforts, her drones might have felt better about their brutality.

There were aspects of being human that Seven would never understand.

Seven continued, "Commander Tuvok will command the mission and provide security."

"And Chakotay wouldn't mind having him off the ship for a while," B'Elanna muttered under her breath.

"There is that too," Seven said.

The women exchanged a look and for the first time in what had seemed like the longest day in Seven's memory, B'Elanna responded with the barest hint of a smile.

"Hey Seven," B'Elanna said softly. "I have a favor."

"Yes?"

"I finished my work on the probe. It's ready to transport to the launch tube."

"You want me to go over what you have done to verify that it works properly."

B'Elanna shrugged. "In a word, yeah. But there's something else . . . She stopped and looked Seven in the eye. "You have to find the Doctor and bring him home. If we're going to put all our lives on the line, do whatever you have to to pull this harebrained scheme off."

"I will," Seven said.

They stepped out of the turbolift, into the shuttlebay. Seven lingered behind, watching B'Elanna greet her teammates, then procure her gear. *My presence is no longer required,* Seven thought. She pressed the button to call the turbolift. A thought occurred. "Lieutenant," she called out.

B'Elanna twisted around to look at Seven.

"Good luck," Seven called out.

A broad, full-mouth smile transformed B'Elanna's face. The engineer gave her a thumbs-up, then hustled up the ramp into the shuttle.

Tom needed all of a few seconds in his new locale to know that Q had sent them to a fun spot. The flashing lights and the tangle of alien bodies writhing to a percussive beat left no doubt in Tom's mind.

"Where in the hell are we?" Harry said, sounding vaguely panicked.

Tom shrugged. "As places Q could have sent us go, this is pretty damn pleasant." *Humid. And a little spongy,* he noted, bouncing lightly on his toes. *But pleasant.*

"But what if we're, like, dinner or something?" Harry's eyes zoomed back and forth across the crowd with a rapidity that made Tom dizzy.

"The best way to avoid being dinner is to find Kol," Tom said. "You saw that image of him on q's desk. You have a better idea what he looks like than I do."

"Cue ball head. Dark black-brown goatee. About your height," Harry said. "The fact that he has a humanoid appearance would make him a stand out in this crowd." A trickle of liquid dripped onto Harry's face. he wiped at the ooze with his finger, held it under his nostrils and inhaled deeply. Wrinkling his nose, he pronounced, "Smells like overripe fruit. What is this place?"

Tom examined the walls and ceilings of variegated pinks and reds, the rounded contours of the chamber sloped and curved without any perceptible pattern. "Some species use organic building materials. We're still in the Continuum—I think—so I suppose anything is possible. Stay focused, Harry."

Both of them paused to study their surroundings. The crowd was in constant flux. Maybe three or four hundred occupied the room, though counting heads (since several aliens had multiple heads) didn't give an accurate measurement. On sight, Tom couldn't identify any of the alien species schlepping around and from appearances, neither could Harry. None appeared humanoid, which didn't bode well for their search. Many had no discernable sense organs or faces, making it difficult to tell whether they minded having their party disrupted because indeed, a party had been under way when they'd arrived.

"If Kol has Nacene abilities, he could change forms," Tom said after several minutes of unsuccessful searching.

Harry groaned. "We're dead."

"Have a little faith, Harry," Tom said, draping his arm around his friend's shoulders. "We just need to work the room, do a little recon and figure out how to find Kol."

"I'm supposed to search the room for someone who, theoretically, could be anyone."

"You make it sound so impossible, Harry. You're a clever guy. You'll figure something out."

"And what will you be doing?"

"q said that Kol was into node racing—whatever that is. I figure I'll start by finding the racers." He wished Harry luck and the two parted ways.

As he watched Harry disappear into the sea of bodies, Tom paused to assess the pros and cons of their current situation. On the con side: Q had sent them off into parts unknown without giving them any idea of what they were supposed to do. Should they fail to find Kol, Tom suspected that Q wouldn't hesitate to damn them to eternity as single-celled organisms. How they'd find the Keeper of the Light among all these aliens escaped him. Especially if the Nacene hybrid was hiding from Fest the loan shark, from the Continuum, and from the Nacene. Tom suspected that the punishment described by Fest was only the beginning of the suffering awaiting Kol—the Continuum never did anything halfway, and he imagined that Q punishment wouldn't be pretty. Kol had a vested interest in not being found.

On the pro side: He glanced down and felt reassured that Q had the decency to dress them for the occasion.

Cobalt blue had always been his color. At least he'd face his doom looking like he'd just waltzed out of a Risan fashion show. He'd have to remember to thank Q for the suit if he lived through the next, oh, say fifteen or twenty minutes.

Probably the single most important factor in their favor was the fact that Q had sent them to a party. There were a lot of things in the universe that Tom Paris didn't know. But parties? Tom knew parties like Vulcans knew self-control.

It never ceased to surprise him that no matter where his travels took him, from the backwater worlds frequented by the Maquis to the far reaches of the Delta Quadrant, the best parties among all species always had three key ingredients: music, intoxicants, and thrills. The formula never varied. Only the Borg didn't follow the formula because the Borg didn't throw parties—a fact, Tom believed, that was part of their problem.

Taking a deep breath, Tom set off in search of the node racers. If they were like most pilots, they'd be gathered where the action was. He scanned the room, trying to discern who might be interested in more than the common delights of partying. *Time to turn on the Paris charm and work the room.*

From the minute he'd appeared in the crowded chamber, he'd barely been able to hear himself think over the noise, never mind eavesdropping. He swore the place vibrated with a steady bass thump-thump-thump. Even a live band would have to put out major amps to make all the walls shake simultaneously.

Part of the challenge of finding Kol was navigating the irregularly shaped chamber; the ceiling height varied from two meters to as high as six and the floor, Tom discovered after nearly skidding down a slope, dropped off without any warning. His first thought had been that the chamber had once held some kind of fluid, but further examination of his surroundings reminded him of the anthills that sprouted up in his parents' backyard every summer—only squishier. Tunnels and hallways branched off in every direction. Tom felt like a fish trapped in some bizarre aquarium.

Tom walked along the perimeter of the room, the moist walls quivering visibly, a gelatinous ooze accumulating on the surface. Multicolored lights never ceased flashing geometric patterns on the ceiling. He squinted through the weak, ever-changing lumination to discern anything of use and found his efforts thwarted. Several deep inhalations of the pungent air had induced woozy numbness in Tom's brain. *Definitely some recreational chemistry going on in this place.* Two or three steps away from resigning himself to failure, Tom noticed that a large, noisy crowd had gathered about five meters in front of him. Shouts and cheers continually came from their ranks. *At the very least, I might be able to escape whatever drug is circulating in the air over here.*

He wiggled past buffet tables and more dancers, discovering that the objects of his search were gathered around large openings in the walls—similar to observation windows—though he couldn't tell what was being watched. In this section of the room, the deafening music wasn't quite as potent nor was the smell quite as brain-numbing. Tom breathed deeply and leaned back against the wall; clarity gradually returned. Resuming his search, he noticed that several dozen aliens perched on chaises and deep-cushioned lounge chairs. A game of chance was under way—tetrahedral dice being shaken and tossed onto a table; chits exchanged hands.

Abruptly, the crowd around the observation holes

tightened. Vaguely claustrophobic sensations squeezed his head; Tom considered leaving for more open climes when he noticed, through a gap in the crowd, several egg-shaped, transparent capsules appearing to be constructed of a membranous exterior enclosing congealed goo. Suspended in the midst of the goo was the pilot—no chair, no gear. The capsules jetted past the window, out of sight, then back in front of the window. Each capsule appeared to be a one- or two-man craft with no discernable engine or guidance system. His previous thought—of being inside an aquarium—had proved to be a good instinct. The party locale seemed to be surrounded by fast-moving currents of viscous liquid, though not water. No surface light could be discerned at this depth. Below the window, maybe thirty meters, he saw the bottom, though of what, he had no clue; it didn't look like any ocean floor he'd ever seen. Thankfully, Tom wasn't claustrophobic.

"You ever seen a node race before?" came a gravelly voice.

Tom turned away from the window, glanced behind him to see the speaker, and saw empty air. Dropping his gaze, he discovered a coral skinned tree-trunk quadruped whose forked tongue flicked rapidly in and out through a circular opening outlined by rows of sharp, pointy teeth.

Not knowing where the creature's eyes were, he spoke to the toothy opening. "What's to know?"

The alien bounced up and down on two of his legs while he spoke. "Two racers are selected. Wagers made. Winners get rich. You want to get rich?"

Tom grinned. "Who doesn't?"

Reaching a tentacle behind Tom's shoulders, he nudged him through a circle of long-necked avians where he would have a better view closer to the window.

"So what's a node?"

The quadruped continued bouncing. "Dark clots—round. Go very quickly. Irregular movement. Pilot hooks one. Races through the stream. Faaaast—" As he drew out the word "fast" his bounce rhythm increased proportionately.

"Say, you ever heard of a racer name Kol?"

The quadruped bounced emphatically.

Tom took that as a "yes." "Is he here?"

The circular opening whirled closed like flower petals tightening at the cold; he leaned slowly from side to side, and then the opening spun open. Tom sensed without having to be told that he'd asked a dangerous question. "Can't say. Watch for now," the quadra-ped said, his volume diminishing to a near whisper.

A bright green light beam shot through the water. The capsules zinged off in the direction of several nodes approaching the vicinity. Hazarding a guess, Tom supposed they had to be going several thousand kilometers an hour—easy. He imagined the rush of going that fast with little more than some plastic wrap between the pilot and the liquid outside and his heart rate leaped.

Tom Paris was smitten. Utterly.

What wasn't to love about a sport where the pilot steered a capsule into the node's wake, launched the equivalent of a grappling hook into the tissue, and then was dragged around behind the node as long as the hook held. Skilled racers, Tom guessed, could actually alter the speed and trajectory of the node; he watched dumbfounded as one of the racers jumped out in front and guided the node around an obstacle course. The quadruped informed him that a successful run meant the racer navigated around an aqueous environment, over, under, and through every obstacle (fields of tall coral-like tubes, waving back and forth with the currents, for example) without the grappling hook dislodging or the capsule spinning out of control and killing the pilot.

The race currently under way began in a field of freestanding chunks—not unlike asteroids. Nodes wove in and out, taking a zigzag course through the dark, craggy objects. Beyond the bobbing chunks, the first racer gained ground navigating between clusters of massive semitransparent gelatinous globules fringed with numerous fronds. Tom watched admiringly as the pilot executed a series of tight turns that he doubted he could manage with the best shuttlecraft in Starfleet. When one pilot brushed too close to the fronds, the globule pounced on the capsule and sucked it into its interior. A spate of groans rose from the crowd at the sobering sight of the pilot being dissolved alive. Tom shuddered.

The last leg of the course appeared deceptively simple: a few larger floating chunks followed by shooting down a deep, dark red opening at the bottom of the course. The racers disappeared from sight when they dove into the tube, explained one of the onlookers. The first one who appeared back at the party won.

Tom realized, however, as his favorite racer—the leader—approached the tube that the node veered dangerously from side to side. The torrential pull of the current would be brutal, especially on an apparently lightweight object like a node. A miscalculation of flow and the capsule would crash head-on into the bottom. Tom pressed closer to the observation hole, crouching down on the ground so he could watch unimpeded. Behind him, he felt the quadruped bouncing gleefully.

Imagining himself in that capsule, swinging wildly in the node's wake, Tom's gnawed his lip, eyes narrowed as he studied the precise motions the pilot took. He curled his fingers around the edge of the observation hole, the squishy substance coating his palms. The racer was coming in at the wrong angle. *Back off, back off,* Tom hissed through gritted teeth. A collective gasp sounded on all sides. He winced, hunching his shoulders up around his ears—

In a split second, the node smacked into the surface, bursting on impact. The capsule followed shortly as the pilot hadn't had the chance to release the tether. Upon impact, the capsule suffered a similar fate as the node; the pilot floating off into the variegated steam flow, tentacles waving frantically as he vanished from view. *Probably drowned,* Tom thought, sitting back on his haunches, still wide-eyed at the spectacle.

And boy did he want to give it a try.

Whoever this Kol was, Tom felt a huge respect for anyone who could successfully make runs like the one he'd just observed and live to tell about it. He suspected, however, that being a pandimensional being might be on the list of required qualifications for spore racing. Beyond lassoing nodes to race, how could a mere human like himself possibly steer one around a race course? He was, however, on a mission for Q. With any luck, he'd been given a little something extra to make his job easier. . . .

"You asked about Kol," the quadruped whispered. "I know someone." The smooth-skinned, squatty creature waved a leg toward an exit. "What can you offer?"

"Offer?" To Tom, the word sounded suspiciously like "bribe" or "bet."

"Kol is off limits. No offer. No talk."

Tom didn't hesitate with his next comment. "I'm a damn good pilot. One of the best anywhere, anytime."

"A racer?" The creature took a long, slow bounce.

Tom answered with a smile few had ever resisted. From his mother to Academy professors to starship captain to his lover B'Elanna Torres, he'd weaseled his way out of a lot of conduit scrubbing duty by turning on the full wattage of the Paris pearly whites.

The tree-trunk alien seemed satisfied. "Follow me."

Following behind his new associate, he maintained a vigilant watch on the crush of shimmying aliens surrounding him, searching both for danger and Harry's whereabouts. The two were typically linked. Tom had no doubt that someday Harry Kim would be among the best officers Starfleet had ever trained. In the meantime, the universe seemed determined to teach him every lesson the hard way. So far, he noted no screams, stripped off clothing, drawn weapons, or other indications of trouble. Tom breathed a little easier. Obtaining legitimate intelligence about Kol would go a long way toward getting them home, never mind saving the universe.

The tree-trunk alien guided him past a platform where several shape-changing aliens morphed between forms to the tempo of the music: the local equivalent of rock-paper-scissors. Their trek through the party ended at an anteroom hidden behind a music-generating machine. Red smoke pouring out of the entranceway made it difficult to see within, but Tom trusted that the tree-trunk alien knew what he was doing. Crouching down to fit without scraping his head on the ceiling, he squeezed in after the alien. Smoke-induced coughing fits and eyes itching and watering with grit assaulted him instantly. He doubled over wheezing, swiping at his eyes to remove the offending particles; he squeezed his eyelids together, hoping to induce enough optical lubrication to avoid near-blindness. Once his discomfort was alleviated, he eased upward, righting himself, and saw Harry, arms and legs bound by thick manacles, his mouth scabbed over with foamy crust. Tom cringed at the grotesqueness of Harry's appearance, but resisted the impulse to look away. Taking a few steps toward Harry, Tom focused on learning what little he could about what had befallen his friend from Harry's abnormally widened eyes and rapid blinks. His friend shook his head violently and jerked his head exaggeratedly to his left. Catching the clue, Tom stopped and glanced in the direction Harry indicated. Through the dissipating smoke, Tom saw an enormous walking stick seated beside Harry. The pincers at the end of one of the alien's eight segmented limbs hovered around Harry's neck.

The creature drilled its multifaceted prismatic sense organs on Tom, the exterior of each of the three melon-shaped globes reflecting endless distorted images. One globe, moving independently of the others wriggled up and away from the brown wavy-plated exoskeleton torso until it hovered in the air like a periscope.

Tom sat stone still while he was examined. Whether the tree-trunk alien had brought him here to be dinner or whether there was a chance of advancing his search for Kol was unclear. The sweat drizzling down Harry's blanched cheeks didn't encourage him. At last, the prismatic globe returned to its place beside the others. The exoskeleton vibrated, quivering with hummingbird speed.

The universal translators rendered the atonal vibrations as language, but Tom heard only disconnected syllables. He glanced at the tree-trunk alien for clarification.

"Pem wants to know your interest in Kol."

Tom breathed a sigh of relief. "I'm not working for one of Kol's creditors, if that's what you're asking. My interest is personal. There's a problem that"—he tried to think of the right word to describe Q—"one of my associates is having that only Kol can solve."

The exoskeleton vibrations resumed in rapidly shifting tones and tempos.

"The other one. The soft body like you," the tree-trunk alien said. "He had nothing to offer. For an offer, Pem will help."

This might be fun. Taking a deep breath, Tom said, "I'll win a race for Pem. In exchange, he tells me where I can find Kol." He pointedly ignored Harry's horrified bug-eyed expression. "And he releases my friend unharmed as soon as I enter the capsule."

Another series of vibrations sounding suspiciously like laughter raised the hair on Tom's neck. He didn't need the tree-trunk alien to translate to know he had a deal.

Surviving long enough to collect the payment was another matter.

Brushing gravel from his arms, the Doctor sat up, stretched his arms and shoulders, and looked around what appeared to be a canvas tent. Definitely a flimsy one: the dingy, coarse brown walls flapped with every passing gust of wind. He could barely discern his surroundings in the shrouding darkness. Beside him on the ground, he discovered a Saracen-style lamp, recalling a prop from the *Arabian Nights.* He touched the polished brass exterior: it was still warm. The lamp must have recently been extinguished. He fumbled around until he found an ignition switch. Moments later, warm light flooded the room.

He observed a plain, utilitarian desk; several scratched trunks closed with large copper fasteners, each large enough to hold a person, if necessary; a series of unfamiliar weapons—perhaps lances or swords. How had he come to be in this place?

A faraway horn sang in rapid-fire staccato.

The sharp tingling in his body prompted remembrance. Ocampa. The Nacene.

Had he been dreaming?

A slit in the wall opened and two men and a woman, all wearing the lily crest, stepped inside, General Lia's slight form sandwiched between them. *The general is back from the field hospital. Perhaps now I can focus on my mission from Vivia. I have to get access to those Nacene. . . .* Anew, he recalled the strange encounter with the hazel-eyed soldier. Perhaps he had reached the wrong conclusion. It had all happened so quickly. . . . For the moment, he chose to put it aside. He scrambled to his feet, confusion forgotten.

With a toss of red-gold hair, Lia snapped an order dismissing her entourage. In a moment they were alone in the tent. She plopped down onto the edge of the cot, resting her hands in her lap. "I never thought I'd get a private moment with you." Lia grinned at him.

The Doctor couldn't help reciprocating her smile, but Lia's smile belied a feverish flush in her pale face—a watery heat in her eyes, which were ringed with bruise-colored half-circles. "You are not well," he said.

"Not you too, Ced, I—" She wavered, throwing a hand behind her to prevent her from falling backward. "Ever since the baron's fortress . . . I haven't felt entirely like myself."

"When was the last time you had something to eat or drink?" the Doctor asked.

"I might have had something in the med tent—"

"Might?"

Lia responded with a noncommittal shrug.

The Doctor stepped over to the tent flap, pushed it aside, called to the soldier on duty outside, and ordered him to have a meal brought to the general immediately. He turned back to the young general, who watched him with affectionate bemusement.

"If you had died back at the fortress—because of me—" Her voice trailed off. "But you didn't. And now you're here."

A twinge of guilt tweaked the Doctor: Lia's loyal confidant *had* lost his life in the fortress. The Doctor was a stranger masquerading as her friend, and that felt suspiciously like a betrayal of her trust. He made a silent vow that he would protect her, for Ced's sake. As part of keeping that promise, he determined that her sorry physical state needed to be dealt with posthaste.

With a thousand years of medical advances at his fingertips, the Doctor knew he could outperform anyone on this world in this era. He informed Lia that as her adjunct, he needed to assess her battle fitness, hoping she would accept that reasoning without question. The Doctor still had little clue of what Ced's day-to-day duties were.

After halfhearted protestations, she submitted to his exam.

The Doctor touched the primary arterial branch in the general's neck to evaluate cardiac function and performed a quick visual triage to assess for signs of internal bleeding or obvious maladies. Other than low blood sugar and dehydration, she appeared fit; the Doctor said so. Medical intuition told him there was more to Lia's poor health, but he lacked evidence to confront her.

"I told you, Ced, you old worrier you." Lia folded her arms across her chest and tucked her hands into her armpits. "A good meal and I'll be as strong as a *lumwa's* back."

Her gesture struck the Doctor as self-conscious—too deliberate. She was hiding something. "Show me your hands."

Averting her eyes, Lia made no move to comply with his request. "Mestof's wizards are in custody. It really was a spectacular maneuver how Balim—"

A soldier pushed back the tent flap and held out a wineskin and a crude pottery bowl filled with stewed vegetables and meat. Lia accepted the food and then dismissed the soldier.

Not even the mention of the "wizards" would deter the Doctor, possessed, in this moment, with memories of his lost friend. Softly, he said, "My liege."

She sighed, placed her meal atop a wooden chest, and held out her hands for him to examine. The Doctor flipped them over to check her palms. A sticky yellow substance oozed from her pores—the *ipasaphor*. Lia had entered the once-in-an-Ocampan's-life fertility period. Having gone through this early in Kes's years on *Voyager,* he knew what to expect. He looked up at her and asked in his clinician's voice, "Has the mitral sac formed on your back?"

Lia bit her lip and nodded.

"Your body is under extreme strain right now, what with the *elogium* as well as what you did on the battlefield. You've been taxed to your limits. You need time to regain your strength." The Doctor eased her back onto the stretcher and pulled a blanket up around her neck. "There. Rest. Recover. This is an important event in your life."

"Compared to what? Saving Ocampa?!" Lia exhaled loudly and kicked off the blanket. "I have no time to be an invalid."

"Think of your health!"

"Scouts have sighted a platoon of Mestof's soldiers heading in this direction," Lia protested. "I must recover if we are to prevent them from retaking their wizards. You know I don't have parents to perform the *rolisisin,* never mind the luxury of six days to form a mating bond."

"How far away is the enemy?" the Doctor asked.

"They are expected before dusk."

The Doctor frowned. Even if he had electrolytic fluids and hypos and optimal conditions to help restore Lia to full strength, he would still want to keep her under observation for a full day and night before she could be released for duty. "The troops should be prepared to fight without you."

Eyes flashing, she snapped, "They will not fight alone."

Even in her anger, how like Kes she looked! The resemblance was extraordinary. The Doctor wondered if perhaps there was some ancestral tie between Lia and Kes. "Mestof's troops, for the time being, are scattered. Attend to yourself! You know as well as I that the *elogium* will happen only once for you."

"Balim's strategy worked then. He said it would. Where is he—" Lia began sitting up, then collapsed back onto the stretcher. She scrunched her eyes together tightly, emitting a hiss through clenched teeth. "I—hurt."

"I know," the Doctor said, wishing for all the latinum and precious treasures in the universes that he had the resources of *Voyager*'s sickbay at hand. "I'll look for something to relieve your discomfort, but you have a more pressing concern: what to do about the *elogium.*"

The general became still. She signed deeply. "There have been signs but circumstances have been so dire . . . I couldn't be distracted. Balim has urged me to take better care of myself, but I haven't listened to him either. You shouldn't take it personally."

"You will need to be distracted now because the window of conception is limited. Do you have someone . . . ? " His voice trailed off. When his Kes had gone through this, she had been in a relationship with Neelix. Lia had repeatedly mentioned Balim. Then the Doctor remembered the hazel-eyed soldier. The one who might be . . . Could they be one and the same, Balim and the soldier? The familiarity between Lia and the soldier had the unmistakable air of romantic entanglement about it. And Lia clearly trusted this Balim, whoever he was. The Doctor's encounter with the handsome soldier had a far less pleasant outcome. As much as he dreaded her answer, he had to know. His heart squeezed painfully in his chest: "Balim? The one with the hazel eyes I met earlier?"

A slight smile curled her lips; a flush pinked her pale cheeks.

The Doctor repressed the inclination to comment. It couldn't be possible—this lovely creature, involved with *that.* She couldn't know his true identity and still share such—he scowled—intimacies with him.

"I know he is yet a stranger to you, Ced," she began, clearly trying to reassure him. "But he is . . . remarkable. Though we haven't yet received the sanction of the priests for our union."

Lia's exceptional powers made more sense if she had a Nacene in her life. By comparison, Kes didn't show such gifts until she had begun transforming. Tanis and his fellow Ocampa demonstrated powerful abilities because of Suspiria's interference. Having a Nacene by your side—in your bed—had its benefits, the Doctor supposed. He glanced at the young general who reminded him so much of Kes. She had a soft light in her eyes. No question, she loved this Balim, whatever he was. How could she be so foolish! This Balim creature was using her!

Another horrible thought occurred: Balim might be the Light, the Nacene the Doctor had promised to stop at all costs for the purpose of saving *Voyager*. He couldn't betray Lia's love without betraying Lia, and yet circumstances might require he make a difficult choice. The Doctor had to know how serious their relationship was. "Are you prepared to have a child with Balim?"

"I love him—"

The Doctor felt ill.

"But I will not conceive a child with him or any other."

"What?" the Doctor said, eyes widening. Yet relief coexisted with sadness for Lia's sake. Knowing what having a child had meant to Kes, what it meant to the Ocampa of the modern day, he had an inkling of what Lia intended to sacrifice.

"We are at war. I live on the battlefield and will not bring a child into this life. Mestof must be defeated and Ocampa restored." She rolled onto her side and stared at him, unflinching. "There is no place for a child."

"Regardless of what you decide, you are in no condition to face Mestof. Rest now or you will be of no use to anyone." The Doctor gently pushed her shoulders back and again drew the blanket up to her chin.

"You are too kind to me, Ced."

"Be kind to me and take care of yourself." Tucking a tangle of dull red-blond braids behind her ears, he placed a paternal kiss on her forehead and rubbed a dirty smudge off her translucent cheek with his thumb. The hollows beneath her eyes bespoke of bone-aching fatigue. Her collarbone was jutting out beneath her thin, coarsely woven tunic. Her chest shuddered with the deep, asthmatic cough of one constantly subjected to battlefield pollutants. The Doctor looked on helplessly, longing for the medicines to ease her maladies.

Lia studied him intently. "I used to be able to touch your thoughts easily, Ced. Something has changed."

I am no longer the person you knew, the Doctor thought. "The battle exhausted you. Do not exert yourself."

"Yes . . . that must be it." Lia yawned, closed her eyes, and drifted into a fitful rest.

He watched her as she slept, wondering if there was a way for this situation to resolve that wouldn't require her to lose the love of her life—or him to be trapped on Ocampa forever. Moments later, the Doctor went in search of the hazel-eyed soldier, the Nacene Lia called Balim.

As a Vulcan, Tuvok had, through a lifetime of self-discipline and understanding, trained his mind to reject thoughts or impulses that might compel him to impose his perspectives on those around him. Their ability, or inability, to live an enlightened existence of self-mastery was not for him to judge. If his input was desired, he would be asked to share it. His rigid adherence to a nonjudgmental worldview was precisely what had earned him his role as Kathryn Janeway's mentor and confidant for many years. Otherwise, her emotionally impulsive tendencies would have driven him to violence long ago. In his present circumstance on the Monorhan vessel, however, he made an exception to his hard-and-fast rule.

He found it unconscionable that sentient beings could survive under these circumstances. As he moved through the compartments, accompanied by Ensign Luiz, he was overwhelmed by the suffering these individuals lived with. The majority of what had formally been living spaces had become mortuaries. Twelve thousand Monorhans, a thousand from each tribe, had left the planet on these ships. Currently, less than half survived. Tuvok doubted whether half of those had the capacity to recover from their ailments. To better their odds, the surviving passengers had abandoned the most damaged parts of the vessel and had moved into the most livable compartments. Overcrowding and resource scarcity had put the qualifier "livable" into question. From what he could tell, however, the dead outnumbered the living on this ship.

At a minimum, hundreds of Monorhans pressed into each compartment he had visited. He couldn't accurately ascertain the numbers because of their emaciated condition: there might actually be far more than what he guessed. Most of the Monorhans were too weak to even acknowledge his presence. He had seen the hands reaching to touch his environmental suit in an effort to secure his attention, but none had the strength to do more than that. Vacant stares followed him wherever he walked. They no longer had the strength to express their misery through tears or wailing. The quiet, save for the rustle of bodies shifting position, permeated every square meter he covered.

Tuvok was uncertain whether *Voyager* could be of much use here. The stench of disease, the decaying flesh and lack of sanitation alone was unacceptable. Compounding the problem was the abundant radiation, starvation, and the limited quantity of potable water. Ensign Luiz did the best she could to assess which Monorhans could benefit most from medical treatment. The larger question was would they benefit at all? A few moments ago, Tuvok had found Luiz kneeling on the floor, hands pressed against her helmet, undoubtedly overwhelmed by the challenge.

"We've barely started and I'm almost out of hypos," she'd said.

Next to Harry, she'd been one of *Voyager*'s most inexperienced crew members when the ship had left Deep Space 9. Her growth curve had been steep. "Do what you can. Sometimes comfort in the face of death is the kindest gift one may offer."

Shortly after, she'd resumed her work, but the problem remained of how useful the away mission would be without more supplies.

Using his mind, he reached out to the Monorhans and sought to learn answers to his questions, the most pressing of which being how can we help you? What he discovered might have collapsed an emotional individual like Captain Janeway; for him, it was profoundly disturbing, though understandable.

All of these passengers had collectively lost their will to live. They had come to accept that death was a kinder fate than continuing to live under such despicable circumstances. He didn't want to violate the privacy of the passengers, but he did discover the barest outlines of their personal stories. How young ones died covered by ulcerated lesions, burning to death from the inside out owing to radiation poisoning, the suicides. Tuvok maintained his impassive demeanor when a Monorhan mind told him the story of the parent who killed her unborn child so as not to expose it to this misery. He saw before his eyes the hallucinations that led passengers to claw the hull plating until their raw fingers bled and broke. The psionic intensity reminded him of the time he spent with Lon Suder. Permitting such a breakdown to occur at this time would not be advisable, given the circumstances.

Tuvok employed all the techniques of discipline and control he had spent a lifetime perfecting so he could shut out emotional and physical suffering pouring into his mind. He succeeded in erecting impenetrable barriers. Even without complete understanding of the circumstances, he knew with certainty that the rations, water, and basic medical treatment *Voyager* offered would hardly suffice. Another solution would need to be devised.

Tuvok's attention had shifted away from the skeletal passengers when a gloved hand—obviously belonging to a member of the away team—reached around the edge of the partially ajar compartment door and tried forcing it open. None of the automated mechanisms on this ship appeared to be working, with all power diverted to life-support. Tuvok did not anticipate any in-person reports when the comm system would suffice.

Neelix squeezed through the doorway and waddled as quickly as he could in his environmental suit through the compartment. Two Monorhans—in better shape than the ones Tuvok had encountered so far—trailed behind him.

"Mr. Neelix," Tuvok said. "Report."

"I've found the leaders of the ship, Mr. Vulcan. The *rih-hara-tan*. Apparently, when things got ugly, the Monorhans sent them to the best-protected compartment, where they were bad off, but not as bad off as most of these passengers." Neelix gestured at the nearly dead Monorhans huddled together on all sides. "They've had enough to eat and drink so they're stronger than most of the passengers. These two are Xan and Tei." At the mention of their names, they bowed to Tuvok.

"You have retained their ability to communicate—to join minds?" Tuvok said.

Xan, whose clothes indicated to Tuvok that this was a male Monorhan, clicked his tongue rhythmically, then said, "We have, though many of our people are too weak to initiate the bond."

"If you would, Xan, help me identify how best we can serve your people," Tuvok said.

"It would be my honor to be in your service," Xan said with another deep, respectful bow.

Neelix rubbed his hands together, his eyes glowing with enthusiasm. "The other *rih* have strong abilities as well, Mr. Vulcan. And they are eager to do whatever they can to help their own people."

"Gracious and noble benefactors," Tei began, the universal translator rendering her voice as high-pitched and feminine. "The All-Knowing Light must have guided your path to us and because of that mercy we will do whatever is required to repay our debt to you."

Tuvok was struck by their regal bearing, even in these miserable surroundings. A more dramatic counterpoint to the conniving *rih* Sem wasn't possible. He reached out ever so slightly with his psionic abilities and found no hint of treachery. *Voyager* had been correct in coming to their aid. He excused himself and Neelix from the *rih*'s presence and took the Talaxian aside to talk privately. "How would you propose that we address their resource needs while considering our own limitations?" Tuvok asked Neelix.

"Ensign Tariq can take the *rih-hara-tan* back to *Voyager*, where they can receive more comprehensive medical treatment," Neelix said. "In total, there are six *rih* and six who are in training. None of them weigh enough to matter. Tariq can make a few supply runs while the *rih* are being treated. Might be able to make a dent in the needs around here that way."

Tuvok raised an eyebrow, communicating his doubt. A fleet of Starfleet shuttles loaded to capacity with supplies would hardly suffice. Neelix, while idealistic, had to be pragmatic enough to realize this.

"I know, I know—they need more than we can give

them," Neelix said, pushing aside Tuvok's concerns with a hand wave. "But I thought that we might be able to help them the way we helped the Caatati—provide them with some bare-bones technology so they take care of themselves until they can reach home."

Tuvok considered Neelix's proposal. It had merit but might not be feasible given current constraints. Ensign Luiz, he knew, would be grateful to be given the chance to be useful. He glanced at Xan and Tei and decided the other option—doing nothing—offended his sensibilities more. He instructed Neelix to take his suggestion to Lieutenant Torres and, contingent on the engineer's response, authorized him to accompany Ensign Tariq and the *rih-hara-tan* back to *Voyager* for medical treatment.

As he walked with Neelix to meet the other *rih,* Tuvok resumed calculating how to distribute what few supplies they had brought. Among those who were capable of eating, he estimated that they had enough to provide each with half a ration bar—about twenty-five percent of the metabolic energy required to fuel a body for a day. The alternative would be identifying those who would most benefit from nutrition and allowing them to have larger portions. Logic favored the latter choice, yet he, an outsider, should not be making such determinations on behalf of a people not his own. He would prefer to follow the directives of the Monorhan leaders—the *rih-hara-tan*—allowing them to make the ultimate decisions. Neelix was correct in his view that helping the leaders would ultimately help their fellow sufferers.

Moments later, his combadge chirped. Torres had a workable suggestion for a portable, self-powered replicator, so Tariq and Neelix would be off to *Voyager* within the next ten minutes. Tuvok consented to Neelix's plan and then resumed his work, since it appeared he no longer needed to meet the remaining *rih-hara-tan*. At least progress had been made.

It wasn't appropriate for him to become personally invested in the outcome of the away mission, save in how it impacted *Voyager*. Maintaining objective distance was critical. But he would rest more peacefully should Neelix's efforts prove to be successful. His combadge signaled again.

"Torres to Tuvok."

"Go ahead, Lieutenant."

"I've got an idea how to get this ship moving again, but I'd like to run it past you first."

Tuvok heard the mischievous undercurrent in B'Elanna's voice. She was about to propose something dangerous. Neelix and the *rih* would be fine without his further involvement. B'Elanna, on the other hand . . . "I'll be right there."

Behaving like a damn fool was part of the joy of being Tom. Only a fool would blatantly ignore common sense and willingly throw himself into the most dangerous circumstances of his life without a clue of how to get out of them. But such idiocy was, in fact, Tom's present reality.

Suspended inside the goo-filled, egg-shaped capsule, he attempted to familiarize himself with the controls as he waited for the next spore race to begin. The term "controls" was a loose definition. Beyond a waist-high filament, there wasn't much to understand. Tom ascertained that he was supposed to hold on to the filament. He supposed that the goo surrounding him would cushion him from any major blows or prevent the liquid's pressure from wiping out someone with his physiology; he could even breathe through the gel, which weirded him out more than had slipping through the semi-permeable membranous exterior into the gel. And the liquid—Tom wasn't sure exactly what he was racing through, but it sure as hell wasn't water. Up close, it appeared to be more like an infinite number of irregularly shaped spheres of various transparent hues adhering together to act as a liquid.

A flashing light inside the party chamber drew his attention and Tom wondered what it might be. Within seconds, he discovered the capsule began churning toward the party chamber. *Back off! Back off!* he said aloud, though his viscous surroundings absorbed all the sound. The capsule stopped. *This thing is thought-guided,* he realized. The nervous realization made him wary about letting his thoughts drift as they typically did when he was piloting. Not exactly the best time to daydream, he decided.

As piloting went, this was the real deal. None of the usual button pushing, advanced algorithmic calculations, or endless hours of staring at monotonous starscape applied. This run was about Tom going *fast.* The minute he'd climbed into his racing capsule, he'd moved beyond adrenaline into a whole new level of high. It was raw and Tom loved it. He would coax this vessel into total compliance with his will.

The capsule hovering across from him was occupied by an alien that had more in common with a moss-colored feather than any living, breathing creature Tom had seen. He wasn't sure the creature had *limbs.* Periodically, he needed to remember that he was playing in the pandimensional leagues—not like a bunch of shuttle jockeys hanging out at Yaga III racing for black-market moonshine or pleasure holoprograms. Out of curiosity, he flicked his index finger against the transparent gel surrounding him. The clear material spread like oozing syrup, then rebounded back into position. *Must be some kind of polymer,* he concluded. *Or not. And this is what will keep me from being drowning beneath dozens of meters of water.* Tom sighed, recalling that not even a half hour ago, he'd *wanted* this chance. And if he were being totally honest, he still wanted it. Simply put, the odds that he'd end up smashed against the floor resembling one of Neelix's leola root goulashes had gone up drastically. Tom had done some stupid things in his life but this, he conceded, was near the top of the list.

In private moments in the dark of their quarters, B'Elanna, playing counselor, had accused him on several occasions of playing a role, cultivating a screw-up, goof-off persona as a way of compensating for his childhood father issues. She knew this, she explained, because she took a similar approach to dealing with her psychological baggage. "You can't disappoint them if they don't expect much" had been her wise observation one night as she curled her body against him. "But I know who you really are." During moments of self-doubt he often recalled that conversation because it buoyed his confidence. Of course, in his more cynical moods he'd reject B'Elanna's words on the basis that intimacy tended to make B'Elanna philosophical and sentimental. He doubted, however, that B'Elanna would explain his current circumstances as role playing. She'd just call him an ass and wash her hands of him.

:*Nodes on approach:* a silky voice whispered to Tom's mind. :*Prepare to launch in ten seconds:*

As the countdown got under way, Tom wrapped the filament around his hand. Off to starboard, he saw the two black-red orbs streaking toward them.

:*Launch:*

Instinct took over. The ongoing dialogue in his head between B'Elanna, his father, and all the other voices who represented his doubts, fears, and triumphs ceased. Pure intuition told him at what angle he needed to approach the node.

Tom loved speed, the weight of the forces pressing his body against the rear of the capsule. He steadily increased acceleration until the surrounding liquid blurred into rippling lights shooting beside him like meteor showers. On approach to the spore, the membranous dome stretched and the curve flattened out. Tom accelerated, the dome flattened further. The bubbles trailing behind the spore seemed close enough that he could reach out and pop one. He flew alongside the node, matching its speed with the capsule. When he reached the proper distance, he thought, *Capture node.* The capsule shuddered. Tom never blinked. He held his breath for the space of an eternal second. A pseudopod-like extension shot out from in front of him, touched the edge of the node, and affixed itself with rubbery POP.

There! The pseudopod thinned out, becoming taut as fishing line when Tom steered the capsule into the node's wake. Like a harness on a resistant horse, Tom focused on maneuvering the capsule with the node, not against its momentum. A split-second break in concentration sent the capsule bouncing erratically side-to-side across the wake; the gel squeezed Tom's limbs until he groaned aloud from the strain. Refusing to yield, Tom dug deep and found focus. He recaptured control and forced the capsule to steady out. His muscles unclenched. *Now to make this baby go where I want it to,* he thought, salivating at the challenge. He discovered by shifting his weight from side to side (even up and down, though how that was possible, Tom couldn't fathom) that the node shifted direction slightly. Experimenting with the technique a few times yielded results. He'd licked the first challenge. The next was before him: the obstacle course. Excitement coursed through him. None of this would be worth much if he ended up losing. Tom knew he had to win or die trying. Feeling confident in his node-control abilities, he risked a side look over at his competitor. Damn it all if that silly-looking creature didn't appear to be several kilometers ahead of him!

He'd have to close the distance through the field of craggy, rocklike solids. How long had it been since he'd piloted a small craft through an asteroid field—maybe the Academy. How different could this be, even though it was liquid instead of space? At these speeds, with fluid gurgling around the capsule, he focused on the terrain ahead the best he could. Calculating the distance between the capsule and the spore, Tom was able to figure out how much clearance he needed to make his way around the required chunks without colliding. He blessed his extraordinary spatial abilities (yes, he'd seen the test scores) because he was capable, with a glance, of plotting an efficient course. *In five . . . four . . . three . . .* Tom swooped into action, whipping in and out of the chunks, easing his speeds around the steepest curves, revving up when he had a smooth stretch. A quick look revealed it wasn't enough—the other capsule maintained its edge!

The deafening shrieks of the capsule streaking through water became white noise. Tom would not be deterred. He took the capsule into an arc above a chunk the size of *Voyager* and then down again, up over another, down beneath another, creating an effortless motion wave. The rhythm of his heart and his breathing synchronized with the capsule's subtle back-and-forth modulations. Instinctually, he knew how to navigate the remaining few seconds of the field. He retrieved from memory the race he'd observed from the party window. The globules with the fronds came next. Not much of a challenge with those except to avoid steering too close. Otherwise, he would take the shortest pathway at the highest speeds to assure that he gained enough on his competitor that he wouldn't lose.

Coming out of the field, he had caught up to the other capsule, now he needed to pull ahead. He counted at least four globule clusters. The up-and-down wave navigation had worked for him thus far so he saw no reason to change tactics now. With more room to maneuver, he gunned his speed, accelerating the capsule to a velocity that he knew, from the ache in his bones, he wouldn't be able to maintain for much longer. In and out, back and forth: the capsule swooped between the globules, the fronds waving flaccidly. Light and shadow, red and brown blurs streamed past him, through the patches of coral tubes and out again. He held his body rigid, his muscles strained to push back against the forces threatening to smash him. Pressure built behind his eyes; sharp pinpricks of pain burst and Tom's view suddenly became red. The logical voice in the back of his brain insisted on reminding him that theoretically, it wasn't possible for a mere human to move this fast. Tom refused to allow logic to interfere with what needed to be done. He'd taken the lead in the race. He wouldn't lose—not now.

Something nagged at him, though, something about the end of the race. Trying to remain composed and in control took all of his resources so he had little brainpower to devote to figure out what it was he'd forgotten. Probably a niggling nuisance type of thing. Up over the last chunk—each one larger than the last—he increased his speed to the maximum that he dared attempt. The muscles in his arms and legs quivered in painful spasms. Tom took risks, pushing to the limit of his capacity, but he knew when to stop. A new energy surged through him when he recognized that he'd almost made it. Then, through the red fog, he saw the small opening at the bottom of the course.

I'm coming in too fast.

At this speed, he could make only minimal adjustments to the degree of his turn. If he had a prayer of shooting straight in, he'd have to make more than minimal adjustments. Tom forced the capsule out of straight vertical into a more horizontal approach. What had been horrific pressure before ratcheted up another notch. Mentally, Tom held steady; his arms, cemented to his sides, felt like they'd be yanked out of their sockets at any moment. His teeth chattered hard, but he maintained his focus.

His brain registered that his competitor was gaining on him, but Tom couldn't let that egg him on. As soon as he dove into the opening, he'd accelerate with everything he had left. Now, he wanted to live another ten seconds. The pressure from the increased depth squeezed the node head. Into the opening—

The pulpy blue-purple walls were unexpectedly narrow. Without warning, the walls compressed—tightening, then releasing—nearly severing the connection between the capsule and the node. The competing capsule bumped against Tom's and nearly sent him spinning out of control. Sweat erupted on Tom's forehead and drizzled into his eyes. The tunnel's rhythm of compression and release continued unabated; each compression reduced Tom's visual contact with the node. He relied on his gut to know where the node was in the tunnel ahead of him. He refused to panic.

Almost . . . almost through, he thought. Between the depth, the liquid, and the compressions, pressure inside the capsule mounted to an unendurable level. Not even a scream could be ripped from his throat, if he could only hold on . . .

The capsule twisted back and forth in an agitating motion. Whatever pretense Tom had made of holding on to the contents of his stomach ended. The raw intuition that made him an exceptional pilot knew the exit was close at hand. He could hold on, he knew he could! Counting down, *five . . . four . . . three . . .* Shooting out of the tunnel back into the open . . .

And he was ahead!

Three quick inhalations and the node shot across the finish line. Tom ordered the pseudopod to release, sending the capsule spinning around like a propeller. Exhaustion overtook adrenaline: Tom's head flopped forward into his chest, then slammed back between his shoulders with such force that stars burst before his eyes. He needed to stop, but scrambled thoughts combined with pain made it difficult to regain control. The capsule shot right past the party chamber and careened straight into a minuscule hole in a barrier directly in front of him.

All went black for the space of several heartbeats.

Tom knew he was alive and conscious, but he had no idea where he was or how he fit into such a teeny space. The capsule emerged out of liquid into air, still spinning around with momentum that even a speed maniac like Tom was uncomfortable with. When the capsule slowed to an irregular wobble, he checked out his surroundings. Sharp yellowing mounds rose up on each side of the domed space—

Wait. Those are teeth. What the—?

A most horrible gacking noise reverberated around him. A projectile of tangled sticky hair exploded through the air behind him and hurtled straight into the capsule. Tom closed his eyes and braced for impact. With a juicy thwack, the capsule adhered to the pellet. The sour, acidy fumes of partial digestion penetrated the capsule's permeable membrane.

Tom cracked open one eye as the hair ball emerged from between sharp, pointy canines, watched by the yellowing eye of Kol's mangy cat, Felix. When the nest of fur and mushy, chewed foodstuffs crashed into the floor, the capsule went with it and exploded on impact, sending Tom Paris flying headfirst toward the ground. His skull hit with a crunch, rendering him unconscious.

Chapter 7

With Seven standing at his left shoulder, Chakotay sat in the captain's chair on the bridge, watching the viewscreen. The "gash," as they'd come to call the phenomenon formerly known as the microsingularity or the rift, filled the center of the screen. Waterfalls of white-blue light cascaded over both sides of the gash. *Voyager* had traveled as far as she could without risking entrapment by the phenomenon. Ayala had scanned the region, discovering, not surprisingly, that the space-time fabric had become riddled with abnormalities that appeared only hours old. Seven appeared to be the only one of the crew unsurprised by how quickly the metamorphosis of the region was occurring. Ensign Knowles had become exceptionally twitchy in the last twenty minutes. Navigation back to regular space would be challenging. But for now, *Voyager* would wait.

"The probe is ready for launch," Seven said. "At your word, Commander."

The risk they'd taken by remaining in Monorhan space came down to this moment. "Launch probe," Chakotay said.

Seven stepped away from her observation position and

took a seat at the engineering console. She tapped a sequence of commands into the control panel.

A trail of yellow-red flame streaked across the viewscreen, aimed directly for the gash. Chakotay never moved his eyes from the torpedo casing bearing the probe, as it drew closer, ever closer, to its target. Mentally, he counted down the time he knew it would take to enter the gash and activate. *Ten . . . nine . . . eight . . .*

"Activating separation sequence," Seven said. "Probe will detach . . . now."

The torpedo casing fell away, disappearing offscreen as the probe veered up and away from the edge, executing a perfect arc above the gash before plunging downward and vanishing amid the cascading lights.

"Probe initiation sequence under way," Seven said. "We should start receiving transmissions within thirty seconds."

Chakotay sat, immobile, hands threaded together on his lap, watching intently. The atmosphere on the bridge vibrated with the crew's expectations. They knew the stakes. Elongated seconds elapsed. Not a sound disturbed the quiet. When, by Chakotay's count, at least sixty seconds had passed, he ordered Seven to report.

"The probe has yet to begin transmitting," she said, her soft, low-pitched voice quavering almost imperceptibly.

"Give it a bit longer. We've never encountered phenomena like this and it might not work exactly to our expectations."

"Yes, Commander," Seven said tersely, and resumed tapping commands into the workstation computer interface.

Chakotay felt awash in sympathy for Seven. She had proposed this mission that Chakotay suspected many crew members wouldn't have undertaken given the chance to object. As captain of *Voyager*, he alone bore responsibility for the consequences of that mission. He wouldn't be able to look his crew members in the eye and tell them he had done all he could to assure their well-being if he hadn't tried to recover the Doctor.

Another minute elapsed. Then another. Seven's fingers still flew over the console with frantic speed.

Chakotay tried to resist the doubts besetting him, but he found them difficult to ignore the longer their wait continued. Knowles unspoken concerns about returning to normal space were justified. *Voyager* would need to be on its way as soon as possible. Taking a deep breath, he prepared to order Seven to abandon the probe when he heard her assault on the console stop. He twisted to look at her. Her eyes opened wide, sparkling with excitement that prompted Chakotay to smile. "Seven?"

"The probe is transmitting data," Seven said.

A cheer rose up from the bridge.

Leaning back into the captain's chair, Chakotay's shoulders slackened, as some of the considerable weight he'd been carrying since he'd taken on the mantle of command dissipated. He felt like a teenager again, approaching the Elders with his request to undertake the rituals that would prove him to be an adult in the eyes of the tribe. Having passed the first test, he knew the second would be more difficult. The probe would endure the conditions within the gash for ninety minutes. For the moment, though, this small victory felt very, very satisfying.

Rising from his chair, he took two steps before pausing to address the bridge crew. "I don't need to tell you all that we have a brief window in which to find the Doctor. Seven, please contact the away team and let them know our time frame. I want them back here before the probe goes dark."

"Yes, Commander," Seven said.

"Once the search-and-rescue operation is completed, we will set our course for regular space and beyond that, the Alpha Quadrant. I'll be in—" He hesitated, uncertain as to which possessive he should use. In his mind, this was still Kathryn's ship. He was, however, the captain. Remembering his recent visit to engineering, when B'Elanna had questioned whose ship this was—his or Kathryn Janeway's—he realized that now, more than ever, *he* needed to provide leadership. "I'll be in my ready room after I'm done meeting our guests in sickbay."

His next challenge: not one, but twelve *rih-hara-tan* and *rih* in training Neelix had brought aboard. When Sem had attempted her mischief with *Voyager*'s gel packs, he had witnessed firsthand what a psionically gifted Monorhan was capable of. The idea of bringing aboard a dozen individuals who theoretically had the ability to wreak havoc on *Voyager* during the sensitive probe operation made Chakotay nervous. He'd already ordered Rollins to maintain extra security around sickbay until the *rih* returned to their ship. He stepped into the turbolift.

Chakotay prided himself on keeping an open mind about places or persons he didn't know. Growing up in a unique human subculture had taught him what it felt like to be judged by strangers—especially those outside the Federation who knew nothing of their history. His desire to come to a greater understanding of the inhabitants of the galaxy had been, in part, one of his motivations for joining Starfleet.

But Chakotay wasn't a fool either. He was fond of his great-aunt's adage "Fool me once, shame on you. Fool me twice, shame on me." Such was his thought as he entered sickbay to meet the Monorhan *rih*. As needy and vulnera-

ble as the Monorhans might appear to be, Chakotay knew
from painful experience that such a perception was inac-
curate.

He had been on the bridge with Captain Janeway
when Sem, a *rih* sent by the Monorhan planetary government as an advisor, had forced her way onto the bridge
during a dangerous operation and tried to interfere. Her
ability to manipulate the gel packs was direr than any virus
the packs might have contracted from one of Neelix's
creations. Furthermore, Sem had violated one of her
culture's most formidable taboos: she'd initiated a sexual
relationship with her *shi-harat*. Chakotay was not so naïve
that he believed all *rih* to be as black-hearted as Sem; he
was not so trusting to believe otherwise.

Sickbay's doors parted, admitting Chakotay to the
crowded treatment area.

"Captain on deck," said Ensign Juarez, a medic, as
he walked past a biobed where she was treating two skeletal *rih*.

"At ease," Chakotay said immediately. Looking around
the room, he found his new "doctor" engrossed in what
appeared to be surgery on an unconscious Monorhan.
Since crewmen were passing in and out of her work area,
he assumed her procedure wasn't too delicate. "Lieutenant Nakano, can you give me a report while you
work?"

In the surgical bay, Yuko glanced up from an instrument tray and waved him over with a gloved hand. When
dealing with unknown aliens, medical staff often took additional precautions—like gloves—lest an unexpected
contaminant cause problems for either *Voyager*'s crew or
the alien. "A minor procedure to excise a pocket of infection. We can talk while we work, Captain."

When Chakotay was situated at her elbow, Yuko began

explaining the various medical undertakings that her team had completed since Neelix and the *rih* had come aboard.

"Have you seen anything I should be aware of?" Chakotay asked in a tone that let Nakano, a former Maquis under his command, know, without him having to state it explicitly, that he had concerns.

Nakano fused the incision closed, administered an anti-infective hypo, then stripped off her red surgical gown and gloves and promptly tossed them in the replicator. "Quite the opposite. Naomi Wildman causes more problems during her checkups than these *rih* do. They are polite to the point of obsequiousness. I've heard more versions of 'thank you' today than I've heard in four years."

Looking around sickbay, Chakotay saw nothing that negated Nakano's observations. "Interesting. Keep up the good work, Lieutenant."

As he passed by a biobed, a *rih* reached out and touched his sleeve. Chakotay paused, and acknowledged the Monorhan with a polite nod of the head.

"You are the captain?" came a treble voice, accompanied by the subvocalizations he'd come to associate with the Monorhans.

"May I be of assistance?" Chakotay said.

"I am Tei, the eldest *rih* among all the *rih-hara-tan*," she said. "Your *haran* has aided in healing our ailments. We are forever in your debt."

What struck Chakotay about this *rih*—as opposed to say, Sem—was the utter guilelessness in her expressions and tones. He was reminded of the holy women of Teplos III who devoted their lives to tending the shrines of their ancestors and pursuing pious endeavors. "I wish we could do more for your people—like transport you home. But our capacity is limited at this time."

"You have already returned our lives to us." She bent

over and took Chakotay's hand in her own thick, heavily bandaged appendage. "I give you a life oath, on behalf of the other *rih* and all our *haran,* that should you require our aid, we will offer it."

Chakotay contemplated Tei's promise as he entered the turbolift; her words remained with him as he dropped into the chair behind Kathryn's desk in her ready room. He toyed with a favorite coffee mug bearing a graphic of a dog. Kathryn must have used it during her last visit to this room. Glancing inside, he discovered coffee stains. He used to wonder why she didn't just throw her empty mugs into the recycler—he'd asked her about it once. She'd told him that she liked having objects in her life that had history, because it gave her a sense of connection to events and people. Sitting here, holding an item that linked him to her, he understood exactly what she meant.

He glanced at the chrono: seventy minutes to go. Waiting was the difficult part, and he had no doubt that the next hour or so would be the longest part of an already long week.

At a future time, when Chakotay reflected on his days as *Voyager*'s acting captain, he would realize how dramatically he'd underestimated how long this hour would turn out to be.

The Doctor asked three soldiers before he found one who knew of Balim's whereabouts. Apparently Lia's chosen mate socialized little with the troops. The Doctor believed he knew the reason for the soldier's reticence: he likely didn't want to be found out.

Balim had last been seen leaving the supper fires and following the switchback trail up to the overlook where the Doctor had watched the battle with Iga. It was believed that Balim had been sent for reconnaissance purposes, since the overlook had the most expansive view in the area.

The watch patrol numbers were doubled as evening came on. Constant vigilance against a surprise attack was required. As the Doctor made his way to the trailhead, he had been met at each tension-filled checkpoint he passed through with questions: Will we be attacked tonight? Can the general lead us? The Doctor admonished them to be wary but to avoid letting fear control them, for otherwise mistakes would be made. His years with Kathryn Janeway had taught him the importance of maintaining composure in the face of adversity. He had been struck, as he reassured the soldiers, by their youth. Indeed, as he asked their ages, few had reached five years.

The long, twisting path up to the overlook gave the Doctor plenty of time to think about Lia, Vivia, and his mission. Regardless of whether Balim was the Light, the Doctor couldn't stand around idly while Lia remained in the thrall of a Nacene Exile. Lia's life would be in danger, and so would the lives of those who served with her. Yet there was no denying that Lia loved Balim. The Doctor couldn't readily dismiss her feelings; he had no right to tell her who to love. Conflict raged within him every step up the hill. No good resolution presented itself.

Trudging up the final stretch to the top, the Doctor once again longed for his holomatrix: no sore muscles and certainly no fatigue. The uncomfortable tingling had returned as well, though not as powerful as before, affirming what he already suspected to be true.

Rounding the last corner, he saw Balim, an ill-defined silhouette, standing at the top of the trail, blocking his passage. Walking up through the soldier's shadow, the Doctor noticed upon drawing closer that Balim carried no visible weapons and wore no armor. Clad in the artless tunic of a peasant worker, Balim appeared harmless enough—on the surface.

Closer observation revealed muscular arms and shoulders; Balim could snap a neck like a twig. His lithe body hinted at speed and agility in running or fighting. He lacked any visible symptom of the radiation sickness that plagued virtually every soldier the Doctor had encountered. *That should have tipped me off,* the Doctor thought. *Traitor.*

"I've expected you," Balim said. "You're a long way from home, creature of light."

His words had the melodious, sonorous roundness the Doctor recalled from their encounter on the battlefield. He probably could sing a competent aria, given the chance.

"Exosia isn't exactly next door, Master Balim." The Doctor stopped walking when he came close enough to look Balim directly in the eye. The previous night's waxing crescent moon had been replaced by the more effulgent light of the first quarter, providing them enough illumination to see by. "I'm here representing Lia's interests."

"Are you sure you don't mean Vivia's?" Balim countered. "You're here to stop me. Call out to Vivia, tell her you've found her archenemy so she can send a cadre of her followers to capture me."

The confession startled the Doctor; he paused, as if struck by a physical blow. *So you are the Light.* He needed only to stop the Light to fulfill his promise to Vivia. *But Lia . . .*

"You should be confused, man of light. You're on the wrong side; you don't see it yet."

"I'm not confused. I'm concerned. What Lia sees in you beyond your handsome face eludes me, but she loves you and I need to understand why she cares so much before I make any decisions about Vivia. You've taken Ocampan form and seduced a vital military leader—that can't be an arbitrary decision on your part."

"The way you explain it makes me sounds so calculating," Balim said, tilting his head thoughtfully. "Believe me when I say I had no intention of involving myself in the affairs of this world."

"You're not denying you're Nacene?"

"If you don't deny you're photonic."

"I've seen what your kind has done to the Ocampans. You reduce them to being dependent children—" Recalling Tanis and the other Ocampans on the array, the Doctor continued, "—or you exploit their psionic abilities."

Turning his back on the Doctor, Balim walked back onto the outlook, gazing out over the battlefield. "Suspiria wasn't always as you found her," Balim said thoughtfully. "Of course, you'll learn that for yourself, so expending energy to persuade you now is a waste of time for us both."

Indignation welled up within the Doctor. How dare this Nacene sound self-congratulatory and so lackadaisical about matters of critical importance! He stormed over to where Balim stood. "That little display on the battlefield—the orb of burning light is what the troops are calling it. Quite theatrical and quite nearly impossible for an Ocampan to sustain such a display of telekinetic powers without help." Remembering Kes's suffering at Tanis's hands because of Suspiria, he could barely contain the impulse to squeeze the life out of the handsome form the Nacene had taken. He took several steps toward Balim, fists raised. "Why can't you leave the Ocampa well enough alone?"

Smiling sympathetically, Balim gently pushed the Doctor's fists down until they hung at his sides. "There is an empathic connection between the Nacene and Ocampa that the Exiles have failed to find elsewhere. What began as harmless interest became, for some of my kindred, far more deadly."

"Some of your kindred? Mestof's wizards?" The Doctor recalled that *two* of them had been taken into custody. "I should have realized that only a Nacene can effectively *contain* another Nacene. Lia is very impressed with your strategy."

"My purpose here is to repair, the best I can, the damage the other Exiles have done."

"How convenient that you can manipulate Lia to accomplish those objectives. You know physically she's been compromised within an inch of her life, but what does another menial life matter—"

Balim drew up to his full height, towering over the Doctor. *How dare you!*

The power of Balim's voice in his mind sent tremors coursing throughout the Doctor's body. He shrank away, anticipating the forthcoming assault.

I could kill you with a thought. He glanced at a towering evergreen behind them and narrowed his eyes. The tree shriveled into a desiccated corpse of singed limbs and browned needles.

"That you haven't *accidentally* slipped off this ledge," he nodded at the overlook, "should tell you all you need to understand about my intentions." Balim angled his face to reveal a deadly calm visage, the operative word being "deadly." "But what about you, man of light? Call Vivia. Tell her you've found the Light. I will not stop you." He removed a coil of rope from his utility belt and tossed it at the Doctor's feet. "Here. Bind me. I won't resist."

His mind racing, the Doctor's eyes flickered between Balim and the coil of rope. *He's trying to trick me. This is my chance.* Voyager *needs me!* Another voice argued for prudence. *Wait. Hear him out.* Indecision gripped him. The coil of rope lay untouched at his feet. He kicked it aside.

"I thought as much. You have honor." Balim said huskily.

"I care about Lia," the Doctor said.

"As do I."

"Prove it."

Turning away from the Doctor, Balim strode toward the ledge.

The Doctor, nervous about Balim's motives, followed a few cautious paces behind. He breathed easier when he observed a natural shelf eroded in the side of the outlook that he believed was Balim's intended destination. The view from the shelf would allow them both to keep watch over the encampment while they talked.

Dropping down onto the ground, Balim rested his back against the rock behind him and extended his long legs out in front of him, his feet nearly dangling over the edge. The Doctor sat cross-legged beside him.

"I joined the Exiles in their fight against Vivia and those like her because I believed that my kind deserved more than slavery. I don't believe the strings need us—they existed before us and they will exist after us. What they need is to be left alone instead of slavishly attended to." Balim picked at and sorted the pebbles on the ground beside him. "The truths that would liberate my people, I believed, would be found Outside."

"Have you found the truths that would persuade Vivia to relent?"

"I am on the path—I spent time in the Q Continuum and was taught a great deal. My fellow Exiles, however, have been useless. Over time they have become self-indulgent, loving only the pursuit of pleasure and the exercise of their powers. Look around you, man of Light"—he held his arm out in front of him, indicating the land spreading out below—"and witness the handiwork of the Nacene."

Balim's sharp sarcasm prompted the Doctor to wince. "So this isn't your doing?"

"My purpose in coming to Ocampa was to repair the damage done by my kind," Balim said, gesticulating with his hands. "Instead—"

The Doctor anticipated Balim's explanation—the immemorial story. "Boy meets girl. You found Lia."

With a deep sigh, Balim nodded. "Lia has powers, man of light. Exceptional powers. You've seen what the Ocampa are capable of in your time. Lia is like the one in your memories." He raked his long fingers through his dark hair. "I focus her abilities, but I don't give her more than what is already there. I fear, however, that I may have unleashed capacities in her that she will have a difficult time controlling." The sculpted, angular lines of his face imbued him with sternness; the moonlight shadowed and grayed his features. "Her best hope of surviving this war is with me by her side. Guiding her. Preventing her from further damaging herself."

"How do I know you have Lia's best interests at heart?" the Doctor said, feeling cornered. "Perhaps sending you away would be the best way to help Lia. Why should I believe anything you say?"

Balim shrugged. "Believe me. Don't believe me. But know this: you are disposable to Vivia. Even if you give her what she wants—me—she'll toss you aside. The strings are all that matter to her. Forget about returning to your ship."

As much as he wanted to believe otherwise, Balim's words had a ring of truth to the Doctor. He had witnessed

Vivia's single-minded devotion—even fanaticism—toward her duty. If Balim was correct about Vivia, the Doctor may have thrown his lot in with the wrong Nacene. He said nothing; instead, he chose to hear Balim out.

"My goal is Lia's goal: to save her people. To that end, whatever needs to be done will be done." Balim's voice rose a note in pitch. "Displaying her powers before Baron Var nearly killed her! Until that time I had aided her from afar, but circumstances forced me to intervene directly *to save her life.*" He clenched one hand into a fist and punched it into the opposite palm, then again and again until the Doctor wondered if the metacarpals would break. "As it is, I know the war is lost. Ocampa will die and Lia . . ." His voice trailed off and he exhaled heavily. Balim's shoulders drooped and he climbed to his feet, heading back onto the bluff. Stopping in front of a mature mountain birch, he rested his hand on the trunk and faced the dark forest.

The Doctor watched Balim for a long moment, listening to the choruses of chirping insects, the faraway gurgle of a streamlet meandering toward the lake. He tried reconciling what he believed to be true, based on Vivia's representation of the facts, with what Balim had told him and came up with only one conclusion. He approached Balim and said to his back, "I can't say for certain whether I believe you or Vivia—the Nacene are nothing if not Machiavellian—but what I know is Lia. Or at least I think I do. She knows her own mind. I don't believe she is easily deceived—even by a Nacene. I choose to believe and trust her love for you."

Balim looked back over his shoulder, his cheeks wet with tears.

The Doctor's eyes widened with surprise. "You love her."

"I didn't plan to. It was a complication that I neither

wanted nor sought. As much as I fought my feelings, my efforts came to nothing."

"That tends to be the way love works," the Doctor said wryly.

"Her willingness to die for her people, her selfless devotion to freedom—to their cause—taught me more about what I needed to do if I were to help my people than any experience in tens of thousands of years." He turned toward the Doctor. "I would do anything for her. *Anything.*"

Balim had a misty, faraway look that a well-schooled romantic like the Doctor recognized. *Well, this is a problem,* the Doctor thought. *How can I turn Balim over to Vivia's custody when his primary motives are not only altruistic, but compelled by love? I cannot betray love!*

Of all the evolutions and enhancements in the Doctor's programming in the past four years, few had left greater impact on his matrix than an increased understanding of love and relationships did. Hadn't he experienced what it was like to love and to lose love? To disregard that life lesson and turn Balim over to Vivia would make him a traitor to his deeply held conviction that true love should be protected and defended. The problem in his time facing Vivia (and the universe, for that matter) would have to be solved another way. "If Vivia wants you, she will have to find you herself," the Doctor said at last.

Balim's lips parted, as if he was about to speak, but he paused. His eyes narrowed, abruptly shifting toward a place over the Doctor's shoulder.

The Doctor twisted around to see what had captured Balim's attention.

The forest surrounding the basin was aflame!

"Mestof?"

"His troops are here, but they did not torch the trees." Balim shook his head. "Lia did. I—"

"Stop her!" the Doctor said, urging Balim on. "You must save her!"

Balim vanished. A gust of wind rushed out of the forest and into the basin.

"Tom, wake up."

Deep inside a delightful dream about B'Elanna, Tom ignored the annoying voice. He wished the voice would shut up and let him enjoy himself. Hadn't he earned the right to luxuriate in a little fantasy? After all, he'd won the spore race. *Wow. Node racing was amazing,* he mused in his half-awake state. Granted, things became a little gross at the end when he'd hurled the contents of his stomach into the gel and the hair ball . . . Tom didn't want to think about the hair ball.

It occurred to him that the whole race and pan-universal party central must have been inside the tabby cat's body. *I must have been DNA sized,* he thought. What a radical twist on the usual party. Shrink to the size of a chromosome and come hang out inside an animal's insides, maybe take a spin through the circulatory system. The topography made more sense: capillaries, cells, chunks of food, plasma. Better than any science class he'd had.

While it lasted, it was the ultimate rush. He could die tomorrow and say, with confidence, that he'd likely seen it all.

Inside the warm, floaty place he was drifting in, the rational Tom recalled, *Oh yeah I won the race so I could get the information about Kol. How'd that work out anyway?*

The call of real life was too strong to ignore.

Cautiously, he raised one eyelid—very slowly, then the

other. The bright overhead lights didn't hurt *too* much. Two blurry faces hovered over him. One was a stranger, but he recognized Harry from the floppy lock of black hair drooping over his forehead. The scabby crust over his mouth was gone because his lips were flapping about finding out where Kol was and—

Finding out where Kol was. Tom sat straight up and instantly regretted it.

"Take this," the stranger said in a tone that indicated that Tom would be wise not to argue.

"This" was a frosted glass filled to the brim with a foamy lime green liquid. *The voice was familiar . . . where have I heard it before . . . ?* Tom complied, instantly puckering and shuddering at the bitter taste. The almost immediate analgesic effect, however, removed all of his apprehensions. He gulped down the rest. "Where's Kol again?" Tom said, wiping his mouth on his sleeve.

"Pem helped him buy his way into a Trinity game at Fortis."

Now Tom realized where he knew that voice from. Whether he should be relieved or terrified, he wasn't sure. He turned to Q, who was smiling at Tom.

"Congratulations, Tommy. You set a new record! Who knew a human had it in him?"

Nearby, Tom saw q still clad in her school attire, and wondered aloud what the hell they were still doing here in Kol's dorm room at Q U. Felix yowled and coughed up another hair ball.

"You think you won that node race solo, flyboy?" she said, her mouth twisted into her patented sarcastic half-smile.

Tom protested, "I'm a damn good—"

"Pilot. I know. You've been babbling about that in your sleep for the past few minutes," q said, snapping her fingers. A clean outfit, at least as showy as the one Q had given him before the node race, appeared between her fingers. She thrust it into his lap.

Tom looked at the suit questioningly.

"Change," she ordered. "No way either of you will go to a high-class place like Fortis in *those* clothes. Q thinks he has an eye for high fashion, but he doesn't."

"I'm insulted, q," Q said.

"The whole Continuum knows it's your favorite delusion," she said.

The issue of the race still bothered Tom. Dammit, he'd worked hard! *"I* won that race."

"I'll grant you, for a human, you're competent," Q said. "But there's no way you could have raced a *Lazi* and survived without a little help from a Q."

He peeled off the stained suit jacket and undershirt and cast them aside. "I was in that capsule alone," Tom said.

Sitting back on her haunches, q rested her hands on her thighs and gave him a look that told Tom she thought he was the most dense creature in the universe. "Not in the capsule, flyboy, in the node." Her gaze flickered up and down his bare torso a few times, her smoldering violet eyes resting on his face. "Q tells me you're with some half-Klingon hellcat. Is that right?"

"Yes," Tom said, holding his cast-off undershirt against his chest.

"Does she share?" q asked.

Sitting there half-clothed, Tom suddenly felt violated and vulnerable. Ignoring her last comment, he said, "I'm not changing with you in here."

"Fine." Rolling her eyes, q snapped her fingers and disappeared.

Tom stood to remove his pants. "That—that—*q,* " he said, perturbed.

"She's a pill, that's for sure," Q said.

"So do I tell B'Elanna that q made a pass at you?" said Harry, who was gathering up Tom's soiled clothing.

"Harry—" Tom hated it when he received female attention that his friend had been seeking. In their early days on *Voyager*, more than a few of Harry's crushes had flirted with Tom. Out of loyalty, Tom had never reciprocated, though it rarely stopped the women from trying.

"Don't worry about it," Harry said. "I'm used to it by now. But I'm confident that once she sees past your superficial hotshot pilot charm, she'll fall for my superior intellect."

Q put a hand to his mouth, stifling laughter.

Tom ignored him. "Do I need to point out that she's a q? That's hardly a relationship that can last, Harry."

"Isn't she amazing? Turns out she came of her own volition. Q didn't send her."

"Harry," Tom said, most softly this time.

"I'm not stupid, Tom," Harry said. "I know I'm being an idiot; there's no realistic way I'm going to get involved with q. But I rather enjoy being an idiot where women are involved."

"In love with love?"

Harry paused, considering for a moment, then said, "Maybe."

"Okay then," Tom said. "I'll stop harassing you. You know I'm just looking out for your best interests, right?"

Harry smiled in reply.

q's voice echoed throughout the chamber. "Are you decent yet?"

"No, but he's dressed," Q said before Tom could answer.

She reappeared in a flash.

"I know what's in it for him," Tom said, nodding toward Q. "But what's in it for you, q?" He fastened the frogs on his tapestry jacket.

"Kol is my friend. I want him found and out of danger as much as anyone." q produced a mirror from an unseen pocket and held it in front of Tom.

"Very snappy, Mr. Paris," Q said.

Tom smoothed his jacket, straightened his lapels. "So what's next?"

"We go to Fortis," Harry said. "According to q, it's the ultimate interdimensional community for games of chance."

"A casino," Tom said.

"Yep," Harry said. "And Q's not coming."

"Why not? We can probably use all the help we can get."

"You don't get to question my decisions, Mr. Paris. I have other pressing concerns requiring my attention." Q rose from his spot on the carpet, making a show of brushing dust from his clothes. "See you soon, boys!" He snapped his fingers.

Once Q was gone, Harry looked cautiously from side to side, then said, "Q can't help us anyway."

"How is that even possible?" Tom said, disbelieving. He was, after all, a Q.

"Q got himself banned from Fortis because he cheats," q explained.

"I heard that," boomed a familiar voice. *"Allegedly cheats. They never proved anything."*

q turned a sour face toward the ceiling.

"So once we get to Fortis—is this gonna be another one of the Continuum's tests?" Tom asked q. "You going to toss us into a backroom game? Or better yet, use us as collateral?"

q snorted. "There's no way you'll get in without me there. Dirts—corporeals—like you two don't even qualify for the help. Before you get any ideas, flyboy, I'm running the show from here on out. You ready to play some games, boys?"

Tom still wasn't certain if this was the wisest move. He looked over at Harry, hoping to find solidarity, and discovered that his friend glowed like a warp core. The entranced expression indicated that Harry was deep in the throes of infatuation. q had Harry on a leash—no question. If Tom argued with q—which would be pointless anyway—he would do it alone. Having spent much of the past four years in the company of strong women, Tom recognized when it was futile to argue with them. "Okay then. Point the way."

q arched an eyebrow and snapped her fingers.

The fire had been extinguished by the time the Doctor reached the basin. A steady line of soldiers carried the enemy's dead to the south end of the basin, far away from the encampment, and piled them up. He'd nearly covered the full distance when the last corpse was tossed atop the heap and the bodies torched. The wind shifted northward, wafting the crematorium stench in his direction. In his lifetime aboard *Voyager,* the Doctor believed he had to have experienced worse than this, but what it was he couldn't recall at the moment. Those of his comrades who remained in camp hunched over campfires, leaning against the shoulders of their fellow fighters, ash smeared faces etched with exhaustion. He saw far too many bodies bearing the lily crest on makeshift biers, awaiting some semblance of a death rite. Many pairs of eyes followed him as he walked. A few called his name. He longed to tend their wounds and offer them comfort. He hated forcing them to wait. They had already sacrificed much.

When the Doctor approached Lia's tent, he discovered that an acolyte had set up several braziers piled with smoldering pungent incense and surrounded the tent with torches whose flames formed a pathway of dancing light. She circled the premises chanting the incantations that would allow Lia to enter the passages to the DeadLands. Inside, he found Lia unconscious on her cot, hair streaming out behind her as if she were a princess on a chaise. Balim, sober-faced, sat by her side and held her hand. The tent reeked of sweat and scorch.

"Mestof's men ambushed ours," Balim began his unemotional recitation. "The attack roused Lia. She left her bed with the intention of invoking a protection shield. She couldn't control her powers and instead set things afire."

"Have the healers seen her?"

Balim indicated that they had.

The Doctor studied Lia's vitals. Without proper equipment, he couldn't pronounce a certain diagnosis, though his medical instincts told him she was gravely ill. He searched the tent for any medical accoutrements that he might use to help Lia. "Can you help her?" he said finally.

"I'm afraid I might do more damage if I try," Balim said, smoothing her hair. "Her condition is grave. You're her only hope."

"I certainly don't have the tools I need to properly help her," the Doctor said. He sorted through a supply chest, setting aside jars of dried herbs, animal parts, and oils to be used in preparing medicine. It was only because of Kes that he had any hint of Ocampan healing in the first place. Being expected to provide expert medical care without proper equipment frustrated him endlessly. He was a doctor, not a replicator! The Doctor unburied a salve he believed would help her pain. He massaged the sweet-smelling ointment into the nerve endings at the base of her skull and into her filth-covered arms and hands. The ointment slowly took effect; Lia breathed easier, her body became slack, though her skin color remained waxen and pale.

Unlacing her torn tunic, the Doctor discovered mottled bruises and weeping blisters covering several broken ribs and her abdomen where she'd been struck by a burning tree limb. Her belly, swollen and hard, indicated internal bleeding. The Doctor touched her forehead, checked her pulse, and determined she ran a fever.

Balim looked at him questioningly.

The Doctor shook his head, offering him little hope. Closing his eyes, Balim rested his head on the edge of her cot, pressing her hand against his cheek.

Shadows lengthened. Outside, the soldiers sang their comrades to the DeadLands. The Doctor ground a rodent's skull into fine powder with a mortar and pestle, then stirred it into a wooden pot along with some Ocampan rosemary and antiseptic oil. He soaked a length of clean, white wool in the mixture. Pushing up her tunic beneath her breasts, he covered the burns on her abdomen with the poultice. Lacking the surgical instruments for repairing her insides, he could only make her comfortable.

Lia coughed, cried out from the pain caused by her lungs pressing into her broken ribs.

Sitting straight up, Balim watched her intently, holding her hand to his chest. The Doctor hovered over his shoulder.

"Balim? Ced?" Lia's hacking cough returned and she winced with each breath. "Come closer. I . . . can barely find . . . my voice." When they had assumed their places crouched down on opposite sides of her cot, she said, her voice raspy, "I see it in your faces. I'm dying, aren't I?"

The Doctor and Balim exchanged sorrowful looks. Balim nodded to the Doctor, who, squeezing Lia's hand, said, "Yes."

She gasped, startled, and tears started down her face. "I knew this was possible . . . I didn't expect it so soon."

Sitting on the edge of the cot, Balim eased her head into his lap. He untangled her hair with his fingers, brushed her tears from her cheeks with his thumb.

"Is there—is there *any* way?" she pleaded. "I—I—I can't fail my people."

Ever since the moment he saw the flaming trees from the outlook, the Doctor had been contemplating what, if anything, could be done to salvage something from the life that was General Lia. He had ruminated over the possibilities every step down the switchback track. Somewhere between the bluff and her tent he realized that nothing in his database could help her. The situation required powers beyond anything he had. More than ever, he wished for the expansive treatment options available to an emergency medical hologram. Lia would suffer because of his limitations.

"I have an idea," Balim said, meeting the Doctor's eyes.

The Doctor sensed without having to be told that whatever Balim proposed would be risky. He steeled himself for the worst.

Balim took a deep breath. "We could create a child together, a child with . . . the best in each of us. In time, the child could resume fighting for our people."

Rocking back onto his heels, the Doctor dropped his hands to his lap, stunned.

Lia, through her pain, protested that such a plan was

impossible, her injuries aside, she would not live long enough to carry a child to term.

If this were a normal circumstance, the Doctor would have to agree. With a Nacene involved, however, he didn't *know* what was impossible. Over Lia's body, he frowned at Balim, reprimanding him with a glare.

Balim accepted the chastisement with a nod, linked Lia's hand with his own, and raised it to his lips. *"Meshanna* I am . . . not what I appear to be. I have . . . powers. Abilities beyond what even you are capable of. With my help, your body would be a momentary vessel."

"How is such a thing possible?" Lia said.

"My life force would enter you and create a body for our child," Balim said simply.

"But you—you—"

"As you know me, I would cease to be."

"Oh please, love," Lia said. "You cannot do this." As she pushed up from her cot, her body shuddered as another spate of coughing began. Stubbornly, she placed her hands on either side of Balim's face and forced him to look at her. "No. I will not let you give your life this way." She coughed again. This time, blood droplets sprayed from her mouth and stained her chapped skin. Balim held her close.

"You'll have no choices if you keep this up," the Doctor said. "Agitation will hasten your deterioration." Among the medicines, the Doctor found what he believed to be a sedative and administered it. She calmed, her eyes fluttered closed. Balim laid her back down. Once the Doctor was assured that she rested peacefully, he turned to Balim. "Is it possible?"

"From conception to birth would be . . . almost no time. The fusion of Ocampa and Nacene would produce a . . . transcendant child, one not bound by the limitations of either species."

"Because his or her body would be born in this dimension, not Exosia," the Doctor surmised. "Such a one could have the power to defy the Exiles . . ."

"And Vivia, if necessary," Balim said, voicing the Doctor's unspoken thought. A sadness filled his eyes. "Ocampa is lost to this generation. There is a time in the future when my offspring would have the opportunity to help it be reborn."

The Doctor sighed deeply. "Lose the battle, win the war."

Balim said nothing.

"You must consider that Lia isn't physically capable of carrying such a powerful life force within her for any length of time."

Balim turned to face him, appearing to study his face intently. "You're quite right about that. But I sense that there is one within my reach who may be strong enough. One who achieved the Second Life. I see her clearly. She is never far from the surface of your mind."

The Doctor's eyes widened. He suspected he understood what Balim was proposing, and the idea simply left him speechless.

"I know how much you want to go back to your people—your ship," Balim said. "I promise you, if you help us, you will return."

The Doctor opened his mouth, prepared to proffer a thousand reasons why this was the worst idea he'd heard since Kathryn Janeway decided to adopt a Borg, but again no sound emerged.

What happened next defied all rules of time and space that the Doctor understood. One moment, he was standing beside the crude medicinals, talking to Balim; the next he was flat on his back, shielding his eyes from a light that nearly burned his retinas. And then, as quickly as it had come, the light faded away.

As the Doctor's eyes readjusted, Balim offered him a hand up. "Prepare her. I have a mission of my own I must fulfill before my rebirth." He stepped through the tent flap and vanished into the darkness.

The Doctor watched him leave, and then returned his attention to Lia. He felt a touch on his shoulder and stood up straight, waiting, afraid to believe. The crashing throb of his pulse filled his ears; his knees weakened beneath him.

"Doctor? Is that you?"

He closed his eyes; her voice played like music in his mind. Swallowing hard, he wet his lips with his tongue and cleared his throat. He dared a glance over his shoulder.

She glowed and shimmered, her glorious image rippling like wind over water, and yet there was no question in his mind who she was, or that she perceived his identity through the façade of his Ocampan body. He smiled at her, and in the same instant, Kes smiled back.

Chapter 8

Tom Paris was not a man who fell for hyperbole. Perhaps his reluctance to rate the places he went or the people he encountered stemmed from a lifetime of discovering that elsewhere in the universe something or someone was always bigger, better, louder, faster, and so forth. There was also the distinct possibility that Tom was too jaded to be easily impressed. Under his present circumstances, he made an exception to his rule. Standing outside the multistory entryway to Fortis Casino, Tom decided that without question, this was the most over-the-top gaudy spectacle he'd ever seen. By comparison, Ferengi had modest taste. Whoever built this place must have emptied out several systems' worth of latinum or gold for the flooring and figured out how to power a star's volume of neon lighting to decorate the exterior. Tom wondered seriously if it was possible to sunburn his eyes if he stared at the ribbons and cascading fountains of lights. And thinking about fountains, whatever phosphorescent liquid was erupting out of the center of the plaza had more in common with a geyser—hell, with Victoria Falls—than with a fountain. Tom observed many visitors, hand-in-hand, threading in and out of the glowing streams, frolicking with abandon. He turned to Harry and q to discern their reactions. q had her nose buried in her wrist bag, apparently searching for a compact; Harry was watching q, completely oblivious of the spectacle about him, though this time, Tom granted, there was something to look at—or rather, little to look at.

Mid-finger-snap, q had shed her severe black school clothes and traded them for a skimpy outfit worthy of a dabo girl. Both the strapless bra top held together with chains of glowing lights and her midthigh mini with slits up to her hips appeared to be woven out of a gem-encrusted, fine metallic mail. A matching cap fitted tightly against her skull. q could strut her stuff as a dancing girl on Risa or a table attendant at the finest resorts on Terisis V.

"Tempting?" q powdered her nose, and winked at Tom.

Tom didn't hesitate. "Nope."

"Your loss." She grabbed Harry by the arm and walked faster than any woman in eight-centimeter heels should walk across the plaza toward the line forming before a pair of bouncers—dragons to Tom's eye. The three of them joined the queue, waiting their turn for admission.

Standing around, Tom had more of an opportunity to study their surroundings. He believed that q wanted to help Kol, but he also knew that Q tended to put self-interest first. Should they need an exit strategy, he wanted to be prepared. Of course, Fortis might not even exist in Tom's universe, so he figured he might as well toss the rule book out from the get-go.

From his vantage point on the entry plaza, the casino reminded him of the orientation exercises in his Introduction to Engineering class. His professor, Sanjin Nu, took them onto a holodeck to study basic starship engineering components. All but the ship's innards were rendered transparent by the program. The class would walk along a deck and be able to see the ship in operation all around. In the parlance of the 1950s comic-book adventures Tom liked so well: it was like having X-ray vision. Now, staring through a seemingly endless number of crystal walls, he felt like he was back on the holodeck watching all the intricate workings of a complex machine flashing and moving. *B'Elanna would love this place,* he thought.

They reached their turn in line. q raised her palm to one of the dragon-bouncers, who scanned it with a phaserlike device. When the dragon raised a suspicious eye to Tom and Harry, q said, "They attend me. Slaves, if you must know. Nothing in the rules forbids them coming with me."

The dragon rumbled, emitting puffs of smoke, then waved the trio into the lobby.

Tom noted that Harry didn't appear to be too concerned about the prospect of being q's slave.

"What's the plan from here?" Tom asked. They followed q over to a display board that had tens of thousands of items listed on it in various languages and colors with a series of numbers after the written item. The numbers changed every second—increasing or decreasing.

"We need credits. Lots of them if we're going to get a seat in the game Kol's playing in. I just need to find out where the action is . . ." she said, systematically scanning the board.

Tom surmised that the numbers must indicate house wins and losses. q would want to find a game where her odds of winning were best.

"Why don't we just ask Q for a loan?" Harry asked.

Raising an eyebrow, q glanced at Harry. "Because the big lug went and got banned from Fortis not long ago. He'll say it was because he was too skilled a player. Management says it's because he cheats. Badly. He shows up here and he'll be in Continuum lockup from now until the next Big Bang." She squatted down and resumed studying the list, paused at an unintelligible line blinking green, and clasped her hands together, grinning. "Follow me," she said, making her way toward a kiosk.

A yellow Lazi (Tom recognized the type of alien from the node race) reached through the kiosk window, took q's hand, and scanned her palm the way the dragon had done. A console behind the Lazi produced a platinum-colored band with a square, green stone in the center; the yellow alien slid the band over q's index finger.

After they left the kiosk, Tom asked q what the band was for. She explained that the band worked as an identification device that would allow her to redeem or borrow credits and would also keep track of what games she entered. "It also registers whenever I use my Q abilities. If the monitors think I'm cheating, they'll impose deterrents to keep me in line."

"Such as?" Harry asked.

"Being spaced to the ninth dimension."

Tom and Harry exchanged quizzical glances.

"Having never been there, you don't realize what an unpleasant experience it is, but trust me: You don't want to be spaced to the ninth dimension for any length of time."

"I'll take your word for it," Tom said

The trio stepped onto an interfloor conveyor beside a group of lavender-colored spherical aliens covered by sea-urchin-like spikes. From what Tom could tell, there had to be at least fifty different conveyors leading to different areas and climbing through the atrium that extended as high as his eye could see. Tom looked down, through the clump of tropical foliage that grew up the center of the building, and watched level after level of entertainment pass by. He noticed a marquee announcing the Tesseract Ballet Troupe in a zero-g performance of *Seductive Geometry* as well as the band Motley Q playing their pandimensional hit single, "Woe Is Me (Omnipotence Isn't What It's Cracked Up to Be)." Based on the length of the line, Championship Gladitorial Calculus seemed to be a major attraction.

"There's a game of Zero-One going on the thirteenth level. If the action is hot, I should be able to increase our stake pretty quickly," q said. "Once I have enough credit, I can buy my way into the higher-level games and find Kol. He won't be playing anywhere beneath the fiftieth floor."

Noting her use of the singular pronoun, Tom said, "What are we supposed to do while you're gambling?"

"Look pretty?" q said dryly.

Tom laughed. "No, seriously."

"For the time being, just stay alert. We're taking Pem's word for it that Kol's here," q said, walking off the conveyor at what appeared to be a gaming floor. "It wouldn't be the first time that overgrown tree branch has lied to avoid a confrontation with the Continuum." She reached into her wrist bag, removed two simple, silver bracelets, and slapped one onto Tom's wrist and then the other onto Harry's; they locked automatically. "Don't take these off," she said, starting down a splashy blue and gold carpet at deadly speed, her stiletto heels never wobbling. "If anyone stops you, these bracelets are encoded to identify you as belonging to me. You'll be less likely to be taken into custody that way."

"Less likely?" Harry asked, chasing alongside her.

"They don't like Dirts around here. You might be cute," q said, tracing Harry's cheek with her thumb, "but that doesn't negate a social order that's existed since the dimensions collapsed."

"Is it safe for us to talk to *anyone?*" Tom asked.

An expression vaguely reminiscent of appreciation crossed her face. "The casino help might be useful. Most of the staff take their breaks in that lounge over there," she said, pointing toward a loose conglomeration of mostly unoccupied tables arranged around an empty platform with a scarlet velvet curtain draping the wall behind the platform. A fur-covered worker wearing a—to Tom's eye, tacky—red vest stood behind the bar stacking glasses into a pyramid. "You're beneath most of the help, but a lot of the creatures who work here would like nothing better than to get back at the Pandimensional Guild. They'll talk to you if they think they can get someone spaced."

"Ninth dimension. Gotcha," Tom said.

Harry placed his hand protectively on the small of q's back. "We should meet you where . . . ?"

Her eyes flashed with amusement at his gesture. "Your bracelets will buzz if I need you. I won't." q paused in front of an arched doorway. "My game's here."

"Good luck," Tom said. He grabbed Harry's shoulder and steered him in the direction of the lounge.

q called after them, "Luck has nothing to do with it. Being a Q does." She flashed her identification to the dragon-bouncer and vanished through the doorway.

"You sure know how to pick 'em, Harry," Tom said after she'd gone. He couldn't say whether he felt sympathetic or awed that Harry would even attempt flirting with a Q.

Harry slapped Tom between the shoulder blades. "Let's find ourselves some disgruntled employees."

Tuvok hadn't liked her idea. He hadn't expressed it in those exact words, B'Elanna granted, as she took her zero-g walk along the Monorhan hull. Vulcans didn't show the kind of emotional attachment to decisions that implied "like" or "dislike." His exact words had been "Your plan involves illogical risks"—accompanied by an eyebrow arched high enough on his forehead that it nearly touched his scalp. It wasn't like B'Elanna was the biggest fan of EV operations either; they tended to make her sick to her stomach. But frankly, she didn't care about logic, because her way was the only way this piece of spacefaring trash was ever going to find its way back home.

Featuring a more primitive version of the technology *Voyager* had encountered a week ago, this vessel's hydrogen ramscoop-style propulsion system was useless. Parts critical to the ramscoop mechanism had worn out. Even more serious, an explosion in the hydrogen-processing system disabled the ship's ability to create usable fuel. As B'Elanna perused the engineering specs stored in the ship's database, she was hard-pressed to figure out how the Monorhans had managed to leave their planet in the first place. Surprisingly, the Monorhan shield technology was exceptionally advanced compared to what she'd seen previously. The shields hadn't been fully functional since the fuel creation system broke, but B'Elanna made a few tweaks that would keep the shields operational—at least for the short term. What she was left with was deciding how best to introduce the ship to Mr. Newton and inertia.

The ship had a similar design to the one Ziv had been captain of: a flattened sphere formed the main hull. Dangling off the back were dozens of blocky passenger containers that, unlike on Ziv's ship, were interconnected by a series of tubes. If she could look at the ship from above, she suspected that it would look like a kite, the passenger compartments hanging off the bottom. Presently, only half of the passenger containers were still inhabited—those farthest from the main hull where the radiation problems were the least serious.

She discovered that the hull was equipped with a mechanism that, when activated, could move the chain of passenger compartments around the perimeter of the hull. The process of moving the passenger compartments described in the database conjured an image from her childhood of her father holding her by her arms and swinging her around in a circle, causing her legs to fly out behind her. B'Elanna could use the cranking mechanism to move the compartments around the hull's perimeter until a straight line could be drawn between the compartment farthest from the hull and Monorha, several hundred thousand kilometers away. Once the compartments were detached from the hull, they could be shot through space like an arrow to a target, provided B'Elanna could come up with the proper force to set them in motion—such as a controlled explosion.

Her first problem was accessing the crank that was mounted on the hull. The solution proved to be simple. Since she was already in an environmental suit, she needed only to go through one of the airlocks and walk from compartment to compartment until she reached the hull. Once the line of compartments was aimed toward Monorha, she would tackle problem number two: initiating a series of explosions in the empty compartments that would act like gunpowder behind a cannonball.

In spite of having the gravity controls set to comfortable, almost *Voyager* levels, the familiar detestable anxiety over zero-g conditions started in on B'Elanna's stomach about twenty meters into her space walk. She ignored it. She managed to cover the length of the first compartment with little effort. When the time came to traverse the gap between the first compartment and the second, she hesitated. She looked down; vertigo assaulted her. Staggering backward a step, she felt overwhelming gratitude that she hadn't eaten in the last twelve hours. *You can't do this, B'Elanna,* she scolded herself. *You're on the clock.* Indeed, she knew she was down to the last forty minutes before their shuttle would return to *Voyager* for good. *Step NOW . . .*

Avoiding the downward glance that had set her awry moments before, B'Elanna took a step, bent into a shallow squat, then jumped, sailing ever so gently over the gap between the compartments into space. When she cleared the distance, she pressed her grav thrusters and landed on the compartment's surface. *Good. One compartment down, four to go before I reach the hull.* Adjusting the visual settings on her helmet, she was able to zoom in on a speck that was the cover over the mechanized cranking unit. Thankfully, it appeared to be intact.

Once she swung the compartments around so they were correctly situated, she would return to the shuttle via the route she was currently taking. As she walked back, she would depressurize the cooling conduits, causing a destabilization that, if her calculations were right, would cause an explosion about ten to fifteen minutes after she'd opened up the valves. She would then uncouple the occupied compartments—save a few empty compartments that would act as cushioning—from the unoccupied ones before beaming aboard the shuttle. Moments later, the explosions would start, cascading until the spherical hull became the last, most powerful part of the chain. She was counting on the final explosion's being a doozy. The collective force of the explosions would launch the compartments toward Monorha. She'd run the physics past Tuvok, who, reluctantly, acknowledged that her plan should theoretically work.

With luck, the shuttle would have several minutes to get out of the way of the explosions. Not a lot of time, but as long as the shuttle escaped to *Voyager,* no one would complain too much.

She continued trudging atop the compartments, making her way toward the gargantuan sphere. She reached the sphere faster than she thought she would and discovered, much to her delight, that the crank mechanism worked beautifully. The compartments swung just the way she thought they would. Now for the fun part: the explosions.

As she walked, she considered how poetic it would be if she lost her life in hard vacuum wearing an EVA suit when, to her reckoning, one of the most significant times in her life had begun on her Day of Honor under circumstances similar to these. An image of Tom flitted through her mind. *Maybe I'll be seeing you sooner than you thought, Flyboy.* Thoughts of Tom kept a smile on her face as she walked from compartment to compartment, preparing the compartments to be launched.

B'Elanna knelt down on the top of the third-to-last compartment and turned the knob that allowed the coolant to vent into the interior. Using her tricorder as a listening device, she waited until she heard the sibilant hissing through the paper-thin hull plating before she stood up and moved to the next knob. B'Elanna enjoyed fixing things, to be certain, but she also enjoyed blowing things up.

"Commander Tuvok to Lieutenant Torres."

"Yes, Commander," B'Elanna said, and unscrewed the next knob. A few moments later, the hissing began. She stood up and moved to the next junction.

"Ensign Tariq needs to return to Voyager *now if he is to bring the* rih-hara-tan *back to their ships in time."*

The implication: they all needed to leave now. No time

to wrap up loose ends on the return trip. She wasn't done yet! To top it off, she couldn't get this damn knob to open. She felt around on her tool belt and pressed the button that released her electromagnetic spanner. Grunting, she worked on loosening the knob. "Look—I need ten minutes. Why not call *Voyager* and have them send a second shuttle with the *rih-hara-tan.*"

"A logical suggestion. I will keep you updated."

The comm went silent. B'Elanna yanked with all her strength on the fastener, but nothing. Even worse, the tricorder indicated that if she continued her efforts, she risked ripping the hull plating. Frustrated, she gave up and started clomping along toward the next compartment. Hopefully the leaks she'd initiated would be enough.

The Doctor knew he wouldn't be able to touch Kes, skin-to-skin, as he had aboard *Voyager.* Ironically, in her current state she had more in common with his holographic self than the organic form he currently took. He hesitated a moment, remembering how Kes's transformation had destabilized *Voyager's* structural integrity, but when he realized that her presence had yet to disrupt their surroundings, he relaxed.

"I've missed you," Kes said, drawing closer to him. "A body suits you." She circled around him, taking in his new look from all sides.

"You think so?" the Doctor said, holding up his arm so he could scrutinize his hand. "This body is a bit . . . hairy—and barrel-chested—for my taste."

Kes laughed.

"I'm relieved you can tell it's me," the Doctor said.

"The body is a shell. I see beneath it." She gazed at the furnishings, inhaled a deep whiff of air scented with the refuse of war. Not even the incense burning outside the tent flap could cover it. "We are on Ocampa, aren't we? Just before the warming. The burnt-soil smell reminds me of the tunnels to the surface." Kes drifted over to where Lia slept and studied her. Her eyes narrowed thoughtfully. "I know her. I have her memories from my imprinting."

The Doctor resumed his place on the stool beside Lia's cot. "She reminds me of you." He took her vitals and examined her wounds; unsurprisingly, her symptoms had worsened. A low-level nervousness seized him as he began to wonder where Balim was. . . .

Kes touched Lia's forehead; the Doctor startled, fearing what such contact would do to the dying woman. The rosy blush that suffused Lia's cheeks lessened his concerns somewhat. Lia shifted in her sleep without apparent pain.

"What did you do? Can you heal her?"

"I can't give life to one appointed to death, but I can ease her passage." Kes glanced at the Doctor, her lively eyes dancing beneath long lashes. "Another life awaits her."

"Like yours?" the Doctor asked. Since Kes had left *Voyager,* he had longed to know—to understand—what had happened to her. Concern for her well-being had been with him continually for many months now.

"Not yet, but someday." Kes turned away from Lia and asked, with such kindness the Doctor's insides ached from missing her, "And what about you? How is it that you came to Ocampa—in this era?"

"That, my dear, is the million-quatloo question," the Doctor said, arranging Lia's bedding so she wasn't chilled. He explained how he was accidentally taken from *Voyager,* his deal with Vivia, and his subsequent journey to Ocampa and his encounter with Lia and her army. Part of the way through their discussion, she held her hand so it hovered over his. His flesh warmed in her presence. All of it, from leaving *Voyager* to being thrown into Ced's body, was worth it to be with Kes again. "And you? Where were you before—" He circled his hand several times.

"I was inside a star, exploring, when a voice called to me. There was a flood of light—as if a thousand stars had burned a hole in the fabric of space-time," she said, her voice husky and soft; to the Doctor, she seemed far away. "A massive energy surge felt like it sliced through me. I thought I was undergoing another transformation. Now I'm here."

"Are you well now?"

"I am."

Sitting in companionable silence alongside her, the Doctor couldn't bring himself to tell her about Balim—at least not yet. Perhaps he wanted her to himself a few minutes longer. Soon enough, she would belong to Balim and to the eternities. So he said nothing until she asked why she had been brought to Ocampa.

The Doctor folded down Lia's blanket and turned Lia's palm so Kes could see the *ipasaphor.* He saw comprehension in Kes's expression.

"General Lia began her *elogium* yesterday. She had no intention of creating a child, because she believed her first duty was to Ocampa." Taking a deep breath, the Doctor prepared for the next part, the more sensitive section. Kes's look told him that she suspected where this conversation was headed, but that she would hear him out. "Now, she can't continue to lead her troops, nor does she have the strength to carry a child."

"There is a story that General Lia gave birth . . ." Kes began tentatively.

"I suspect that may be the case," the Doctor said.

"But I have no memory of Lia taking a mate."

"Her lover has unique gifts that can help Ocampa. He believes that his and Lia's child could save your world."

"The lover . . . he called me here—"

"Balim is his name."

"I have only the barest recollection of him. He's a shadow in her memory."

"He is not like you or I. Perhaps he is more like you are now, but he is not like Lia."

Kes contemplated the Doctor's words for a long moment; her eyes widened. "He's Nacene!"

The Doctor nodded. "He loves your people. As the Caretaker did—more, even. I believe he loves the Ocampa as much as you do and that is why I overstepped my bounds and allowed him to call you here."

"Can I trust him?"

"I believe so."

"What should I do? What do *you* want me to do?"

The Doctor looked at Kes, struck not only by her loveliness and grace, but by her confidence in him; she entrusted her destiny to his judgment without hesitation. A word from him and this whole charade would end. Lia would die and Balim would continue his fight alone. The Doctor would have to find another way to *Voyager. Perhaps Kes could help me.* As much as he longed to take Kes and escape this nightmare, he knew what he had to do.

Inhaling deeply, he said, "I can't choose for you, but I believe this is a just and good cause. I won't pretend to know the future, but Ocampa's destiny may hinge on the outcome of this decision. Whether for the better or not I can't say. I can only admonish you to trust your heart." He met her unveiled gaze directly. Kes saw through him. She'd been his first best friend and that was why he owed her the truth.

"I need a private moment with Lia," Kes said finally.

Excusing himself, the Doctor rose from his stool and went to the tent flap. He slipped through the opening unobtrusively and waited outside.

Balim stood a meter or so away, talking animatedly with two shrouded figures he didn't recognize. The now familiar electric tingle hit him, but with less power and force than it had before. The Doctor realized this pair must be the Nacene prisoners—Mestof's wizards. He waited, listened.

"For your penance, you must be their Caretaker," Balim said to the taller one, who the Doctor surmised was male based on the clothing. "They will be helpless without water, without land. Unless you can build a home for them away from the surface, the Ocampa will die out. Do you understand?"

He nodded.

"And you, Suspiria. You are young among the Exiles. You must help your mate until the day when my heir will return to repair the damage our kind has done."

Suspiria! This is where the Caretaker came from. This is the beginning of the chain of events that brought Voyager *to the Delta Quadrant!*

For a moment, he toyed with an irrational thought. If he prevented the Caretaker and Suspiria from fulfilling their promise to Balim, *Voyager* would never be taken from the Alpha Quadrant. Knowing he was at a place where he could forever change history exhilarated and terrified him. But the momentary megalomania passed: he would not risk Kes's future or the futures of any of her kind. Besides, where would he be without the Delta Quadrant journey? Another EMH module waiting around in a database until he'd be decommissioned when the better version came along.

From inside the tent, the Doctor heard Kes calling

him. He'd raised the tent flap when Balim addressed him. The Doctor turned back.

"Is it time?"

"I believe so," the Doctor said, and slipped inside.

Kes was kneeling beside Lia's bedside, holding the general's hand in her own. Lia had awoken and was talking intently to Kes in the quietest of tones. The Doctor cleared his throat, warning the women of his presence.

"I need . . . to say goodbye . . . Ced. To you and Balim," Lia said, her breathing labored.

"Then you've decided?" the Doctor asked them both.

Hand in hand, Kes and Lia exchanged looks; then Kes said, so softly he almost didn't hear, "For Ocampa."

Lia's eyes closed. The Doctor heard a distinctive rattle in her chest indicating that she had little time left. He pressed a kiss on her forehead and asked whatever power in the universe that looked after the souls of Ocampans to guide Lia's passage.

The tent flap rustled and parted, admitting Balim.

The Doctor never had fully comprehended how tall Balim was; he barely cleared the tent's ceiling. He stood at least an imposing two meters by the Doctor's estimation. And while he considered his holomatrix to be handsome, the Doctor had to confess that by torchlight on a bleak and lonely Ocampan night, Balim had much in common with a rather dirty, plain-garbed Lancelot. He glanced at Kes, gauging her reaction.

She was transfixed.

He stepped inside and knelt beside Kes, bowing deeply from the waist. "I am Balim." He raised his head so Kes could better see him.

"I thought you were a fairy story," Kes said, her eyes never leaving his. "A legend."

He answered with a sad smile.

"You were—are—Lia's companion. Her lover."

He nodded. "You understand why I called you here?"

"To give Lia a child." Kes placed her hand over Balim's. "You should say goodbye."

"She has slipped into the twilight between life and death. When the child is formed, I will know her again."

"Then I am ready," Kes said.

Twining his fingers with hers, he murmured words only Kes could hear. He raised her hand to his lips and placed a kiss on her palm.

The Doctor felt like a voyeur standing idly by as Kes and Balim sought, and found, a connection. Part of him wanted to linger to protect Kes from harm the way Ced had failed to protect Lia; another part of him wanted to flee, to have no part in what the Doctor knew would be a painful ordeal for her.

With wide, radiant eyes, Kes studied Balim's rugged face, still grimy with blackened smudge from the battle. Her eyes became moist and she placed her hand on his olive-skinned cheek. "She loves you so much."

The Doctor watched, transfixed, as Kes became . . . someone else. She transformed beneath his gaze and her awareness of the person he knew receded. He didn't know how Kes would join Lia nor did he want to. Not even scientific curiosity would prompt him to seek to understand such intimacy.

Unwilling to further violate their privacy, the Doctor slipped out of the tent unnoticed. Out in the chilly night air, he pulled his cloak tightly around him as a defense against wind-stirred dust haze. Where was he supposed to go from here? He could hear the distant cannonade, having no idea where the fighting was under way. He could smell the smoke of discharging weapons and singed bodies. Increasingly powerful winds swept down from the hills and disturbed the parched, gritty basin the camp had been built on. Gray thunderclouds grumbled with empty promises of rain. He settled on a stump sitting beside a dying cook fire.

The urgency of his predicament pressed heavily on him: he had no idea where he was relative to his own time continuum. A day in Exosia could be millennia in his space-time, and he'd been away from *Voyager* for at least two full Ocampan days. The Doctor couldn't risk being lost to *Voyager* forever. If what Balim told him was true, Vivia might abandon him here if he failed to fulfill his mission. Expediting his return was critical, though he didn't know how such a thing would happen until Lia's child was born. Meanwhile, he needed to find a place to sleep. Damn these organic bodies. So needy and inefficient at times. Dropping down on the ground, he pulled his cloak hood over his head to shield himself from the wind. He squeezed his eyes shut and rubbed them with his fingers, trying to remove the grit that had caught beneath his eyelids. He opened his eyes—

And was in an ornate nineteenth-century Parisian-style theater.

He'd returned to Exosia.

An electrical tingle coursed through his limbs; his head burned as if fire burned through his scalp. Placing his hands on his temples, he massaged them until the sensation faded. Spinning around, he found Vivia floating behind him.

You may go home if you wish, she said. *Your people are looking for you and we have devised a way to send you back. We sent them . . . a bit of a message that let them know you were here.*

"What will happen to the Light—to Lia."

She dismissed him with a hand wave. *I will finish what*

*you were too weak to do. How cleverly the Light overcame the ob-
stacles placed in his path! But sentiment has overcome reason—he
has become vulnerable in joining with the woman.*

Horror overcame the Doctor. She had to be referring
to Balim and Lia—now Balim and Kes. "You won't—you
can't—"

Their child can never be born. He will destroy Exosia.

q had been correct about Fortis workers being willing to
gossip about the patrons. Tom and Harry hadn't been in
the lounge fifteen minutes when the bartender connected
them with a dealer who had more than a few grievances
with the monitors. It seemed that the alien—an amphi-
bious Namian—had been demoted from the "big" by-
invitation-only games that happened on the fifty-second
level after he'd complained about a Rutillian gambler who
liked "destroying things" when he won. When pressed for
clarification about what "destroying things" meant, the
Namian would only say that even pandimensional beings
should exercise a modicum of restraint. The Namian
hadn't had direct contact with Kol, though he'd heard
about a Nacene hybrid who liked taking big risks.

"He lost big," the Namian said, sucking up algae
through his fingers. "But he won big too. Reckless was
what the other dealers called him. Jaded, even for an entity."

"What do you mean by jaded," Tom asked, pushing another plate of algae toward the Namian. He'd quickly
learned that the more he fed the dealer the more the dealer
talked.

"Dirts have a reputation for being easily amused," the
Namian said. "Doesn't take much to thrill you lesser life-
forms. And while most of these hotshots around here act

all blasé about rearranging planetary systems and making stars go nova, the truth is, simple games of chance entertain them endlessly. I've seen Q sit at the slots for days, shoveling in their chips and pulling the handle to see if the primordial DNA combinations the box throws at them might create life and allow them to win the jackpot."

"Winning is fun," Harry said, pushing around a drink coaster. "No matter what dimension you come from."

"Because it's the one thing these pandimensionals can't control. It's all about choice and chance and it gives them a kind of rush to not be in control for once." The Namian pushed aside his third emptied algae plate and signaled the bartender to bring him a Pondwater—a potent cocktail, from the dealer's description, that featured ground-up hallucinogenic snail shell. Both Tom and Harry passed.

"But this Nacene hybrid guy. Nothing fazes him. He'll sit at the table for hours, win or lose, and he doesn't react. He throws away planets and rare elements like they were common Dirts—nothing personal," the Namian apologized.

"Is he here now?" Harry asked.

The Namian shrugged. "Maybe. The bosses on Fifty-two are pretty protective about their clients. You can't know for certain unless your mistress"—he indicated the bracelets Tom and Harry were wearing—"earns her way into a game up there."

"I have confidence in her," Harry said brightly.

"What a surprise," Tom muttered.

"What's that supposed to mean?"

A hand alighted on Tom's shoulder. "Miss me, boys?" q said.

Harry leaped into action. "We have news on Kol."

"That's good, because I was going to have to decide

whether to borrow against my account to get into a game upstairs."

"Not too much luck at Zero-One?" Tom asked.

q shrugged. "The table was slower than I'd hoped."

Touching her arm sympathetically, Harry gazed up at her. "How much are we short?"

"All of it," she said.

Tom blinked.

"But I can get enough of a loan to get us into a game of Trinity. That's the game Kol typically plays."

The Namian exhaled loudly and clicked his long, flexible tongue against the roof of his mouth. "If your mistress is into Trinity . . ."

"Keep your opinions to yourself, Namian," q snapped. "Or I'll turn you into one of those concoctions you're drinking. Ever tried life as a hallucinogenic snail? I hear it's mind-bending." Placing her hands on the table, she leaned forward, touched her nose to his nostril holes, and glared him straight in the pulsating eyeballs.

Shrinking back into his chair, the Namian cradled his Pondwater close to his chest and slumped down sullenly. "You Q are all alike."

"Hey, that's q to you."

Having spent a few minutes in the Namian's company, Tom had no doubt that the dealer was a low-life malcontent, but he had little reason to question the alien's assessment of q's choice of games of chance. Harry and q left the table headed in the direction of an unmanned kiosk. Tom ran after them.

"Why do we need to play Trinity, q?" Tom said. "Let's find out where Kol's playing, call Q to come pick him up, and then go home."

"If that were possible, every loan shark and low life hood in the universe would extradite from Fortis," q said impatiently. "This is a protected outpost. Once you're in, you're in to stay until you leave voluntarily or you're booted by the management—like Q was."

Harry said, "So we ask Kol to come with us. We explain the situation and—"

"You think we're going to get Kol to leave a game willingly?" She snorted. "No. We force him out by making him lose everything. Then we negotiate when he's vulnerable."

"If we lose, then what?"

"We won't lose," q said.

Tom took a deep breath. "*If* we lose . . ."

"You might spend a century in detention while I pay off the debt, but it isn't like you'll suffer my fate."

"Ninth dimension?" Harry said.

q shuddered. She inserted her hand beneath a reader. The machine paused for a moment, and then spat out a stack of chips as tall as Tom's forearm. She studied them for a long moment before gathering them up and dumping them into her bag. "There's not enough here. We won't even make it through the door." Resuming her fast, focused pace, she shot across the floor toward the conveyor. Both Tom and Harry jumped to catch up with her; closing the distance between them proved tiring, especially since Tom realized it had to be at least thirty-six hours since he'd had any sleep.

"I still say we should contact Q," Harry said, meeting Tom's eyes over q's head.

She stopped dead and gestured for both of them to follow her over a grouping of high-backed, overstuffed green satin-covered chairs.

Once they sat down, q said, "Q steps one foot in this place and alarms will go off from here to the end of the universe. So scratch that one off the list right now. What few options we do have are iffy at best and come with huge risks. Most of them require that we leave Fortis unless I keep gambling until I come up with a stake to get us into Kol's game. Even that's not a sure thing. For all my blustering to the contrary, I can't make you stay and help me. I'm sure Q's given you the whole chance and choice song and dance routine. It's his favorite number—especially for corporeals."

"He's said something along those lines, yes," Tom said.

"As a Q enrolled at university, my options are limited," q said. "I can put a third eye in your forehead, give you a snout, stick you in a cell with a grumpy Nausicaan, but I can't do anything that can't be easily undone by another Q. So if you all have anything useful in those little brains, now's the time to speak up."

"If we leave now," Harry said, "we lose our best shot at Kol. Everything we've done so far would have been pointless."

q nodded her head.

A trio of uniformed and helmeted security personnel burst through the door behind them. One of the officers raised his wrist to his mouth. Most of his words were unintelligible, but Tom caught "Nacene hit man" and "secure perimeter immediately."

Leaping to her feet, q rushed over to an information terminal and whispered a command into the console. Tom and Harry followed behind. Moments later, the screen flashed several rows of green text. They scanned the contents. Tom blanched.

A groan, followed by a sigh and a swift kick to the information terminal expressed q's reaction to the information. "They've found him. Those self-important sporo-cystian prima donnas dispatched someone to take him out. I didn't think they'd get this far! Arggh!" She kicked the terminal again.

For the first time since he'd met her, Tom felt a sense of what q was up against: reduced power, odds stacked against her, no backup from the Continuum. He admired her for sticking to her resolve and not falling back on her superiors to bail her out. *B'Elanna would like her,* Tom realized.

"We can't let the Nacene get him. There has to be another way," Harry said.

"There's no time!" q shouted. "We'll have to force our way in." She pressed her hands against her temples. "Or something."

Harry touched her arm. "Don't worry. We're in this together."

"That's sweet, Harry, but it's not comforting," q said.

They started for the interfloor conveyor. Out of habit, Tom slipped his hand into his pocket and found something hard and metal inside. Midstep, he paused. "Wait," he called out to q and Harry, who were several meters ahead of him.

"What is it?" q asked.

He removed the metal box from his pocket and held it up so he could better see it. Flipping open the lip, he read: Monorha. A glance inside revealed the marble with the planet spinning inside. He held it up for q to see. "Can I gamble this somewhere? Fast?"

"Tom, we don't have time for this," Harry said.

"We don't have time for anything *else,* Harry," Tom said. "It's our one chance to get into the game quickly." He looked back at q.

q stared at him blankly for a moment, and Tom wondered if she thought he had lost his mind. Suddenly, she pointed over his shoulder. "There! A slot machine!"

Tom looked. On the wall opposite where they'd met the Namian, he saw the gambling device. It wasn't particularly fancy, and pretty easy to miss in the midst of all the grandeur and opulence of Fortis. Tom would have preferred a dabo wheel, but this would do. He ran toward it. When he reached the slot machine, he caressed its cool silver edges, appreciating the fine workmanship as only a gambler could. Gingerly, he removed the marble from the box and rolled it into the betting slot. "Let 'er rip!" he called out as he yanked down the handle. He heard Harry's nervous squeal and refused to let it dampen his mood. The slots spun around dizzily, colors flashing. "Come on, baby, come on! Give me the goods," Tom chanted as he rubbed his hands together.

"This is, without question, the most stupid thing I've ever agreed to " q said.

Tom ignored her. The first slot stopped. A cherry. "Straight cherries, honey, I know you want to give it to me. Cherry cherry!"

A second cherry. And a third. When the fourth slot stopped on a cherry, Tom thought his heart might have stopped beating. Even q had shut up and was standing at his shoulder, watching the slot intently. Tom took a deep breath, waiting for the final wheel to stop. He squeezed his eyes together, unwilling to look.

It clicked to a stop. Tom dared a peek—

The bells and sirens started at once.

Tom's face split into a grin as the credits, deeds—including the one to Monorha—jewels, and currency spilled out of the slot machine onto the carpet. He grabbed the machine by the sides and placed an enthusiastic smooch in the center of the cherries.

Mouth agape, q stared at the machine, her spike heels rooted to the floor. "If that isn't the finest display of dumb luck I've ever seen . . ."

"Can we play Trinity now?" Harry asked as he scooped credits off the floor and shoved them into his pockets.

Tom paused from his lovefest with the slot machine long enough to look over at q. "Choice and chance, right?" She smiled.

Chapter 9

"You're making a mistake," the Doctor said to Vivia. "The Light isn't the enemy you've made him out to be. He's trying to repair the damage done by the Exiles. What he's doing can not only save Ocampa but help you deal with the Exiles."

Vivia tossed her auburn hair. *I am running out of patience with you, foolish creature. I owe you no explanations.*

The Doctor knew he should simply accept Vivia's offer to be returned to *Voyager* and allow fate to run its course, but he refused to take the risk of abandoning Kes—and Lia and Balim—to a horrific end. "You don't know the future, Vivia. You see shadows and possibilities, but until the choice is made the outcome is uncertain. Allow the child to be born!"

Only the fate of the strings concerns me. The Light made his choice when he joined the Exiles.

"You have a chance to make a different choice, Vivia. Something besides the Nacene default to containment or destruction." Opening his arms, the Doctor approached Vivia, pleading. "If you destroy the Light's child, you are no different than the Exiles who know nothing but pursuit of their own selfishness. Do you want to be like them or—"

Vivia whirled in the air, her eyes wide with rage, her arm raised above her head.

The Doctor gasped; dullness seized him. He tried lifting his legs to walk but they refused to move. The theater spun dizzily around him and his grip on this reality weakened. Stumbling forward, he dropped to the stage. Tightness squeezed his innards; pain shot down his arm into his fingertips.

You will be contained.

Must stop Vivia . . . he thought. Balim had been right all along. And now, he may have sent Kes to a cruel death at the hands of a vindictive Nacene. *Think, man, think,* he thought. What are Vivia's rules? How does she operate . . . ? How did I break through her containment before . . .

The unthinkable happened. He heard Seven's voice as clearly as if she were standing beside him.

"*Voyager to the Doctor. Please acknowledge. Direct your program to coordinates 56-2-1-V. Repeat. We will bring you home.*"

Seven wasn't one who typically paced. She found it to be an inefficient way to expend cellular energy and rarely believed it accomplished its purpose—to help relieve anxiety or to express stress. As she stood before the astrometrics console, waiting for the viewscreen programmed to receive data from the probe to go active, she discovered she had an unexpected impulse to pace. This annoyed her.

She turned her back on the viewscreen. She would ignore it. She would be productive. Watching a blank screen, waiting for it to crackle to life, was a ridiculous waste of time. The probe would not transmit information unless it fell within the parameters programmed into it by Seven and B'Elanna.

Instead, she focused on developing updated navigation coordinates for Ensign Knowles. The problems in Monorhan space were accelerating, and it was vital that *Voyager* avoid piloting into one of the many wells and folds that were continually appearing like—*like Borg implants sprouting out of the newly assimilated,* she thought. She asked the computer to compile the latest sensor readings and to adjust the route *Voyager* would follow out. Obligingly, the computer produced the appropriate graphic, displaying the best route of five minutes ago with the current route. *Statistically insignificant differences,* Seven concluded. She had just wasted three minutes redoing a task that didn't need to be redone.

Waiting was seriously beginning to irritate her.

Looking around astrometrics at the various blinking consoles, Seven realized that everything in the room was operating as it should. No critical tasks remained. She decided that she would offer her services to the commander. On a ship this size, someone always needed help—perhaps engineering, since Lieutenant Torres was on the away mission. Even better, she probably should make her offer in person so she wouldn't have to stand around astrometrics *waiting* any longer. "Computer, location Commander Chakotay."

"Commander Chakotay is in the ready room."

Too far away to be efficient. She reached for her combadge and heard an unfamiliar chirp. *My badge must be malfunctioning,* she thought, and looked down. To the naked eye, there was nothing troubling. She touched it again, "Seven to Commander—"

The chirp sounded again. Spinning around, she saw

the viewscreen blinking bright blue. The probe had matched the Doctor's parameters loaded into its memory with something inside the gash. Stunned, she stared at the viewscreen rapidly filling with lines of data.

"Yes, Seven?"

"I believe we have found the Doctor," she said. When her shock abated (mere seconds later) she took two long steps over to the console and tapped in the commands to send the information to the bridge. "I'm transmitting the information to your ready room."

"That's incredible news, Seven. Don't share this with anyone until we can confirm it."

Seven could hear the smile in his voice. "I too am pleased."

"Get up here immediately so we can go to work."

She was out the door before he finished his sentence

"Good thinking, Tuvok, I'll get right on it. Voyager out." The comm chirped off. Chakotay called down to the shuttlebay to Chief Clemens and asked him to ready a second shuttle. He touched his combadge and ordered Knowles to find another pilot to take the rih-hara-tan back to their ships. The added benefit was that additional supplies could be provided for the Monorhans.

The door chime sounded.

"Come in, Seven," Chakotay said, barely able to maintain a calm veneer as the doors whooshed open. He hadn't been this hopeful since the day he'd asked Susannah Many-Feathers Moryoquai to the summer-solstice celebration.

"Commander," Seven said, and strode over to the nearest workstation. "I will show you the latest operation the probe has undertaken."

Chakotay rose from behind the desk and went over to

huddle with Seven over the workstation. He studied the data carefully. "So what the probe is doing now is emitting a field that will capture anything that matches the Doctor's photonic signature."

Seven nodded. "Exactly. The field will not hold all the photonic energy within range, only energy that matches the programmed specifications. The field will capture as many datablocks of the Doctor's program as it can find and hold them until it has found all the datablocks we asked it to look for. Or—" She hesitated and glanced at the chronometer on the viewscreen.

"If time runs out," Chakotay finished for her.

"We are down to about fifteen minutes," Seven said. "And all I can say for certain is that the Doctor was taken into the gash. Beyond that . . ."

"We might not be able to fish him out."

A burst of static erupted over the comm system, followed by garbled noise and more static.

Chakotay felt his pulse quicken. In the midst of all the aural clutter, he swore he heard something intelligible. "Run that through filtration, Seven. Now." He needn't have asked: she was already at a console, fingers flying over the keys.

"Playback commencing . . ." she said.

A burst of static, a series of high-pitched squeals, then a distinctive *"Voya—"* static *"help—"* The transmission cut off.

"Computer: Voiceprint analysis," Chakotay said.

"Voiceprint belongs to the Emergency Medical Hologram."

Overtaken with incredulity, he opened his mouth but no words sufficed. An involuntary blurt of laughter surprised him. He shook his head, disbelieving. "Is it possible? Could the computer be confusing something the probe is transmitting with the actual Doctor?"

Seven's forehead furrowed with concentration. She cocked her head to one side, pondered, and said, "No, I don't believe so."

"Haha!" Chakotay crowed and raised his arms up in the air, out of deference to the Great Spirit—wherever, whatever, that all-powerful force might be. Without thinking, he threw his arms around Seven, enveloping her in a massive bear hug.

Awkwardly, she touched his upper arms with stiff, uninspired pats.

When sense hit him, Chakotay felt how tense her body was and immediately disengaged himself. "I apologize, Seven. The moment carried me away."

"The sentiment is understood and reciprocated. No apology necessary," Seven said flatly. She turned away and linked her hands behind her back.

Chakotay, however, swore he saw a slight upward curve crease her cheek before she turned away from him. He had never realized how a smile illuminated an already beautiful face. "Shall we tell the crew?" He watched her. It was almost as if he could see the gears of her mind whirring and spinning. Before she could even answer, he knew what she'd say. "Never mind. Bad idea. We won't say anything until we're more certain."

"I believe that would be best," she said. "After all, we don't—"

BAM. The first shock wave hit.

"—the hell?!" Chakotay exclaimed.

The red-alert Klaxons sounded.

q explained Trinity on the way up to the fifty-second floor as a game of high risk and high payoff. When she described it that way, Harry envisioned *tongo*, dabo, and the old Earth standby poker. He had no idea how juvenile humanoid gambling was until he heard about Kol's favorite pastime. On his way from conveyor to conveyor, Harry replayed her words in his mind in an effort to put them in terms he could understand.

The basic structure of the game involved three teams composed of up to three players each, though teams with equal numbers of players wasn't required. Some players—like Kol—tended to play solo, because the payouts were higher. Each team rolled six-sided dice to determine what colors—red, orange, or yellow—of three-sided playing pieces called "triads" the dealer would give them. The team would then slip the triads into empty slots on a triangular board. Rolls continued until all nine slots on the board were filled with the colored triads—the last single slot being called "the crown." Each team placed their bets, and the team with the largest stake determined how many slots of each team's pyramid would need to match the pyramid generated by the house (a.k.a. the computer) in order to stay in the game. Matches ranged from two triads to a full pyramid, though q explained that calling for a full-pyramid match in the first round of betting was very rare. If all teams lost, the house won. Rounds continued, pitting the teams against the house and each other, until the entire pyramid was revealed or the winning player halted play.

The probability equations involved in Trinity staggered Harry. He attempted to calculate the odds that certain colors would be rolled over the course of the game; statistically where the ideal placements would be for the colored pieces; and the odds for two, three, or four triad matches, based on where the pieces were placed in the pyramid.

His headache started sometime during his contemplation of the dice rolls.

During his first year at the Academy, he'd gained a reputation as a weekend cardsharp by using his mathematically inclined mind to count cards and improve his odds at winning the occasional dorm game of Texas Hold 'Em poker. Harry's forays into gambling happened during vacations and school breaks; he never took a trip for the purpose of playing cards. He much preferred his clarinet or logic games. Gambling—card games especially—was relaxing, even entertaining to Harry, but that was the extent of his interest.

By contrast, Tom fancied himself a gambler, but if the two of them compared month by month who won more, Harry's winnings usually outpaced his friend—not by much, but by enough. Tom might have the charm to wheedle the goods and services he wanted, but Harry could acquire the *resources* needed to obtain goods and services. He was rarely in anyone's debt. Inevitably, this was why Tom usually owed Harry more replicator rations than either of them bothered to keep track of. Harry had grown to expect Tom's good-natured ribbing about his crushes, his bad luck with women, and his horrible tendency to be the *Voyager* crew member most likely to be mutilated at the hands of hostile aliens. But Tom could never give him a hard time about being a loser at games of chance. Listening to q's explanation, however, took Harry aback. He had no idea how he could be useful to q in making the kinds of strategic choices that would be required to stay in the game.

Pouring on the charm, q managed to sweet-talk her way into finding out which game Kol was involved in, because he was, indeed, as Pem had claimed, involved in a high-stakes game of Trinity.

"So we found him. What now?" Tom asked, his eyes watering from holding back a yawn.

"We play," q said.

irsthand experiences, by the way—that when a guy pends his life carousing and gambling, he's running from omething."

Plopping down into an overstuffed chair beside Tom, l peered intently at him, then leaned back and threw her arms out to her sides, draping them over the top of the chair. "You'd be running too if the fate of the universe depended on you. He was created to save his people—both his mother's and his father's. There's never been a moment in his life where he's been free of that burden. So he plays as a way to escape."

"I get that," Harry said, grateful to momentarily put aside his statistical studies of Trinity. Being the much-longed-for only son of doting parents, he also understood the burdens of parental expectations better than most. Still, he wasn't impressed by how easily Kol appeared to shrug off his responsibilities. "What I don't get is how indifferent he is to what's going on around him. I mean, the whole universe is ready to unravel, and he's goofing off."

"He cares about some things," q said. "Take Ocampa. He has a soft spot for Ocampa because of his mother. He's had the deed to that world since birth and it's been his most treasured possession as long as I've known him."

Harry started at that. He had a vague recollection of Q mentioning that Kol's father, the Light, had fallen for a "small town" girl, but Q had never explicitly stated where the girl came from. It made sense that Ocampa fit into this puzzle, considering what Harry had experienced with the Nacene *Voyager* knew as the Caretaker. He wondered if th Caretaker had anything to do with Kol, but then dismiss that thought. Hadn't the Caretaker brought individual his array from all over the galaxy in his efforts to re duce—to create a successor? If he'd known about J

Tom suddenly appeared more alert. Harry, on the other hand, was still trying to figure out how it would possible for them to play Trinity and win. The proba of success seemed far too remote for him to feel comf able pressing forward. A glance at q revealed that would be no dissuading her. In a split second, he deci to throw his lot in with q—not because of her attrac ness, but because in some deep, illogical gut-level pla sensed it was the right choice to make. Heart thuddi his throat, he reached for q's hand and squeezed it g "We're with you."

"Good," she said, and left both men so she could cuss the terms of their entering the game with the ro attendant.

Luck was with them: no other players had requested join Kol's game. Once a team was eliminated, they wo be invited into the Trinity Suite. The room attendant vited them to wait in an opulent antechamber, furnish in plush, overstuffed furniture; several servers hove around, carrying trays of refreshments—liquors, canap and bite-sized desserts. Harry took his cues from q, suming that whatever she ate would be safe for him. Wh she rescued him from a close call with a raw piece of T nak codfish, Harry decided to lay off the food.

Time droned on.

At last, Tom broke the quiet. "You know, q, the o thing I don't understand in all this?"

q raised an eyebrow.

"What's the deal with this Kol guy? He must ha some major malfunction to be throwing his life away t way he is."

"And what would you know about what it means to b a pandimensional being?" q snapped back.

"Not much," Tom admitted. "But I do know—fro

been part of Kol's creation, wouldn't he have simply called on Kol to help the Ocampa?

After a long, thoughtful pause, q said softly, "When it comes to what matters, he does the right thing. And he's a good friend. I hope he's okay." She slapped her thighs and jumped up from her chair, effectively ending their conversation. She started walking the perimeter of the room, occasionally stopping to check in with the room attendant, ostensibly for security updates.

The knowledge that somewhere in the vicinity of Fortis a Nacene hit man closed in on Kol lingered in their thoughts—at least in Harry's. No question: the urgency of the situation ratcheted up the tension in the room. The speed and strength of q's gait and the unemotional expression on her face exuded stress. A few times, Harry invited q to come sit by him, hoping it would help her relax, but she rebuffed all his overtures. Seeking a distraction, he resumed his analysis of Trinity.

Tom, on the other hand, seemed immune to the tension in the room and decided to take a nap. He had been sleeping peacefully for almost a half an hour when the door separated. The losing team shuffled through the waiting room. q paused from her pacing long enough to study the players on the off chance that Kol had been eliminated. Harry couldn't determine whether she was relieved or nervous that he remained inside the playing chamber.

A gangly, hunched-over alien loped through the doorway. Harry presumed he was the dealer, since he wore a fancier version of the red vest that Harry had seen employees sporting downstairs in the lounge. With a ropy arm, he waved them toward the gaming room. q marched through the opening, mail skirt swishing with every swift step.

Harry took Tom by the shoulder and shook him. He

groaned in protest and slapped at Harry's hands before allowing Harry to pull him to his feet. Groggily, he stumbled after Harry into the game room. The door smashed closed behind them with a *shhoop*. Noting the two empty gray upholstered seats behind q, Harry pushed Tom into the one nearest the door, and then took the seat off to q's left for himself.

Trimmed with light strips, the silver and black game table, shaped like a four-pointed star, was partitioned into five sections. The four triangular-shaped arm sections, composed of a hard, transparent polymer and lit from beneath, were the "pyramids"; each pyramid had nine slots in which they would insert the colored playing pieces that "built" their pyramids. The dealer, representing the house, sat at the fourth "pyramid" section. The leftover square space in the table's middle, a solid black color, served as the area where the dice were cast. One team was stationed at each pyramid. The dealer stood at Harry, Tom, and q's right.

Seated at their left was a player the dealer identified as a Rutillian—who preferred not to share his name. He was an alien with skin of the palest white-gray and a single yellow eye in the center of his cylindrical head. His appearance reminded Harry of a character that might be found in one of the mutant zombie holovids that Tom occasionally dragged him to. The Rutillian's luxuriant robes of dark purple hid most other anatomical features, save a clawed hand emerging out of a heavy satin sleeve. Harry immediately wondered whether this was the gambler who had brought about the demotion of the Namian dealer they'd chatted up in the lounge. The prospect of having an opponent who "destroyed things" didn't offer much reassurance to Harry. The dealer then introduced Kol, who sat directly across from their pyramid.

"We know each other," q said in a clipped tone.

Kol offered a tight-lipped smile in return but otherwise gave no sign of emotion.

Harry was uncertain about what game these two were playing, but the chilly interchange between supposed friends surprised him. Ever more surprising, however, was the Keeper of the Light himself.

After hearing stories of Kol's wild streak—his recklessness and irresponsibility in accumulating gambling debts and being a node racer—Harry had formed a picture of a callow, irresponsible playboy in his mind: flashy clothes, thick gold rings stacked on his fingers, half-naked females hanging on his shoulders. What struck Harry the most about this, his first in-person encounter with the Kol, was how ordinary he appeared to be. He evinced a monklike asceticism in his choice of clothing, a dark blue, coarsely woven tunic with no embellishment. Appearance-wise, q was showier than Kol. He, with his smooth, bald head, dark brown eyebrows, and neat goatee, might pass for the humblest of Bajoran vedeks, even without the rhinal ridges. If Harry had passed Kol in the streets anywhere on Earth, he wouldn't have given the fellow a second look. Only Kol's green eyes flashed with the vivacity Harry would have expected from a being of such power. Surprising, though, were Kol's Ocampan ears, which Harry had somehow missed earlier when he'd viewed the holo back at Q U.

With all the introductions made, the dealer explained in unruffled tones the order the rounds would be played. The Rutillian, who had been the most successful in previous games, would make the first roll of the dice and receive the first playing pieces. Kol would go second and q last. Neither Kol nor the Rutillian played with a team.

The Rutillian took the dice cup, shook it several times, and threw the silver-edged dice out onto the game table. A red and two yellow faces appeared. He slid his three pieces into position on his pyramid. The dealer passed the dice to Kol. Kol's roll was equally unremarkable. Once his pieces had been slotted where he wanted them, the dice cup moved again, and this time to q. She chose one piece; Tom and Harry each selected one. The dice cup continued around the table until all three teams had filled their nine-slot pyramids with colored building pieces. Now the tension began in earnest: betting.

The Rutillian dropped the chips he was betting into a slot at the base of his pyramid. Each time a chip dropped, the slot lit up. When he finished placing his bet, the room darkened. A dazzling starscape holoprojection filled the room. Harry stared, overcome with the sensation that he had it within him to reach up and pluck a star from among the billions that surrounded him.

A silky female voice said, *Aquilleus Minor nebula,* and a dark green circle appeared around a cluster of stars floating above Kol's head. The projection zoomed in, providing close-up detail of the stacks of dark dust and cool gases rising like stalagmites out of the nebula. Ultraviolet light from nearby stars lit up the celestial gases wreathing the towering stellar nursery in gold. Text, readable to Harry, scrolled beside the nebula, and included recognizable chemical formulae for the matter found in the nebula.

The silky voice continued. *Pararonsian asteroid belt.* This time, when the projection zoomed in, Harry wasn't surprised. After a few moments, the text scrolling began and it became apparent that the Rutillian offered asteroids rich in tyrillium ore and other heavy metals. His other chips included another nebula and several dead moons.

q whispered in Harry's ear that the real prize in the Rutillian's bet was the asteroid belt—the rest was showy, but not too valuable. "We should be glad that his bet was so conservative," she concluded. "We won't be eliminated straight out."

Kol's bet was similar to the Rutillian's save that he threw in at least half a dozen Keys to Gremadia. Harry startled at the revelation of the chips after having witnessed back on *Voyager* what disastrous events had been unleashed by Captain Janeway's possessing the Monorhan's Key to Gremadia. How Kol could so casually toss in items that held such power and meaning for "lesser" life-forms gave Harry insight into the Keeper's personality that he hadn't had before. It was as if he saw the universe as a theoretical construct whose pieces were to be shuffled around a board—like in a game of Trinity. Where was the Keeper's moral compass? Harry dared a direct look at Kol. The Keeper lifted his eyes. Any hint of vivacity had vanished: all emotion had become opaque. Now he understood why simply finding Kol wasn't enough. Based on what Harry observed from the Keeper, he wasn't sure if Kol could be persuaded to *care* about their current dilemma by words alone. He had to trust that q had a plan to get through to him. If nothing else, he was learning, through this experience, to disregard his former assumptions and realize that what he thought he knew to be real could conceivably be light-years from the truth. Harry sighed deeply.

q entered their bet into the slot. When he saw their chip pile decrease by half, it took a great deal of self-control to stop from questioning the wisdom of q's choice. But she seemed to know what she was doing, and what Harry knew about Trinity could fit in a thimble.

The dealer turned to the Rutillian. "What are the match terms?"

Without hesitating, the Rutillian said, "A three-side match."

q smirked.

Harry leaned over and said, "What's so funny?"

"Stop being such a worrier, Harry," she replied, but there was lightness in her voice he hadn't heard since they'd entered Fortis. "Pay attention, though. You'll be taking a turn soon."

"What!?" Harry whispered.

q brushed him aside with a wave of her hand.

The dealer activated the computer. After the dim light of the stars, the flashing white table lights hurt Harry's eyes. Several seconds later, the house's pyramid appeared. All three teams breathed a sigh of relief: they had all matched three side slots with the house. An illuminated outline appeared beneath each of the matched slots. Six slots on each pyramid game remained unlit.

Kol requested a four-slot match, any direction.

Theoretically, Harry wasn't sure what the likelihood of success was—he still hadn't figured out a satisfactory probability model—but what he could calculate didn't favor any of them. Moments later his concerns bore fruit: none of the teams made a complete match. Kol and q made a two-slot match. The Rutillian matched three. Four unlit slots remained on q and Kol's boards; three remained on the house's board.

The losing teams owed a penalty; the dealer poached a chip from both Kol and q's team. Two of the Keys to Gremadia vanished from off the board and one of q's nebulae was circled in silver—the house's color. The Rutillian's loss amounted to one of his dead moons.

As Harry understood it, q and Kol both needed to contribute more chips to the pool if they wanted to remain in the game. Both teams had four unlit slots to play against the computer's three remaining slots. The only possible outcome for q and Kol at this point was to survive to play a second round: neither of them could beat the house or the Rutillian. Theoretically, however, the Rutillian could still lose or tie both q and Kol.

q slipped one chip into the slot and requested a two-slot match, any direction. Kol met her bet and thus stayed in the game. If both of them matched, they would continue playing. Moments later, the computer flashed their fate.

Harry swore that q shuddered with relief when they made the two-slot match. *So much for a sure thing,* he thought. Kol, too, made a match and stayed in the game. Because the Rutillian matched only one slot, he gained only one chip from the house—hardly a confidence-building win. The dealer indicated the Rutillian's win, a pulsar, by circling the blinking star in green. Seconds later, a chip—the deed to the pulsar, Harry guessed—popped out of a slot beside the Rutillian's chair.

"Have fun betting that waste of space," q said, sneering at the Rutillian from across the table.

His yellow eye twitched.

"What do you mean by that?" Harry whispered in q's ear.

"That star's hardly worth the hydrogen it's made of. Not a significant gain."

The Rutillian pointed a finger at the blinking star.

The bright white explosion had the blinding brilliance of a supernova. Harry shielded his eyes with his arm and waited for the light to fade before raising his head.

"What-I-think-just-happened-didn't-just-happen," Tom said, his compressed speech barely intelligible. "Right?"

Skin blanched, q leaned backward in her chair so both Tom and Harry could hear her sotto-voce reply. "He destroyed the pulsar."

Her voice had a tone of incredulity that worried Harry. "You mean he destroyed the representation of the pulsar." His mind rejected the notion that thoughtful, highly advanced beings would find entertainment in the arbitrary obliteration of stars.

"No, I mean he *destroyed* the pulsar—a real star— somewhere in the Pretagen quarter. I need a drink. Does anyone else need a drink?" she said, her effort to sound flippant and casual failed miserably. With a trembling finger, she touched a button on the table and a tall, smoking mug emerged from beneath. "You want one of these?" When a wide-eyed, decidedly paler Tom shook his head, she took a long pull off the rim and then wiped her mouth on her hand.

Harry was still trying to wrap his brain around the idea that the Rutillian, with a point of the finger, could wipe out a star. "Why'd he do it?"

"Because he can," q said, and took another, longer drink from her mug. "And if that doesn't give you an idea of what we're up against here, I don't know what will."

Openmouthed, Harry collapsed back into his chair, still trying to comprehend the implications of such power. He couldn't shake off his stupor through the whole second round of building the pyramid. This time, when q asked both him and Tom to slot the pieces earned off two of the rolls of the dice, Harry hardly bothered to put any thought into his choice. Harry still was in a fog when the betting began. Because the Rutillian was the only player who had earned anything off the last round, he opened the betting. The now-familiar starscape appeared, and as the green circles were drawn around stars and planetary systems, Harry wondered which of these would succumb to the same fate as the pulsar.

Next up, q placed their team's bet. One by one, her

chips went into the slot. Their stack was down to almost nothing.

"Here, take this," Tom said, and slipped the metal box containing Monorha to q. "It's good luck."

She nodded and added the box to their bet. "If Kol wants to stay in the game, he has to pony up the goods. We'll break him faster that way—he'll be forced out of the game and we'll have a shot at convincing him to leave with us."

Across the table, Kol slid his chips into the slot.

A circle appeared around a Class-M planet. The zoom-in view showed a serene world that seemed familiar to Harry. The text narration began scrolling. When he saw "Ocampa" among the garble he rose from his seat and whispered, "No."

The room stopped.

q reached back, grabbed Harry by the sleeve, and pushed him back down into his chair. "Stay out of it, Harry."

"You said he wouldn't risk Ocampa!"

"This isn't your fight," q said through gritted teeth.

"Listen to her." Tom placed a reassuring hand on his arm, but Harry could see that his friend was every bit as distressed as he was.

Raking her hair with her fingers and fidgeting in her chair, q appeared to be attempting to calm down, though not successfully.

Harry glared at Kol across the table as if by a look he could force the Keeper to awaken from his indifference. *You are part Ocampan!* He wanted to shout.

Kol's eyebrows knitted together; his eyes flickered between q and the planet Ocampa.

"What are you thinking?" q asked coldly. "I mean, I've defended you. I've had your back all this time, and for what? So you can be a bastard like that guy over there?" She jerked her thumb at the Rutillian.

Kol fixed his stare on q, the shadow of a frown darkening his face; he remained silent.

"If you can callously throw away something *I* know matters to you, you've gone past the point where I even care what happens to you. Good riddance. I hope the Nacene get you—you deserve it."

"Is there a problem?" the dealer said smoothly.

Straightening her jewelry, q touched the panel and another drink appeared. "Problem? No problem. Why would you ask? Let's resume play, shall we?" q tipped back her glass and sucked down her drink to the dregs.

Harry crossed his arms across his chest. He'd be damned if he went along with this charade. There had to be another approach. Maybe q could take out that bastard Rutillian. Snap her fingers and reduce him to smithereens . . .

As if he could sense Harry's thoughts, the Rutillian's grotesque glowing yellow eye fixed on him. The hairs on Harry's arm prickled.

"Game play will resume," the dealer said.

Like the last time, the Rutillian chose a three-side match. Because it was the first round, all of the teams matched three slots easily, allowing them to breeze through to the next round. The win forced the house to add to each player's coffers just enough to instill a sense of confidence—or that was how Harry read the table. *Lure in the prey with a promise of more to come, then snap the trap.*

The dealer was saying something, though Harry couldn't understand what. Nor did he care. Probably Kol choosing how many slots the teams would need to match. It was all so much choice and chance that he'd given up trying to beat the system.

Until now, he'd happily played along with q's plan because he didn't believe he had another choice. And admittedly, there was his personal interest. But now . . . now he'd lost the stomach for it. Tilting back his chair, he studied the stars projected on the ceiling above him. *So which of you are going to be blown up because a pandimensional being decides to play dice with the universe?* The pinpricks of white starlight against the blackness of space reminded him of the view from *Voyager*'s bridge. Homesickness beset him. He'd been so caught up in the throes of infatuation, he hadn't given *Voyager* much thought since they arrived at Fortis. Damn that Q!

Feeling eyes upon him, he tore his gaze from the starscape. Both Tom and q looked expectantly at him. He couldn't figure what they might want from him and said so.

"You get to select the next match," Tom said.

Harry blinked. "I don't want to."

"That's not how the game works," q said, sighing deeply. "I chose last time. You choose this time. Tom chooses next time, assuming there is a next time. This is why we play as a team; otherwise one player shoulders all the risk."

Exhaling a lungful of air, Harry then gnawed his lips. "I don't have a clue." Shaking his head, he said to q, "Use that marvelous Q-ness you omnipotent types brag about to give me a clue."

"That's not how it works," q said. "Choice—"

"—and chance," Harry finished for her. He could continue to protest, though from the look on the dealer's face he suspected that if he did so his team would forfeit the bet. He glanced at the game board. The first round had illuminated three slots. The second—Kol's bet—had illuminated two left-side slots. None of the teams had won the second round so each had forfeited a small number of minor credits. All credits with the level of Ocampa's value remained on the board. Harry studied the colors, the lights, imagined what his best odds were and came up with nothing.

Harry considered his choices. What would Tom do in this situation? He wasn't a logic gambler, he was an emotional gambler. Tom would make a meaningful bet based on a personally significant fact or just gut instinct. The system—or lack of one—worked pretty well for the pilot. While Harry wanted to run all the scenarios and crunch the numbers, Tom gave a lot of credence to personal intuition.

Only one aspect of this damnable situation felt intuitive: his personal tie to Ocampa, *Kes*.

Harry smiled. His gut told him he was in the right place. "Three-slot match." He'd known Kes for just a bit more than three years, but since 3.2 wasn't an option, he rounded down.

q twisted back to look at him. He didn't need to hear her say "Are you sure?" because the dubious expression in her eyes told him she thought he was making a mistake.

The dealer repeated Harry's request, waited for Harry to confirm it, then initiated the house reveal. Lights flickered and pulsed across the table. Harry drilled his eyes on their pyramid. His arms hung at his sides, hands clenched into fists that he pumped up and down with the rhythm of the lights. "Come on, Kes, don't let me down. . . ."

Hand in hand, the Nacene Exiles formed a ring around Monorha's outer atmosphere. Phoebe, of course, had taken her position at the head of the Circle. She had organized her followers according to their strength, making certain that weakest among them stood between the strong. Their efforts would not be foiled by the vulnerable. She would do to them what had been done to the Enaran if necessary.

Once all the Exiles had assumed their places, Phoebe reached out to them, gently penetrating the barriers that defined their individuality. One by one, she separated them from their rigidly held grasp on their singular states and invited them to flow into her. In return, she flowed into them until they became a greater whole. The gloriousness of the energy intoxicated Phoebe. Since Exosia, she had never approached such a complete, pure state of being. She shared the magnificence of this with the others, promising that such sensations would be endless once the gateway had opened.

As one Exile ceased to be alone and joined the many, another was brought into the Circle, and so on until each of the survivors had been fused together. For a time, they remained in this state of wholeness until an equilibrium had been attained. What they were about to undertake required perfect unity and an exact exercise of will.

On Phoebe's cue, they began exploring the life force of the planet Monorha. Much satisfaction filled the Circle as they recognized elements of long-forgotten comrades and allies buried in the memories of plants and animals—in the elements of soil, rock, and air. *We will take you home,* the Circle promised. *We will restore you.*

The Circle's will poured into the spaces between atoms, gaining knowledge of all the planet's matter and energy. Soon the Circle understood the intricate, inexorably entwined vibrations that created the music that sang the planet Monorha into being. Because this place came from the Nacene, the familiar refrains tantalized them with possibilities of home and the music of Exosia. The Circle explored until all knowledge of Monorha was shared among them. They accepted the knowledge, made it part of their core beings. With that final task completed, the time had at last arrived for the Circle to create the Key.

The will of the Circle converged on Monorha. With knowledge of the song, the song could be changed. The Circle closed subatomic spaces, compressing particles together, transforming an atom. The energy created from fusing particles together rippled into adjoining particles until a cascade of transformation was under way. The Circle coaxed the process along, guiding the music to suit their needs. Momentary discord was expected as Monorha's subatomic structure underwent a dramatic metamorphosis, but the Circle would restore harmony. They would take the life force of every entity on the planet and create a dazzling symphony.

The first energy wave emanated from the planet, infusing the Circle with new power to continue their task.

The Key would not be formed instantly. Collapsing a planet took time. But what was time except a limitation imposed on the Circle by this primitive dimension? Few of these restrictions would hamper the Circle for long.

Exosia awaited them.

Tom shot a glance at Harry at the mention of Kes.

The lights stopped. The house pyramid glowed warm red, yellow, and orange.

The knot from his throat moved to his stomach, rolling around like a lead meteor. Dropping his head, Harry groaned aloud. He couldn't bear to witness the catastrophe.

He'd failed to match.

I was so sure, Harry thought. *I just knew it was the right thing to do . . . how could we have lost?* Over and over, he reviewed his choice. He had felt *guided.* This wasn't possible!

"This is the last time I trust corporeal life-forms to do *anything*," q muttered under her breath.

Harry dared a glance up at the starscape. All the chips had been shifted over to the Rutillian. He shook his head, trying to understand the implications. A moment later, he realized that Kol must have lost too. Unless Kol had more chips, he was out of the game too.

The Rutillian linked his hands together, flexing his thick, clawed fingers.

Harry stopped breathing; neither Tom nor q made a sound either, all of them watching the Rutillian's next move.

Don't do it, don't do it, Harry chanted mentally.

q threaded Harry's fingers with her own and squeezed tightly.

The Rutillian's finger leisurely drew invisible circles as he contemplated his choice. He turned a yellow glowing eye on q's team and fixed his finger toward Monorha.

The Doctor writhed on the floor, Vivia's containment field pressing against his matrix. *Voyager*'s message replayed several times, taunting him. He focused his energy, trying to push through Vivia's barrier the way he had when he'd first been captured, but discovered he was incapable of breaking through. He struggled to understand what had changed when a realization struck: he was clothed in Ced's flesh.

Vivia looked on placidly, watching him suffer. Clearly she wanted him to relent—to admit that she was right, he was wrong—or he would never return to his ship. The Doctor thought of Kes. He would hold on for her sake. He couldn't allow Vivia to hurt the child. The sizzling heat of containment strangled his matrix; the Doctor shrank away from the field, remembering what agony

Vivia could inflict on him. One last time, he tried to reason with her, crying weakly, "Don't . . . be . . . like them!"

Vivia hovered beside the orchestra pit, the bland, repetitious music of the strings punctuated by *Voyager*'s static message. He could see the conflict warring on her face. That she hated—no, loathed—the Exiles was without question. But she made no move to free him from the energy field that pressed closer, ever closer with every passing second.

Give up and you will go home.

Crackling, jagged threads brushed against his matrix like sharp-edged knives, peeling his skin away layer by layer. A single thought remained in his mind and he willed Vivia to know it: *I will not betray Kes.*

She answered him with a hard look.

The Doctor braced himself for the end.

The field collapsed.

Vivia's head jerked from side to side, searching for the culprit who had thwarted her plan.

"This isn't your choice to make, Vivia," a new voice said.

Panting, the Doctor rolled over onto his back and sprawled out on the stage.

Q strolled out of the wings, hands linked behind his back. "Get on your feet, man. There are great things afoot. Get it? Afoot—feet? I just keep 'em coming."

How dare you! Vivia raged.

"How dare I?" Q said, raising an eyebrow. "How dare *you*. You know better than to fiddle with the timeline, Vivia. You can't negate the consequences of others choices simply because you're a little bothered by a few photons." He reached down and gave the Doctor a hand up.

The Doctor brushed the dust from his uniform. "Thanks."

"You've got a decision to make," Q said. He pointed to the ceiling, indicating the loop playing *Voyager*'s message. "Return to that tin can you call a starship or to that adorable Ocampan you're so fond of. It's up to you."

How easy it would be to leave this hellish dimension and return to live among the people he loved—people who needed him. The penultimate question: Once the Light was reborn, what would happen to Kes? Balim's words came back to him. *I promise you that you will return to* Voyager *if you trust me.*

He sighed deeply, whispered words that he hoped beyond hope that Seven of Nine would hear, and made his choice. In a blink he disappeared.

No one understood how difficult it was, Vivia thought, to be the caretakers of the strings. The Q could be cavalier about the Nacene duty: they weren't bound to any one dimension. They could do as they pleased. Spoiled children.

Q folded his arms and walked over to the edge of the stage where Vivia hovered above the orchestra pit. She pointedly ignored him.

"You should know better than to tamper in the big game, Vivia. But he was right, you know, the Doctor. You should think about what he said—while you're waiting for your company to arrive." He snapped his fingers.

Vivia spun around to face him but Q had disappeared.

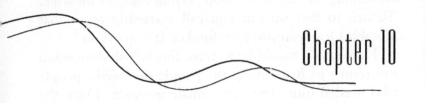

Chapter 10

Seven and Chakotay rushed onto the bridge.

"Report!" Chakotay ordered, before he'd even taken his place in the captain's chair.

Seven walked straight to the engineering station.

Ayala read from his console. "Class-five energy wave originating in the vicinity of the third planet. Sensor readings are inconclusive."

"Shields down to eighty percent," Rollins added.

"Can we expect another wave?" Chakotay said, studying the data pouring into his own viewscreen.

"I don't know, sir," Ayala said. "Initially, it appeared as if an explosion took place. But on a second read, it seems more likely that something is collapsing at such a rapid rate that the result is a massive release of energy."

"Has the away team been hit?" Chakotay asked.

"Can't say, sir. Communications have been disrupted."

Chakotay knew enough of his own species' history to recall Earth's twenty-first-century experimentation with hydrogen fusion, both as an energy source and as a weapon. Ayala's interpretation of the data helped clarify his own thinking. No doubt in his mind that matter fusion was under way in the Monorhan sector.

"Another wave of that magnitude will drop our shield strength to fifty percent, maybe less," Seven said. "Our ability to successfully exit this region will be compromised."

"Ayala, I want the long-range sensor data on Monorha. What is the planet's status?" Chakotay said, feeling his stomach twist with anticipated dread.

"Sir, the shields—" Rollins said.

"I'm well aware of the shields, Mr. Rollins," Chakotay said.

"I have to concur with Mr. Rollins," Seven said. "Once we have resolved the outstanding issue we discussed in the ready room, a speedy departure would be advisable."

He met her eyes across the bridge. *The Doctor!* In the panic of red alert, he'd almost forgotten. "Seven, focus your attention on the probe. Resolve that situation as soon as possible." His unspoken meaning: *Do what it takes to get the Doctor back.*

Seven nodded, almost imperceptibly, and returned to work.

A few seconds passed as Ayala complied with the order. Chakotay knew that the anomalous character of the region made every task take longer than any of them would prefer.

Finally, Ayala rose from his station, his mouth agape. "Sir . . . I don't know how to say this, but it appears that Monorha is imploding. The planet . . . it's collapsing in on itself."

Before he could make a final determination of what course to take, Chakotay needed one last piece of information. "Scan the planet. Are there any unusual energy signatures?"

Ayala ordered the computer to perform the task.

The answer chilled them all.

"*An incalculable number of Nacene are in the region of Monorha.*"

Chakotay opened a channel to Tuvok. "Away team, this is *Voyager*. Get back here. *Now!*" As he walked over to Seven at the engineering station, he ordered Knowles to prepare her navigational coordinates for immediate departure.

"The *rih-hara-tan* are in the shuttlebay," Rollins said.

He paused in midstride. His first inclination—to curse—quickly gave way to a realization that the Monorhan leaders might yet prove to be useful. "No one leaves *Voyager*. Tell Neelix to stay with them and stand by for orders." Braced against the engineering console, he leaned over and said so softly that no one but Seven could hear him, "Are we going to be able to bring the Doctor in before Tuvok and the away team return?"

Words proved to be unnecessary: the worry in Seven's eyes answered his question.

Klingons weren't known as perfectionists, save where weapons technique—say, with the *bat'leth*—was concerned. Nothing but indifference could explain Klingon cuisine. So B'Elanna blamed the impulse driving her back to the compartment where she'd had problems with bleeding the coolant on her human heritage. Theoretically, what she had done should have destabilized enough of the volatile chemical that an explosion would follow. The "should" part bothered her. She had neither the time nor the room to make a mistake. The chain reaction she'd carefully orchestrated needed to work the first time: there wouldn't be a second chance. Besides, the last she'd checked with Tuvok, the shuttle wouldn't be departing for another fifteen minutes. Plenty of time.

B'Elanna reached the edge of the compartment. The

damnable gap she had to jump across. She'd done this what, a dozen times over the last hour and survived with a minimum amount of adrenaline-induced apprehension. *Get a grip, Torres,* she thought, and took the jump.

Midway across the gap, B'Elanna was struck from behind.

Her mind had only a few seconds to process the severe blow—akin to a belly flop into water off of a thirty-meter cliff—before the force expelled the air from her lungs. Breathless, she gagged; futile gasps drew nothing into her oxygen-starved body. The starscape before her helmet spun round and round until all the flecks of light blurred into jagged streaks. Disoriented, she reflexively threw her arms out to her sides, seeking a sense of up and down so she could right herself, but the spinning continued. Warm, dark lethargy relaxed her: she welcomed the relief.

She blacked out.

Before Commander Chakotay had finished giving his order, Tuvok had started walking toward the airlock where Ensign Tariq was waiting with the shuttle. Ensign Luiz had joined him a few moments ago. Lieutenant Torres had requested additional time that Tuvok felt was unnecessary. Recognizing the engineer's determination, he allowed her to remain working with the understanding that she would be transported aboard the shuttle at the soonest possible moment. The range and effectiveness of the transporters in this disturbed region favored Torres's request for more time, however. Tariq would have to pilot the shuttle within visual range in order to assure that there wouldn't be any problems with the matter buffer. She would be pleased.

The last of the supplies had been loaded into the passenger compartments moments ago. The rudimentary portable replicators that B'Elanna had asked for from *Voyager* were placed in central locations. Tuvok had explained their use, the best he could coupled with a demonstration, to the strongest Monorhan he could find in each place. It would be a good thing when the *rih-hara-tan* returned and could provide proper guidance.

He touched his combadge. "Commander Tuvok to Tariq. Time to depart. Has Lieutenant Torres returned?"

"She said she had one last compartment to check out and she'd—" The com signal stopped unexpectedly.

Before Tuvok could wonder why, the compartment he was traveling through quaked violently, swinging sideways, then back again, like a watercraft careering on the Sea of Tears on Vulcan. On every side, hull plating groaned; Tuvok watched the metal bow before his eyes. Monorhans clung to whatever foot- or handhold they could find. Debris flew through the air, crashing into whatever and whoever was in its path. The lights blinked off and on. Tuvok heard screams echoing throughout the ship, the thuds of bodies being hurled against the walls. He clung with one hand to a metal support that connected the floor and ceiling. "Tuvok to shuttle *du Châtelet.*"

Static answered him.

The tremors stopped.

Moments later: *"Commander, this is Tariq. Shock wave of unknown origin just hit us."*

"Lock on my signal and prepare for transport as soon as I'm within range."

"Transporter standing by, waiting for your command." Tuvok resumed his trek toward the waiting shuttle. He had only five or so meters before he was in transporter range. For the first time since arriving in Monorhan space, he keenly felt the inconveniences caused by the abnormal spatial conditions. It would be far more efficient if Ensign Tariq

could simply remove him from the premises, especially in red-alert conditions.

A vision of Lieutenant Torres in an EVA suit working on the outside of the ship flashed before his eyes. He touched his combadge. "Torres?"

No answer. He contacted Tariq.

"Sensors can't find her," the pilot answered. *"She's not where she was supposed to be. The shock wave must have thrown her from the ship."*

Tuvok had been counting the steps until he could leave this unpleasant and dangerous location. He checked his chronometer: the explosion had to be imminent. The shuttle needed to have cleared the area by the time the detonation sequence began. The second Tuvok stepped into range he ordered the shuttle's transporters to beam him out.

The first words out of his mouth after he rematerialized were "Find Lieutenant Torres. Now."

Well-orchestrated chaos on the bridge reminded Seven of those moments in the collective when all the voices spoke simultaneously. Her comfort in these circumstances aided her concentration. As subtly as she could, she slid open a door to a nearby storage compartment, removed a small earpiece, and slid it into place over her outer ear, the bud sliding into her auditory canal. Manually, she ordered the computer to send all the probe audio to her earpiece. She would not risk distracting Ayala, who sat nearby, by allowing the newly appointed bridge officer to hear the exact nature of the broadcast.

Granted, most of what Seven could hear was static and unintelligible garble. She had no doubt that someone inside the gash was attempting to communicate, but whether that communication was directed to her or at

Voyager was what she needed to determine. Lacking the time to filter out the background noise, Seven had the computer record all of the transmissions so she could study them later.

As best she could, she multitasked, keeping a watchful eye on the events transpiring near Monorha. Best she could tell, the Nacene had attacked the planet, though for what purpose wasn't readily apparent to her.

The probe indicated that it had nearly located all of the Doctor's datablocks. All that needed to be done was to initiate the transfer. Seven wanted to allow as much of his matrix as possible to be identified before the rescue started, so she watched the green bars climbing on her screen for the optimal level to be reached.

A red light flashing on her console drew her attention. She raised her eyes to the sensor readouts. She glanced sideways and saw Ayala, looking at her; their eyes met. An unvoiced question passed between them: *Who tells the commander?*

Seven nodded encouragingly.

Ayala spun away from Seven. "Commander Chakotay, a second shock wave is heading in this direction. We have five minutes before it arrives."

Since the green bars on the screen remained unchanged, Seven permitted herself a moment to study Chakotay's solemn, stern face. How he would protect *Voyager* from the inevitable damage to the shields was not a problem he had the luxury of time to solve. He paused for a long moment, then touched his combadge. "Neelix, I'm ordering an emergency transport of the *rih-hara-tan*. Mr. Rollins, lock in on the Monorhans and send them to main engineering."

"Sir?" Rollins sounded confused.

"Do it," Chakotay snapped.

Very clever, Commander, Seven thought as Chakotay's plan took shape in her mind. *I don't know that I would have thought of that approach.* As tempting as it was to try and be involved in the emergency goings-on, Seven directed all her attention to the probe. If the identification rate continued as it had thus far, she expected to initiate transfer within seconds.

Another blurt of garbled noise erupted into her earpiece. Something amid the noise—an intonation, the modulation—sounded familiar. She knew how close they were to restoring the Doctor to *Voyager.* Her hand hovered over the button that would bring him home—

The green bars vanished.

Seven blinked, wondering if her eyes were playing tricks on her. But no, the screen remained empty. Trying to remain calm, she studied the datafeed, wondering if the probe had gone dark, if the shock wave had interfered with the transmission—anything that would explain why she had the Doctor a moment ago and now she didn't. Out of the corner of her eye, she looked at Chakotay, who was barking orders at Neelix and the *rih-hara-tan.* She couldn't tell him now. Not when the risk to the ship was so great. She shifted her attention back to the probe.

"Shock wave will arrive in three minutes," Ayala said solemnly.

She had never understood the human expression "having the rug pulled out from under me" until now. In this moment when it seemed all her best efforts had failed, it felt as though the deck plating had dropped out from beneath her feet, dragging her digestion and circulation with it.

The Doctor awoke to lightning dancing across a sickly, gray-yellow sky, answered by growling thunder. The air, thick with humidity, promised rain, but there would be none for this dying world. The Doctor knew this story's ending. Nacene interference would destroy Ocampa, and its people would spend millennia held hostage deep in the ground because of unlivable surface conditions. Looking around him, it was as if these soldiers—Lia's army—could sense that fate would rule against them over the long term. They packed their gear, collapsed their tents, and prepared to leave for the next battleground. The Doctor had made it known that Lia would not recover from the damage she suffered in the last attack. Junior officers had assumed command. He had no idea where they were headed or what their plans were other than actively pursuing Mestof's soldiers. He had not involved himself in their decision making, choosing instead to devote all his attention to Kes.

Pulling his cape closer around him, he sat up and huddled into the rock wall beside the tent, seeking protection from the dust and wind. At least Kes was protected from the elements, inside. Last time he checked on her, shortly after Vivia had returned him to Ocampa, she had slept as peacefully as a female could in the final stages of gestation. How many hours had that been—six? Seven? And truth be told, he wasn't exactly sure how to think of the woman who rested behind the tent flap.

In his dealings with her, he spoke to her and treated her as he would Kes, though she had explained to him that the physical body he interacted with belonged to Lia. Lia's weak and fragmented life force had temporarily grafted onto Kes's. Being already accustomed to complex and intense neurological energies, Lia's Ocampan physiology readily accomodated Kes's highly evolved life force.

There was no question in the Doctor's mind that had

Kes not agreed to intervene, Lia would have died. Lia's life force would linger as long as Kes sustained her. For now, Lia existed, but not independently.

Before his current experience inhabiting Ced's body, the Doctor may have been dubious about Kes's explanation. Now he understood from firsthand experience—at least in part—what Kes and Lia were going through. One of his few regrets was that he would not know Ced the way Kes knew Lia; in this he envied Kes a little.

He felt around his person until he found the weapons Ced usually carried for protection—a dagger and a fire lance. He drew out both from where they were buried in his robes. Though he doubted that either of these items could harm Vivia should she decide to confront him here, he might have a fair shot at holding back any deserters or marauding villagers seeking to ease their suffering through scavenging whatever had been abandoned by the departing soldiers. Among those left behind were an aging Ocampan soldier plagued by gout and arthritis and a pregnant female—hardly a match for the desperate.

On the positive side, the Doctor believed that the Caretaker and Suspiria had already begun creating their protective web for the Ocampa and by so doing were protecting him as well. From what he learned from Kes, the pair had accepted the punishment Balim imposed before the Light had departed. By Nacene standards, they were the youngest of the Exiles. For agreeing to his terms, Balim had protected Suspiria and the Caretaker, preventing them from being discovered here by other, more opportunistic Nacene like Vivia's Exile counterpart, Phoebe. He didn't know what was worse: being on a dying world or being out where Phoebe must be waging her own war of attrition. Both Vivia and Phoebe had chosen the form of a rampaging Janeway female. There seemed to be something vaguely appropriate about that choice, though the Doctor wasn't exactly sure what.

A low, throaty groan came from inside the tent.

Without examining her, the Doctor knew the time had come to bring the Keeper of the Light into the universe. He gathered up his possessions and entered the tent. Once inside, he laid his pack flat, opened the flap, and removed the ropes he would use to tie up her arms to facilitate delivery, as well as the oils that would be massaged into her delivery canal. On a professional note, he'd never before delivered a hybrid Ocampa-Nacene, so he believed the experience would be educational.

Throwing the cape back over his shoulder, he pushed up his tunic sleeves and then squeezed a few precious drops of water from the water sack to wipe the dust from his hands. He poured a quantity of wine from another skin over his hands and lower arms, hoping the alcohol content would adequately sterilize his skin.

Another groan, deeper and more prolonged, emerged from the cot.

Though the gestation period had taken hours because of the Balim's Nacene energies, the delivery, alas, would still be of normal duration. By lantern light, the Doctor worked with Kes long into the night, coaxing her to breathe through the pain. He massaged her back and arms, placed water on her tongue, and rubbed ointment into her parched lips. Sometime after the moon had set, she began hallucinating, rambling on about an amalgam of lives and realities that the Doctor couldn't follow. A fever began.

The Doctor considered emergency surgery, uncertain whether Lia's body could survive such a procedure. In the half-light of early dawn, the child, the Keeper of the Light, was finally born. He cried loudly, with powerful lungs.

Kes wrapped him in the Doctor's cape and clutched the child to her breast. The Keeper of the Light had breathed the air of his native Ocampa for only a few minutes when the Doctor heard noises outside. He slid the dagger out of its hiding place and peeked beneath the tent flap.

"Knock, knock," a familiar voice said.

The Doctor sheathed his dagger. "Nice to see you again, Q."

Q strolled into the tent, a buxom blonde coiled around his arm. "Well done, Doctor, and you too, Mommy." He nodded toward Kes. "Can I see the little guy?"

Still lying on the makeshift bedroll the Doctor had created for her when the cot had become too confining, Kes tightened her grip on her child. "You've come to take him, haven't you?"

Q squatted down before Kes. "You know I have to. For his protection and yours," he said gently, resting a hand on her blanket-covered leg.

Kes blinked back tears. "May I have a moment with him?"

Jerking his head toward the entrance, he motioned for the Doctor to follow him. "Don't ever say I'm not an old softy, Doc. I am nothing if not the paragon of the sensitive modern male of the universe."

The Doctor rolled his eyes and followed behind Q.

Shortly thereafter, Kes emerged from the tent. "You'll take good care of him?"

"The finest education the Q Continuum can offer. I already have a spot for him at Q U."

Taking a deep breath, she passed the squirming bundle off to Q, who offered the baby an index finger to play with. "The kid has a death grip, Kes. What did you feed him?"

She laughed in spite of her sorrow.

"You'll see Uncle Q in a minute, little guy," Q said,

rubbing the newborn's nose. "I've just got to take care of your mom first." He passed the baby back to the buxom blonde, who vanished with a snap of Q's fingers.

Covering his mouth, he mumbled to the Doctor, "Wet nurse," and raised his eyebrows suggestively.

"Q . . ." The Doctor was most certainly not in the mood. "You know you could have just taken care of all of this from the start."

"I know. But there are those pesky issues of choice and chance. Can't fight those, I fear. I can only clean up when the smoke clears."

"So are you going to send us back to *Voyager* now?" the Doctor asked, his mood souring rapidly.

"Not quite yet. I figured Mom here would like to see how junior turned out."

Snap.

When the light from Monorha's destruction faded from the starscape, both q's team and Kol watched expectantly, wondering whether the Rutillian would obliterate Ocampa. Tom suspected that Harry might have a nervous breakdown any moment, while he—well, Tom just felt guilty. How cavalier he'd been in tossing down Monorha, gambling the lives of all those individuals *Voyager* had fought so hard to save. He'd foolishly dismissed common sense, believing that he might get another one-in-a-billion break.

Expressionless, the Rutillian raised his hand, pointing his finger in the direction of Ocampa—

A profane exclamation escaped q, who slumped down in her chair; she reached out for one of Tom's hands and one of Harry's and gripped them tightly. Across the table, Kol's eyes sought and found q's. Tom couldn't see q's face but he could sense from her body language how intently she focused on her friend.

The Rutillian's finger hovered in the air for a long moment when he abruptly jerked his elbow, as if he were about to unleash the destruction and just as abruptly pulled it back. The fake-out prompted q's team to jump in their chairs.

Mouthing "Pow!" the Rutillian displayed a scraggle-toothed grin.

Tom closed his eyes: he couldn't bear to watch.

"No."

Tom opened his eyes; q straightened up and leaned forward, watching intently.

Kol had tossed his stack of chips—including a pile hidden beneath the table—over the surface of the Rutillian's pyramid. "I'll buy it back."

"How unlike you, Keeper," the Rutillian said, his voice like rock scraping against rock.

"Ocampa means nothing to you," Kol said.

"But it evidently means something to you, which makes me believe that it is a bad idea for me to hand it over so blithely. Perhaps I should keep it for the next round. See if a more *competent* player can take it from me."

"Whatever you want for it." Kol pushed up his sleeves, unfastened several bracelets and tossed them on the chips. "I'll borrow more."

"Your credit is worth nothing. Everyone knows it." The Rutillian cackled. "You've given me a lovely story, Kol. No one will believe me when I tell them that you've suddenly grown a moral compass. How many times have we gone cavorting through galaxies together, blasting planetoids and causing tsunamis on pathetic little worlds—worlds a lot like this one!"

"Whatever the price, I'll pay it." Standing to his full height, Kol opened up his arms, as if in a pose of surrender. "Search me. Take whatever you find."

The Rutillian sniffed. "I'm bored now. This conversation becomes more taxing by the moment." He raised his arm, pointing his finger at Ocampa—

Kol stepped from behind his side of the table and walked over to the dealer. "The Rutillian is a cheater."

"Are you filing a formal complaint, Keeper?" the Dealer asked, hand hovering over a bright red security button.

The Rutillian paused. "Don't be foolish, Kol. If you insist on taking that course, you know how it will end for you."

"I don't care," Kol said to the Rutillian. To the dealer he said, "Yes, I'm filing a formal complaint."

"How do you know for certain that the gentleman is cheating?"

"Because he taught me," Kol said. "And this is how he does it—"

The Rutillian reached into his stack of chips, removed a thick one, and tossed it over to Kol. "Take your precious toy back." He brushed the stacks of credits on the table into his hands and shoved them into his pockets. "I'm done here," he said, and left the table.

Kol stood beside his chair, staring at the Ocampa chip in his hand. He glanced up at q; a smile cracked his face. For the first time since he'd laid eyes on him, Tom could see hints beneath the surface of the person Kol had the potential of becoming. The Rutillian pushed by Kol, brusquely bumping into him. Kol responded with an exaggerated bow of politeness.

A pair of humanoids with bone-white skin, clad in gray

mandarin-style tunics and matching pants, appeared in the doorway. Each wore dark glasses and stood with hands on hips. "We have a pickup."

Tom heard q chuckling quietly. He leaned over and asked her what was so funny.

"They're security. The Rutillian will have plenty of time to think about his Trinity game in the ninth—" She scooted away from the table. "Let's get out of here before they start asking us questions." She grabbed Harry's arm and guided him toward Kol's side of the table. Tom followed close behind. He extended a hand to Kol, intending to congratulate the Keeper. Just as the Ocampa-Nacene took his hand—

The four of them stood inside the aft compartment of the *Homeward Bound.*

"Games, children, such games!" Q said, opening his arms expansively and wrapping one around Kol. "The trip to Fortis was supposed to be fun. Why all the Sturm und Drang? By the looks on your faces, one might assume that instead of having fun, worlds were at stake." Starting a stroll around the cluster of them, Q paused and slapped his palm lightly against his cheek. "Why, I suppose they were. Why is that? Is it because Mr. Kim made a predictably foolish bet?" Q circled Harry, bringing his face within a nose's length of Harry's. "All these choices. All these chances and all these consequences." His expression turned dark. "Isn't it lovely?"

"I told you he loves that song and dance," q muttered.

"Did you say something q, because I don't recall inviting you to speak?" Q snapped.

She stuck out her tongue in response.

Ignoring her, Q continued, "As much fun as it is to ponder the mysteries of the universe, I believe you've done what I asked and found our AWOL friend here. Isn't that true, Mr. Paris? And yet the universe is still careering on a path to destruction."

Tom indicated that that was, indeed, the circumstance they faced.

"I suppose we should do something about that," Q said. "You've still got work to do. Computer, set a course for the Monorhan system."

"Acknowledged."

The familiar voice of the computer was music to Tom's ears. *At last, normal,* he thought. He waited for the warp nacelles to come online, but they never did. Q must be propelling them by other means. And then it occurred to him: Who was piloting the shuttle?

Before Tom could ask Q why he didn't simply snap his fingers and will them back to *Voyager,* Kol collapsed into one of the shuttle's passenger seats and exhaled loudly. "I had no idea . . ."

"It would hurt so much?" Q said.

Kol nodded. "How could I have been so careless?"

"You had to learn. Loss hurts. Not those chips you toss around like spare hydrogen molecules." Q rested a hand on Kol's shoulder. "Loss. Real loss becomes part of who and what you are."

"I'm ready. For whatever my father, my mother intended for me," Kol said.

And from his tone, Tom believed him.

"You had to learn first, Junior. Next time, there won't be a second chance," Q said. "You'll have to accept the consequences without your Uncle Q riding to the rescue."

"What's next?" Kol asked Q.

"Like I'm going to make it that easy for you?" Q made an irritable hand wave. "I'll give you a hint: You're going to have to give your Nacene relatives a good reason to get out of Exosia so the strings can be set right. Tell them they've won the lottery—or, better yet, an all-expenses-paid vacation to another dimension."

Kol smiled. "I think I know what to do."

After a long moment of companionable silence, Harry said, "So I was right. To place the bet."

Q scowled at him. "Must it always be about you, Mr. Kim?"

"Well . . . I mean . . . of course not . . . I mean—" Harry stammered.

"Obviously you aren't learning your lessons—remember choice and chance? You made a choice, took a chance, and we ended up here. So I must reluctantly admit that you chose correctly."

Tom slapped Harry between the shoulder blades. "Good work, Harry."

"On your way back to *Voyager,* you can discuss your educational advancements with a couple of friends of yours." Q snapped his fingers.

Harry had barely processed the words "back to *Voyager.*" Seated in the pilot and the copilot seat were—

Rushing forward, Tom cried out, "Doc? And—"

"Mother," Kol said. He took several long steps toward the diminutive woman seated in the passenger chair, dropped to his knees, leaned his face against Kes's tunic, and closed his eyes.

"Talk to the 'little minds,' " Neelix told Tei, the *rih-hara-tan.* As the healthiest of the bunch, the squatty, garrulous female had become the Monorhans' primary spokesperson. "Use your mind-speak to help them deliver more power to the shields. The ship's protection system."

The *rih* gave him a look that reminded him of the well-meaning, genial expression of a pet *roogalo* he'd once had. Dumb as a *lomp*'s tail, that *roogalo,* but the most snuggly pet he'd ever had—hardly ever shed! "Do you understand?" Neelix asked.

Tei clicked and thrummed a few times, but none of the others appeared to understand the *rih*'s suggestions. She gave Neelix a desperate look. "I am sorry. But they have a difficult time comprehending your . . . your . . . technology. It is far more advanced than ours."

Neelix glanced at his chronometer. Commander Chakotay had given him almost no time to use his carefully honed diplomatic expertise to teach the *rih-hara-tan* how to help *Voyager.* But wasn't that the crux of diplomacy? A carefully constructed foundation of friendship and mutual understanding so that at one critical juncture, everything worked. Well, this was a critical juncture if ever Neelix saw one. Other than Tei and Xan, the blank looks on his guests' faces concerned him—deeply. Neelix threw up his arms in frustration. "The shields are like a shell that surrounds *Voyager.* The shell protects the insides where we are. If the shell cracks, the insides break. Like your ship. The *rih* must tell the little minds that they need to work as hard as they ever have to keep the shell intact."

A veritable percussion section of thrums and clicks followed as the *rih* chattered, presumably about Neelix's request.

They spoke so quickly that the universal translator could barely keep up. Neelix didn't care. "I'm sorry, honorable *rih,* but we don't have time to discuss!" Neelix said, jumping up and down to get their attention. "*Voyager* is going to be in big trouble if we can't get those little minds to work together to be stronger. NOW."

Tei peered at Neelix, blinked twice. "I believe I understand how to teach them." She took two of his fellow *rih* by the hand and guided them toward the center of main engineering. The others followed after in their characteristic loping gait until all the Monorhans formed a line that bisected the room right in front of the warp core.

The humming began.

Neelix watched, feeling hope, but definitely understanding the dubious expressions on the faces of the engineering staff. He was confident, however, that the Monorhans knew what needed to be done. He'd already seen them demonstrate their powers, though he wasn't about to volunteer that information to Commander Chakotay.

When they first arrived, the *rih-hara-tan* had only been able to identify the irritating (to them) cacophony of noise emitting from the bioneural gel packs. It had brought them discomfort, as it had the Monorhans who had visited the previous week. Thankfully, in the intervening days since Ziv and his group departed, Neelix had been able to figure out a logical way to explain the phenomenon.

Neelix had asked each of the *rih* to focus on one specific aspect of the noise—one characteristic. Once that was accomplished, he helped the Monorhans comprehend that each unique noise represented an individual component of a group—like a *hara*—and that the noises were emitted by members of the group. When that comprehension dawned, one of the more eager *rih* had apparently "talked" the gel packs into increasing the room temperature in sickbay by two degrees Celsius. A small thing—not worth bothering the commander about—but definitely proof that the *rih* understood the gel packs.

Atonal humming began. At first Neelix believed it was a group meditation. Soon, the pitch varied within the group until the humming became an ornate fugue in a minor key that became impossible to ignore. Engineers throughout the room paused from their tasks and studied their alien guests, uncertainty written on their faces. What couldn't be denied, however, was the quiet metallic buzzing that was nearly imperceptible. Initially, Neelix thought it was just another one of those engineering noises. When the deck plating began vibrating, however, no one in the room could ignore it.

A smallish corner of Neelix's heart was fearful. Not too long ago, a Monorhan *rih* had nearly destroyed *Voyager* because of her interference with the autopilot. But only in this smallish corner did Neelix believe that these *rih* had the same black intentions as Sem. No, Neelix's heart swelled as he watched them, overwhelmed by the blessing that fate had sent them in the form of a ship of Monorhan refugees.

He would later swear that the glow from the warp core became brighter and that for a moment he believed the Blue Eye had been resurrected on their ship. Most dismissed it as one of Neelix's exaggerations. Most—but never the engineers. Whether or not the glow was real or imagined, no one ever question the reality of the words coming over the comsystem:

"Shields are at full strength and climbing. Keep it up!"

Neelix could hear the smile in Chakotay's voice.

Tuvok had never been one to be as impressed by the accomplishments of sentients as he was by the powers of nature. The wind and rains that could carve away stone with patient ministrations, for example, or the continental plates that could reshape a landmass within seconds by shifting ever so slightly.

Yet the Monorhan ship, even by Starfleet standards, was undeniably awe-inspiring. The persistence and devotion to duty that would motivate them to build a central hull that would dwarf fifteen *Enterprises* had to be admired. Perhaps it was the difficulty he was having finding Lieutenant Torres against such a colossal creation that had prompted his admiration. Against such a backdrop, she would be as a speck of dust, as Tuvok was quickly discovering.

Tariq was piloting the best he could, since they were both relying on visual. The shock wave had damaged the shuttle's sensors, so their reliability was suspect. He insisted on muttering under his breath—repeatedly—"Just don't know how we're going to find her out here."

Tuvok found Tariq's sentiments less than helpful in resolving their current predicament. The chronometer readout on the piloting control panel assured that Tuvok knew that they had mere minutes before the explosion started. Perhaps six or seven if the crudeness of Monorhan technology reduced the accuracy of Lieutenant Torres's calculations.

Tuvok studied the instruments, wondering what, if anything, these broken tools could do to help resolve the challenge before them. The wisdom of one of his *Kolinahr* masters returned to him: the mind knows all it needs to know and can, with logic and self-mastery, succeed where all else fails.

Lacking the time to undergo a full meditation and recognizing what was at stake, Tuvok forced his unruly thoughts into order, rejecting the distraction of the computer consoles, the chronometer, the texture of his uniform, the dryness of his mouth—even the heat pouring off Tariq's body in the form of copious sweat and smell. Ensign Luiz was far less emotional, and thus less distracting.

He visualized the Monorhan ship, the compartment where B'Elanna had been working and the shock wave—

unseen but felt. Stripping away the surprise component of the shock wave, Tuvok considered the momentum, the wave pattern the energy must have taken to cause the compartment where he'd been to move as it had. He overlaid his image of B'Elanna with what he had experienced with the shock wave and allowed his mind to process the information, fuse it together until the answer appeared.

Somewhere, outside him, Tuvok acknowledged that Tariq had begun counting down out loud. He, naturally, rejected the distraction of limited time and allowed the pictures to fuse together. . . . *Become one,* he thought, *become one.*

Tariq drummed his fingers on the computer console, accompanied by a tone-deaf whistle.

Tuvok opened his eyes. "Go to starboard. Follow a forty-five-degree angle up from the base of the central saucer."

Tariq glanced at Tuvok for a split second before tapping the commands into the computer. As the shuttle followed the programmed trajectory, a red light on the console began flashing.

"*Incoming shock wave. Impact five minutes,*" the computer intoned.

Luiz gasped.

Swearing under his breath, Tariq tried, unsuccessfully, coaxing more power out of the engines. The inability to go to warp frustrated him, as the veins bulging from his forehead clearly indicated.

Tuvok viewed Tariq placidly, then shifted his gaze toward where he believed Lieutenant Torres would be found.

"Ensign Luiz, have emergency medical supplies ready to go. Lieutenant Torres may need assistance."

The first compartment exploded, followed shortly by the second.

"Monorhan compartments have started on desired trajectory. Several more explosions and they should be well on their way," Tariq said. "Lieutenant Torres did her job."

"Of course she did," Tuvok said. "She is extremely capable." *Breathe . . . two . . . three . . . four. . . . Breathe . . . two . . . three . . . four. . . .*

The third explosion rocked the rear of the shuttle.

Tuvok ignored the distractions, looking for the tiny speck of white against the starscape that would be B'Elanna Torres. Logically, the energy-processing mechanism in the saucer hull would explode shortly after the fifth compartment. It would be in their best interest to be on their way to *Voyager* at that point.

The fourth compartment bucked into the air.

"Shock-wave impact, three minutes."

Tuvok observed a white spot spinning where a star would not be moving. "She is there." He pointed with his finger. "Preparing for emergency transport."

Tariq moved into range just as the fifth compartment exploded.

"Initiating transport," Tuvok said.

The shuttle escaped the exploding hull with a minute to spare. Reaching *Voyager* before the shock wave would be another matter.

Behind him, Tuvok heard Ensign Luiz crack open the medical supplies.

Tuvok opened up a channel to *Voyager*. "Starship *Voyager,* this is shuttlecraft *du Châtelet*. We are en route. Can you close the distance between us?"

"We'll do what we can, Tuvok," Chakotay said. The channel clicked off.

"Ensign Luiz, report," Tuvok said.

"Can you help me lift her?" Luiz asked.

Tuvok rose from the copilot seat and walked several steps back to find the unconscious engineer flopping off the transporter. He lifted her effortlessly and placed her where Ensign Luiz could tend to her needs.

Luiz had already unfastened her EVA helmet and exposed Torres to regular oxygen levels. She showed him the medical tricorder reading indicating mild hypoxia and internal injuries from the shock wave. He returned to his copilot seat as Luiz administered an emergency hypo—a stimulant to her circulatory and respiratory systems.

On a deeply philosophical level, Tuvok realized the last exchange he had with Commander Chakotay had profound implications beyond the matter at hand. Indeed, the words, when taken less literally, were applicable to the estrangement between them. The mind knows what it needs to know indeed, Tuvok thought, grateful for the wisdom of his masters.

Suspended in space by the combined will of the Circle, the Key hummed with life. An ignorant being would see a crude chunk of meteorite or an unremarkable volcanic rock. Phoebe wrapped her hands around the Key. She caressed the pocked surface, feeling the energy charges coursing throughout her entire being. The Key whispered a lullaby of Monorhan death cries as those small lives combined to give her this gift. She had given their lives meaning; how lucky they were to be part of something greater than themselves!

And so the Key bound itself to Phoebe and Phoebe to the Key. Janeway had denied her this before but now . . . now what had been her right was restored to her. A lesser creature might have been inclined to forgive Janeway's transgression, since the balance had been restored by the birth of the Key. But Phoebe was not a lesser creature. Her power, her glory, had been kept from her by the *human*. Such choices required consequences. Whether Janeway had any life force remaining after opening the conduit was questionable—Phoebe granted that. But Janeway's followers needed to be taught the lesson that their leader obviously never understood. That lesson would serve to teach others who might be tempted to follow Janeway's example. Lower life-forms who interfered in the realm of superior life-forms faced swift retribution. Phoebe was obliged to correct the humans so that in the future all others would conform their will to those whose rightful place it was to rule the universe. It was all very simple, really. Punishing *Voyager* would not only serve the greater good, it would meet the Exiles' needs. She congratulated herself for being so efficient.

Holding the Key above her head, she allowed her fellow Exiles to bask in the glory of their creation for a long moment. She felt their envy and longing to touch the Key, though they knew such covetousness would not assuage their desires. The Key was hers until she could find a lesser one to be the conduit. Through it she would satisfy their deepest longings. In exchange, they would serve her unquestioningly.

The Key lacks only a conduit, my fellow Exiles.

The Circle rumbled with anticipation. Phoebe felt the nearby planets trembled at this expression of their will.

Go. We will take Voyager *for our conduit. The gateway to Exosia will be ours.*

"How long till we can bring in the shuttle?" Chakotay asked Ayala.

"I'm doing the best I can, sir," Ayala said, trying to split his attention between two consoles.

Later, he would apologize to the unseasoned officer. For now, he needed him to focus. "Your best isn't enough. I want that shuttle protected." He heard a "yes, sir" from Ayala's general direction and turned his focus to Seven.

"Where are we at on the probe, Seven?"

"I have nothing new to report," she said. "However, I believe that if the shuttle comes within range of our tractor beam, we will be able to pull it in close enough to extend our shield envelope around it."

"Do it," Chakotay said. He forced himself to face forward, ignoring the impulse to walk over to Seven's station and see whatever progress she'd made with rescuing the Doctor. Hopefully, *Voyager* would survive long enough to return him to sickbay!

Sitting straight up in the captain's chair and tucking his legs against the base, Chakotay visually surveyed his bridge crew to make sure everyone was prepared. So far, so good. Knowles had proved to be a real asset in the trenches. Rollins kept his head. Ayala was back on track.

"Shock-wave impact in forty-five seconds."

Chakotay had yet to resolve the question in his mind about whether or not it was better to know when you were about to get clobbered or whether it would be better to tell the computer to shut the hell up on certain occasions. Every time he heard that calm, unemotional voice announcing what might be their impending doom, he felt his blood pressure climb.

"Shuttle within tractor distance," Rollins said.

"Bring it in," Chakotay said, feeling a huge weight lift from his shoulders.

"Done, sir," Rollins said.

"Extending shield bubble," Seven said.

"Shock wave in twenty, nineteen, eighteen . . ." The count-down droned on.

Chakotay opened a shipwide channel. "All hands, brace for impact."

". . . nine . . . eight . . . seven . . ."

Not that it would do any good, Chakotay closed his eyes, offered a brief plea to the Great Spirit, then opened them. He would face his fate straight-on.

". . . two . . . one . . ."

Ayala's console blew instantly, throwing him backward into the bridge railing. Chakotay tried to leave his chair to help him, but the energy pounding *Voyager* came with seismic force. Even Seven turned away from her console and covered her head with her arms.

Rollins shouted out the shield reports, but couldn't be heard over the high-pitched whine emanating from the bridge computers.

In that strange, detached place his mind sometimes went when stress became too much to process, Chakotay wondered if his teeth would shake right out of his jaw.

And then, when he couldn't imagine how he would endure another moment, the tremors stopped. Acrid smoke wafted through the bridge. Groans and sighs surrounded him. Before he could ask, Rollins reported that Ayala needed to be transported to sickbay. Blurts of buzzing and pops from the equipment punctuated the updates. Because Rollins was assisting Ayala, Knowles provided Chakotay with the shield update: They'd held. No breaches, no external damage. Even the shuttle had touched down safely.

"What happened out there, can we tell?" Chakotay asked Seven.

"Not precisely, but I believe the planet Monorha is gone."

Tension-filled silence engulfed the bridge.

Chakotay said gruffly, "Knowles, can we get out of here?"

"Yes, sir. Main engineering said we're good to go."

"Then do it," he ordered, making a silent promise to himself and every person on this ship that they wouldn't stop until they'd cleared Monorhan space. He looked over at Seven: her face was blank. Whether this was her characteristic Borg-on-duty face or not he couldn't tell.

"Seven?" Chakotay said quietly, all he wanted to ask implied in simply stating her name.

"We have nothing," Seven said.

Chakotay stared at her. How could this have happened? They were so close—he'd seen it himself!

Seven placed a hand over her ear and listened intently to something coming through her earpiece. "Wait," she said, her composure serene.

"I—" Chakotay began.

She held up her hand to silence him, then: "Correction. We have one thing."

"And that is?"

"A message. Two words."

"Is it from . . . ?" Chakotay was reluctant to say the name. Drawing attention to their mission's failure at this time would not help morale.

"Yes. He said, 'Not yet.' "

Chakotay blanked. "Which means?"

"I believe the operation was nearly successful, but a choice was made, not by *Voyager*."

The implication infuriated Chakotay. The Doctor chose not to be rescued. The EMH had a chance to return to *Voyager* and he'd willingly refused the opportunity. Chakotay felt unprepared to sort through these feelings in front of the crew. "I'll be in my ready room," he said, rising. He'd taken two steps before Ensign Knowles said the one sentence he dreaded.

"Sir, I believe there's something you need to see."

Not looking back, he said. "Tell me, Ensign."

Knowles took a deep breath and said, "Nacene. At least a thousand. They're coming this way."

Chapter 11

"We can't outrun them. We'll have to stand and fight," Chakotay said, answering Knowles's question about where she should take *Voyager. We've survived a war between the Borg and Species 8472. We can survive the Nacene.* Upon returning to the captain's chair, he touched his combadge. "Chakotay to Tuvok."

"Tuvok here."

"Status report on the anti-Nacene weapons."

"Twelve toxin-loaded torpedoes configured and ready on your orders."

"Split them between the front and rear launchers. Once they're ready, I'll see you on the bridge. Rollins, let me know when they're in targeting range." He turned to Seven, the outline of a plan formulating in his mind. "The shield bubble you devised for protection from the shock wave—can you replicate it?"

Seven tilted her head thoughtfully. "With the additional power from the gel packs, yes."

"How large is this bubble?"

"Theoretically, we may be able to extend it as far as a hundred meters."

This might just work, Chakotay thought, feeling hopeful

for the first time. "When I give you the signal, Seven, I want you to initiate the shield bubble. Extend it as far as you can. Once we have the Nacene where we want them, make sure all excess power is rerouted to main engineering. We'll need it there."

Seven acknowledged the order. Chakotay listened with satisfaction as Seven contacted Neelix and the *rihhara-tan* down in main engineering to prepare them for the next attack.

Moments later, Tuvok arrived on the bridge and Chakotay asked Rollins to step aside to allow Tuvok to manage weapons and security for the duration. Rollins would assume Ayala's post at ops. Chakotay and Tuvok devised a simple signal that would be Tuvok's cue to launch the torpedoes loaded with the anti-Nacene toxin. With a complement of twelve, the weapons would have to be used judiciously. They wouldn't get a second chance with the Nacene. Once the most pressing issues had been put to rest, Chakotay asked Tuvok about B'Elanna.

"Lieutenant Nakano is repairing her injuries. She will recover, but not in time for this fight," Tuvok said.

Chakotay made a conscientious effort not to reveal what a blow that was, having their chief engineer out of the game. He placed his faith in the *rih-hara-tan*'s ability to fortify the shields one more time, at least long enough to get them through the first wave of attack.

"Do we know what the Nacene want?" Rollins asked as he settled in at his new station.

"Considering that they just destroyed a planet, I doubt their intentions are benevolent. But I'd like to give them a chance to explain themselves before we blow them out of the sector. Begin transmitting on all frequencies." Chakotay decided to have this conversation standing. "*Starship Voyager* to the Nacene on course for our location."

At first, nothing happened, neither on the communication channel nor in the surrounding space. Chakotay had begun to wonder whether this was a case of shooting first and asking questions later when a cluster of whirling specks in the viewscreen grew close enough to reveal itself as a chain of aliens, some known, some not. At the head of the chain appeared the figure of an auburn-haired woman. Having spent much time in Kathryn's ready room, he recognized her superficial resemblance to Phoebe Janeway instantly; the cruel twist of her mouth and the coldness in her eyes distinguished her as an impostor.

"How good of you, Chakotay, to surrender instead of requiring us to take Voyager *by force,"* Phoebe said, drifting to and fro across the viewscreen.

"We humans tend to be reasonable people. We like to talk things through and try to work out our differences, if possible." Chakotay smiled.

Phoebe's lips twisted into a condescending scowl. She wasn't buying it and neither was he. *"Being reasonable with your captain didn't work. She denied me what rightfully belonged to my people. It's only fair that her crew provide me with the replacement. So I'm allowing you to make it up to me. You can be my conduit, as was your captain."*

"I'd rather not, if you don't mind."

Phoebe cackled. *"Unless you've suddenly acquired the ability to rebuild Gremadia, I don't believe you have a choice, Chakotay . . ."* she carried on, proclaiming her indignation at the injustice foisted on her and her fellow Nacene Exiles by Janeway's stupid decision.

Chakotay listened politely, interjecting with the occasional "That's too bad" or "I see." He was counting on wasting time long enough for the Nacene to draw closer to *Voyager.* That Phoebe might be employing the same delaying tactic occurred to Chakotay, but he couldn't let it worry him. He needed the first strike if he was to have any chance of *Voyager* emerging alive from a battle with the Nacene.

It appeared, for the moment, that his gamble was paying off. As she spoke, more Nacene came into view, many in forms that Chakotay recognized from their travels in the Delta Quadrant; others were unknown to him. One by one, they joined limbs and formed a line across the viewscreen. Chakotay assumed that if *Voyager* wasn't surrounded, it soon would be. Using the crudest of geometric formulas, he calculated the distance between the closest Nacene and *Voyager*. He discovered that if the Nacene continued to approach at their current velocity, they would be within range of the shield bubble in a matter of minutes.

"So I take it you're not interested in peace negotiations?" Chakotay said, counting down mentally how much time he'd have before he could signal Seven.

"I will not waste time negotiating for less than what is my right when I can take what I need much more easily."

"That's too bad, because I have no intention of making this easy for you." Chakotay nodded to Seven, who activated the shield bubble, and then to Tuvok, who entered the commands that would launch the torpedoes.

Chakotay closed the communication channel and dropped down into the captain's chair to watch the fireworks. The Nacene would be slowed—perhaps some among them incapacitated and incapable of damaging *Voyager* further. As he watched the Nacene recoil helplessly as they encountered the toxin, he felt a small measure of satisfaction. But Chakotay would not deceive himself into believing that victory was possible. The Nacene would invade *Voyager* and they would attempt to use it in whatever nefarious scheme they were devising. Chakotay knew his greater responsibility required that he place the needs of the many above the needs of the few. In this case, the few were *Voyager*'s crew. Soon enough he would be forced to make the most difficult decision of his life. For the moment, he would watch and wait, silently pleading with the Sky Spirits of the Rubber Tree People for aid and asking the spirits of his ancestors to show him another path.

When the shimmering blue shield surrounded many of her Nacene followers, Phoebe wondered what kind of silliness the humans had in mind. The shield might stun or momentarily disable a few of the weaker Nacene. Beyond that, the shield was a nuisance. Surely they must know that a mere energy field could not contain a Nacene! The torpedoes launching prompted a similar reaction. Phoebe's first impulse was to dismiss *Voyager*'s pathetic efforts at self-defense as the desperate attempts of weak creatures. *Why are they wasting their time?* Such weapons were useless against the Nacene. It was—an image of an experience she'd had came to her from one of her forms— like a small child hitting an adult with a skinny stick and expecting the adult to collapse. She threw back her head, laughing.

The first cloud of toxin touched her feet. She gasped, a reflexive gesture that Phoebe didn't understand but was her human form's way of responding to unexpected stimuli. Her feet and legs stiffened as the toxin stilled the spinning atoms of sporocystian energy of which her body was made. If the rest of her body was exposed, certain damage if not partial disintegration would result. Using her arms for propulsion, she spun around, forcing her human form away from dissipating toxins. *The shield isn't meant to contain the Nacene, it's meant to contain the toxin,* she thought bitterly, conceding that Chakotay had devised a clever means of disabling the Exiles.

Frantically, she looked from side to side, assessing the state of her kindred. Limp bodies spun lazily through space. Others dissolved before her eyes. She despised them for their weakness, for not being clever enough to outwit the machinations of a primitive species. Every individual lost depleted the strength of the whole. Vivia would laugh at such an infantile, meager attack! Stupid, stupid creatures, they were. All of them—like those ignorant photons Vivia fought so hard to protect the strings from. Good for nothing but causing damage and making her quest more difficult. Phoebe imagined the Exiles flying through Exosia's gateway, being plucked off one by one by Exosia Nacene.

Oh, how she hated the human's words, but with every passing minute, she discovered her ability to assert her Nacene nature diminished, so she was forced to resort to their clumsy, inadequate expressions. Anger drove her like fusion fueling a star. Escape became her only goal. Pumping her arms with all the strength she could muster, Phoebe sought to propel her body up toward the shield and as far from the toxin as she could manage. She would break through the barrier out into open space. The toxin had not paralyzed her, merely slowed her. Phoebe accepted the toxin into her system and explored its chemistry until she understood it intimately. So empowered, she overcame the toxin and negated its effects. She called out to her fellow Exiles, enjoining them to follow her example so that they too would defeat *Voyager*'s meager weapon. She bid them to follow her by whatever means necessary.

She would gather her kindred around her and they

would attack *Voyager.* They would not be so kind as to give them the gift of the swift, painless death they had given the simple Monorhans. No, Phoebe would take her strongest followers aboard *Voyager* where they would destroy Janeway's crew person by person. A superior choice presented itself: creating the conduit while the crew *still lived.* None of the humanoids had the capacity to survive such an energy surge. Consider what happened to Janeway! Yet they would live long enough to know agonizing death. Phoebe burst through the shield bubble and "swam" into open space.

Drifting off of *Voyager's* starboard side, she stretched out, studying each thread of plasmatic energy in her form with her mind. The few that had been damaged she isolated and carved them away from the other healthy energy threads. As much as she regretted having to reduce her power, she risked vulnerability if she allowed any of her compromised energy strands to remain. Alas, she knew this process would make it difficult, if not impossible, to return to her sporocystian form. A sacrifice, to be certain, but the knowledge that Exosia awaited her tempered her bitterness. She urged those around her to purge themselves as she had done. A damaged army was unacceptable.

She sent her memories of being Phoebe Janeway aboard the starship to her fellow Exiles along with a picture of what she expected them to do. *Voyager,* virtually undamaged, glowed like a miniature moon reflecting the light of a sun.

Not for long, Phoebe vowed. *Voyager* could not stop the Nacene.

Seven of Nine had her orders: protect main engineering at all costs. Every bit of power that could be spared would be available to her. If the Nacene captured the warp core, the fight would be over. From the minute Chakotay had given her the assignment, her Borg neurological processors examined all the potentialities of their current situation with a speed that no human could manage. Few satisfactory solutions had yet emerged. Even weakened Nacene had advantages that *Voyager* couldn't match. She exited the turbolift and headed toward main engineering, uncertain of what her strategy would be.

During *Voyager*'s opening salvo against the Nacene, Chakotay had told the crew in no uncertain terms that the next round would be fought aboard the starship. Every person aboard needed to be prepared to fight. They had a few weapons: at the same time Tuvok had worked on the torpedoes, he also modified enough compression phaser rifles to arm two or three security teams. It would not be enough for every crew member to be armed. Seven carried a case bearing three of these rifles loaded with enough toxin to keep the Nacene at bay for a short period of time, but not indefinitely. Other measures would have to be taken and that is what kept Seven's mind busy. The vast collection of Borg knowledge offered little help; the Borg had never successfully assimilated a Nacene. Beyond the calculations, stratagem, and scenarios, Seven's mind was preoccupied with Chakotay's last words.

Chakotay had pulled the senior staff into the ready room for an ad hoc discussion of what their options were. Knowles confirmed that there was no way for *Voyager* to outrun the Nacene given the obstacles of Monorhan space. From a security and weapons perspective, Tuvok and Rollins confirmed that they would need a nearly limitless supply of toxin to contain the sheer numbers of Nacene they faced.

"Can we release it into the environmental systems, distribute it throughout the ship?" Chakotay had asked.

Tuvok confirmed that they could, but that such efforts would only be a momentary deterrent. All the staff agreed that any and all tactics must be used.

And then Chakotay had told them what Seven suspected would be *Voyager*'s final recourse. She paused before the doors of main engineering, as she remembered.

"We know from Seven's analysis that the disturbances in this region threaten the cohesiveness of the fabric of space-time on a much larger scale. Whatever these Nacene have planned, I suspect will accelerate the process currently under way." Chakotay had looked to Seven for confirmation and she'd given it to him. It had been less than an hour since Monorha had been destroyed and already the damage to the region was visible. Whatever would come next would be worse.

"We will fight a good fight, but we cannot allow the Nacene to succeed. If we reach a point where our defeat is inevitable—"

Our defeat is inevitable, Seven had thought.

"—we will autodestruct *Voyager*. I cannot initiate the destruct sequence without Commander Tuvok's confirmation, but I want to make sure that we're all in agreement before I put this contingency into play."

Not one member of the senior staff had objected.

Chakotay issued his orders, the meeting had been adjourned.

Now Seven was left considering what, if anything, could be done.

The Nacene could penetrate the ship's hulls at will. All of *Voyager*'s nonessential energy could be redirected into the shields but such a measure would delay their attackers for only a few moments. The Nacene would then stroll onto the bridge, into main engineering, or into any other area servicing critical systems, main engineering being chief among them. What the Nacene would do once they were aboard was unknown, though Seven had a guess, though not confirmation, of what the Nacene might be contemplating.

While Chakotay had been baiting Phoebe into a protracted conversation, Seven had been watching the Nacene, studying her and discovering that Phoebe had in her possession an object that reminded Seven of the Key to Gremadia that the Monorhans had given Janeway. Phoebe hadn't held the Key where it was noticeable—she had hidden it in the folds of her clothing. No one on *Voyager* would have noticed save a Borg with an ocular implant with the ability to visualize energy fields. And the object Phoebe had hidden was leaking radiation like a warp core losing containment. Considering that Phoebe had a Key, she was likely trying to open up something— Exosia, Seven hypothesized. Since Exosia was sealed from this dimension, the Key would fit into something that would force the gateway to Exosia open, something that could conduct enough energy through it to break down a subspace barrier.

Seven believed that Phoebe and the other Nacene planned on using *Voyager* as the energy source that would facilitate a conduit (Chakotay, if Phoebe was to be believed), using their Key. This could not be permitted. The commander was correct: an energy discharge of that magnitude would hasten the deterioration of subspace.

Taking a deep breath, Seven charged through main engineering's doors, discovering the Monorhan *rih* encircling the workstations and warp core. To an individual, the *rih* appeared fatigued. *You are not finished yet,* she thought.

She searched the room until she found Lieutenant Carey, who was busy instructing his staff on what gel-pack relays needed reinforcing. When the engineers were dismissed, Seven briefly outlined the first part of her plan for protecting main engineering. Carey concurred with her approach and went to work on the modifications Seven had requested.

Seven then sought out Neelix, who, along with the *rih,* would manage the second part. She found him deep in conversation with a *rih* named Tei, whom Seven had met earlier.

"We must prepare for the Nacene attack," Seven said brusquely, stepping between the pair. A voice in her head instantly reminded her that Lieutenant Tuvok had taught her that a key to being an effective leader was not to be so abrasive. The Borg side of her reminded her that politeness in an emergency was inefficient. "The shield bubble will not be effective protection. Instead, we must establish and fortify a forcefield around Main Engineering, particularly the warp core. The *rih-hara-tan* must assist us in this effort."

Tei's tongue clicked and whirred with a speed that Seven's universal translator couldn't keep up with. The translator produced garble in Seven's ear.

"Can they comply?" Seven said, wondering if Tei had comprehended her request.

"I believe so," Neelix said. He seemed to have adjusted to the rhythmic, guttural speech more readily than most of *Voyager's* crew. "I think I caught something about her taking your request to the other *rih.*" He further explained, "She wants to know what happened to her people during the shock wave—the ships that Tuvok and B'Elanna were going to help."

Seven reassured the *rih* that their scans indicated that the shock wave had appeared to have had minimal impact on the Monorhan ships. She had little knowledge of Tuvok and B'Elanna's time on the damaged vessels, but she had learned that B'Elanna believed their shielding capacities to be up to the task. As far as she knew, the refugee Monorhans still lived.

"Praise be to the Blessed All-Knowing Light," Tei murmured and bowed her head for a moment. Standing behind her, her fellow *rih* cried out variations on this invocation.

Her moment of reverence over, Tei lifted her head and explained to Seven (whose universal translator had finally synchronized with the Monorhans' speech) that the *rih,* of course, were prepared to continue to boost the gel-pack output but that she had another suggestion to consider: allowing the *rih* to engage the Nacene.

"Neelix has told me that we live because of these creatures. We may not be as easy for them to—" She paused, contemplating her words. "—take life from. Kill."

Seven considered Tei's logic for a moment, found merit in her suggestion, and then agreed to the proposal on the condition that *rihs'* maintain the forcefield first and only engage the Nacene if the forcefield or gel packs failed. Tei loped back to her fellow Monorhans, her percussive speech emerging from her mouth with incomprehensible rapidity.

"Neelix, you will report the gel-pack status to me from workstation gamma," Seven said.

"Happy to do it, Seven. Happy to do it." Neelix fired off a salute to Seven, then walked off to assume his post.

Joe Carey waited patiently at her elbow. Seven acknowledged him.

"I've rerouted all the auxiliary power to Main Engineering and reprogrammed our system to permit for increased field-generating capacity. I should be able to give you a level ten plus. There's still a few safeties that need to be dealt with, though, if this field is going to last for any length of time. The field frequency you gave me is . . ." Carey frowned "Pardon me for questioning, but are you sure it will work?"

Seven said thoughtfully, "No. But in the Borg's experience with plasmatic life-forms, this frequency appears to be the most damaging. They should not be capable of stepping through the walls of main engineering without difficulty."

"I'll trust you on that, Seven," Carey said.

The overhead com chirped.

"Chakotay to the crew. They're here."

"Activate the forcefield," Seven ordered.

"We'll need a bit more time to bring it up to full capacity," Carey said as he ran toward a bank of consoles.

"Do what you can."

The *rih* resumed their circle around the warp core, the rhythmic monotone of their chants keeping time with the thrum-thrum-thrum of the core.

"Gel packs at one hundred and ten percent of capacity," Neelix announced.

Moments later, the clanging against Main Engineering's doors began.

Phoebe had chosen her strongest warriors to accompany her to *Voyager*'s engineering room. The initial impact of the toxin in the air proved bothersome. Overcoming the humanoid's meager efforts to halt them proved distracting, but not disabling. Phoebe had lived far too long and experienced more than any of these creatures. They would have to do far more to thwart her efforts. Anticipation tingled within Phoebe; she almost forgot that she had a human shape, the sensation, reminiscent of her plasmatic state, was so vivid and tantalizing. The conduit would be hers—*was* hers. Nothing could stop the Exiles. Certainly no *humanoid.* As they progressed through the ship, it was tempting to toy with the Voyagers, to enjoy the momentary pleasure of their suffering. She didn't yield: once the energy source had been secured, she would take her chosen conduit and use the Key at will.

The ship's warp core was an irrelevant blip when compared to the powerful singularity that fueled Gremadia but it would suffice as source of energy. Where the humanoids had been clever was in their use of bioneural gel packs. Individually, they mattered as much as a single-celled organism might. But when the gel packs were placed under the control of the Nacene mind, their capacity would grow exponentially. *Voyager* would become a thinking entity, not merely a space-faring container. The ship would be taken to the gateway. Once there, all those Exiles strong and brave enough to survive would receive the spore they'd rightfully earned. In their transformed state, they would fuse their will to the gel-pack mind. *Voyager*'s warp core would be exposed and the Key placed inside.

Exosia would be opened.

Gliding through *Voyager*'s walls on her way to engineering brought unpleasant recollections of Janeway. She knew that somewhere in this container, Janeway's husk remained viable. It occurred to Phoebe that as much as she would savor the opportunity of dealing with Janeway herself, she could not be indulgent when far more urgent matters pressed upon her. She called out to one of her favorites—a Nacene who remained in Dfaaryan form and bestowed upon him the honor of destroying what remained of the captain. *Find her and obliterate her,* Phoebe ordered.

Phoebe and her warriors approached the cordoned-off

area housing the warp core. As she approached the wall, a high-pitched humming noise alerted her that not all was as it had been when she had last come to this place. She ordered one of her warriors to step through the metal barrier. When he demonstrated reluctance, Phoebe forced the issue, physically propelling him toward the wall. His tentacles vanished—

The effect was instantaneous: He collapsed on the ground, his form quivering from molecular destabilization. The warriors surrounding him stepped back, their fear palpable.

So they're trying to keep us out, Phoebe thought and ripped a panel from a wall that didn't vibrate with the high-pitched humming of a forcefield. She wrapped her hands around the edges of the gray metal and channeled her energy into the matter. She came to know each molecule and atom and she excited them with her will. The panel glowed red with heat beneath her hands. She ordered the cowards to also grab hold of the panel and direct their energy into it. They would overcome the forcefield by disrupting it, no matter how long it took.

Together they slammed the panel into the engineering wall, the hollow clang of metal on metal echoing throughout the hallway. Phoebe sensed the forcefield wavelength altered just slightly when their panel encountered the forcefield. They would not bring the forcefield down, they would disrupt it just enough for Phoebe and her warriors to pass through to the other side. And as they continued their assault on the forcefield, Phoebe realized, from what she knew about *Voyager,* that they lacked the capacity to generate and maintain an energy barrier such as the one they were encountering. Something else must be aiding them, boosting their capacity. Tentatively, she reached her mind into the room beyond . . . *Now, that's interesting,* she thought as she found a presence, not unlike the Nacene, communicating with . . . the gel packs.

The bridge was the calmest place on the entire ship. At first, Chakotay had been surprised that the Nacene had not attacked *Voyager*'s nerve center first. As the ship began moving toward the gash without any navigational interface, he realized that the Nacene didn't need the bridge controls to take *Voyager* where they wanted it to go. Knowles's fingers danced over the helm controls but command after command was overridden.

Voyager would go into the gash and they were helpless to stop it.

Already, the ship's photonic energy drained away. Lights blinked off and on as the effect of the gash increased with every kilometer. Reports came pouring in of holodeck buffers destabilizing and phasers malfunctioning. Futile though it was, Chakotay ordered all nonemergency light or holographic systems offline. He felt like the boy who tried to save his tribe from flood by using a bucket to bail water out of the river. By his calculations, he theoretically had a few more minutes to determine whether or not initiating the autodestruct sequence would be necessary.

He exchanged looks with Tuvok. He knew without having to ask that the Vulcan had already accepted what Chakotay had hoped to avoid. He longed for the time to explain, to apologize for the mistakes he had made, for the way he had behaved toward the Vulcan whether outwardly or in his heart. From the expression in Tuvok's eyes, Chakotay knew that all had been forgiven.

"Computer, queue autodestruct sequence by order of Commander Chakotay, authorization beta-mu-five-eight-six."

Tuvok spoke clearly and calmly. "Second authorization provided by Lieutenant Commander Tuvok, authorization alpha-two-six-four-one-three."

"Acknowledged."

"Begin silent countdown in five minutes," Chakotay said. Still time to cancel the order but at least it would be in place if, for some reason, none of them lived to implement it.

Harry loved his parents and shared affection with them, but he felt embarrassed watching Kes and Kol as they both stood. She was so much tinier than Kol that he rested his hands on her shoulders and she wrapped her arms around his waist. As much as he didn't want to intrude on their moment, he remained so stunned by Kes's presence that he could barely rip his eyes away. He had so many questions—where had she been since she left *Voyager*, would she return and rejoin the crew?

Tom, on the other hand, seemed content to sit by and enjoy sharing her company again. He had moved to the pilot's chair, occasionally looking back and exchanging smiles with Kes.

The Doctor sat down beside Harry, medical tricorder in hand, scanning him from head to toe. "Standard operating procedure," he said cheerfully. "Examining members of an away team upon their return."

"You're taking this all very casually," Harry said, watching the Doctor at work.

"You mean Kes?" He flopped his hand in a dismissive gesture. "We've been together for ages."

Harry's eyes widened. "Oh really. So I take it you know why Kol is calling her 'Mother.'"

"Of course I do. But I'm a doctor, not a gossip monger, so you'll have to get your update elsewhere." The Doctor examined his instrument. "Other than elevated hormone levels, which I assume can be attributed to her—" He jerked his head in q's direction. "—you're fine."

Blushing, Harry rested elbows on his thighs and his face in his hands. q scrutinized him; Harry couldn't tell if she was interested or amused. Tom was right. Emotional involvement with a Q was a bad idea on every level. He left his passenger spot and took the copilot's seat beside Tom.

"Nice of you to join me." Tom slumped back in the chair and stretched out his arms to their full span before placing his hands on his neck, elbows in the air.

"Aren't you supposed to be piloting?"

"Engines don't work." Tom jerked his head toward Q, who waggled a few fingers at Harry. "He's in charge. How else would we cross thousands of light-years in mere moments? Whatever propulsion system he's got going, I'd love to share it with B'Elanna."

The conversational volume between Kes and Kol increased. Both Tom and Harry turned toward what appeared to be an argument. "I will deal with my father's people in my own way."

Kes shook her head. "You can't merely *deal* with them. Their fundamental existence will need to change—they cannot remain with the strings. The Nacene have had access to what they need to evolve past their current state. Because of their stubbornness, they literally haven't seen what's right in front of them."

"Persuading them to embrace the very thing they have been so vigilant against will be difficult." Exasperated, Kol threw up his hands and took a few agitated steps back and forth.

Placing her hands on his upper arms, Kes forced his attention back to her. "All creatures within Exosia, and the Nacene and Monorhans outside, will accept their destiny.

The universe will never be safe otherwise. The only way they can fulfill the measure of their creation is to evolve. They will see that. But only *you* can open the gateway to their next life."

Saying nothing, Kol leaned back against the wall, engrossed in thought.

"You know I'm right," Kes said quietly.

Kol took her by the hand. The tender gesture made Harry feel once again like a voyeur.

"Be my emissary to those in Exosia?" Kol asked.

Kes smiled. "And you will persuade the Exiles."

Harry had forgotten how radiant Kes became when she smiled.

"When all is done, Mother, come with me?"

Raising a hand to cup Kol's cheek, Kes touched him tenderly. "When the time comes, I will choose the path that I am meant to."

That's my girl, Kes, Harry thought. *You'll come back to* Voyager.

Kol shot a pleading look at Q. "Surely you can make her see reason."

"My life is out there," Kes said, indicating the starscape spreading before the shuttle. "I have my own path to follow."

The realization that Kes wouldn't be returning to *Voyager* twisted Harry's heart.

"Interfere with free will? I?" Q did a fair job of appearing insulted. "Besides, you know how it goes, my boy. Choice and—"

"Chance," q finished for him. "We get it."

"Go back to school," Q said.

q yawned. "Good luck trying to make me—" She paused. "Can Harry come along?"

Harry perked up.

Q considered Harry for a long moment. "As long as Mr. Kim is agreeable to this . . . this . . . *liaison*. And if you promise to have Mr. Kim back in a few minutes."

"You game, Harry?" q said, quirking one of those sexy-as-hell half-smiles.

"I'll serve as your chaperone, of course," Q interjected. "After all, someone needs to make sure Mr. Kim's honor will be preserved."

Before Harry had a chance to respond—though the giddiness that had suddenly overtaken him was answer enough—Q had snapped his fingers.

Seven remained calm as the reports of injuries and hull breaches mounted. Voices conjured faces. She could visualize Crewman Lang, fingers flying frantically over his console as he tried to seal off damaged areas and the expression on his face as the Nacene assaulted him. Part of her wished that the communications channel could be shut down, but she knew that she needed to know what was happening elsewhere on the ship. The modulating forcefield frequency would take a few minutes to overcome but not more than that.

Ripping open a panel, she reached her hand into the nest of tubing that Carey wanted her to recalibrate. Starfleet had placed safety sensors in the system to initiate automatic shutdown if energy levels climbed too high. Inserting her tubules into the computer interface, she systematically disabled every built-in safety protocol she encountered. The built-in redundancies frustrated her, consuming precious seconds as the clanging grew louder. When the last barrier came down, Seven called out to Carey to pour all their power into the forcefield.

The computer transmitted data to Seven indicating that the conduit temperatures had risen several degrees past the safety zone. By her calculation, the overload would not trigger cascading systems failure for at least five minutes. The forcefield would keep out the Nacene for a few minutes longer.

Or Seven's modifications would make the auto-destruct sequence unnecessary. Portions of *Voyager*'s crew had always suspected that Seven might be part of some larger Borg plot to destroy the ship. They might feel satisfaction that at last, they may be proved correct and that Seven's presence could prove *Voyager*'s undoing.

She listened to chatter over the communication system and remembered the thousands of times she had participated in a Borg attack.

"There's too many of them! Our rifles are out of toxin—"

"Hull breeches on decks seven, twelve, and fifteen."

And the screams . . . the screams took Seven back to the assimilation chambers aboard a Borg cube.

The computer beeped. Seven queried the system, asking for a status report and learned temperatures had dropped. She asked for an explanation.

"General gel-pack relay failure in sections—"

"Run diagnostic," Seven snapped irritably. *Gel-pack relay failure. How was that possible? The* rih *were tired but that shouldn't be enough to—*

Hearing a dull thud behind her, she glanced over her shoulder.

A Monorhan had collapsed onto the floor, unconscious.

Across the room, Neelix called for a medic and when no one was forthcoming, he pulled the emergency kit off the wall mounting and rushed to the *rih* himself.

Another Monorhan collapsed.

Carey shouted that the forcefield was failing.

Engineering doors slid open.

Seven reached for her compression phaser rifle and crawled behind a console where she was hidden from view.

The Nacene had arrived.

With a hand wave, Phoebe threw the humanoids aside. She didn't want to kill them lest she be denied the pleasures of watching them suffer. Instead, she would incapacitate them so they couldn't interfere. And there they were, the Monorhans who had caused so many problems for her, encircling the warp core. She threw out her hand to shove them out of the way as she had the others but she met resistance. She exerted her will again but found more strength than she'd expected. *Of course they are strong: they come from Nacene.* This realization failed to dissuade her. Nacene or no, Exosia awaited.

Out of my way.

At their center, an ugly glob of flesh, the organic form of the abominations said, "You will have to destroy us before we move."

Then we will destroy you.

A poof of toxin exploded into the air, felling two of her warriors. Phoebe shrieked, broke ranks, and launched into the air, where she would elude the poison. A humanoid had snuck up behind them, she saw. He pointed his weapon at her again. She reached into his body and exploded blood vessels in his brain. He clutched his head and toppled onto the floor.

Phoebe turned toward the Monorhans. She would not ask again. This time, she coaxed the gel packs into dropping the temperature below freezing, then further. The crude creatures could not endure under such conditions. As she suspected, the physical hardship made it impossible for them to defend against her, so as their resistance collapsed, she probed their bodies, found the air sacs that allowed them to respire. *Yes, yes,* she thought, gleefully squeezing each sac until it collapsed. She heard them gasping for breath, sensed their desperation as they suffocated. Toying with the Monorhans amused her for a few moments but then she grew bored and ordered her warriors to continue.

The warp core glowed blue, thrumming and pulsing with promised life. Phoebe removed the Key from within her robes, holding it before her. She approached reverently. None of the humanoids attempted to stop her—all of them had been dealt with. Their resistance impressed her, but in the end, they were an irrelevant distraction from the greater goal.

Partake of the spores, she ordered the Exiles.

As much as it would be a fitting fate for Chakotay to serve as conduit, she did not have the time to hunt him down and bring him here before these Voyagers did further damage. She would have to find another to take the Key. Reaching behind a lump of metal in her path, she discovered a human cowering. *This one will do.* Yanking the human up by the neck, she threw him down in front of her and pinned him to the ground with her foot.

The *thrum-thrum-thrum* of the warp core became the tempo of her energy. She would no longer be bound to this weak and pathetic form. She would return to a state of pure energy and thought. With one hand, she held the Key, with the other, a spore. She closed her eyes, parted her lips, and raised her hand to her mouth—

The toxin overtook her before the spore touched her lips. Phoebe frantically tried sending her thoughts to the Exiles, but paralysis had overtaken her. She knew she could defeat the toxin, but it would take time . . . precious time . . .

A humanoid stepped out from behind a console, holding a weapon. Phoebe recognized the Borg. She had seen what they had done on worlds across the galaxy. They were formidable opponents.

"I will take the Key," the Borg said.

With what energy that remained in her form, Phoebe refused to release the Key. The Key could be surrendered only to a new owner willingly. She would not grant a Borg or any other creature such a privilege. If she could just hold on a bit longer, the toxin would wear off and she could continue—

The Borg again fired the toxin. "Surrender the Key," she said, as calmly as before, and took several steps toward Phoebe.

Looking around, Phoebe saw none of her warriors willing to draw close enough to her to risk being exposed to the toxin. *Cowards.* Except . . .

A shimmer flickered behind the warp core. Hope flared within her. Another had entered the room . . . one of her Exiles! The conduit was not lost to them. She sought to know her rescuer, but discovered the toxin had scrambled her awareness to the point of confusion. Beyond sensing his Nacene nature, she knew nothing for certain.

Release the Key to me, the new one said. *And I will keep it from the Borg. I can open the conduit.*

She wanted this honor for herself. She had earned the right to be the liberator of the Exiles. And yet . . .

The Borg fired her weapon again.

Phoebe dropped the Key onto the deck. She couldn't see her rescuer, but she felt the moment he retrieved the Key.

"Now it will end," her rescuer said aloud. "The Keeper of the Light has come."

~

The voice was quiet, yet spoke with such calm, confident authority that all fear drained from Chakotay. Though Chakotay couldn't see the speaker, his words pierced through to the center of his being.

Now it will end, he had said.

Looking around the bridge at his crew, Chakotay noted the dissolving tension. Knowles's arms dangled at her sides, her face composed. An aura of serenity surrounded Tuvok; he had a faraway look in his eyes. The placid expression on Rollins's face suited a lazy afternoon better than a starship battle. Chakotay followed their gazes. The sight of hundreds—if not thousands—becalmed Nacene hovering in front of *Voyager*—had mesmerized them. Their attackers too had stilled at the spoken command.

Glancing at the armrest consoles of the captain's chair, Chakotay saw that the self-destruct countdown had paused—suspended between tenths of a second. *Voyager*'s journey to the rift had also halted as had the firefights throughout the ship. The ship-wide comm bridge broadcast only silence. Even the temperature in main engineering had returned to normal. Chakotay could find no sign of a warp-core breach.

Curious, Chakotay said, "Computer, status of structural integrity."

"Structural integrity is normal."

Believing the computer's assertion presented a challenge for Chakotay. The data updates scrolling on the screen before him indicated that none of the hull breaches had been repaired. *How is this possible?*

"Computer, how many Nacene are aboard *Voyager*?"

"None."

Chakotay looked up at the viewscreen. As each moment passed, more Nacene appeared to be congregating together. *They're awaiting him,* Chakotay realized. *Just as we are.*

In the midst of the Nacene, a Starfleet shuttle suddenly appeared. Chakotay shook his head, wondering if he was hallucinating. He didn't recall having launched any shuttles after he'd brought Tuvok's away team aboard and yet there it was. Not daring to hope, he touched the control next to his chair, his heart skipping a beat. *"Voyager* to shuttle. Identify yourselves."

The viewscreen flickered briefly, dissolving into static; then the view of the Nacene was replaced with a smiling face. Chakotay nearly fell out of his chair.

"I know you wanted us to feel welcome, but you really didn't need to send a homecoming committee," Tom Paris said.

"I know how much you love a party," Chakotay said, playing along.

"We brought company," Harry said, a grin on his face the size of *Voyager* itself, and took a seat in the copilot's chair.

Tom looked at Harry, clearly surprised. *"You're back?"*

And there between Tom and Harry sat the Doctor. *"It's good to see you, Commander,"* he said.

Dumbfounded, Chakotay slouched back into his chair.

"You'll never believe where I've been—"

Tom clamped a hand over the Doctor's mouth. *"Goes double for me and Harry."*

"We're a little shorthanded, so I'd appreciate it if you'd show up for your duty shifts a bit early," Chakotay said dryly. *B'Elanna will be overjoyed,* he thought. *Give her a reason to recover quickly from her injuries.*

"Yeah . . . about that," Tom said. *"It's a long story, but we don't actually have any control over the shuttle at the moment. Beam us aboard?"*

"Done," Chakotay said, and ordered the transport, savoring a moment of satisfaction. Not all had been lost. Before Chakotay could contemplate how Tom and Harry ended up back in Monorhan space, his attention was drawn away by a ball of light hurtling toward the gash. In the center of the ball was a dark object that resembled an asteroid. The ball followed an arc trajectory, then swooped down into the gash.

"What the—" he said, scooting forward in his chair.

A dazzling eruption of white flames sprayed from the gash. Chakotay turned away from the light and saw Rollins scrunched up in his chair, trying to shield himself from the painful brightness. As the brilliant flash faded, incredulity overtook Chakotay as he realized that what he had assumed to be flames were, in actuality, beings of light. The ghostly visages of millions of Monorhans had joined the Nacene army surrounding *Voyager,* their shadowy forms like wisps of interstellar dust before the geyser of photonic energy pouring into the gash. Chakotay raced through the connections. *When the planet was destroyed by the Nacene—the Monorhans must have become part of the Key—which had to be the ball that had dove into the gash. And now they've been freed . . .*

I am witnessing the end of days, Chakotay thought, mindful of thousands of years of apocalyptic tales that prophesied just such a resurrection of the dead.

Neither the time to question what he saw nor to fear for *Voyager*'s safety was granted him. In the midst of the masses rose a figuring glowing like starlight. Chakotay's first thought was that a Nacene in its sporocystian state had arisen, but the figure had a humanoid form. The Nacene and Monorhans watched him rise, their upturned faces illuminated by the light radiating from his being.

Come out of Exosia, he called. *Accept your fate and be transformed. I offer you a new way.*

And then Chakotay knew what had just transpired: The gateway to Exosia had opened.

With dread, Vivia watched the Keeper of the Light hurtling toward the gateway. He had obtained the Monorhan Key from Phoebe and would use it to destroy the delicate membrane that protected Exosia from the other dimensions. The photons would invade, the balance would be irrevocably altered, and she was helpless to stop it. Hadn't Q warned her?

All of her existence—all of her efforts to protect and care for the strings—had brought her to this moment where she would witness the undoing of all things.

There would be no closing the gateway this time.

She couldn't understand why Q was so cavalier about this catastrophe. Collapsing the dimensions would mean catastrophe for the Continuum. Q could have stopped the Keeper of the Light, and yet he didn't. All his talk of choice, of allowing the future to be the result of consequences, chosen or not, rang hollow when such destruction followed. He should have forced the issue with the Keeper. Imprisoned him in the Continuum. Contained him.

She didn't need to see the photons to know their presence. The music changed instantly, the tuneless predictability of the song shifting into a melodious complexity that rattled every sporocystian atom within her. No effort would be enough to shield her senses from the cacophonous racket. She would remain in Exosia, looking on helplessly as the photons poured in from the Outside, irrevocably changing the music of the strings. There were too many photons for the Nacene remaining in Exosia to contain. What form space-time would assume now was unimaginable. Vivia could no longer do the impossible. Her energy dimmed; her will to fight dissipated. She would await her fate. The disquieting song of the strings would relentlessly remind her of her failure. It was a fitting penance.

This isn't the end.

Vivia turned to see her visitor, assuming that this latest presence had arrived when the photons had broken through. She recognized the humanoid instantly. The face had haunted her from the moment she had become part of the tapestry of choices that brought them to this point. The Light had found her beautiful, though Vivia couldn't understand what would be desirable about any creature with so many orifices and so few limbs. To create a life with her had been unconscionable! And the reddish filaments hanging down her back carried a stench with them that Vivia found offensive. The Light had chosen such an odd emissary. She carried his protection—Vivia could sense it. Whatever efforts she or the other Nacene might expend to contain or destroy her would ultimately be futile.

You can still protect the strings from the photons, she said.

And how would that be? Vivia drifted to the place where the creature stood. The cheek, this creature had, informing she who had a nearly limitless view of time and space that she had understanding Vivia didn't. She would indulge the creature.

The Nacene have the capacity to make the photons part of themselves. To incorporate them into their sporocystian energy.

Vivia's tentacles tensed. The creature spoke blasphemy. *Such an action will destroy us. You want to rid this dimension of Nacene so the Exiles can gain dominion.*

The creature's largest orifice twisted peculiarly, but

Vivia ascertained that she was amused by Vivia's suggestion. *Absorbing the photons into your energy will transform you. A
pathway to another dimension beyond Exosia will open. You will
no longer be a slave to the strings.*

But who will care for them? Vivia questioned the creature
whose thoughts startled her.

*The strings existed before the Nacene. They will exist after. Let
them be as they once were back before time began. You, however,
can become more than you are.*

She had not considered the possibility that she might
have an existence other than what she knew in Exosia. On
rare occasions when Vivia contemplated what would have
happened if she had chosen the Exiles' path instead of
duty, she castigated herself, condemning herself for even
having those thoughts. Now a stranger stood before her
tempting her to walk away from the strings, luring her toward the same destructive existence as the Exiles.

The stranger's words that intrigued Vivia, however, re-
garded the photons. If she spoke truly—that the Nacene
had the ability to absorb photonic energy—perhaps Vivia
should take in as much photonic energy as she could stand
as her final effort to defend the strings.

Others had detected the stranger's presence and had
gathered around her. Vivia heard their whispers in her
mind. Some argued for containing the creature as they had
the abominations. Many voices clamored in fear for the
strings. The photonic energy flooding Exosia surrounded
them on all sides. Balance had been lost. A few asked if the
stranger could be believed: Could a door to another dimension be opened?

The stranger chose not to respond to their questions,
instead sending reassurance. *The decision,* she said, *rests with
Vivia.*

The creatures that had once been Monorhans

swarmed around the stranger, their wings fluttering anxiously. *Can we go?* they said to the stranger. *Is this place for us?*

The stranger told them that the gateway had opened to all that was Nacene, and that all Monorhan life force would be offered the chance to make the crossing.

Fearlessly, they soared away, flying toward the light and away from Exosia.

Vivia watched them leave, marveling at their . . . their *faith* in trusting the stranger. Where did this leave her?

Rejecting the stranger would not restore the Balance. On the other hand, if all of them accepted photonic energy, perhaps the strings could resume their song. Whether or not the stranger's tales of another life beyond Exosia were true or not mattered little to Vivia. Her duty came before all else.

Vivia opened herself to receive the light. She allowed the barrier that defined her plasmatic energy to become permeable. Becoming vulnerable to her enemy disturbed her more, but she remained open for the sake of the strings. *I exist for the sake of the strings. I will cease to exist for the sake of the strings.*

At first, the mingling of her sporocystian essence with photons created unfamiliar sensations as the disparate energy waves encountered one another and conflicted. Her control weakened. She hadn't felt so disconnected since before the War with the Exiles—when she shifted between alien forms. Vivia felt energy draining away from her. Before her, the stranger contorted her face in the same obscure fashion; Vivia knew she was pleased. Of course she was pleased; the emissary of the Light presided over the end of the Nacene. Revenge, indeed, would be satisfactory. Vivia no longer had any control over the photons pouring into her. She yielded her remaining will to the invading energies. *Let my sacrifice have purpose,* she thought, the last vestiges of her self draining away as the photons wrapped her sporocystian body in glossy filaments.

The energy waves synched.

Vivia exploded from her cocoon singing the song of the strings and the strings joined their harmonies to hers. With her wings, she soared, experiencing pure energy and thought in a way she could never have fathomed. She called out to the other Nacene—to every creature whose energy she could touch, from the Monorhans who had been part of Phoebe's Key, to the Exiles and those Monorhans who yet lived Outside: *We are free!*

A fountain of light burst out of the gash as the Nacene of Exosia burst their bonds, transformed. They surrounded the Keeper of the Light, singing. With Harry beside him, Chakotay watched their dance; he longed to celebrate with them, sharing the joy of salvation and liberation. The Nacene who had attacked *Voyager* as well as the Monorhans who had been slaughtered in the creation of the Key swarmed in through the gash. Chakotay knew they too would be granted the gift offered them by the Keeper of the Light.

Chakotay knew that he should be worrying about how he would repair the damage to *Voyager* and if or how they would ever be able to navigate their way out of this region but the scene transfixed him.

After innumerable transformed beings had emerged from Exosia, the Keeper of the Light opened his arms to the darkness, speaking an incomprehensible incantation that could be heard only by the mind—and heart. Before Chakotay's eyes, dark space rippled and shimmered like a mirage on a hot day, becoming as clear as glass. Though he could not see what lay behind the glass, he knew joy awaited those who eagerly made the passage to a new place.

The turbolift doors opened behind him. Chakotay heard shuffling footsteps, then saw Tom ease a pale B'Elanna into the engineering-station chair. He crouched down beside her, draping an arm around her shoulders. Neither of their gazes ever left the viewscreen.

Shortly after Tom and B'Elanna had arrived, Seven of Nine entered the bridge and assumed a position behind the captain's chair. Indeed, as the moments passed, many of *Voyager*'s crew members—including Neelix—came up to the bridge and sat on the floor or stood where they could. To a person all of them were transfixed by the sight unfolding before them. They had sacrificed so much, suffered incalculable losses in recent weeks. Chakotay knew that this family needed to understand that their suffering had meaning, that at the end of the journey, hope was not lost.

And when the last creature—Nacene or Monorhan—made its passage, the mirror clouded over, the passageway closed. Those watching from *Voyager*'s bridge issued a collective sigh. Chakotay knew when he was an old man he would look back on this memory and hope that his passage to the next life would be as beautiful.

"Where are the *rih?*" Chakotay asked Neelix.

The Talaxian flashed a toothy grin. "The Keeper of the Light invited them to ascend to the next life with the other Monorhans who died when the Nacene destroyed their planet. Even the ones Lieutenant Torres sent off into space were asked."

B'Elanna snorted and muttered something about "all that work for nothing" under her breath.

Chakotay looked over at Tom, prepared to ask him to

relieve poor Ensign Knowles at the helm. He was met by a ridiculous grin on Tom's face.

"It's not over yet. Just wait."

Before Chakotay could ask for an explanation, a pillar of light descended from the ceiling.

The Keeper of the Light materialized on the bridge.

Chapter 12

The Keeper glanced over at Tom with a look Tom was beginning to recognize as his "time to be serious but not too serious" face. One of the traits he admired the most in Kol was the ability to have a good time. He might be a pandimensional being with godlike powers, but Tom had to respect a guy who could save the universe *and* run a mean node race.

"Glad you dropped by," Tom said, acknowledging Kol with a nod. "I was wondering if you'd have time to say goodbye before you returned to Q U." As soon as the mention of Q escaped his lips, Tom regretted it, considering the furrows that instantly appeared on Chakotay's forehead. Tom should have kept his mouth shut—any chance he had of his debriefing lasting less than a week had just ended.

"My coursework is complete," Kol said.

"I take it you passed?" Tom gestured toward the viewscreen that now displayed Monorhan space and the decidedly smaller gash, the flood of photons having slowed dramatically.

"Not quite yet. My final exam won't end until we've cleaned up around here."

"I'm relieved to hear that," Chakotay said, apparently overcoming his surprise and finding his voice.

"After all you have done, I would be remiss if I didn't complete the task at hand." Kol stepped toward Chakotay and bowed deeply. "I am honored, Commander, to make your acquaintance."

"Would I be impolite if I asked exactly what your intentions are?" Chakotay said.

Kol shrugged, lacing his hands together behind his back. "Your captain should come first."

Tom might have imagined it, but he believed he saw tears form in Chakotay's eyes. He couldn't say for certain, because the commander headed for the turbolift and presumably toward sickbay without another word.

B'Elanna nudged him. "Is he going to do what I think he's going to do?" She had given Tom the outline of the captain's medical condition.

Tom placed a kiss on B'Elanna's forehead. "Yep." He wrapped his arms around her and pulled her into his chest. Since he'd last seen B'Elanna, he'd taken part in a harrowing race inside a living organism, traversed the universe with Q, gambled with q, and witnessed the destruction of Monorha. He'd had enough wonders to last him awhile. All he needed to be happy was B'Elanna in his arms and *Voyager* to be safe. He had one and Kol would soon take care of the other.

No man in any galaxy could be as content as Tom Paris.

In the entirety of this medical database, the Doctor had never seen a brain having suffered the damage that Captain Janeway's had recover from injuries. But there it was, on the monitors above Janeway's biobed: normal brain activity.

Kol removed his hands from her face and stepped away

from her biobed, studying Janeway thoughtfully, inscrutable, as always. The Doctor still couldn't believe this was the baby he'd delivered what, yesterday? Time travel made him positively loopy. He would be content to be a mere hologram for a time, his biggest concern being Neelix cluttering up his supply shelves and Mr. Paris sneaking out of his sickbay shifts to visit Lieutenant Torres. Making decisions when the fate of worlds hung in the balance was exhausting work.

Kol asked the Doctor and Chakotay if there was a private place they could talk. The Doctor guided them into his office and asked the computer to place a privacy shield on the room.

Kol explained that Janeway remained in a coma and would for several more hours as her neurons knitted back together and regained the capacity to once again transmit and receive messages from all parts of her nervous system. At the end of her recovery time, she would awaken.

"Will she return to normal or will there be residual effects—like personality changes or side effects of brain damage?" Chakotay asked.

"For the most part, Kathryn's life will continue as it always has and she will continue as the person she is. She will be fully capable of commanding your ship. There will be no lingering physiological damage—" Kol hesitated.

"But?" the Doctor said.

"Becoming the conduit for the Fourteenth Tribe altered Kathryn at a molecular level. Such changes cannot be fully undone."

Chakotay crossed his arms across his chest. "How will this molecular change affect her?"

"There will be times when her emotions will become erratic—when melancholia or anger will seize her and you won't understand why. Her actions, from time to time, may seem atypical. Such occasions will be rare and may not be attributable to this trauma, but you will never know for certain."

"Can this molecular disturbance be treated?" the Doctor asked.

Kol shook his head. "There is only one action you and every member of your crew must take to assure her ongoing recovery: She must never be told of what happened since *Voyager* entered Monorhan space. I have sealed those engrams so they can't be accessed. You should wipe your computer database of all the specifics regarding her experience. All she need know is that *Voyager* encountered some unexpected difficulties when it went to study the binary. Otherwise, the consequences of her learning about this experience will undo all that I have done."

"All right," Chakotay said. "I'll take care of it before she awakens. But while I believe most of the crew will be able to follow this order without a problem, I'm concerned about Naomi Wildman. She's a child and can't be expected to—"

Kol held up a hand. "Done. Her memories will be sealed as the captain's have been. But there is another situation in need of fixing that will also affect *Voyager*. This region of space must be stabilized for the strings to return to normal."

The Doctor, recalling what the journey into Monorhan space had been like, wondered how many more casualties of radiation sickness—or, worse, molecular destabilization—would end up in his sickbay before they would be well rid of this place.

"How will that impact *Voyager*?" Chakotay asked.

"Forever sealing Exosia to the Nacene and restoring normal space will alter the fabric of space-time. Consequently, what happened in this region will vanish from the timeline and will be replaced with thousands of years of history. The resultant spacetime fabric will be as if it has always been. Life will adapt it. Other civilizations will be aware of it and travel through it.

"What about the gash?" the Doctor said, fearing for his matrix.

"It will be sealed, as part of closing Exosia. The photonic energy that was lost, however, cannot be restored. There will be a void. A large one. *Voyager* may have to traverse it for months, perhaps years."

"It will be easier than navigating Monorhan space," Chakotay said. He extended a hand to Kol, who readily took it. "Thank you, I should say, for cleaning up the mess we made."

Kol shook his head. "All this needed to happen. The Monorhan prophecies foretold this hundreds of years ago. For all the talk of choice and consequences, I've found the universe has a lot of self-correcting mechanisms that it employs to maintain balance."

"Whatever the case may be, you restored Kathryn to us. For that, we will always be in your debt." Chakotay bid goodbye to the Doctor and Kol and left the office, leaving the Doctor and Kol alone.

The Doctor's gaze swept over Kol from head to toe. "You remind me of your father—"

"He's part of me. His life became mine," Kol said.

"But the earnestness—that's your mother," the Doctor chuckled. "You're lucky to have met her."

Sadness clouded Kol's face. "She has yet to return from Exosia. Or if she has, she has not come to me."

The Doctor touched Kol's sleeve gently. He knew and understood Kol's grief, having lost Kes not long ago. "Kes has always been an independent spirit. She's had a different path from all of us. Be grateful for the time you had with her."

Kol sighed. "Perhaps our paths—my mother's and mine—will join again someday. For now, I must resume the work that I was born for. I am grateful for having known you, man of light."

"And I you," the Doctor said.

In a blink, Kol was gone.

Though it had only been days by the reckoning of the dimension where she had been born, Kes had missed the glory of her existence as energy and thought. In Exosia, she was reminded of that life and knew that she was eager to resume it. She had no regrets for joining with Lia to help Ocampa. But Lia deserved to at last find the peace she had never known in life. And Kes? She would resume the journey she had been on before the Light had called her.

The last of Vivia's people had departed, leaving Kes alone with the strings. She had heard their music before in the light and color of nebulae, in the birth of a star, in the harmonies of the planets. To be this close and to feel it intoxicated her. She understood why the Nacene loved their existence here.

Kes sensed a change in the energy behind her; she felt hostility—fury. *Reveal yourself.*

A Nacene, in the form of a human with auburn hair, appeared before her, eyes narrowed. *You betrayed us. You lured my kind away from Exosia. But I will not be denied what is rightfully mine.*

The body that contained her—Lia's body—convulsed. Kes doubled over, curling into a ball. Blood burned in her veins, the heat blistering her skin; her neurons seized, making it nearly impossible for Kes to wrest control of the body away from the vindictive creature. The Nacene had reached into the sub-cellular level of this body with the intention of destroying it. DNA strands unwound, malignant tumors grew on Lia's lungs and organs.

Kes ordered the body to resist but discovered that being enclosed in flesh inhibited her ability to fight the Nacene and make repairs at the same time. Failing at either task would be disastrous. Separation from Lia was an option—for Kes. Without Kes's strength, however, the body containing Lia's weak life force would never be capable of leaving Exosia, a fate akin to damnation for the young general. Yet the Nacene could not be allowed to remain in Exosia. Q had made that clear.

Refusing to allow circumstances to defeat her, Kes struggled against the Nacene while simultaneously searching for Exosia's boundaries. When she discovered that Kol had yet to close the gateway to the Outside, Kes made a desperate choice: she would first save Lia, though at cost to herself. Kes risked being trapped here. But to her mind, such a gamble was a small one to take in the face of such high stakes. Every moment she hesitated, the enraged Nacene gained an advantage. Sacrifice was required.

In the space of Lia's breath, Kes fused threads of her own energy with Lia's, shoring up the general with enough strength that Lia's body could survive independent of Kes. She then separated her remaining energy from Lia's body. When the separation was complete, Kes looked upon Lia, saw a shadow of herself in Lia's eyes, and felt cleaved in two. The connection between them was indisputable: Lia felt Kes's pain, her anger, and would share her memories. The reverse was also true. Kes hoped that she could contain this Nacene before the gateway closed; she could not foresee what the consequences would be for her other self should the dimensions separate them.

Gathering all of her strength, Kes expelled Lia out of

the gateway and into the closest available place: the shuttle that Q had used to transport them to the Monorhan system. The vindictive creature would not find Lia there. For the time being, Lia would be safe. Kes turned her attention on the Nacene, who shrunk back from her. *The gateway is still open. Depart or you will be destroyed.*

The Nacene attempted another attack, but Kes blocked it, throwing the energy back at the instigator.

I will never leave!

Then I will contain you, Kes informed her Nacene attacker. Kes had never relished destruction but she had made a promise to the child she had helped create—and to Q—that she would not break. This Nacene must be made to accept the consequences of her choices. Recalling the lessons she had learned about fusion from living in a star, Kes directed her energy at the Nacene, collapsing the creature's subatomic structure one atom at a time. She remembered what happened to the Caretaker. She intended the same fate for this Nacene, though she found nothing but pain and anguish in the task. The Nacene would be destroyed and would be expelled from Exosia.

Kes sensed the gateway closing but she would not be rushed. One slip of concentration and she risked losing containment of the Nacene. No matter how worrisome it was, she could not allow the thought of her other self outside the gateway to distract her. She had to believe there was a plan, that if she chose rightly a way would be open to her.

A crackle of energy caused Kes to shiver.

"They just don't seem to play nice do they?" Q said in Kes's ear.

"Q—I'm trying to—work here." Kes grunted from the effort of speaking aloud.

"Oh, don't mind me. I'm just checking in. Seeing how

things are going, but I can see that you have it all in hand."

"Gateway—" Kes struggled to maintain control as the Nacene's sporocystian plasma began collapsing.

"Oh, don't worry about it. There's a backdoor. Always is. One of the least-known truths of the universe: there's always another way out. Take your time—you'll find it." He rubbed his hands together. "Well, my work is done. It's been nice working with you, my dear. We should collaborate again sometime. Ta!" A flash and—

He was gone.

In spite of the strain she was under, Kes managed a smile. That Q. Quite a rogue. Her concerns about escaping before the gateway closed assuaged, Kes focused on the issues at hand.

Once this Nacene was destroyed, she would take its remains and carry them with her until she found the backdoor. On the outside, she could dispose of them properly, thus fulfilling her promise to rid Exosia of the Nacene. Another concern plagued her. The thought of her other self, vulnerable and alone on the other side, was not so easily solved. As long as she was in Exosia, Kes could do little but hope that an opportunity to set things right would be afforded her. Someday, Kes would be whole and Lia would be free.

In the meantime, she would live among the songs of the strings until she found her way home.

Kathryn Janeway sat up in her bed, examining the padd that Chakotay had given her containing the reports during the time she had been recovering from her injuries. He had been so calm during their briefing—even for Chakotay—that Kathryn felt like a fragile old lady: fussing over her pillows, asking not once, but three times if he could replicate something for her, contacting the Doctor at least one time during their conversation. One might have thought she'd nearly died, for all his solicitousness. She had to admit, though, that she took a small measure of pleasure from the attention. Knowing she mattered, knowing she was missed, made the lonely starship captain's job a bit less isolating.

It felt strange, reading the reports, knowing that so much had happened around her and not having any memory or connection to those events. Who would have thought that a seemingly straightforward trip to explore a binary star system could go so awry? And the casualties! Janeway scanned the list of the injured and the dead: a tremendous price to pay for so little knowledge gained. A certain degree of danger was associated with any exploratory venture, but Janeway had begun to wonder if they'd tipped past equilibrium on the cost-benefit scale and the risks had finally begun to outweight the benefits. The question would have to wait to be answered until the next crisis, if then. Time for *Voyager* to get back to normal, which was to say abnormal—nothing about their lives on this ship was typical.

Take this void they were several days into. No one on the ship had ever experienced anything like it before. Always a new challenge! There was the question, however, of how many of these "challenges" were bad luck and circumstance and how many were the result of choices, primarily Kathryn's choices as captain.

Kathryn rarely regretted her choices, believing that once a decision was made, there wasn't much point in analyzing it to death, but in this case she admitted, if only to herself, that she may have made a mistake in taking this last detour.

She dropped the padd onto her lap with a sigh. So *Voy-*

ager had survived another near disaster to continue on her way to the Alpha Quadrant. What now?

Most of the time, when she was recovering from a medical ailment, be it a nuisance infection or an injury, she couldn't wait to get back to the bridge. The Doctor practically had to chain her to her bed. This time . . . she felt . . . disconnected, hollow.

Her door chime sounded.

"Enter."

Neelix stepped through the door holding Naomi Wildman's hand. Twisting free of his grip, she pattered across the floor toward the captain's bedside, clutching a piece of paper against her chest.

"Commander Chakotay said you wouldn't mind a visitor," Neelix said cheerily.

"I have a present for you," Naomi said, twisting her body from side to side.

"Since I'm not supposed to leave my bed, why don't you bring it over and show me?" Kathryn asked, patting a spot on the blanket beside her.

The child looked at Neelix who encouraged her with a smile, and then scrambled up onto the bed.

Kathryn draped an arm around Naomi's shoulders and squeezed her up close against her. Moments such as these were rare; Kathryn treasured them, especially since she had her doubts that she would ever have a child of her own, depending on how many decades their journey would take, never mind the odds of her being around nieces or nephews before they grew up. "So what do you have to show me?"

Naomi laid down a crayoned picture of at least seven or eight individuals, primarily in Starfleet uniforms. "This is me and my mom," she said, pointing to a small figure with bright yellow hair who held the hand of a taller figure with bright blond hair and eyes fringed with straight line eyelashes. "And this is Neelix . . ." She went on to identify the members of the senior staff.

A figure at the center towered over the rest of the crew. Kathryn pointed this out. "I presume this is me."

"Uh-huh," she said, nodding her head. "And I made you taller because you're kind of like the mom to everyone else since all of their moms are far away in the Federation."

Every once in a while, I need to be reminded that it isn't just about the destination, it's about the journey, she thought. "So I guess we're a family?" Kathryn said.

"Yep. We are," Naomi said. "Now let me tell you about the lesson I just had with the Doctor . . ."

Tom waited in the mess-hall line with the Delaney sisters, chatting casually about his Captain Proton holodeck project.

"So it's in black-and-white? Is there something wrong with the buffers that you can't project color?" Megan said.

"No," Tom said, explaining for the fourth or fifth time today that the program was a homage to ancient Earth entertainment. If the blank expressions on Jenny and Megan's faces were an indication, they didn't quite get that part of it. Lieutenant Ayala finished getting his lunch and left for a table, placing Tom first in line.

"You had something for B'Elanna?" Tom asked. He had no intention of spending his first full day back on a stomachful of *leola*-root surprise.

"Of course! Right here! I made her some *gagh* soufflé. They say it strengthens the constitution." Neelix passed over a plate with a jiggling, gelatinous mass of liver-colored goo set atop a flaky pie crust. "Tell her I hope she feels better."

"Thanks, Neelix." Tom began thinking about who

owed him replicator rations, because B'Elanna was definitely getting a pepperoni pizza. He was about to leave the line when a thought occurred. *I wonder if anyone has told him about Kes.* He paused in midstep and turned back to the Talaxian, leaping about the kitchen, humming a cheerful snippet.

Neelix must have noticed Tom's confused expression, because he slid a pot off a burner and returned to the serving area. "Did you need anything else?"

He seemed so happy flitting from pot to pot, stirring this, tossing that. Sharing news about his long-lost love right now, especially since Tom didn't know what happened to her after she went into Exosia, might not be the most thoughtful decision. Maybe this was one of those things that was better off left unsaid. At least by him and for the time being. Probably wasn't his place. The Doctor would be a better resource anyway; he'd suggest it to the Doc during his next shift. There was enough gloom going around with relentless emptiness of the void ahead of them that Tom didn't want to put a damper on Neelix's mood. "Nah. It's nothing. Thanks for the soufflé."

Tom exited the mess hall and headed for the turbolift where he ran into Harry.

"Headed for my first shift since being back," Harry said.

"Taking care of my girlfriend." Tom pointed to the bloody glob on the plate. "Wait a sec—you might know what that's like nowadays. You never told me how it went with q."

Harry did a poor job of squelching a grin. "She was great the last time I saw her, but we broke it off. Decided to just be friends."

"If it was great, why not continue a good thing? She

could drop in," Tom said. "Give us a little nudge toward the Alpha Quadrant from time to time."

Harry blushed.

Tom raised an eyebrow. "*Harry!*"

"She got tired of having to resurrect me every time we, you know—" He blushed to the roots of his hair.

To Tom's mind, there wasn't a good comeback to Harry's confession, and frankly, the visual kind of disturbed him. "Ah. Okay. Well. Have a great shift," he said, and decided to take a different route to B'Elanna's quarters.

When he arrived, Tom discovered she'd gone out, which surprised him considering that the last time he'd seen her—ten minutes ago—she'd been sound asleep. On his way to toss the *gagh* pie into the recycler, he noticed the message light on the console flashing red.

"Computer, play message."

"*Tom—sorry I missed you. Maybe we can do dinner? I decided I needed some exercise, so I took off for the holodeck. It was great . . . being with you last night. I really missed you.*"

Tom sat down on the edge of the bed. Something was up with B'Elanna. He couldn't put his finger on it, but it was like she was there only half the time. The other half? She went somewhere else. Except when they made love last night. She'd been there. But even that was different, because *she* was the one who wanted to play rough. When she got hurt, broke her arm in two places totally by accident, she hadn't even wanted to fix it at first. It was only after Tom threatened to emergency transport her to sickbay—in the nude—that she agreed to let him repair the bone. And now she was in the holodeck. Again. She'd gone there straight after the Doctor released her from sickbay, claiming she needed to unwind while Tom and Harry were debriefed. . . .

When she returned, he'd ply her with some pepperoni pizza and a merlot he'd been saving for a special occasion and see if he could get her to open up. He loved her, though he probably didn't tell her that enough, and her happiness meant everything to him. Whatever it took, they'd get through this, and the next thing and whatever came after that. He wasn't going anywhere.

He slid into the chair by B'Elanna's workstation. "Computer, open file Paris Proton One."

"Paris Proton One is now open."

Pulling up the character specs, he examined them with an eye to which one would be a good fit for B'Elanna. *That Arachnia . . . now, she's a hot one. B'Elanna in high heels?* A smile plastered on his face, Tom went to work.

The Doctor finished the last of Crewman Chell's diagnostics and sent the Bolian on his way. A series of culinary catastrophes had led Chell to believe that he suffered from a neurological ailment that made him clumsy. The Doctor had the unfortunate task of informing Chell that eye-hand coordination wasn't the problem: inadequate cooking skills were. He admonished the Bolian to take a few holocourses in basic cooking technique before he again attempted to cross-train with Neelix.

A quick review of the computer queue revealed that there were no more diagnostics or tests pending. Lieutenant Torres would return at the beginning of alpha shift for a checkup, but if her surliness at their last meeting was an indication, her health was markedly improved. *Oh— that's interesting. Lieutenant Nakano wants to start Starfleet's pre-med courses,* the Doctor thought. *Pleasant enough girl. Would be nice to have someone other than Mr. Paris around.*

The chuff-chuff-chuff of the air circulating through

sickbay, disturbed by the occasional bleep or burble from the computers, was not companionable.

He drummed his fingers against the console, considering what self-improvement project he could tackle next. Not in the mood for learning another opera libretto, he considered sculpture, horticulture . . . All of it seemed like much ado about nothing. He hadn't glanced at Shakespeare lately, though he had enjoyed playing Bendick last round and Beatrice—

Kes had been Beatrice. And she had done a lovely job. Stumbled a bit over the iambic pentameter but who didn't the first time. By the end, she'd really gotten the hang of it.

The Doctor didn't want to add another skill to his formidable list: he wanted companionship, and not just the programmable kind he could find in one of Mr. Paris's holodeck scenarios.

He missed Kes. Opening her eyes to knowledge and experience, the way he now did for Naomi Wildman, and sharing her excitement as she learned something new. He missed her stories, her kind, thoughtful ways with the patients. Filling his time with self-improvement regimens (he was already an expert at everything) didn't satisfy him the way it once had. If it meant he could be with Kes again, the Doctor would consider returning to Ocampa and inhabiting Ced's body again with all its creaking joints, aching muscles, and decidedly limited processing speed.

Or maybe not. He liked being a hologram.

But Kes . . . there was no question in his mind that missing her was what ailed him. Sighing deeply (and missing the satisfactory feeling of release that accompanied the exhalation of air out of the lungs), he tipped back in his chair and stared at the ceiling. Counting the plates didn't help alleviate his mopeyness, because his visual sensors calculated the total as soon as the thought crossed his mind. He was even an expert at being bored.

The Doctor sat in his chair for a long time, contemplating. Wallowing was not a suitable option. Pushing off the desk, he stood up, clasped his hands, and looked around sickbay, searching for a way to be useful. Mr. Neelix had been pilfering equipment again. Replicating and organizing should take him awhile, especially since Mr. Paris had begged off working a sickbay shift until B'Elanna was "back on her feet." Teamwork tended to make laborious chores go faster, a truism he had learned with Kes.

As he cleared partly used and empty ointment tubes, he whistled. He must have heard the song before though he couldn't recall where. The strangely atonal melody—hardly pleasing to the ear—wasn't typical of his taste, but he found it familiar, comforting. It came back to him: he whistled the song of the strings.

The memory of standing before the orchestra pit, leading hundreds of string instruments was not an unpleasant one, especially now that he knew how the story ended. As he imagined himself conducting the music, guiding the instruments in the song of the strings, he heard a husky alto voice singing the counterpoint to the strings' melody. The strands of music wove together, creating a harmony so lush that he wanted to weep for the beauty of it. How long he stood before the cabinet, lost in the daydream of Exosia.

The rhythmic click of boot heels against the deck plating alerted him to a visitor. Holding up a hand, he said, "A moment." He closed his eyes, allowing the harmonies to decrescendo into silence.

The Doctor quickly assumed his finest clinical posture. "What may I do for you today—" he said, turning.

"Ah. Seven. Need an implant tweak. Human physiology competing with your Borg physiology?"

"Not at this time." She tipped her head thoughtfully. "Commander Chakotay asked me to deliver the complete casualty report during the time of your absence. He said something about 'not entrusting it to the main database' and requested that once you've retrieved the information, that you clear this padd's memory."

"Oh," the Doctor said, and scrolled through the data. "I'll let Commander Chakotay know that you did as he asked." The data became part of his matrix within seconds, as always.

She continued to stand beside him, implacable as ever.

"Is there anything else, Seven?"

"I perceive"—she wrinkled her forehead—"a degree of irritability in your matrix. Perhaps it was damaged when you were away from the ship?"

His first inclination was to tell her she was misinformed, but then he thought differently. "You might have a point there. I'd appreciate it if you'd help me run a diagnostic."

"Preserving efficiency is paramount," Seven said. "I shall return tomorrow after you have had time to finish your assessment of sickbay."

She'd made it three steps before the Doctor stopped her. He wouldn't stoop so low.

"My matrix is fine, Seven. I just wanted"—he loathed admitting this—"company."

"You wanted me to keep you company? To make— small talk."

"Yes, isn't that what I just said?!" the Doctor snapped. Asking Seven to socialize would be like attempting to make meaningful conversation with the replicator: a bad idea on all fronts. Worse, however, was the humiliation of having to grovel. He wished she'd leave. Take her cat-suited self and vamoose!

Seven paused, clearly contemplating a response. "At present, I have no pressing duties. I can remain here."

Taken aback, the Doctor did a double take. "I'm not feeling sorry for myself. I don't need your sympathy."

"And I have none to give. I've learned in recent weeks that my social skills are lacking and if I am to make a meaningful contribution to this crew, I need to master some of these niceties that are alien to Borg experience."

"I concur, Seven. It shows how much progress you've made that you are capable of recognizing your own shortcomings." He indicated that Seven should be seated at a nearby workstation.

Linking her hands in her lap, she looked at him expectantly.

"Well . . ." the Doctor began.

"Yes?"

The Doctor blinked, considered what to say next, and drew a blank.

Seven shifted a few times, adjusting her position in her chair, and sighed.

Uncomfortable silence filled the space between them.

It shouldn't have to be this difficult! the Doctor thought, resisting the impulse to shoo Seven out of sickbay. What form of delusion—or desperation—had overtaken him that would make him believe that this hyperrational former drone could be a friend? And to take Kes's place? A faint faraway refrain beckoned. Oh, how he wanted to recapture that feeling of being connected to something greater than himself, to become part of the music once again . . .

Seven arched her eyebrows, took a deep, but quiet

breath, and said, "Is there a topic you would like to discuss? I haven't prepared anything, and I doubt my dilithium efficiency research is of much interest to you."

The Doctor bit back his initial, decidedly sarcastic response, and glanced over at Seven. Her wide blue eyes watched him intently. *She* was *trying. Which is more than I can say for myself,* he thought, stinging from the realization. Her clumsy attempt at conversation came from a place of childlike trust, and he had nearly verbally bludgeoned her for not being facile or fascinating enough. *I don't deserve a friend. I should surrender due to my own incompet—* He paused. Perhaps it was the tilt of her head or the way the light glinted off her blond hair, but he was reminded, if only for a moment . . .

"I must confess that dilithium efficiency has little bearing on the workings of sickbay," the Doctor said, smiling kindly at Seven, lest she feel foolish for suggesting the topic. "I have thought, however, that you might benefit from knowing more about *Voyager*'s recent history. For example . . . How much do you know about Kes?"

The music began anew.

Epilogue

Three years later

When she had lived on this world, she knew only two sides of its personality: sunlight and darkness. The landscape never changed, for without water or seasons only the wind was left to gnaw away at the rocks and stir the sands. The land had died a thousand years ago, the complex web of interconnected life-forms shattered. Her people would have become extinct along with the animals and plants that once flourished in this sterile place had the consciences of their destroyers not been stirred.

Standing on the sandstone plateau, looking out past the red rock canyons to the horizon, she watched pale pink be washed away by pale blue. Sprigs of stars glittered to life. Since leaving this place, she had come to know those stars, their lives, and deaths: they had names that she knew and called them by. She had become so much more than the child who fought her way to the surface. She had fulfilled nearly every dream she had ever had. How many among the billions of lives in the universe could say the same? And yet, for all she had seen and done, she longed to return to the beginning, to the people she loved.

Upon her arrival home, she had observed her people from a distance and had discovered that they had made tentative steps toward self-sufficiency. This pleased her. The Caretaker's gift of energy had been consumed, but her people had risen to the occasion and had found a way to ensure ongoing survival, however meager. Soon, they would break through to the surface and find a new world that she would help her child create. One final task awaited her before she could give herself fully to her people's cause. She needed to become whole as well as free another.

She had taken only a few steps toward the cave entrance when he walked forward and greeted her with a deep bow.

"I knew my work would someday be your work," her child said. "Your wanderings have brought you home. Welcome."

When she'd seen him last, he had opened the gateway and invited his father's kindred to pass into a new life. By so doing, he'd fulfilled the first of two purposes he'd been created for. He'd matured in appearance since then, his features etched with wisdom and compassion. Seeing him now, on this world where he was born, she couldn't help but remember the baby she had carried with the help of another. She also remembered his father. How like him he was!

"She has waited for you too," he said. "So she could rest at last." From out of the shadows, he guided the frail, broken body that had carried the child, a body that still contained a part of her life force, her other self. Because of the connection between them, she knew that experience had not been kind to this missing part of her.

She knew that the other self, feeling only fury, had recently directed it against *Voyager*. She had wrought havoc, caused sorrow. Janeway, in the end, had shown mercy and asked Kes's other self to remain with the crew. Perhaps sensing her incomplete journey, her other self had chosen to return home.

Just as I have, she thought. *What is it about home that continually pulls us back?* Gathering her other self into her arms, she promised: *We will become whole again.*

Gazing upon the child she had helped create, she understood, in part, why she needed to return. She wanted to bear witness to his fulfilling his other purpose, the promise made to renew this world.

"I have a gift for you, Mother."

Kes smiled.

"Look at the sky."

She lifted her head, felt the chill in the air, a breath of wind and—

Rain fell on Ocampa.

THE END

ACKNOWLEDGMENTS

There are two people who made sure this book was written.

First, and most importantly, Kirsten Beyer, who did everything short of cowriting the book, was there from the outline's beginnings through the last frantic week of rewrites. I survived the detours and disasters along the way because Kirsten kept a cool head and clear perspective. She is one of my dearest friends, and I look forward to the day when we can be old ladies hanging out in Palm Springs. She has been a fabulous writing partner since the beginning of this *Star Trek* journey.

Second, my sister Laurie who, by not being there, saved the day. Laurie and her husband offered their home for me to use while they were on vacation. Were it not for the hours spent sitting at her kitchen counter or in my brother-in-law's den with my laptop, this book would have "written by Kirsten Beyer" on the cover. The presence of *Extreme Makeover: Home Edition* nearby was a definite plus, since it kept my daughters entertained for hours on end.

There are many others who deserve mention: Jeff Lang for leading off the trilogy in brilliant fashion as well as bringing the funny; Mikaela Dufur for bringing the ice cream and the Café Rio pulled-pork salads; Susannah and Bethany for the Comic Con swag and friendship. My editor, Marco Palmieri, was a good sport along the way and deserves big thanks for his continuing faith in me.

Writing this book was a rough outing for my family. We learned that summer deadlines don't work very well for us. In spite of this, all the girls were good sports about the long days, the heat, and their mother's generally crabby mood. My husband, as usual, was the backbone of my life.

In no particular order, the following deserve thanks or acknowledgments for their role in providing either inspiration or sanity: Jane Austen, Coldplay, Veronica Mars, J. K. Rowling and *Harry Potter and the Half-Blood Prince,* Toyota, *Battlestar Galactica* on Sci Fi, In-and-Out Burger, podcasts, and *Gilmore Girls* on DVD.

And finally, I would be remiss if I didn't acknowledge the creative forces behind *Star Trek: Voyager,* especially Jeri Taylor and the stellar cast, who gave us a fun sandbox to play in. Tremendous kudos need to go to the *Voyager* fans who have stuck by these characters through the years, in spite of perpetually, in the paraphrased words of a famous comedian, "getting no respect." I spent many years in *Voyager* fandom in the company of such great folks as Jim "Reviewboy" Wright, M. C. Moose, Jamelia, D'Alaire, Katie Redshoes, Marianne "Lil' Cheese," and Dangermom Patti Heyes. They always encouraged me to pursue my writing and supported me through all my early endeavors. They deserve a huge thank-you for the gift of their inspiration and their friendship.

ABOUT THE AUTHOR

Heather Jarman lives in Portland, Oregon, where she supplements her day job as a tired mommy with her writing career. Her most recent contributions to the *Star Trek* fiction include "The Officers' Club," the Kira Nerys story in *Tales from the Captain's Table,* and *Paradigm,* the Andor novel in *Worlds of Star Trek: Deep Space Nine, Volume One.*

By night Heather flies to distant lands on black ops missions for the government, where she frequently breaks open industrial-strength cans of whupass on evildoers.